INEVITABLE

SHAIN ROSE

Inevitable

Editing: Amy Briggs
Proofreading: Bookish Dreams Editing, KD Proofreading
Cover Design: Book Cover Kingdom
Book Formatting: Stephanie Anderson, Alt 19 Creative

DEDICATION

To all the purple shoes that have been found
and to all the purple shoes still missing
And
To all those who have lost, who have experienced that sleepy
fog in the valley between unconscious dreaming and reality
only to be awoken by the hurricane of remembering

AUTHOR'S NOTE

All characters are fictitious throughout this story. The places, the characters, the events are all from my imagination.

I am forever grateful to the women who dedicated their time by sharing their stories. They will remain anonymous.

I would also like to call attention to the fact that no tribe or home is named within this book. This is to again keep all identities anonymous.

For more information on why I included some events within this novel, please research Missing and Murdered Indigenous Women (MMIW).

CHAPTER ONE

AUBREY

THE FORCE OF his tackle knocked the wind out of me. Jax Stonewood wanted a reaction from me. I was brought up to never give one though. At fifteen, in a household where restraint was a key to survival, I had a pretty good handle on how to control myself when someone surprised me.

I controlled my desire to look at the boy who sat on top of me, ready to smash a snowball into my face.

I took my time looking up at the clouds and the snowflakes dancing around instead. They glittered and sparkled, mingling wildly. With liberty. And a freedom that I envied.

"Aubrey, I thought I told you the last time it snowed that face washes are a tradition if you get caught on Stonewood land," Jax said.

Finally, I turned my gaze toward him. "Don't you dare."

He smirked, one of his dimples revealing itself. Even catching my breath while lying in the snow, my heart still somehow melted.

Jax freaking Stonewood. My walking, talking sex-on-a-stick neighbor *always* warmed my blood even though I'd never admit it. Jay, his younger brother by two years and my senior by one, did little to nothing for me, but he was my best friend.

"Jax, come on, man. Mom said if you facewash anyone else, she'll lock your ass in your room for the rest of winter." Jay sounded out of breath, like he'd run up right beside us.

I wanted to thank Jay for coming to my rescue but couldn't take my eyes off of Jax.

I never could.

The three Stonewood boys moved in next door four years ago, and our quiet, undisturbed block morphed into a revolving hangout for kids our age. The Stonewoods drew attention, and I didn't have much choice joining in when Jax and Jay tackled me one day to steal my candy. Their older brother, Jett, couldn't be bothered with their antics.

I admit, I cried to my mother, and they ended up having to apologize.

Jax and Jett tolerated me tagging along when they were in the neighborhood. After all, I was the homeschooled girl that their little brother had formed a bond with. Maybe the bond formed because we were close in age or because Jett and Jax left out their little brother a lot. Either way, it just happened.

Over the years, my crush for Jax just happened too.

Even right then, knowing he was going to smash snow in my face, I thought winter couldn't have agreed with him more. His normally broody, calculating eyes glittered like the snow with mischief and fun. The cold reddened his cheeks just right, and the wind tousled his dark hair to look unruly. The wind, the cold, the snow loved him like everything else in the world.

The only people immune to his charm were his family, and I appreciated that Jay tried to shield me from it. "You know Mom's not kidding either. She's going to be pissed if she finds out you facewashed Brey."

Instead of Jax acknowledging his little brother, his eyes stayed on mine. Then, they moved to my hat. With the hand that wasn't holding snow, he ripped it off. "What's with you and this bun all the time?"

I started to wiggle under him. "Let me up. My clothes are getting soaked from the snow."

"Right." His eyebrow quirked. "I guess I can't mess with your pretty little face."

My stomach dropped.

He was teasing me. I knew that. None of the Stonewood boys saw me as pretty. I'd seen the girls that paraded around them and in comparison... Well, there was no comparison.

They were tall. I was short.

They wore shirts that showed off their cleavage. I didn't have any cleavage to show off.

They were women. I still felt like a girl.

I wanted to believe him if just for a second though. I wanted him to want me even though I knew he was older, hotter, and had much better-looking options to choose from.

That thought ignited my temper.

I bucked under him, trying to get him off. His smirk thinned, his blue eyes darkened. His head tipped closer, and I felt his breath on my lips. I could smell the mint of the gum he always chewed. He stared at my lips and then glanced back at me, like he was assessing everything in me, figuring out what made me whole. For a second, I thought he might even lean the extra whisper closer to touch my lips with his.

Instead, he squeezed his eyes shut and crushed the giant snowball I forgot he was holding into my hair, grinding it just hard enough that my bun fell apart.

I screamed. Jay groaned.

Jax rolled off me, laughing hysterically.

My cheeks heated with embarrassment, and then it got even hotter as my embarrassment turned to rage.

Instead of dusting myself off and trying to save my bun, I scurried to scoop up as much snow as possible and slammed it into his face, smearing it all around.

"You're such a jerk!" I yelled.

Jay hauled me back quickly as Jax made a grab for me. He whispered in my ear, "Don't make it worse, Brey. Just go inside and get cleaned up. My mom just made lunch for us."

Jax was standing with another snowball ready to launch and glaring at both of us. "Would you stop babying her, Jay? After winter break, us upperclassmen get to teach the underclassmen a lesson. You know Sophomore Kill Day includes her too."

My eyes widened.

I'd heard about the water balloons launched at underclassmen on their way to school in the fall.

I'd heard about lockers being filled with pudding and about the lockers being stuffed with underclassmen as well. The high school administrators turned a blind eye to the bullying that happened. They called it just a little bit of good old fun.

I called it torture and wanted no part of it.

I whipped my head to Jay. "Please walk with me to school next week?"

Jay smirked at me like I was silly. "I got you. Don't worry about it." Jax grunted. "You can't walk her to school. It's tradition," Jax said, abandoning his snowball to glare at us like my idea was outrageous. "He can do whatever he wants," I screeched.

"People are going to start to think you two are dating with how protective Jay is of you."

Jay and I shrugged our shoulders in unison. Jay never really cared much about anything. He just wanted to have fun and wanted everyone to have fun around him.

For the first two years their family lived next door, he was the one who never asked why he couldn't ring my doorbell or why he couldn't come over. He mentioned once that he wanted me to hang out later than normal. When I said I couldn't, that my dad would be home, he didn't ask why that mattered.

After being homeschooled for so many years, he was the first friend I could trust and the breath of fresh air that I'd needed for a long time.

I begged and begged my parents to go to a public school after getting a taste of friendship. When they finally agreed, the darkness lightened up a bit, the clouds cleared.

The first day of sophomore year opened my eyes though.

I hadn't realized how mean people in school could be and how territorial girls were of the Stonewood brothers.

Jax distanced himself immediately. He didn't have time for Jay or me when he was captain of everything and enjoying every girl who looked his way in school.

Jay didn't miss a beat though. Our friendship was an immovable force even when every one of the girls he hooked up with hated me. His friendship made me unpopular. Girls didn't want to be my friend even when they realized my father mingled in all the same circles as their parents. I was the girl whose dad owned a big local business and who got to live next to the Stonewoods. That made me enemy number one.

I was a threat and a target.

And Sophomore Kill Day was going to be difficult to suffer through.

I felt the panic seeping in. It wasn't being stuffed into a locker or getting hit with paint-filled balloons that scared me. I could handle all that. I didn't even care if I got made fun of or picked on. If I came home from school looking a wreck or a phone call from the office was made, my father would resort back to claiming homeschool was the best option to raise a proper lady.

I knew better. He'd find something wrong with the studies my mother put together or he'd find fault in my work ethic.

He already found fault with so much.

Jay put his arm around my shoulders and told me he would walk me to school, that I shouldn't worry.

Jax grumbled behind us, "What the hell's she so quiet for? It's just one day out of the year."

I inhaled deeply, remembering that self-control was my friend. I grasped at that control so I wouldn't snap at Jax—until I saw my hair in the foyer mirror of the Stonewoods' house.

I froze and Jax ran right into me.

"What's wrong with you?" His voice rose, but I didn't glance at him.

My eyes were on my hair. My long, wavy brown hair had escaped the tightly tied bun that took a concentrated amount of time to do.

Both Jax and Jay stood on either side of me exchanging worried looks. My green eyes widened, glassing over as they stared back at me in the mirror. My face paled so much that it contrasted sharply with the dark brown nest that sat on my head.

I frantically started combing my fingers through it. "Oh my God. Do you have a brush? I need a brush."

They both stared at me like I was crazy.

"Okay, if you don't have a brush, I'll take a comb. I need to fix this right now."

Jay shook his head, and Jax stepped back.

"You guys, I need something! Anything!" Anything to make this look better. I felt control slipping through my fingertips. "Oh God. My father is going to kill my m—"

Both the boys kept staring, first questioningly, then with what appeared to be pity.

"Please!" I practically screamed.

I felt the air escaping my lungs. I squeezed my eyes shut and tried to focus on twisting up my hair to wrap it close to my head.

"Brey." Mrs. Stonewood appeared in the mirror. She stood behind me on the large staircase. "I have a brush right upstairs. Why don't you follow me?"

I tripped and almost fell at the bottom of the stairs. Jax's hand caught my elbow, and I turned to say thank you, to grab at any dignity I may have had left. When I saw his confusion at my panic, I couldn't bring myself to say a word.

He started to walk up the stairs with me, his hand still on my elbow.

I didn't care. I just needed to get my hair back in order.

"Jax, this is just us girls," his mother said, her voice stern.

Jax's hand left my elbow and for some stupid reason, I missed it. Probably because I knew after this, he wouldn't touch me with a ten-foot pole.

I followed her up the rest of the white marble stairs and down the hallway to a gigantic bathroom that I probably should have just run to the moment I saw the mess on my head.

She went to one of the drawers and pulled out a brush. Turning me toward the mirror, she calmly started brushing my hair without offering me the brush to do it myself.

I stiffened, staring at her head over mine in the mirror. Her eyes were the same blue as Jax's and they glistened with sympathy.

I didn't want it. I didn't need it. I had done just fine with my mother and my father so far. I stepped closer to the speckled granite countertop. "Thank you for finding me a brush."

Her brow furrowed. "I can help you with your hair."

She'd read my silent plea right. I wanted her to leave, but she wasn't budging.

"Is there a reason you can't wear it down?"

She knew the reason. Adults like Mrs. Stonewood were easy to read. They all held the same expression. The first time I encountered that look had been a day my mother picked me up from grade school. My teacher had seen a bruise on her arm when my mother reached for me.

She had gasped and we both stiffened. My mother pulled down her sleeve quickly but my teacher's eyes had already changed. They flicked to our car nervously, and she asked if everything was all right.

On the way home, my mother said she wasn't going to be dropping me off anymore, that I would have to walk. I read her thoughts. That day, I nodded my head in total agreement. Soon after, I was being homeschooled.

Now, Mrs. Stonewood begged me with her eyes to tell her something as she stroked my hair and brushed away the curls.

I didn't answer her.

She'd always been a sort of friend to me, the type of mother I never had. She yelled at the boys for me, let me eat cookies, she even told me to call her Nancy instead of Mrs. Stonewood. At this moment though, knowing that she wanted the truth, I figured not answering was my best answer. I just couldn't bring myself to lie to her.

She began to fold my dark curls over one another and said, "Whenever you're ready, we can talk. Just us girls." She always said 'just us girls' when she wanted me to understand it would be our little secret. My throat constricted and when I looked away from her, I felt wetness slide down my cheeks. I wiped the tears away quickly, hoping she didn't see.

If she did, she didn't say a thing. "All better."

I looked in the mirror and saw that my hair was French-braided, and it looked classy. Father wouldn't mind this. No curls. No frizz. No hair out of place.

"Thank you," I mumbled.

"Don't thank me when two out of my three boys did this to you." Her third and oldest son, Jett, was in college, living near his father. Thank God because I didn't think all three Stonewoods here would be good for the female population.

I let out a sigh and smiled a little. "Only Jax, really." We started our way back down the hallway.

"I'm going to have to ground him for eternity at this rate. To think, he's seventeen and facewashing girls. I doubt there's hope for him."

I laughed a little, feeling the weight of my braid swinging and realizing I felt a little freer with this hair style. "Not this time, Nancy. I got him good after he did this to my hair."

"Snow to his face?" Her eyes met mine again and they no longer appeared sympathetic, she was trying to make me smile.

I laughed a little and nodded.

"All right. He's off the hook this time. Go beat them in some of those video games." With that, she turned a corner and disappeared.

I made my way down the hallway and found both Jax and Jay sitting in the middle of their rec room, two empty plates beside them as they played a video game.

I moved to grab the plates to take them to the kitchen. Littered with crumbs, those plates would have been grounds for a fight in my home.

Jay grabbed my arm and yanked me down. "We'll clean up later."

I stared at the plates for a second longer, willing away the itch to clean it up. When Jax pushed another controller in my hand, I welcomed the distraction. "If you pick the character Peach again, I swear I'm going to make it my mission to throw every question mark I get at you," he mumbled.

I smiled, realizing that neither of them were going to comment about the hair incident.

I didn't care that both he and Jax got annoyed with me picking to be Peach every time. I didn't care that they would tease me the whole time. I only cared that they would be my friends knowing my faults. It mattered that they acted as if my panic attack hadn't happened at all. Real friends accepted you for who you were, not who you pretended to be. "You're just mad because I beat you every time I play her."

Jax groaned when I picked her as my character, like I always did. "Do you want to be her or something? We at least switch our characters. You are obsessed with her!"

Truth was, I wouldn't mind being her. She was a princess. "Whatever."

After a round I lost, Jax leaned toward me. "How's it feel to be losing, Peaches?"

I scrunched up my face. "Her name is Peach, and I'm not her."

"No. You're not. You're Peaches." He laughed to himself as he focused back on the screen. Jay started to laugh along with him.

"Peaches kinda fits you," Jay said.

Jax groaned. "Find your own nickname for her, man. Quit copying me."

"It's not a nickname!" My voice came out high and irritated.

"You kinda screech like her too."

"You want me to call you Bowser?" I said trying to get the upper hand, but as he crossed the finish line in first place, I slumped.

"No, Peaches. You can just call me winner."

I glared but kept my eyes on the screen. "You'll always be last place in my book. L.P. L.P. rolls off the tongue quite nicely too."

He grumbled something about showing me what could roll off my tongue nicely but I ignored him, so happy with my quick work on a degrading nickname for him.

We bickered and played again and again. Before I knew it, the sun was setting. I finished in first place only to throw my controller down, "I gotta go!"

Jax rolled his eyes. "You can't leave just because you finally won."

"Get over yourself, *L.P.* I won like ten times in the last hour."

He stood to his full height and crossed his arms, trying intimidation. "Peaches, let's be realistic."

Maybe it was the way everyone backed down from him or the way he commanded everything around him but I never wanted to give in to him, to let him have anything without a fight. I put my hands on my hips and stood a little straighter. "L.P.,"—I mimicked his tone—"realistically, Jay beat you last time, and he's the worst."

"Hey!" Jay jumped up. "I'm way better at Jax in most things. He plays this way too much."

I patted Jay's arm and glared at Jax for making me indirectly insult Jay who always stood up for me. He was the sweet one, the one I would call my friend. I held Jax's eyes. "Of course, Jay. We both know you're better than Jax at most *everything.*"

Jax's eyes widened as he took a menacing step forward. He searched my face again, analyzing me. "What the hell does that mean?" he ground out, a gravelly tone in his voice sending shivers up my body.

I stepped back quickly and turned as if unaffected. I didn't answer him because I didn't really know what it meant. Jay and I were friends, nothing more. I didn't know if he was better at any-thing than Jax, other than being my friend.

He was the absolute best at that.

"See you guys later!" I yelled over my shoulder as I bounded down the stairs.

Halfway out the door, Jax yelled from the stairs, "See you on Sophomore Kill Day."

I winced at the reminder.

Jay would protect me. I hoped.

What Jay wouldn't be able to protect me from was walking into my kitchen and seeing my father sitting at the table, glaring at the door.

"Where's Mom?"

"You mean Mother?" he asked, his voice louder than even his normal yelling voice. "I'm asking the questions, Aubrey."

I nodded, frozen in the doorway.

"Close and lock that door. You are letting in the cold."

I turned and did as I was told. I had no choice. Not when I didn't know where my mom was.

As the lock clicked into place, I felt my body start to shake. I couldn't turn back around. I willed myself to pivot, to face my father.

I pled with my self-control, begging it to help me stop shaking, to give me the courage to ask him again where he'd locked Mom up this time.

Control, that little friend of mine, wasn't needed though. Instead, my father yanked me back by my French braid and spit out, "What the fuck is this? She let your hair grow this long?"

Tears stung my eyes from the hair pulling.

The tears spilled over when he reached for the knife block and slid a large butcher knife from it. The metal glinted in the light. It shined as if it had been sharpened and primed for just this spe-cific moment. When the metal sparkled as it swung toward me, I wondered if blood made it shine more brightly.

I wouldn't find out that day because my father only sliced it fluidly across my braid.

My hair unraveled and hung shoulder-length. He threw my twelve inches of braid into the trash and the knife into the sink.

The sounds of the metal hitting ceramic and the knife ricocheting forcefully around the sink drew my focus to the sharpness of the blade. How quickly it sliced through every strand of the hair. Gone, it was all gone.

"Don't blubber in my house," my father yelled and slammed his open hand upside the back of my head. I flew forward, seeing black. Just barely, I caught myself on the countertop.

The blade was closer now, my teeth just inches from the side of the sink.

My father, such a smart, successful man. People said we were lucky to have him. He'd saved my mother, Tala, from that home she'd lived in on the reservation.

That home though was my mother's sanctuary. Father didn't let her talk much about it but she shared with me how it saved her when her own mother vanished. One night, her mother went to work and the next she was gone like a beautiful star burning out in the galaxy.

"Go clean up your mother. She's in the office," he grumbled as he pulled the keys from his slacks and threw them at me.

I stood there wondering what he would do if I said no. If I didn't back down and pushed him just a little further.

My father, such a smart man. He never hit us where it would leave a mark for anyone to see.

His eyebrows raised. My shoulders sank.

Control was my friend and my enemy. I hated it for making me a coward and loved it for saving my mother and me from more pain.

My mother laid like a wounded animal on the floor when I opened the door. I hurried to her and smoothed her hair back. I slid my hands over her face as she cried and ran her fingers through my hair. "Oh, my little dreamer. All your dreams have been cut away."

Yes, every strand of my hair held another dream, another identity, another hope. My mother taught me those sorts of things about our heritage behind closed doors when my father wasn't around to listen. How the wind whispered to me to make me strong, how the water could wash away most anything, how my hair held a piece of me that connected me to every part of those before me, to her. A part of me I would never ever get back.

She cried for my loss.

I cried when I saw what he'd done to her ribs.

She cleaned up my hair that night as best she could. I cleaned up her back and ribs.

Nights like those, we were the closest and furthest from each other. No other person in the world could know exactly what we were going through in those moments. We were also so lost in our own nightmares, we were too scared to speak them out loud to one another.

I always thought our bond was indestructible, a desolate pair who would always make it through the worst trauma together.

CHAPTER TWO

AUBREY

JAY CALLED SEVERAL times over the next week during our winter break from school, but I avoided him. I took care of my mother and kept an immaculate home instead. I didn't give my father a thing to complain about over the rest of my vacation.

Sophomore Kill Day descended on me more quickly than I would have liked, especially when I had no interaction with Jay. I couldn't be sure if he would walk me to school or if I would be on my own.

I put on makeup like it would help camouflage me. I wore the cutest skinny jeans I had and a dark flowy top to look nice, but not so showy as to call unwanted attention to myself. I pulled on some boots that would weather the snow and my puffy winter jacket. I'd mastered tying my hair in a bun that mirrored the same one I'd had before it was cut. I thought I looked good.

I could make it through the day as long as Jay helped me. When I left my house that morning, he stood at the end of my sidewalk, beaming.

He walked up like we'd been talking about this every day and swung an arm around my shoulder. Then he grabbed my backpack.

"I can carry my backpack, Jay."

"Not if the water balloons start flying once we reach school grounds," he said.

My eyes must have widened because I felt his chest shaking while he chuckled at me. I smacked his chest. "You're a jerk."

He squeezed my shoulder and reassured me. "No one's going to bother you, Brey."

I breathed a sigh of relief. "Thanks for walking with me."

"Wouldn't have walked with anyone else."

"You sure?" I teased, skipping ahead to face him and catch him in his lie. "Melanie or Sophie didn't want to walk with you? They weren't mad?"

He looked just past my shoulder toward our school coming into view. "They'll get over it."

"Probably, but I'm guessing your walk to school could have been much more fun this morning." I wiggled my eyebrows.

His eyes, such a lighter blue than Jax's, danced with humor. Then, he dropped my bag and lunged for me. He grabbed me around the waist and knees, carrying me like a baby where he hovered right over a snow pile. I screeched, "Jay, you better not."

"Say you enjoy walking to school with me just as much as I like walking to school with you. Or else."

I batted at his arm and tried to hold back my laugh. "Are you kidding right now?"

His smile widened. "Say it, Sass Pot, or I'm dropping you."

I laughed a little harder as he fake swung me toward the snow pile and screamed, "Fine. Fine! I love walking with you."

"Say you know I like walking with you too."

I chuckled as he set me down when I confirmed what he wanted.

Then we were walking again and I mumbled, "Guess I have to protect myself from you on Sophomore Kill Day too."

Another laugh exploded from him. "Yeah, what a monster I am."

I just smiled up at him. "You need to stop growing. You're already a whole head taller than me."

"Yeah, or keep growing so I can fight off the asshats that are lining up to bother you."

I rolled my eyes. "Yeah, just hundreds of them."

No guy had approached me all year. I wanted someone to make me forget about Jax next door. I wanted a Prince Charming, one who would overshadow Jax's effect on me. I'd dreamed he would bump into me on my first day of school, we would both have stars in our eyes and we would fall madly in love.

Instead, every guy pretty much ran away from me or ignored me. Jay mumbled more to himself than me, "You have no idea."

I blew a raspberry. "I do. The notches on your bedpost are at about a bajillion and mine … well, are none." I shrugged.

He held my backpack to his stomach as he bent over to laugh.

The genuine happiness that belted from him was infectious and made me forget how nervous I'd felt getting ready for school that day and how anxious I'd been to see him after a week, how terrible I felt the whole week without him.

He sighed and patted me on the back as we walked on, approaching the front doors of the school. "There's my girl."

I looked at him quizzically.

"Don't act like you haven't been jittery and nervous this whole morning."

I sighed, more relaxed when I admitted, "Well, it's supposed to be a rotten day for us sophomores."

He nodded and when we reached the school entrance, he stepped in front of me, ready to open the door. He hesitated, then turned to me as he cleared his throat. "When you're ready to talk about why I didn't see or hear from you all last week, I'm ready to listen."

I saw the hurt in his eyes. I could see him warring with himself over bringing it up and guilt washed over me. It was the first time he brought up that I hadn't returned his calls for a week or that I ignored him when he came to my house and threw stones at my window. He deserved for me to be as good of a friend to him as he was to me. "I'm so sorry, Jay."

He looked at my hands which were wringing themselves out. This was unspoken territory for us. I'd ignored him in the past when my father had lost his temper but never for this long.

He'd never called me out on it. We would simply pick up where we'd left off.

He pulled me to his chest for a hug and mumbled, "Missed you, Sass Pot."

When he pulled back, his megawatt smile was back in place, and the concern behind his eyes had disappeared. One day, I owed him an explanation, but relief washed over me knowing that he wouldn't push me anymore.

The first bell rang as I made it to my locker and Jay set my bag down. "You gonna make it the rest of the way?"

I rolled my eyes. "Thank you for walking me, Jay."

"A thank you from Brey." He held a hand to his heart. "Day's officially made now."

"Go to class, you idiot."

"See you at lunch." He spun to walk down the hall and within two steps, five people surrounded him. Shaking my head at how popular one person could be, I didn't think much about opening my locker.

When I swung it open and heard the hiss though, I jumped and looked toward the sound. Coiled in the corner sat a green snake. I stared at it as it stared at me, neither of us ready to make the first move. Its tongue darted out, and I jerked back. The snake probably took my movement as a threat and launched itself at me.

I screamed, flying back and trying to catch myself as I stumbled over my backpack. I wasn't sure if the snake was poisonous, but I acted fast as I fell to the ground and scrambled across the floor, trying to put distance between us.

When I glanced back at my locker, the thing was slithering toward a corner of the hall.

Away from me.

Thankfully.

I sucked in a relieved breath and closed my eyes as my panic subsided.

That's when my embarrassment set in as I heard the first laugh bubble up around me. I knew when I opened my eyes, they would all be staring. A hallway full of my classmates would be ready to get the best of their Sophomore Kill Day prank.

One chuckle I heard distinctly though. It was low, melodic like a siren's song, beautiful enough to lure someone in, but dangerous enough to ruin them as well.

When I searched out that laugh, I found him. Jax stood in the middle of his friends and slapped one of them on the back. "How'd you get Ms. Gering's snake in there? You went above and beyond, man. Above and beyond."

They high fived, and I saw red.

I shot up, snake and embarrassment completely forgotten, and stomped toward them.

They both stopped laughing as I shoved in between them and looked up at Jax.

His friend said from behind me, "Welcome back. Don't take offense, Sophomore Kill Day applies to everyone."

I wasn't paying him any attention. My tunnel vision was aimed directly at the boy in front of me whom I wanted to hate so badly but had a crush on instead. We were a breath apart, and I could smell his spearmint mixed with some sort of sandalwood aftershave.

I hated how he treated me, and I hated how I didn't hate that smell. "Do you have no shame?" I seethed, looking up at him.

His hand shot out, too quickly for me to dodge, and ran through my hair.

The angry red that I saw melted to black and white as I realized my bun must have come loose when I'd fallen. The rage pumping through my veins turned ice cold as Jax's gaze—always so calculated—flashed so many emotions in a second, I couldn't read even one.

Jax whispered so softly that I barely heard it, "Your hair, Peaches, what happened to your beautiful hair?"

The tears that hadn't come in days, that hadn't fallen when I combed my newly short hair or when I looked in the mirror or even from the embarrassment of falling in front of everyone at school, began to fall then.

I started to curl in on myself.

I felt my heart seizing from the cold in my veins, everything was black and white but him and me, and I wanted so badly to just tell someone.

To tell him.

I was ready to give in.

An unlikely ally showed up to save me from spilling my secrets. She had bright yellow and black hair, chopped lethally right at her chin. She looked like a bumblebee ready to sting when she stepped in front of Jax and shoved his hand away from me. "You are a piece of shit, Jax Stonewood," she seethed.

People were looking on, and I realized I'd lost a few tears in front of them. I turned away from them and toward her. This girl stood tall, ready to go to war for me even though we'd never talked before. Her anger radiated through the hall, blinding us with its brilliance.

"Next time you want to take Ms. Gering's snake, I'll make sure there's a poisonous one to inflict some serious pain on you. Get off your high fucking horse for once and act your age."

Everyone stood by silently, probably in a little shock that this girl was attempting to tell off the most popular people in our school.

Then, the guy who'd slapped Jax's hand before stepped forward. "Katie, it was just a joke. It's Sophomore Kill Day."

Katie just scoffed at him. "What are you? Ten? Don't come near me after school today, Nate. We are done."

Then, to my surprise, Nate looked crushed and stepped toward her. "Please, Katie…"

She just held up her hand and turned to look around on the floor. She saw the snake had slithered to a corner and badass that this Katie was, she hunched over and held out her hand. The snake slid up onto it and wrapped itself around her wrist.

The snake whisperer walked toward me, and I started backing up. I mean, she was holding a snake, but she was quicker than me. She hooked her free arm in mine and whispered, "Don't let them see your fear."

I stood a little taller and started to walk with her. "Thank you."

I looked back one last time to see Jax still there as everyone else disbursed. He looked a little shaken and a lot more interested than he ever had before. When he mouthed, "I'm sorry," I knew I was in trouble because I'd already forgiven him.

Katie and I walked to our first class together, because it turned out we had nearly the same schedule.

After thanking her one too many times, she looked over from her desk with her lightning yellow and black bob swinging my way. "You apologize too much, Aubrey."

"Oh, you can just call me Brey."

"Well, Brey, you're kind of too nice."

I cleared my throat and sat a little straighter in my desk before our third period bell rang. "I'm just being polite and thankful."

"K." She shrugged her shoulders. "Stop now though. It's creeping me out."

"Why?"

"Because, no one is ever that nice unless they're hiding something. Clowns and shit are nice."

I smiled, thinking it over. "Kind of like the people who whistle down the street."

"Exactly."

"How about Mr. Larson?" I mentioned our teacher. "He's extremely nice."

"Yup. Creepy as fuck." She finally cracked a smile. With that smile against her caramel-colored skin and her petite frame, I figured out why Katie had Nate pleading to forgive him. We were sophomores and usually guys like Nate and Jax didn't dabble in underclassmen.

"So." I glanced toward the door to see if anyone else was listening to our conversation. "You and Nate?"

"Ugh." She groaned. "Don't remind me. It was a fling, something to pass the time and kind of a place to sleep for a while."

I must have looked confused.

"Guessing you don't gossip much?" she asked somewhat surprised. "You seriously are the real Goody Two-shoes deal, aren't you?"

"Wha ... what are you talking about?"

"You know? You're the homeschooled Whitfield everyone keeps talking about. I'm the foster kid who jumps from home to home. It's a small school, Brey. You haven't heard the shit these idiots think up?"

The teacher started setting up the materials in the front of the room and I watched him, realizing how stupid I must look. "I guess you could say I avoid gossiping to people and people avoid gossiping to me."

She shrugged. "Whatever. I'm done with that asshole."

"He seemed sorry."

"He's immature. I mean, for fuck's sake, I'm a sophomore and I had to tell him to grow up." She shook her head and her hair swung with her. "So, what happened to your hair?"

Man, she talked so fast and jumped topics so quickly, I had to hope I didn't get whiplash. "I'm sorry, what?"

"Jax was mumbling about your hair. What happened?" She didn't beat around the bush.

I smoothed my hand over my newly formed bun and shifted in my seat.

"Got it. It's private, I understand." She turned to face the front, and then her grayish eyes glanced at me sideways. "You can wait till lunch to tell me."

My lips thinned. "I just got a haircut."

She stared at me for a second. Then, burst out laughing. "Okay, you're officially one of the worst liars I've ever seen."

I just shrugged and wiped my now sweaty palms on my jeans.

She leaned in a little over her desk and whispered, "I think I like you. I think we're going to be really good fucking friends. So, I'll tell you a secret. I've been in foster care for a long time, seen a lot of shitty things, and I can tell when something is wrong with someone the moment I meet them."

My eyes must have been wide as I sat there, frozen, listening to her and not knowing what to say.

Her look altered from one of the fierce stinging bee she portrayed to a more wounded, understanding animal. "Your secrets will always be safe with me."

We stared at each other for a beat. For the first time ever, I sat next to another girl that shared the same look I did. I wanted to tell her everything right then and there. Maybe it was her brashness, the way she held herself tall as if neither of us had to be ashamed and we could be something more than the abuse that went on in our homes. I smiled at her and nodded in understanding.

For the first time ever, I wanted to tell Jay. I didn't even listen in my next two classes because I was planning a way to tell them both.

When the lunch bell rang, Katie and I weaved our way through the halls to the cafeteria.

Taking a table with our lunches proved to be easy as we were early. Katie's mile-a-minute mouth was going over our last class when I looked up and saw Jax approaching. A couple girls called out to him but he'd set his eyes on me. I could feel their determination across the room, raking over my face and trying to read me the way he always did.

As he neared, Katie glanced up and then grumbled. "Oh, for fuck's sake, doesn't he have a girlfriend? He's practically obsessed with you."

"Katie!" I whisper-yelled.

Before she could answer, Jax leaned against our table and set a peach in front of me. "Peace offering, Peaches."

I would have said thank you. I would have accepted it and we would have parted ways amicably. No lines would have been drawn. No people would have had to witness the war beginning.

Jay had other plans, as he barreled up to us and shoved Jax so hard, he stumbled into the other table.

"What the fuck, man?" Jax roared, stabilizing himself and coming back at him.

No one stepped in between them like I assumed some of their friends would. Everyone around us was fine with these beautiful guys destroying each other's faces.

"I told you not to fuck with her." Jay pointed to me, and it seemed everyone's heads in the lunchroom turned my way. "You gave me your word."

Jax glanced at me and back at Jay. His gaze hardened as he eyed his brother again. "Well, I'm sorry, Jay. Didn't know the little pixie was so important to you. If you'd have told me you two had a thing—"

Jay shoved him hard again, but this time Jax was ready and shoved him back harder. They were both strong, too strong and too charged to be in each other's faces.

Katie must have seen my panic as I slipped out from my seat and jumped between them because as I faced Jax to push him back, she faced Jay and pushed him back.

My hands were on his chest and I felt his heart beating so hard, I rubbed him there like I had the right to. "It's all right. Please stop, okay?"

His hands flexed into fists and his eyes remained trained on his brother, but Katie had reined him in. She spun around to me and spoke loudly, "Brey, were going. Leave these fuckers to their own shit."

I glanced at Jax again. His eyes were still on his brother. They held something other than anger though. His brows pulled down like he was acknowledging something, like he was worried.

The color drained from Jay's face as he glanced from Jax and then to me with wide eyes. I lifted a hand to smooth back my hair and realized it had slid from my bun again. My short hair was loose and Jay finally noticed.

Without another word to Jax, I rushed toward Jay.

He'd always known something was amiss in my household. Everyone did. I'm sure he'd assumed but the look on his face right then said his speculations were confirmed. It was recognition, and I knew that if I didn't tell him today and talk him down, he'd share his suspicions with someone he thought would help.

As I grabbed his arm and stormed out of the back doors of the lunchroom, Katie followed and brushed off anyone who tried to talk to us. When we sat at a secluded picnic table, I started at the beginning.

I confessed that the first time I remember my dad hitting my mom, I did nothing. Every time after, nothing. I ended my excruciatingly long confession with the shame of still not doing anything every time he hit her.

Jay asked about my hair, and I told him I deserved it and that I should have hidden it better because my mom paid a price for my negligence later on. He looked mortified, but Katie nodded her head solemnly, like she completely understood.

That day, none of my stones were left unturned and none of my secrets were left unsaid. Those stones built a wall between us and everyone else in that high school. My secrets fortified our friendship and lifted so much weight off my shoulders that I honestly believed I had enough strength to fly away from the problems I had at home.

Some problems though weighed enough to keep me firmly grounded.

CHAPTER
THREE

JAX

SUMMER FINALLY CAME after what had been a damn long year. That Sophomore Kill Day prank caused something to happen to my relationship with Aubrey. I saw her for more than just the little girl my brother hung out with and as part of my life.

Or part of me. I couldn't figure out which. Without her around, and with Jay protecting the hell out of her, I freaking missed the little spitfire.

So, week after week, I'd played nice. I said hi to her in the halls, I walked with her and Jay to school, I tried to eat lunch with them when Katie wasn't around.

I'd made a fucking effort the rest of the school year, even got her to go to a few parties with Jay and me.

Not that I needed her or him to talk to me or anything. Life was just better when she did. Plus she was my friend too.

Kind of.

I'd found during the rest of the school year, I sort of saw red every time she was with my brother alone.

So, about a month into summer, I took another step in making peace. I called her to invite her to a bonfire party.

Aubrey's dad was the one who answered the phone. He never answered.

He must have come home early, and I was shit out of luck because he said she couldn't do anything. Frustrated and confused, I hit end on my cell phone harder than I wanted.

Jay came up behind me. "Who'd you just call?"

"I called Aubrey's house. Thought maybe she'd want to go to the party. Why doesn't she have a goddamn cell phone?" I mumbled, still staring at my phone.

"She coming?" Jay said, climbing up on one of the kitchen barstools.

"No, her dad answered."

"Frank answered?" he almost yelled. "Yeah, man. Weird, right?"

Jay looked a little panicked. Then his mouth snapped shut like a locked box. He shrugged his shoulders and looked away.

"What's wrong?"

"Nothing." He scooted off the barstool and headed toward the foyer. "Let's go upstairs and get ready for this party."

I grabbed his arm. "What aren't you telling me?"

He tried to yank his arm free, but we both knew I was stronger. Jay wasn't weak, but I was still older and meaner. Jay had always been the baby, the one everyone loved, the perfect child who never got into fights. Fights had their benefits though. I could beat Jay in a fist fight any day.

He glared at me when my grip tightened. "Jax, you're eighteen. Act like an adult. Let go of me, and let me get ready. I'm not telling you shit."

My baby brother's eyes iced over like mine did when I was set on something.

"Fuck," I mumbled and let him go. I knew I wasn't getting anything out of him.

We both got ready and went to the party in silence.

We pulled up to a huge bonfire in the woods and saw two kegs set up, our friends all drinking. Bottles of liquor had been scattered around the fire, and everyone looked like they'd been partying most of the night. The moon was bright, the bugs were staying away, and beautiful cheerleaders had put on their shortest dresses to dance around the flames. The scene should have made me happy. I should have been throwing back a drink and smiling when one came up to slide her arms around my waist. I should have been happy as hell that Jay had found one of the other cheerleaders and was cozying up next to her by the fire.

Instead, I couldn't shake the feeling of dread. Something wasn't right.

Aubrey's dad never answered the damn phone.

After an hour, I knew my mood wasn't going to change. I found Jay and nudged his shoulder to stop his make out session. "I'm going home, bro."

Jay looked confused. "We just got here."

"I'm not feeling it."

Jay ran his hands through his dark hair, most likely torn between wanting to fuck his cheerleader and making sure I got home. Times like this reminded me of how great a brother he was. He never fucked anyone over. He cared. I knew ultimately if I didn't give him a way out, he'd drive home with me to make sure everything was all right.

"Jay, I didn't drink. You can stay and hitch a ride later or call me." He squinted at me trying to gauge the situation.

"Seriously, man. I'm fine." I laughed to diffuse his concern. "You wanna smell my breath?"

He relaxed then. "No, dude. Don't be a dick. I was just making sure." He pulled his cheerleader for the night closer to him. "Text me when you get home."

I nodded and left the party.

The drive back was quick and quiet. My Ford F150 drove like a dream. I hadn't been surprised when my father gave me the gift once I turned eighteen. I'd been begging for a truck since I started driving, and after pulling good grades for a year and doing some research on investments, my dad claimed I'd earned it.

Technically, I hadn't because my dad's associates, who included my older brother Jett, didn't actually invest the money where I'd recommended them to do so. Instead, they'd patted my back and told me I'd done good work and research. Come to find out, had they invested where I'd said to, they'd have been all the richer. Investment, risk, and math came easily to me. My dad finally witnessed it, and the man probably would have bought my ass anything at that point.

I rubbed my hands over the steering wheel and smiled to myself. The long nights of research had been worth it. I planned to take care of this truck for years. It was special to me, the first real thing I'd earned.

So, when I turned the corner to our block and hit the gas full speed—not thinking about whether or not I'd crash or worrying about rocks flying up and denting the metal—it was for a damn good reason.

I saw fire. Fire dancing like a tyrant taking over Aubrey's house. Red.

Scorching.

Burning.

Fire.

I should have called 9-1-1. I should have stood back and waited for the fire department. Instead, I floored the gas, drove right up her driveway and jumped from the truck.

It wasn't heroism that fueled me, but fear. It damn near swallowed me up, flooded my lungs and drowned me. My fight to get to Aubrey was a fight against that fear. It choked me and had me struggling to break free. She could be in there. She could be hurt. She could be ...

I didn't think about anything but her.

I ran towards the door. I heard someone in the distance yelling my name, but I didn't turn, I didn't hesitate. I tried to open the door but it was locked. I roared and kicked it in near the handle.

Smoked billowed out of the house and I plowed in. I paused in the living room, realizing I had no idea of the layout of her house. I had never been in it. The fire swayed, furious with the wind that had entered the room with me. The smoke invaded my lungs and eyes immediately. I scanned the room, trying to make out hallways, searching for Aubrey. The flames and smoke created a maze, one I wasn't sure I could navigate. As I stood in the middle of the room, overwhelmed with my dilemma, the flames seemed to crackle in laughter at me.

Through a cough, I yelled, "Peaches, where are you?"

I heard coughing coming from a room to my left and darted for it down a short hallway.

"Aubrey?"

I heard a whimper on the other side and tried to open the door.

It was locked. Triple locked. I stepped back to kick it in, but it didn't budge. The door echoed a metal sound back at me. It was as if the door was sarcastically saying to me, "I'm made of steel, dumbass," while the fire continued to roar in the background.

Smoke joined in, taking over the hallway. I coughed harder and harder. I tried to take in a breath but choked on it.

I sunk to the ground and whispered, "Aubrey, the door. It's locked. I can't get it open."

Another whimper.

"Peaches," I coughed. "Where are the keys?"

All I heard was, "Dad."

Everything clicked then. The weird phone call. The anger on the other line. How weird Jay had been acting.

Her father was a fucking psychopath.

We all knew it. We just didn't know it to this extent. I crawled farther down the hallway to another door. This one was unlocked and as I opened the door and crawled in, I realized the air wasn't saturated with smoke but with the smell of alcohol. I welcomed it as I gasped and gasped until I could stand.

That's when I saw Frank—passed out facedown on his bed—completely oblivious to the chaos engulfing his home. A bottle of

Macallan was tipped over next to him, and it looked like only a few drops had made it onto the floor rather than down his throat.

Finding those keys had to be my top priority, even as I considered pummeling him over the head with that empty bottle. I snatched them from his pocket and turned to make my way back to Aubrey.

Some might hope I thought over my choices, weighed leaving a man to die, or that I considered my decision.

I didn't.

The only hope I had for him was that he burned to death.

I took my shirt off, put it over my nose and ran back to the locked door. I unlocked it and shoved it open. She was curled up by the door, her face too swollen to even see her eyes. Her mother's face was worse, if possible. I picked Peaches up and whispered, "I got you." Then to her mother, I yelled, "Let's go!"

The woman just paced back and forth in front of the window that was barred on the inside. "He will come. He will come," she mumbled.

The smoke invaded the room like a snake of fury. It slithered in, ready to attack any space it could. I kept beckoning to Aubrey's mother, but she wasn't snapping out of whatever the fuck was wrong with her.

With Aubrey still in my arms, I lunged in front of her mother's pacing. Her dark eyes clashed with mine and I saw recognition ignite in them.

"My husband didn't come?" She all but accused me.

I just shook my head and coughed out, "We have to get out of here." She glanced at her daughter in my arms and a silent plea passed between them. It was the first time I saw Aubrey really communicate with her mother. I noticed the fake conversations she had with her in front of us all the time, the poised looks, and the hollow smiles.

This time, I felt her body curl in on itself and saw her clenching her fists. Then, she spread her fingers like they might give her the courage she needed. Aubrey's green eyes widened, even with the swelling around them. They held determination and strength through pain. And I'd be damned if they didn't beg her mother to feel the strength too. The look warped to bleeding desperation though, as we both saw the resignation in her mother's eyes.

Aubrey reached her arm out and started to lean toward the fire and her mother, who was backing away from both of us into it. "No, Mom. Don't."

Her mother's eyes snapped to mine. "Take care of her."

With that, she darted out of the room and down the hallway.

Then, Aubrey started screaming. She was a daughter losing her mother and she fought me like it.

I ran for the front door, opposite the direction her mother went. I didn't waste energy comforting her. I saved it to keep her safe, all while she wailed on me and squirmed to go after her parents. The maze of flames had grown, and I decided to make a run right through it.

We burst through the front door, Aubrey crying in my arms, fire trucks pulling up, and my mother crying on the front lawn. I dropped to my knees on the grass beside her, and we exchanged knowing glances. She must have seen something in my expression because instead of crying tears of joy that we'd made it out alive, she laid her hand on Aubrey's cheek and shushed the screams coming from her.

That night, those screams ricocheted through my very being and they became the ones that haunted my sanity, making me question everything. I kept hold of her until she calmed down.

Paramedics continued to check our vitals and ask questions. I would never remember what they asked me, but I remember staring at that house. I remember the crackle and popping of wood that descended once Aubrey stopped screaming.

She didn't look at me, and I didn't look at her.

We stared at the house, and I felt my mom wipe tears from my eyes when firefighters appeared with two bodies, neither of which looked like they had life in them.

"She left us, just for him," Aubrey said. Her voice cracked and sounded numb, void of emotion. It didn't sound like her at all. Her mother's decision had changed her.

My decision changed me too. I left both of Aubrey's parents to die to save her. I left them to burn to death, and I felt void of guilt.

That was the day I realized I'd do anything for that girl.

It was the day I realized I loved her.

CHAPTER FOUR

AUBREY

SOMETIMES, I WONDERED if I was living in a dream. That maybe I hadn't attended my mother's funeral just the day before. After a week of living in the Stonewood's home, I wondered if I would ever wake up.

At first, no one bothered me other than Jay and Katie.

Katie's demons influenced her reaction to my hell. A few days ago, she'd pushed the door open without knocking, and without saying a word, crawled under the blankets with me. When I didn't move away or closer to her, she wrapped her thin arms around me and whispered, "It doesn't really get better for a while."

My throat constricted and my eyes watered a little.

She smoothed my hair and followed up with, "It doesn't really get worse, either."

I gasped, laughed, and then cried.

She held me until I calmed down and mumbled, "Don't hole up too much longer. Call me when you're ready."

She flew out of the room as quickly as she'd come in. I didn't see her after for a long time, but I knew she'd done that to give me the space she would have wanted.

Jay, on the other hand, came to my door every day and tried to get me out of their guest room.

One day, he stood in the doorway, leaning on the frame and looking at me with such pain in his eyes that I almost comforted him. My body wouldn't move though. It seemed every part of me had been drained of energy. I just stared back at him as I lay on my side, trying to will myself to look less depressed than I felt.

"How are you?" he asked and then winced. "Shit, don't answer that."

I just kept staring at him, despite his discomfort. It wasn't the first time I'd witnessed how my best friend wore his emotions on his sleeve for everyone to see. He was so easy to read, so open and transparent. So normal.

"Why don't you come downstairs with me and I'll make you something to eat?"

He had to know that his mother placed food on the nightstand for me every couple of hours, she came in to buzz about and talk even though I only nodded along as I ate.

I didn't taste any of the meals she brought to my room. I went through the motions. I thanked her, listened to a story, and chewed the food. She asked how the room was, I answered that it was great. She asked how I felt, I said tired. My responses were automatic. Controlled. Control was, like my mother had always said, my best friend.

I shook my head at Jay and mustered up the strength to at least answer him today. "I just can't, Jay."

He rushed to the bed, needing just the inch I'd given him to take a mile. "You have to, Brey. You're going to go insane in here."

I stared ahead.

He sat down on the bed and squeezed my hip. "You're losing weight and you barely move. That means you aren't eating enough or the paint in here is such a shitty shade that it's eating you alive."

His attempt at a joke for some reason brought tears to my eyes. This terrible dream had me featured in it as the unstable, crazy girl. Nothing made sense. Not my emotions, not my thoughts, not my life.

"Shit, Brey. Don't cry. That was supposed to be funny." He ran a hand through his hair, uncomfortable. "I'm saying all the wrong things today."

I wanted to comfort him, tell him he was my best friend and that it wasn't his fault. But it felt like everyone's fault. No one understood.

Everyone was normal.

And normalcy was suffocating me.

I jumped when I heard another voice in the doorway. "You're saying all the right things, Jay. She's just acting like a child, and you're treating her like one."

Jay whipped around to look at Jax. His body went rigid and his hand squeezed my hip again. I couldn't see how Jay looked at his older brother, but I knew what his expression would be. "Come on, Jax." His voice came out strained and mixed with a plea.

Jax's family had no idea how to act around him. Or me, for that matter. We were an enigma to everyone who hadn't been through our trauma.

Jax handled what he went through differently from me though. He didn't flinch when someone mentioned the fire like I did. He didn't shy away from confrontation. When the police asked us to come to the station to give our statements, I imagine he'd handled the interrogation as if he were giving an interview, showing every single expression everyone expected to see.

When they asked him those difficult questions about that night, I had a feeling that he'd been sad when they'd asked him about my parents, scared when they'd asked him about the fire, and humble when they'd asked about his bravery. He emerged smiling and patting one of the officers on the back.

Our stories must have corroborated because after they asked me a few questions they let Mrs. Stonewood take us home.

When we reached the car, Jax didn't slide into the front seat like he had on the way there. He opened the other back door and folded in right next to me. When he turned to look at me, for the first time since I'd known him, he stared at me like there was something he couldn't read about me.

His hand went to my thigh and squeezed.

It was the worst time for my body to react. We'd just been in the station telling the police how my father burned down my family home. In that room, my statement of how he'd beaten my mother and me before saying he was burning the whole place to the ground would be the statement that solidified his guilt. That along with evidence of lighter fluid and a match found in our home. They'd moved quickly on pressing charges against him so that my mother's reservation would feel they did her justice. They wanted me to feel justice too, or so the investigator told me.

Yet, I wasn't worried about any of that. I was a lover seeking her first thrill. Exhilaration shot through every one of my veins from where his hand laid. When he squeezed, it was like he injected me with a stimulant. My breathing picked up, my heart pounded faster, the hairs on my arms seemed to sway toward him.

He stared at me, his eyes shifting back and forth like he was trying to see through me. Typically, he could but I wasn't usually this guarded.

Then he sighed as if in defeat. He raked his gaze up and down my body. When his eyes met mine again, he mouthed, "Okay?"

For the first time, the man couldn't seem to read what I was thinking. He couldn't see through the mask I'd made after being questioned by the cops. It was the first time I thought he cared about me.

And right there, in that car, I fell tragically in love with him.

I thinned my lips, pulling them between my teeth and nodded.

The whole way home, his thumb rubbed a circle on the inner seam of my thigh. The movement was slow, soothing, and reassuring. We were in this together, I thought.

I was mistaken. I didn't see him for a whole week after that.

Jay and Mrs. Stonewood would come to my room throughout the week, but he never would. I thought he forgot about me and that twisted the knife deeper in my nightmare of a life that week. I mourned the loss of my mother and him.

Like I'd had him. As if he'd been mine.

When I wasn't contemplating my hell, I was overthinking how stupid I'd been for thinking he'd ever been interested.

So, when he stood in the doorway calling me a child, something different shot through my veins. It was better than being numb and feeling like I was in a nightmare. I let it course through me and fill my heart, making it beat faster and faster.

"I need to talk to Aubrey, Jaydon," he commanded his little brother, never one to ask. "Give us a minute."

Jay hesitated, for the first time, unsure of what to do with Jax and me. Before, it'd been Jay and me against the world, and now this new dynamic created instability. He looked to me for guidance and I had a new fire that he probably saw in my gaze. I nodded and he conceded, leaving us alone.

"The family's worried about you," Jax said, once he closed the door behind his brother. He seemed bigger in the enclosed room, like he was taking up all the damn room in there. I sat up, trying to embody just as much space and power as he exuded.

"I'll be fine."

"I know you will," he stated matter-of-factly. I narrowed my eyes at him.

"But, they don't." He pointed toward the closed door. "You need to start acting like you'll be fine, Whitfield." His words cut through the air, loud and deep. He strode toward me, like he wanted to shake me and then paced back. With his back to me, I saw him pull at his hair before he turned back around.

"I can't!" I yelled at him, waving my hands around the room. "You think this is easy for me? You think you can relate? I just lost both of my parents."

He stepped up close to me and bent down, putting a hand on either side of my hips. "That man never deserved to be called your parent, and he'll rot in prison thinking just that. Let's be real, Peaches. You lost one parent. And at least you fought me to save her."

He whispered the last words. I saw the change in his eyes. The blue in them lightened like they had iced over and froze all his emotions in.

I couldn't help it. My hand went to his jaw to soothe him. I rubbed over the ticking muscle.

He looked right through me as if he was haunted by something from that night.

"Jax," I whispered because we were so close. I felt his breath on my lips, I could practically taste the mint he'd just had. I knew that if he didn't back away, I'd make a fool of myself.

He seemed to know it too, because he snapped back out of my touch and focused a steely, determined gaze on me. "Mom's in shambles because she thinks you're suicidal or some shit."

The callousness of his words shot me out of bed. I got up in his face. "Fuck you. That isn't what she's thinking."

"You got a mouth on you all of a sudden, huh?" I just glared at him.

His eyes shifted back and forth, reading every line on me as if he was putting it all together. That look, I started to realize, was the way he looked at me when he needed to know where we stood, when he needed to know everything about me.

The slow smile that followed his assessment had me putting my hands up to his chest to shove him out of the room. He caught them, as if he'd read my next move already.

"Go for a jog with me, Peaches." His voice was like sugar granules, sweet and rough at the same time.

"I'm not going anywhere with you, L.P." I tried to yank my hands away, but he held them on his chest with little effort.

"Come on," he coaxed, but he wasn't looking me in the eyes. He was looking at our struggling hands.

"Jax, let me go."

"Not until you agree to come for a jog with me. It's the least you can do after shoving and swearing at me."

My anger subsided quickly with his words as my embarrassment set in. What had gotten into me?

He pushed further. "If we stay here any longer, you know I'll make you swear more. Just a jog?" It was the closest to a plea I would get from him.

For the first time since coming into that bedroom, I wanted out of it. I conceded, and he left the room so I could change. I put on compression leggings and a sports bra that I covered with a T-shirt. I didn't have many clothes that I exercised in because, truth be told, I didn't exercise much.

When I met him downstairs, he just nodded. We walked past a gaping Jay and Mrs. Stonewood toward the back of the house. No news stations had access to the acres of land behind the Stonewood estate and we could run there freely.

Our first run together, and most every run we'd shared that summer, started quietly.

The crunch under our feet, our rhythmic breathing, and the nature around us allowed me to meditate. I thought about life without my parents on that first run. I thought about my well mapped out plan for college. I thought about my mother.

My beautiful, sweet mother. She loved her family and my father so much and said we'd been fortunate to have him. She saw him as a good man. It blinded her to all of his flaws and to what our future held. Maybe my father loved her too, in his own brutal, vicious way.

My breathing quickened, but I didn't care. I picked up the pace and pushed myself harder.

My father—that man—had been, and still was, a monster. Controlling, vindictive, and mean, he only cared about three things: his business, his appearance, and himself. How many times had he locked us in that room because we'd said the wrong thing or his business's stocks didn't do well enough or my mother donated too much to her charity? How many nights did we spend in there, locked away?

Locked away.

I stopped like I'd crashed into the steel door that kept us prisoners. I gulped for air but couldn't seem to take any in. I bent over, trying hard to breathe, but I felt smothered, like I was in that room suffocating all over again.

God, I was all alone now. All alone and for some reason, I couldn't think of any other word, everything disappeared except me.

"Alone." I choked it out, trying to find other words, other things, trying to grasp at anything else.

"Alone. Alone. Alone. I'm all alone." I sounded pathetic even to myself.

I heard Jax telling me to breathe, but he was so far away. I crumbled down onto the dirt of the path, and then Jax was kneeling in front of me, holding my face and making me look in his eyes. "Fucking breathe, Whitfield. Watch me." He pulled in a breath and pushed it back out. He did it again, and I followed his lead.

I shook my head. No air was coming in.

He must have realized it wasn't working because his blue eyes flared. His jaw clenched. I knew he was trying to read me, but I was starting to fade. All I saw was the tunnel vision narrowing in on just him.

Then, he crashed his lips onto mine. Hard.

No apologies and no coaxing. He took my lips like he owned them, and I gasped, forgetting my panic. His hands threaded into my hair, loosening it from the ponytail. I didn't care how it might look, because my intake of air was euphoric. My head swirled. The dizziness, I knew, wasn't from lack of oxygen.

Later in life, I'd attribute it to that.

But in that moment, Jax Stonewood's lips tasted mine, explored them, breathed life back into them. I tasted his usual mint in a whole new way, and I clung to that taste, to him.

To us.

Like he'd given me mouth-to-mouth, like he was my lifeline, I finally gasped in air.

He moved back to let me breathe and get a handle on the situation.

He pulled my hair fully loose and then gripped my upper arm. He leaned in to whisper into my hair, "You're not alone."

I looked out at the woods we'd found ourselves in. My vision blurred with tears. "Please don't baby me, Jax."

He stood up and lowered his chin. His tongue ran along the teeth of his closed mouth. "You're beautiful when you're sad, Peaches." Then, he spun and started to go down the path. "Let's finish our run."

Much later that night, I muddled through trying to figure out our relationship, wondering if he wanted me, if we were more than friends, if we were even friends at all.

Every morning after, he came to my room around the same time every day.

First it was, "Get ready. We're going running."

The next morning, he asked, "Why aren't you dressed? We gotta go running."

Then, he didn't have to say much at all. I would meet him in the hall.

Some runs, we talked about our lives. Other days, we'd run and then he'd grab his guitar from his room to take me down to the lake in his backyard. There, he'd sing songs for me that he'd written and claimed to have never shared with anyone else. Those days, I wondered if I was as special to him as he was to me.

One day, he found out I loved watching Disney movies. By that night, he'd gotten ahold of *Beauty and the Beast* and watched me while I watched it. Another day, I found out he hated everything about school, that all of it bored him to death except his music and business classes.

Some runs we talked about how we were coping. My confessions would come in spurts. I'd slow to a walk and just tell him I hated how normal everyone was. He'd smile sadly at me like he just got it. It was all I needed.

Some runs we didn't talk at all. We just absorbed each other, because that's what you do when you fall in love with someone.

Every run, he kissed me senseless.

I didn't ask him what we were. I didn't even mention the kisses. I just took what Jax Stonewood was willing to give.

I fell madly in love with him.

The night he took my virginity, he let me be awkward. He soothed every imperfection and worry I had, like he knew every one of them. He'd found every weakness of mine and made me feel like it was a strength.

That night, he told he needed me. There was a rarity in Jax Stonewood needing anything from anyone. I naively thought that would keep us together.

CHAPTER
FIVE

AUBREY

FOR A MONTH after the fire, I woke up in that sleepy fog, the one in the valley between unconscious dreaming and reality. The mind can't be bothered with pain or traumatic events in those few moments. For just seconds, I didn't remember the loss, the fear, the loneliness. But like a hurricane, reality would roll in and push the fog out. It invaded and emptied my soul at the same time.

I willed myself to sit up and look around. I took in the soft sheets and the sun shining. Beautiful, expensive trim lined the walls and door to the bedroom. I felt like an outsider in a perfect home with a perfect family. None of it was mine. Even if they kept saying it was. And yet, everything I used to wish for when I came to visit, now *seemed* to be mine.

No more screaming or fighting. No more hiding or lock-ins. No more mother. No more father.

I breathed in, hoping to suck in some energy to get through the morning, but nothing felt right. So, I got ready for a jog, knowing that would be the only thing to center me. Then, I went searching for the one person that made me feel like I could cope.

It should have been Jay. Or even Mrs. Stonewood. They'd both welcomed me into their home. Jay had always been the friend who'd known what to say to make me laugh or knew when to shut up when I cried. He knew how to handle everything—except this summer, except me and Jax, except the fire. Over the past month, Jax and I had formed an inseparable bond that no one really understood.

That morning, I didn't admire how the hall opened up to the second-floor view of the entryway. I wasn't focused on the marble staircase, the sleek banister, the dome-shaped ceiling, or the humming outside the two oak front doors.

I just looked for him.

Except instead of Jax, I saw a newspaper lying on the table near the front doors.

The Stonewoods had been very quiet about the scandal my family made. They'd kept the TV off and told me not to go on the internet. I'd listened for practically the whole summer.

That day, with the start of school nearing and knowing I would have to face the world soon, something in me couldn't stay away from it. I needed to know what people were saying. I was pulled to that newspaper so quickly I didn't even remember running down the stairs.

I remembered the headlines though.

I remembered the picture of my father, my mother, and me, posing so elegantly in all white, imitating the picture-perfect family. What a contrast that picture made to the charcoaled, burnt frame of our house next to it. What a contrast to the headline that read, "Whitfield Husband Charged with Attempted Double Homicide." Under the headline, in smaller lettering it read, "Wealthy Stonewood Family Fights for Custody of Whitfield Daughter."

I stared at it as if I could make my mother real again. Her long black hair, her wide smile, and the way she leaned into my father and me like we were her world, she looked like the happiest wife. Her sweetness permeated onto that paper. Her love for us was a reminder of what had made her so blind to him. My father's head was turned toward us, as if not even a professional photographer could sway his love for us toward the camera.

Little did that photographer know my mother was bruised underneath her white dress and I smiled as wide as she did for the picture so my father wouldn't lose his temper when we got home.

The start to the article had me holding my breath as I read:

> *The Whitfield family home, owned by Frank Whitfield, CEO of Whitfield Candy Company, was set ablaze by Whitfield himself two months ago. Authorities confirmed that Tala Whitfield, wife of Whitfield, suffered fatal injuries. Frank Whitfield suffered minor burns. Aubrey Whitfield, their daughter, was rescued by neighbor, eighteen-year-old Jax Stonewood, before emergency responders arrived on the scene.*
>
> *Today, forty-five-year-old Frank Whitfield has been charged with murder, attempted murder, conduct endangering life, and arson. His trial is to take place in the following months.*
>
> *These charges are being made by the state and have the Tribal Nation's full support. Tala Whitfield was a Native American tribe member when she married Whitfield. She held charity events for multiple causes within her reservation. "She was always quiet and humble with him. I only met her once in passing because she never came to the charity events. Now we know why," a source…*

That page had me shaking, wanting to rip everything to shreds, to scream. My emotions were overloaded and I didn't think through my actions, I just went to open the door when the bell rang. Opening the door to a ringing doorbell had been automatic as I took in my whole life written objectively in just black and white.

I realized my mistake with the screaming of questions and the flashes of light that went off.

Before, coming from the Whitfield family, I would have smiled and answered every question. I was properly trained in handling this type of attention. That day, each camera flash shined light on my terrifying reality.

Newspaper reporters were camped outside a home that wasn't mine, waiting for me.

Flash! Flash! Flash!

All I could do was wonder if their camera lenses picked up the text from the newspaper article I was holding.

Each flash turned into another headline later that week. I knew because, after that day, the Stonewoods figured they couldn't hide it from me anymore.

What got the most attention was my "rescuer" rushing in again. Each news outlet caught the look of determination on Jax's face when he yanked me back into the house before slamming the door.

They didn't catch the rage in his blue eyes when he spun me around and gripped my upper arms though.

"What the fuck, Whitfield?" he yelled in my face.

I closed my eyes, trying to get rid of the bright flashing dots in my vision. "I didn't realize—"

"You didn't realize there would be cameras outside?" He shook me a little, gripping me a little tighter. "I told you not to open the door. I told you to get me if you wanted to go out. You haven't wanted to go out the front door this whole summer. We always go out the back and—"

He stopped abruptly, looking down at where I gripped the newspaper to my chest.

His hands dropped and eyes widened. "Where did you get that?"

"They're writing about us," I whispered.

"I know, Peaches." His eyes softened. He tried to take the newspaper away.

I stepped back, holding it tighter. "They say my family is

prominent and yours is wealthy, as if it defines us. They called my mother a Native American, as if it defines her. They ... "

He ran his hand through his ink black hair and stepped closer to me. "They don't know anything. Give me the paper."

"I think I need to read it, Jax." I tried to stand up taller, like it would make me look less broken.

"I don't think so." His voice was low in warning.

"Jax."

"Whitfield," he mimicked.

"Don't treat me like I'm glass. Your brother and mom are already doing that."

"Yeah, well, my mom treats all of her kids like that and you're one of them now. Have been ever since we moved in next door. And you're Jay's best friend. He thinks of you as a little sister."

"And you?" I looked everywhere but in his eyes.

I worried he just saw me as the girl that needed saving. The whole summer had changed us. He'd ignored me until that night, treated me like his little brother's friend, a nuisance. After the fire, after he tore through that house to find me and bring me out with nothing but a small burn, he'd become my protector but also something more. Some part of me I couldn't comprehend but also couldn't seem to live without.

He didn't have me worrying long. He just stepped into my personal space and crushed his lips to mine. He slid his fingers over my neck and rubbed his thumb down the length of it as he devoured me. Hesitation and caution weren't a part of that kiss, just domination, claiming, power pushing me to accept him and meet his passion with mine. I gripped his shirt in one hand and held on, meeting him as best I could. I forgot everything except melting into him.

When he pulled back, he had the newspaper in his hand and was smiling. "How about we make you some tea and walk down to the lake through the backyard?"

"But I need to read—"

"Down there, we'll read it together."

Picking my battles, I brushed past him into the kitchen to put water on the stove. Waiting for it to boil, I mixed milk, brown sugar, and vanilla creamer together while he moved around me to mix cinnamon, ginger, allspice, and sugar in a glass bowl. We operated in silence, the newspaper on the table speaking volumes for each of us.

Once the water started to boil, Jax put everything in two mugs and held them out. I poured the liquid over it. I took in the earthy, sweet scent.

Jax moved each mug over to top off with the cream I had stirred and then sprinkled a little nutmeg on top. Something so simple calmed both of us. He handed one mug over and I smiled at the steam wafting from the mugs.

As I met his eyes, he didn't look at the mugs at all. He kept his eyes on me and smiled back. "I figure you're only as sweet as your favorite spice and yours is cinnamon. Sweet as sin."

When he talked like that, I didn't care about the news, or the people outside, or what anyone thought of us. I just cared about that moment. I rubbed my lips together, trying to center myself.

"Keep looking at me like that and we won't get down to the lake," he practically growled and then grabbed the newspaper. He didn't spare a backward glance, just opened the door for me, checked the gated backyard to make sure no one had gained access and tipped his head to motion me forward.

I went willingly but slowed down as I brushed up against him, hoping that maybe he'd deliver on his threat. Only weeks after the fire, we'd given into each other, but there was a restraint in him, one I was sure he didn't have with other girlfriends. I'd heard a cheerleader once say he'd thrown her into a wall and fucked her so hard she couldn't walk without pain for days.

With me, he took his time. There was something gentle about the way he handled me. For once, I wanted to be the temptation he couldn't resist, for his coiled restraint to snap. I needed him to see me not just as the girl he'd saved and needed to protect, but as the one he wanted.

The only one.

When I brushed against him, his jaw ticked. I barely hid my smile, so proud of my seduction skills.

"Whitfield," he warned, his voice low.

"Yes?" I whispered, inches from his lips.

He didn't lean in, as if not even tempted by the bait I was trying—unsuccessfully I might add—to dangle in front of him.

"Stop toying with me."

"What do you mean?" I tried to sound innocent.

"You know exactly what I mean. Move your ass down that path, or I'll shred this newspaper."

"You're a jerk," I blurted. Although I knew I was being childish, and my mother had always taught me never to call anyone names, I couldn't control myself around Jax.

I stomped all the way down to the lake. He stomped his way down there too. Both of us mad for much different reasons.

Jax sat at the same rock he always did, and I sat next to him just like I always did. It was a good representation of who we were. Jax gravitating toward the most logical choice and me gravitating towards him. We stared out at the lake and sipped our tea, ignoring the newspaper at first.

The water laid our anger to rest, like always. The sun made it glitter and sparkle, almost as if putting on a show for us. The trees surrounding the small lake moved in a natural sync with the glimmer, showing off their reflections to anyone who would look.

I loved it right there, breathing in the cinnamon of my tea, the smell of Jax, and the moisture of the lake. Each scent mingled and filled me with comfort, with security, with something I could never have had before.

"You marched all the way down here on a mission to be a pain in my ass and now..." Jax leaned over to brush his thumb over my lips. "You're smiling. What are you thinking?"

I shrugged, embarrassed that he could read me so easily. "Nothing important."

One side of his mouth kicked up. He set his tea down, turned toward me and cocked his foot up on the boulder. "Humor me."

Those words, his lopsided smirk, and that gravelly voice could have made me do anything for him. I wanted to humor him, rub against him, kiss him, and look at him for eternity. With the perfect backdrop, he wasn't just dangerous, he was devastating. His blue eyes sparkled just like the water, and his jet-black hair looked like it was begging to be tousled again. I wanted him more than I wanted my next breath and he had to know it.

That made me snap back away from him and answer as neutrally as I could. "I just like this spot on the lake."

"Why?" he asked, digging further.

I shrugged. I couldn't keep making a fool of myself with him. It'd been more than a month since the fire, and we'd shared a lot of secrets. I shared every thought I had and had opened up my soul to him. There were times I thought he could see right through me, to even the parts of me I didn't know.

I couldn't tell him I was consumed by him, that I loved everything about him.

That I loved him. Period.

I wasn't stupid. I saw the way every girl looked at him, knew that most had probably shared they loved him at some point. I wanted to think he'd stick around longer if he couldn't figure me out completely. I wanted to be the equation he couldn't calculate, the problem he couldn't answer.

I wanted him to stay interested.

I wanted him to just. Stay.

I leaned around him to grab the paper. "Shall we?"

He groaned. "Can't we finish our chai first?"

"No. Your family won't tell me anything. Jax, something is happening if the cameramen are back at your front door."

"Our front door. You live there now too. And my family won't tell you anything because they don't want you to worry," he grumbled back. I ignored him and took in the article again. Skimming through it, I shot off the one question that scared me the most. "You think your mom will get custody?"

He sighed into his cup and the steam curled around him, accentuating his strong bone structure. "It's mostly already done, Peaches. It might not be right, but my family has a lot more pull with the system than anyone else. Money talks."

The breath I'd been holding whooshed out. I couldn't shake the sense of guilt that came with knowing I would get out of the system so quickly. So quick, I would never have to see it. And that I would never have to go live on the reservation even if my mother had such a strong bond with it.

At this point, everyone was aware that my father didn't want her associating with the reservation. Growing up, I never bothered to think about it. Now, it overwhelmed me.

"She gave them so much. Her charities raised millions, Jax."

"Okay," he said cautiously.

"People probably think I should want to get to know them or live with them. They could fight to have me stay on the reservation," I whispered.

He didn't say anything.

"Sorry," I hurried to apologize. "I shouldn't burden you with—"

"Don't apologize for letting me see you." He sounded offended and took a breath before he leaned toward me. "I want to see every part of you, even the parts you hide from everyone else."

The way he looked at me when he said those words made my heart race.

I looked down at my hands. "No one wants to see those parts. They're uncomfortable and ugly, Jax."

He pushed my chin up with his fingers. "Sexiest parts about you, I promise."

I pulled away and licked my lips, trying to get a grip. "It's just that people think I should act a certain way with all this, or want to—"

"You shouldn't worry about what they think. You want what you want and do what you do. Who gives a fuck what other people think?"

I looked over at him and his hardened gaze told me I shouldn't argue.

I continued on anyway. "Dr. Pope says it could help to meet them." Dr. Pope was the therapist Jax's mother had forced upon both of us, saying we needed someone to talk to.

Jax rolled his eyes and shoved off the boulder. His muscles were coiled tight as he walked to the water's edge. "Dr. Pope says a lot of things."

"Like what?"

"Aubrey." That low warning always sent shivers down my back, like him saying my name commanded my body to do whatever he wanted. My body belonged to him, the traitor.

"I know we aren't supposed to talk about our sessions," I admitted.

The truth was that formalities and following the rules were dying a quick death in me. I wanted to know if our therapist was telling Jax the same things she was telling me. I wanted to know if he confided in her like I did.

Was he scared in the fire? Did he blame my parents? Was he mad about being in the spotlight all summer? Was that why he stuck around? To be the hero?

I took the last sip of my tea and placed the mug next to Jax's empty one along with the newspaper. Then, I met him up at the water's edge.

When I turned to look at him instead of the water, his stormy expression made me want to step back. I stepped out of my sandals and into the water instead. I let the coldness of it wash over me and moved directly into his line of sight. He towered over me, fierce and magnetic. I set my hand on his chest and knew that spark that I felt every time I touched him wasn't going to subside.

"I told her I'm not sure what you think about us. She asked me if I thought things were going too fast."

He grunted, not saying a thing, just reading my eyes.

I continued. "I know that can't be right. I know how fast you can work."

He started to say something, but I cut him off. "Do you think we're enabling each other like she says we are?"

It was that question that snapped his control, unbound the knot that coiled all his muscles together, because he lunged for me then. I gasped and he didn't hesitate, just took it as an opportunity to kiss me hard. I gripped his shirt as he enveloped me, not worrying that his clothes were getting wet. I jumped up and wrapped my legs around him, holding nothing back. I wanted him so badly, and because I could feel every hard inch of him, I knew he wanted me too.

Later on, I realized he never answered the question.

CHAPTER
SIX

JAX

I DIDN'T STAND A chance at avoiding her now that she lived in the same damn house as me.

I'd made up my mind when I grabbed her from the fire that day. I chose to leave her parents behind. I chose to leave my friends and everyone else who didn't understand behind. I chose her and no one else. Life and death situations like that make things crystal clear.

But other parts of that night were murky and opaque. Like the fact that Aubrey's mom didn't make it out of that fire, and we'd left her. Frank's lawyers focused like hell on it and tried to pin the blame on me.

My parents and their team of lawyers aided the district attorney in arguing back that I was the only reason anyone made it out alive.

Clearly, I'd made my choice. Deep down, I knew I'd chosen to leave two people to die and only saved one. I didn't feel guilty about it. I accepted it. I wanted to be able to live with that and move on.

It just hadn't occurred to me that I wouldn't have a say in moving on.

Instead, the girl who reminded me I was capable of risking my life to save another and leaving someone for dead now lived with me. I saw her every day and every night. We were two broken souls trying to piece each other together and make one. None of it was healthy. Yet, when she stood in front of me in that lake looking lost, like she needed me with her next breath, damn it, I wasn't going to disappoint her.

I should have, because what Dr. Pope said about the enabling shit was true.

Aubrey and I sat in the house all day together. We escaped from the realities of everyone else, including the newspapers and tabloids, by focusing on each other.

Her focus centered around loving me and using me to get through the worst time in her life. She built me up to be the only person who could save her. I could see it when she looked at me, when she gave herself to me.

My focus was nimble. It darted from emotion to emotion. I couldn't keep up with it. Sometimes, I thought I loved her, would risk everything for her, even murder for her. Other times, I hated her for the constant reminder that I'd already done all those things. That I was capable of doing anything.

For her. Just for her.

I hated that every time she looked at me with those green eyes, she saw her savior instead of her demise. So, I ignored all of it and focused on knowing that I possessed her. If she was mine, I could at least contain the emotions that swept through me with her. I'd graduated that year and I didn't give a shit about this little town, except she was in it. I needed to own her and be with her to figure it all out.

Dr. Pope thought we were unhealthy. What she didn't understand was that Aubrey and I were so much worse than unhealthy. We were protected from reality by the thin glass house where we hid. In it, Aubrey put me on a pedestal. And I wouldn't step off because I wanted to watch her from above to make sure no one got too close to the one thing that made me tick.

Aubrey had to go back to school though. She had to face the town, and she would have to face it without me, the only person she thought was helping her stand.

I knew I had to jump off the pedestal for both of us. I also knew the jump would shatter the whole damn house and our relationship with it. So, when she'd uttered that question, standing barefoot in the lake that I deemed ours, I wasn't about to resist her. I needed one last time with her in that glass house, just us.

I grabbed her neck and brought her to me tasting her intoxicating lips. No doctor, newspaper, or city was going to keep me from her in that moment. She gave in, like she always did. I flicked my tongue over her lips. She opened them, letting me take control. I dove in because the truth was, I'd lost my control with her a long time ago.

She ran her hands over my biceps as my hands slid to the bottom of her shirt. As I slipped my fingers underneath, she moaned, and the sound went straight to my dick.

I wanted to slide my hand into her shorts and find out if she was wearing that scrap of lace she claimed was sensible underwear. There wasn't any sense to them at all. They covered nothing. I definitely knew they wouldn't cover how wet she'd be for me, how ready. She always was, and that moan was her signature tell.

It felt like my body sucker-punched me when I pulled back, but one of us had to keep it together. She'd always been the one to stay in control in the past, but ever since we'd been together, she'd snapped. Her lack of control should have been some sort of signal to me to back off. Maybe it was fate telling me this wasn't meant to be.

But let's be honest, I'd never been a superstitious person.

I focused on the facts. Laying them out, there was no evidence of fate or divine intervention. The only evidence of our destiny was her standing in front of me. The way I felt every time she looked my way, my heart pumped like it was ready to leap out of my chest to offer itself up to her.

I was fucking doomed when it came to her. She was the only thing I believed in. She was my heaven and hell.

"Let's go inside, Peaches."

Her eyebrows came together as she panted in front of me. She ran her hands down her wrinkled shirt and put them on her hips as if standing tall, ready for battle.

I took her in, flicking my eyes down her body. Her dark hair was wavy and a little messed up. Her eyes blazed a deep green, letting me know just how revved up that kiss had gotten her. And I knew all too well where every curve on her body was. I'd run my hands over every part of it more than once. Damn, she was the most beautiful creature I'd ever seen.

And the scariest.

Because as a small smile started on her face, she slid her shirt over her head, and my knees nearly buckled despite the control I tried to force. I wanted every part of her, and she didn't want to deny me.

I couldn't have given a fuck that we were enabling each other or that one of us needed to restrain ourselves. If we were the storm causing each other disaster, I wanted to be the most devastating one. If we could ruin one another, then I figured we'd leave a trail of our destruction neither of us would forget.

I crashed into her and grabbed a handful of her hair just above her neck. "This is your idea. Don't get pissed later that I fucked you out here."

She smiled wider. "Fuck me? Is that what we've been doing?"

I stepped back and pulled my shirt off while she unbuttoned her shorts. "You're baiting me again."

Standing in just a black bra and her scrap of next to nothing lace panties, she didn't shy away. "Just asking. I never seem to feel fucked after." She said the words bold and low. My dick jumped at her swearing, so ready to give her what she asked for. The girl in front of me rarely swore. When she did, I could barely contain myself.

Part of me held back though. I always held back with her because even when she stood tall, spoke boldly, and swore fluently in front of me, I remembered how conservative she'd been months earlier. I knew what she came from and didn't want to cross that line.

"You need to watch your mouth around me, Peaches," I warned, "You're asking for something you've never had before."

Her chin lifted. "I asked for sex too, Jax. At one time, I'd never had that before either. Remember?"

I growled at the reminder that I took her virginity from her and grabbed her wrist to pull her flush against me. "You feel that?"

I looked down, and already her hand was unbuttoning my shorts and shoving them down so she could grip my cock.

She moaned and I went on. "That's evidence that I remember. I remember the first time with you, taking what was mine, *is* mine, and will always be mine. Fucking you is all I think about."

I slid my hand in her panties. She whimpered, looking down at the picture we made, getting one another off. She whispered, "I want you to let go and fuck me harder."

I let go of her wrist and threaded my fingers through the hair at her neck. Then I yanked it, pulling her gaze back up to mine. "You really are sweet as sin. Don't tempt me, Whitfield. We're already going too far by doing this at the lake."

She squeezed my cock and then started sucking on my ear as she whispered, "You've done things in public before. Please."

"Shit. You know I can't resist you begging," I groaned.

Her smile was victorious as she stepped back, undid her bra, and slid out of her panties. I glanced up at the house and back to her again as she walked away from me and over toward the rock we normally sat on. Instead of lying on it or giving me a chance to figure out how to take her gently, she bent forward over it and stretched her arms forward to place her hands down for stability.

Then, she whipped that dark hair around as she looked back at me. "Please, Jax."

Any guilt, any remorse, any caution that had helped to coil up my control snapped away. Tunnel vision overtook me. Aubrey naked. Bent over that rock. In the sunlight. I lost my boxers as I walked toward her, ready to dominate every part of her.

No one knew her like I did. I ran my hands over the exact parts I knew would give her goosebumps. I grabbed her hair and wrapped it around my fist to pull her head back and make her arch, just for me.

I leaned over her to growl in her ear. "You asked for this, and fuck it, you're mine. I'm starting to realize I don't treat what's mine gently. I push them over the edge."

With that, I shoved into her, hard.

She gasped, but I didn't wait for her to recover. While I kept her arched with one hand in her hair, my other hand went around her neck and squeezed. "So small. I could break you … Break you, and you'd still be mine. Fuck, sweet as sin. Sweet, sweet sin."

When she moaned, I knew she had too much air, so with my next thrust, I squeezed harder and pulled her hair back even more. She whimpered, but I felt how wet she was, felt her pushing back into me with each thrust.

Beside that lake, I did the most selfish thing I could have ever done. I fucked her, branded her as mine, and took everything I could, knowing I would break her by leaving her behind that night.

I just didn't know I'd be breaking myself too.

CHAPTER SEVEN

JAX

THAT SUMMER WAS filled with sorrow, pain, and handling legalities after I left her that night. Going to live with my father—hours away from my mother, little brother, and Aubrey—had always been my plan. I didn't want to stick around and go to college like every other person in that small town. I wanted and needed more.

That night, we laid together after I snuck into her room. I pulled my guitar out and sang lyrics I'd written for her after us being on the lake.

> *"Sweet Sin, Sweet Sin,*
> *You pulled me in.*
> *Taste of cinnamon,*
> *Sweet as ever and mine forever*
> *Sweet Sin, Sweet Sin,*

I can't avoid this now
Meant to be waking up and sleeping next to me."

She cried like they meant everything to her, and then we made love like we were meant to be. In that moment, my desire to be everything to her nearly did me in. She was the one girl who'd made me feel everything—good and bad, all at once.

When I got up to leave, I'd thought about bringing her with me, but when I looked at her lying in bed as I grabbed my duffel, I knew I couldn't wake her and ask her to come. Her smooth skin glowed in the moonlight, her lips parted just enough to keep their natural shape and show the plump upper lip that bowed. Her hair was undone and the dark waves clashed with the white sheets my mom thought looked so nice. Little did she know how much of a bitch it was for me to clean when I'd taken her virginity there.

Damn, I wanted to wake her up and look at her emerald eyes one last time. But if I did, I would give in to their sadness and do what I knew I shouldn't.

I wouldn't enable her or myself any longer. We needed to heal from the tragedy we'd both experienced. She needed to learn I wasn't there to save her, and I needed to learn what fucked-up emotion I was dealing with when I looked at her.

We needed to grow the fuck up without one another because, at this rate, I wouldn't let a soul near her. I was ready to knock more than a few heads together to shield her from the shit that was being said about that night.

Already had.

More than that, I needed to protect her. I could do that from farther away. I'd do that by doing the one damn thing she was sure to never forgive me for. I'd do it by leaving her and by visiting the damn man that lit her life on fire.

THE NEXT DAY, I was patted down after walking through metal detectors. When a boy, who's supposed to be a man at eighteen, shakes from the clash of culture shock after walking into a prison, he realizes one thing about himself. He's a pussy.

That prison shaped the rest of my life, maybe for the better or maybe for the worse.

Aubrey's father sat across from me, such a different man than I thought he was.

Looking back, the signs were there. The way she never made a mistake, the way she entered a room almost too quietly. How her face lit up like she'd never seen a happy home every damn time she came over or how her clothes were never out of place. But shit, she hid the turmoil of abuse well. Or maybe I was ignorant, not realizing that most families hide those secrets so much better than others.

So many years ago, I remember how she would panic. She didn't say much, but when she panicked it was fucking scary. Jay handled her panic attacks better, knew how to soothe her, handled her better in general. Which pissed me off.

I'd never been jealous of my little brother until I saw how Aubrey looked at him. He was her protector, and she was the treasure he would kill me over. Even if neither would admit it.

The only other time as a kid that I'd questioned Aubrey's home life was the day I found that her hair had been cut after she'd panicked at my house. When I saw her at school the next week, I almost collapsed in shock. Her hair was cut into a bob, and something in me just knew she hadn't wanted it cut that way. Something in me, even stronger, made me forget. No one wants that shit on their conscience and I was young and stupid.

I wasn't being stupid this time around.

Aubrey's father must have seen that in my eyes, read me better than I was ever able to read people. After we stared at one another—his green eyes so much like Aubrey's, but colder—he leaned back in his chair and smiled.

How closely the girl I loved resembled the man I hated scared the shit out of me. When he smiled, I saw Aubrey, but I also saw a sort of menace Aubrey could never have.

"You here to apologize?" he asked so softly. Yet, his words reverberated so loudly through me.

I shook my head, trying to clear it. "Apologize for what, Frank?"

"We aren't on a first name basis yet, boy."

My jaw clenched, and he saw it. He was waiting for it and pounced.

"But maybe we should be, huh? It seems you were in the company of my daughter enough. Maybe we should have met on a more regular basis."

"What your daughter and I do is not really your concern anymore." I smiled and looked sweepingly around to emphasize my point. The man would be behind bars for a long time.

His eye twitched a little then. I'd struck a chord and he knew it. "You think these walls can protect my daughter from me?"

"Your daughter doesn't want anything to do with you." My voice was low.

"My daughter doesn't get a choice. I'm her blood," he spat the words out smugly.

I started to rise. "I'm glad I came to witness this. You're right where you belong—"

"Sit down," he hissed.

"Maybe you forgot, but I'm not locked up in here. I can go whenever I want," I reminded him, still standing.

Somehow, the man seemed to rise above me even as I stood over him. He stayed sitting and showed his hand, the one he'd been sitting on, the one he knew was the trump card. "Aubrey thinks she's donating her mother's trust fund to that little charity, doesn't she?"

"Who the fuck cares what she does with it? If it makes her happy—"

"Oh, I'm aware it makes her happy. You know she lives for that? Doing something for someone else. She and her mother were just so alike. So giving."

"Fuck you, old man."

"No, no, no." He shook his head slowly. "You and I have a lot of business to do together and you talking to me that way just won't do. Now, let's remember, I didn't give Aubrey's mother any money."

I narrowed my eyes at him. What he was saying didn't add up.

I could always read people though. They were an equation that could always be solved. Frank was no different. His plan was as clear as day to me immediately.

My face must have paled or turned red, I don't know. I didn't hide my disgust so easily back then and knew Aubrey would never accept the conclusion I'd come to.

"Ah, you understand." Frank smiled at me, teeth so white and perfect, they just called to be knocked out. "So, you see why we'll be working together. You can't possibly be all right with me telling my daughter she's spending your parents' hard-earned money. That trust fund is a little lie they spun to make sure she was comfortable."

"You piece of—"

"Sit down," he hissed again. This time, I listened.

"Now, we've got stocks to talk over and you've got algorithms to look at for my company. I expect my business to still be running smoothly by the end of my time here."

"I'm not a businessman or an investor." The walls of this place started to seem as though they were closing in. "And you'll never get out of here."

"Then you'll be investing my stocks for a long time, won't you?"

"Like I said, I'm not a business—"

He cut his hand through the air to silence me. "I know your worth. I've read about you in the news. You've worked closely with your father and have made some of the best investing decisions possible in your first eighteen years of life. Don't play dumb with me."

"Aubrey won't care," I replied, but my voice sounded panicked. "Maybe not. But she'll care that you're responsible for her mother's death. That you left me when you grabbed those keys that night."

My poker face went up like a motherfucker then. We both knew I would never admit to anything like that. Not here or anywhere.

"You don't have to admit anything, but it doesn't matter how much I had to drink. I always kept my keys on me when I locked them up."

I almost vomited at his blatant confession of abuse.

"So, when can I plan on seeing you next? I need to make sure my company gives you access to my finances."

The prison I thought I could freely walk out of seemed to mock me.

I walked out that day in my own personal lockup, chained to a monster that happened to be the father of the girl I loved.

SIX YEARS LATER

CHAPTER
EIGHT

AUBREY

VOICE MAIL: *"Peaches… Damn, I miss your voice. I… things are fucked up. I shouldn't be calling, but I… well, Dad had me meet with a record label, and it went well. It went so well, Peaches, and the only person I wanted to talk to was you. I know it doesn't make sense. I know you're mad. You sounded so damn mad. I wasn't gonna call. I shouldn't be calling this late after, well, I don't have a right to anymore. You're back in school and I'll be here and I know this isn't right but… I love you. So fuckin' much it hurts. Peaches, you're still mine. You'll always be mine. Remember that."*

IT HAD BEEN six years and I still had the same stupid voice message saved. The one time he called even though I tried to contact him countless times after he left. Someone may wonder how that's possible. Well, after a not-so-proud moment of Googling how to forward it to an email, I had it saved on my laptop.

Pathetic, yes, I know.

I could tell someone where every sigh was in the message, when he slurred the words together, and how clearly he announced he loved me for the first time.

Those three little words. They were a sort of battle cry, the first one I'd ever heard. I found myself in a war with my own heart because it belonged to the enemy.

I listened to Jax's drunken voice as I took another swig of Macallan.

He sounded sincere, disoriented, ruined.

I blinked back the tears I sure as hell was not going to shed. Tonight, the words that sounded so sincere over a recording rang hollow, because tonight, Jax was on TV. Jax Stonewood, the guy I had tried to get over, was singing on TV. He was singing to a girl on TV. Then, he was hauling her up on stage, kissing her, and singing some more to her.

The crowd roared. I contemplated throwing my bottle at the screen.

My little friend, Control, reminded me of the obvious—waste of alcohol. I tipped the bottle again. Another swig and burn as I listened to that horrendous song.

When I said horrendous, I meant beautiful and heart-wrenching.

This was the song I could have sworn was written just for me, until he pulled the same damn woman on stage every time he sang it.

How many times could he sing this stupid song and get on TV for doing it?

It had been six years since he left and then called me to leave that message. Which meant six years ago, the record label started working on his album. Four whole years ago, it released and set the world ablaze. The album went triple platinum more quickly than any other, and he sold out every concert. Magazines claimed him to be the most eligible bachelor, and

Rolling Stone titled him the Hot Male Version of Adele. He was Adele's equal because he didn't intend to come back or make another album. The spotlight, news outlets claimed, had been too much for him.

Seriously? After four years, they couldn't give it a rest when he didn't even want to be in the spotlight?

I tried to soothe my anger over the fact that he had only made the one stupid album. His fans had to start forgetting about him soon.

Right?

Right.

Except now he was creating a music app that was about to take over the whole damn world. He would get to be behind the scenes of the app and push other musicians to the forefront. Some of the marketing for it had him performing this same song.

Vick and Rome walked into my apartment and found me in my drunken stupor.

"Brey, you didn't lock the door again," Vick announced as she dropped her purse on the table. Then she spun around and saw me. "What the hell happened to you?"

Code for I looked like crap.

I continued staring at the TV.

She looked over and then snapped up the remote to turn it off. "You don't need to be watching this!"

She and Rome were like overbearing, helicopter parents disguised as friends when it came to my history with Jax. So, I wasn't surprised when Rome snatched my bottle of booze away and united with Vick in her Battle Jax Out of Aubrey's Mind campaign.

"You need to stop focusing on this prick. And lock your damn door," he grumbled.

I sniffled and smeared the mascara that I was sure had formed a raccoon mask over my cheeks. "I know."

God, the pity in their eyes almost suffocated me.

"Just leave the alcohol, will you, Rome? I don't need this from you two tonight. You were both out drinking. Why can't I sit at home and drink?"

"Because you're drinking alone and wallowing in misery!" Vick practically screeched as she swiped her hands through the air.

"You're being dramatic," I deadpanned. "You're being destructive again," she mimicked. I rolled my eyes and turned to Rome.

He studied me while I studied him. Black tattoos snaked around his arms and wrapped him up into one delicious, mysterious package.

Katie had egged me on when we first met him while he was bartending, saying he looked like sex on a stick. And she was right. I knew when a lethally gorgeous man stood in front of me. Rome, he was beyond lethal. His body was cut and he towered over almost everyone. His dark hair and eyes both looked unruly and untamed.

Yet, none of that pulled me to him. I didn't care about how hot any guy was really. For years, no one sparked anything in me like Jax had.

Rome though, hooked me with his dark eyes, so black I couldn't make out where the pupil ended and iris began. Most of the time, those eyes were just as empty as they were obsidian. They pulled me into their abyss, as if I could fill them up for just a night. I could make him whole because I knew how empty he felt, being just as broken as him.

"You going to give me back the alcohol?" I finally asked.

"You gonna drown yourself in Jax being with another woman after all these years?" Leave it to Rome to twist the knife in quickly, even if it was as blunt as ever.

"I don't care that he's moved on." Rome crossed his arms and waited. I just glared back at him.

And because Vick could never take a second of silence, she burst out, "Oh my God. Who cares, Brey? We know you're mad because he's finally settling down with that Isabel chick. I would be too. He's ridiculous and he'll come to his senses!" She waved her arms around as if the news of him being ridiculous was obvious. "We know it, you know it, even his brother knows it."

I sighed. "Can we not talk about this?"

"Well, we wouldn't be if you weren't watching his concert," Vick retorted.

They'd know tomorrow anyway. Telling them now would just prepare them for when my alcohol-induced haze wore off the next morning and I had to face my nightmare. "Jax is coming to Jay's graduation tomorrow," I whispered.

Saying it out loud, even when it was barely loud enough for anyone to hear, sped my heart up. My nightmare was becoming a reality, because somehow, I'd always made sure it was just a nightmare, seeing him again.

Which was stupid. Jay was my best friend and his brother had to be in his life sometimes. Unfortunately.

Somehow though, we'd avoided crossing paths and if we did, we didn't speak.

Jay's graduation would be different. His graduation would make gossip magazines. Jax's presence, along with the Stonewood parents being there, would solidify that. With people watching, our interactions not isolated to a private place and the family's celebrity status, I would be on display. Conversation between Jax and me would be necessary because of how close I was to the rest of his family.

I was doomed.

Rome and Vick exchanged looks. A worried silence saturated the air around us. I wanted to scream loud enough to make it all go away.

Rome plopped down onto our gray couch right beside me. "You sure?"

I nodded. "Jay stopped by today to tell me."

"And then he left?" Rome erupted.

"Well, I'm just fine!" I said as I threw up my hands, because it was exactly what I had to convince Jay of before he left.

Vick rolled her eyes. "Sure. You look just fine to me."

Rome stared at her and then cut his eyes to me, as if deciding something. "Fuck it. I'm joining you in your wallowing."

He took a long pull from the bottle, wiped the back of his arm across his mouth and then handed the bottle back to me. "Damn, that's some shit."

Vick looked mortified. "If he's coming tomorrow, you can't just drink yourself into oblivion! And Jay's premiere is coming up. You have to—"

"She doesn't *have* to do anything, Vick."

A glaring contest ensued. Would it have been wrong to just let them fight it out and sneak to the back room with the bottle?

"I have my alarm set, Vick. I'll be ready." I sounded like I was going to war.

Who was I kidding? I was going to war and it would be bloody.

Both of them looked like they wanted to say more. Instead, I turned up the TV and let it fill the silence. Then, I shrugged and took another swig.

Vick's eyes bulged. "You'll look like crap tomorrow if you keep drinking."

Rome chuckled. "Who gives a shit?"

"She does!" She pointed at me.

"No, I don't!" I yelled back, now just as pissed as her.

"Now, now," Rome chided as if we were his two children. "You're both drunk. Vick, go sleep it off. I got this."

She narrowed her eyes at him. "I'll just bet you have it." With that, she whipped around and stalked out of the room, her long blonde hair waving behind her furiously, as if to show me how aggravated we'd had made her.

I sighed and slumped down into the couch.

Rome threw his arm on the back of the couch and rubbed his thumb up my shoulder. No spat with Vick ever really phased him. Instead, he flicked through some channels and settled on a rerun of *House*. We watched in silence as House cracked another case, saved another life, and went on playing the piano.

On a commercial, and after handing the bottle back to Rome for another swig, I announced, "I wish I had a physical illness that House could cure rather than a broken heart."

Roman laughed quietly. "You're an idiot, Brey."

"What? It would be easier. Someone else could just figure out what was wrong with me, and poof, I'd be cured. Instead, I know what's wrong, but no one can cure me."

I leaned my head onto his shoulder.

He smoothed my hair like he wanted to soothe away my pain. "It takes time."

"Is that really all it takes?" I was alluding to Rome's demons, and I felt his muscles tense under me.

You see, he and I were one and the same. We didn't trust easily, and when we did, we trusted with our whole soul. It was the reason I couldn't get over Jax. I trusted him with everything. My whole fucked-up life, my whole fucked-up self, and he'd abandoned me.

He'd abandoned me just as Rome had been abandoned after he'd shared his fucked-up life with someone too.

When I looked at him, his eyes were inviting me into their abandoned void.

I licked my lips.

He whispered into my hair, "Walk to my place with me?"

He caught my eyes flicking to the back room where Vick had disappeared to.

"She's passed out by now. Don't let her take-no-shit attitude fool you. She's small as hell, and the shots she had at the club tonight would have brought her to her knees had I not taken her home."

I smiled a little. "That why you came home so early?"

"That and I knew you'd be here to fuck."

I should have said no. I should have told him it was wrong to sleep with someone without your heart being involved. I didn't really believe that though.

We'd complicated things so much already by sleeping together for so long, because what else does a person do when they're broken? They find solace in another broken person. Misery loves the miserable.

That I believed with all the broken pieces of my heart.

I took Rome's hand and followed him out the door. My blood was already rushing just knowing I could get lost in someone other than Jax.

I'm sure Rome's was rushing for the very same reason.

CHAPTER
NINE

AUBREY

WHEN I LEFT Rome's apartment to walk down the hall to mine the next morning, I wasn't prepared for Vick to be sitting at my small table like a sergeant.

She greeted me with as much venom as a blonde fairy could muster. "Well, I was right. You look like shit." Then, she shoved a thermos of coffee my way because, truth be told, Vick couldn't be rude to anyone for long.

I also had a hard time being rude to anyone and could never turn down caffeine even if it came with an insult. So I mumbled, "Thanks."

"Katie will be here any minute. You want to talk about your walk of shame?"

I took a long drink of the scalding hot coffee and then lied through my teeth. "It wasn't a walk of shame. I just watched a movie over there."

"Fine. But Katie's right. You *are* a terrible liar." Her honey-colored eyes said everything she felt about me and Rome.

Katie barreled through the door at just the right time. "Saved by your warrior princess," Vick mumbled.

"What the hell are you going on about?" Katie asked as she threw her keys on the counter and beelined for the coffee pot.

Coffee addiction ran rampant through my friends.

"She doesn't know." I waved away Vick's comment. "Are we starting this early?"

Vick put some music on her phone and pulled out a chair for me. "You bet we're starting this early."

I groaned and fell into the chair that would be my torture chamber for the next few hours.

"Don't worry, I will somehow make this mop look like it did once upon a time." She picked at my messy bun as if it was diseased. "Katie, go get my hair kit bag. I left it in Brey's bathroom yesterday."

I tried to jump out of the chair. "You never said we were going that far! That hair kit bag has things in it that will keep me tied down here for days, Vick!"

Vick shoved my shoulders down to keep me seated. "Don't be dramatic."

Katie laughed as she walked down the hall. "Coming from you, that's rich, Vick."

Vick ignored her. "Your hair is a disaster, Brey." She motioned for me to move the chair over to the sink.

Reluctantly, I did. Katie handed over her bag and she dug through it while I told her, "Just wash it. You can't cut it today anyway." If Vick brought out that bag, I figured that's what it meant. She'd cut hair part-time while in undergrad. Now, she was focused solely on completing her law degree.

"Cut it?" Vick shrieked.

Katie winced. "Brey, remind me how we ended up becoming friends with someone who can't hear how loud she is. Have the neighbors complained about you having her over yet?"

I snickered because after only a month in the new apartment, I'd received a complaint.

Vick just waved her off. "Someone has got to be vocal about her hair being the perfect length, Katie, and we all know it isn't going to be you."

Katie snorted and for good reason. She sported a pixie haircut with black-and-lavender highlights. It matched her bold, take-no-shit attitude.

"Sure. I know, you both don't care," Vick continued. "But guys love long hair. You can't cut it, Brey. You can, however, never put black temporary dye in it again." She squirted about ten different products in my hair and then leaned my head back into the sink to start scrubbing.

"That feels much better than I would have thought today. I need this every day after a hangover." I sighed in bliss.

"Yeah well, from my end, this is absolutely gross." I looked up to see the temporary dye smeared up on her wrists. "No offense, Katie. You pull it off just fine but Brey has the most gorgeous natural hair color, and quite frankly, I don't know what your natural hair color is."

"Neither do I," Katie deadpanned.

I started to giggle when I felt Vick pause and hesitate. Vick reminded me of a roadrunner on speed when she talked. She couldn't even keep up with the words that were coming out of her mouth half the time, so she'd shoot off something offensive and catch herself too late.

Katie and I actually loved that about her, but it didn't mean we wouldn't give her hell for it. And Katie was never one to pass up a joke about not knowing her mother. She loved making everyone else feel awkward. Growing up with her, I was immune, but Vick still tiptoed.

When Vick realized Katie and I were barely containing laughter, she yanked my hair a little too hard as she wrung out the water and started to towel dry it. I let out a yelp. "Serves you right. Why I keep you two brats in my company is beyond me."

Katie shrugged her shoulders, still laughing. "Vick, it's just too easy."

"Yeah, well, be happy I'm not doing your hair today. Brey, remember I *am* doing your hair and you have to hang out with the equivalent of America's royal family."

That killed the mood. Katie grumbled something along the lines of "who gives a shit" because she'd grown up around them too.

I spoke up with, "Don't remind me."

"I know from both of your stories that he's an ass. I get it, and I'm not even saying he's worth your time, but don't you want to look so good that you knock him on his ass when he sees you?"

Katie stopped her. "She'll already knock him on his ass without all this." She swung her hands around the room. "I'm telling you, Vick, he could never take his eyes off her. He—"

"That was years ago, Katie. Honestly, I just want to look good enough for Jay's graduation and for him. He has to be seen with me, and who knows what the paparazzi will come up with this time. Can we get this over with?"

They exchanged looks as if battling with what they wanted to say. I knew how it went. We all had our weaknesses, and they knew mine was the Stonewood family, a specific Stonewood to be exact.

"Well, I'll reiterate, you should never cover up this dark auburn color. It looks fantastic and it's really hard to achieve. You could ruin it by continuing with the temporary dye." She shoved a piece of it in my face as if I didn't know my real hair color. "Did you know the chemicals in—"

"Vick!" I winced at my own loud voice. "Can you save it for a different day?"

She rolled her eyes. "You shouldn't be hiding this hair or that body of yours." She continued on as if I hadn't just asked her to stop. "The fact that you have the greatest ass in the state and work to keep it should be evidence enough that you shouldn't be wearing clothes that hang to the floor. No one can tell that you even work out."

I snorted at her ludicrous way of thinking. Vick worked with what God gave her. And boy, did she know how to work it. She looked like a sex kitten everywhere she went, and it got her a lot of attention. She didn't understand how someone could not want that attention.

I could try to explain to her why I didn't want to be noticed, that being noticed for the wrong reason and being a local celebrity for my father's crime wasn't exactly rainbows and roses. But Vick was different in a brilliant, blinding way. She would have probably taken that tragedy and turned her life into a reality TV show.

For a few more hours, I submitted to Vick's torture of getting ready.

I submitted to my hair being curled. I submitted to blush and eye makeup being put on. I submitted to Vick complaining about being a hairstylist until she could merge into the legal field. I even submitted to a rub-on tan while Vick whined about getting an A minus on her last exam.

After one hour, I wanted to scream.

After two, I definitely did not want to put on the strapless flowy dress Vick picked out for me with wedge sandals.

Three hours in, I wanted to kill Katie because she was trying to ditch with some excuse about having to go to another pre-commencement gathering. I knew it was a lie. Vick mentioned Rome was coming to get us, and she practically beelined for the door.

"You told me we were walking, Brey!" she accused when Vick informed her.

Vick snapped her head around to bug her eyes out at Katie. "You think I'm walking all the way to the ceremony in these heels?"

I sighed. "Vick, take it down a notch."

Katie and Vick started to bicker over how walking would be just fine. I smiled at their useless argument as I examined the specimen that stared back at me in the mirror.

She didn't look like me. She looked happy, light, pretty. Her hair fell below her chest in soft waves, shining a little hint of dark red when the light hit it just right. Her green eyes popped a little more as if trying to win the fight for the most attention against the long hair. The pastel-colored dress she wore clung in all the right places, flowing out just above the knee.

I sighed, realizing Vick had done her job. I would look the part, and I was thankful for that. I wanted to look as though I could hold my own in front of the equivalent of America's royal family. Today, after gruesome hours of hard labor, I guess I looked it.

"I'm leaving," Katie chimed from behind me.

I looked over my shoulder through the mirror to meet her eyes.

She must have seen my panic because she wrapped her arms around my waist and squeezed the life out of me. "You look hot as fuck, best friend. I promise you'll get through this and if he makes it difficult for you, you tell me and I'll gut him like the floppy fish he is."

I squeezed her wrists. "I can walk with you. We don't have to go with Rome."

She rolled her eyes. "I hate the guy." Her voice got loud enough for Vick to hear. "Don't know why you two hang out with his dumbass."

I snickered. "You told me to hook up with the hot bartender when we first met him."

"That was before I knew he was the owner of said bar and an egotistical ass."

I sighed. "I'll walk with you."

She shook her head. "He's an ass but Rome will look good on your arm today. Plus, you guys have killer chemistry. It'll make Jax sick."

I rolled my eyes this time. The woman was evil.

She swung open the door on her way out just as Rome arrived.

Their usual stare down happened. Rome raked his eyes over her body like he did with every woman, and honestly, Katie could have a sign that said Keep Away or I'll Shoot You on her shirt with holstered guns strapped to her, and men would still look. She surpassed Vick's sex kitten and my blandness by miles. With her combat boots, cut-off black top, and denim shorts that left little to the imagination, she looked like a badass *Tomb Raider*.

Although we didn't know her ethnicity, we knew it was a phenomenal mix. Her eyes slanted a little and their gray color contrasted nicely against her caramel skin. On top of that, she rocked a Victoria's Secret model body with a little less height.

Rome and her didn't get along but he eyed her up like he wanted to eat her alive. He leaned on the doorframe, blocking her exit. "Going somewhere, Kate-Bait?"

"Yes. So, move."

He flicked his gaze to Vick, not listening to Katie at all. "I thought I was driving all of you."

Katie didn't wait for Vick to answer. She just shoved him hard enough in the shoulder to slide past him.

He smirked as her body grazed his and grumbled, "What a waste."

She mumbled something along the lines of him being a dirty asshole. Then she was gone.

Rome snickered to himself at his own antics.

When he looked up, the hours seemed worth it. His jaw dropped open so wide, I almost asked if he was trying to show us something in the back of his throat.

He growled and moved toward me. "You look hot and fuckable. You sure we have to go to this graduation?"

My eyes bulged as I snapped my neck around to see if Vick had heard him.

"Vick's in the next room, Brey," he whispered. His hands slid around my waist, and he was already licking my ear.

I slapped him on the shoulder, and then slid my hands down to his chest. "I told her we aren't sleeping together anymore."

His jaw ticked as he pulled back from me. "Is that the truth? We stopping this?"

I sighed. "I don't know. Do you want to?" He eyed me up and down. "Absolutely not."

"Rome, are you thinking with your head and not something else?" I smirked and looked down.

"Brey, I'll stop if you want. We do it because it's a release for both of us. I care about you and you know that, but I can't do relationships. Every girl I sleep with knows that. If you're thinking that you want a relationship … " He trailed off, looking heartbroken.

I placed my hand on his chest and sighed in relief. His words were the comfort I needed to hear. "Vick keeps making me think you may want something more like a relationship, and then I'll hurt you or you'll hurt me. I can't do more than what we are doing now either. I like what we have."

"Vick's just being over protective."

"She protects our little crew even before there's a problem." I laughed as Rome cringed like he hated being a part of it.

Things were good between us. We reveled in each other sexually.

Yes, Rome could have other women, he *did* have other women.

I liked that. I liked knowing I wasn't anything special to him and he knew he wasn't special to me either. He was just safe and hot and easy. He'd been the only other guy I'd trusted myself with and the only one who hadn't hurt me.

Was I close enough for him to hurt me? No, but that was the point. Because, today, I was facing the one man who'd hurt me the most. We were in the car, about to face my worst nightmare.

I had to see each and every Stonewood today.

I had to see my heartbreak. My first love. My ultimate ruin. Jax Stonewood.

Thankfully, Jay had requested tickets for Vick and Roman, also. We were the first to show and it gave me a moment to get my bearings.

"Vick, you sit on this side of me and Rome you sit on this side." I motioned as I took a seat.

"Seriously?" Vick looked at me, hands on hips. "You look cute as hell. Leave this spot open and hope he sits down right next to you. Make him sweat it out. You have nothing to be embarrassed about."

"Cut her some slack," Roman grumbled and looked at me like I was pathetic. He plopped down next to me and swung his arm over my shoulders. "Want me to act like your boyfriend?"

Vick huffed. "You two might as well be dating. You eat together, you watch horrible television together. I also know for a fact you are still sleeping together … "

I flinched. "Vick, come on! You know that is none of your business."

"Why the hell not?" Her arms flailed along with her blonde ponytail. "You're my best friends and you guys are barring yourselves off from real relationships so you both can wallow in your past fucked-up ones."

Rome stopped her by leaning forward and glaring at her. His glare stopped traffic if it needed to. "Vick, not your business. We're all fine. No one's getting hurt. So leave it alone."

Vick's ponytail swished through the air like a white flag, giving up for now but letting us both know she didn't agree as she slammed back into her seat with her arms crossed.

I tried to relax under Rome's arm and let the sun warm me while we waited. The breeze kept me cool in my light sundress and rustled the budding trees.

We should have all been enjoying the comfortable weather while we waited for the ceremony to start. Instead, people buzzed through the seats, trying to get the best ones, and the graduates sat as straight as they could, sporting their caps and gowns.

I searched out Jay. I smiled to myself as I saw him talking to the person next to him and then that person laughed along at whatever he'd said. Jay deserved this moment more than anyone I knew. He'd never stopped making everyone around him laugh even as he studied through school.

Roman whispered in my ear, "You gonna miss him?"

"Like the deserts miss the rain."

He laughed, shaking his head. "Sade?"

"I only quote the best." I patted his leg. "You'll miss him too. He's been just as good of a friend to you as Vick and me."

"And I'm barely either of your friends at the moment," Vick mumbled at my right.

"His filming in LA starts in a few weeks, right?" I sighed. "Don't remind me. I'll barely see him."

Rome squeezed my shoulder. "If you need me to, I'll go to his movie trailer and drag him back here."

I shrugged. "If not, we'll just have to go see every rom-com he's in for the next two years."

"He's booked for two years?" Rome's voice went up in disbelief.

I nodded. "He'll come visit. He's starting to get time off when he asks for it."

Vick and Rome didn't look convinced.

"I'm serious! After being in three blockbuster movies, they have to give him time off set to decompress."

Vick nodded, staying positive. "You're totally right."

Like a breeze bringing in a storm, whispers started to travel around me. Goose bumps formed on the back of my neck. My heart raced as if my body was preparing for battle.

As I turned, I knew who I would see, but bracing for an explosion never worked.

The Stonewood family walked toward us from a distance. The crowd that buzzed before, rumbled with excited whispers.

Celebrities were in their presence. Men in suits fanned out around the family, and although it wasn't obvious, I knew they were bodyguards.

Nancy Stonewood stood at her estranged husband's side, a small smile on her lips as her dark hair waved in the wind. She wore a white dress that matched Senior Stonewood's white tie. As she looked up at her husband, his blue eyes twinkled like he held the secret of the world and shared it with only her. She smiled like she knew it too.

Jax and Jett walked beside them, sunglasses shielding their gorgeous eyes. Both were dressed in suits that probably cost more than my entire wardrobe. They mirrored each other with their dark hair and sun-kissed skin. Jett stood stiffer, like the weight of the world rested on his shoulders.

Jax, on the other hand, moved like molten lava. I knew firsthand how dangerous it was to be in his presence. He warmed everyone he passed, could make them feel alive. And yet, if someone got too close, he'd singe them. He didn't carry weight on his shoulders, he swallowed it all up and formed it into a power to wield as his own.

I crossed my legs as they all made their way over to us, and I reminded myself that I hated him. I hated everything about his confidence and the attitude that made him not worry about a thing. It allowed him to leave me behind to become a rock star who slept with another woman every night without a second thought. It was that attitude that had made him a billionaire mogul investor who could get whatever he wanted.

I stood to greet them as they neared. Nancy Stonewood rushed forward.

"Brey, you look beautiful." Her hand ran through my hair. She pulled me in for a hug. "I always loved your natural hair color. Keep it, okay?"

I smiled as I hugged her back. "Nancy, you told me you liked my dark hair."

"Honey, I lied," she whispered, pulling back to look over at my friends. "You all look so good. Much better than the last time I saw you."

All three of us threw glances at one another. Last time Jay bought us all a little too much wine. Vick faced it head-on. "Ugh, I don't remember a thing from that night, Mrs. Stonewood."

"Me either." Her candid, bright response had us all laughing hard enough that I forgot about who was around.

She moved to hug me quickly again. "Lunch soon?" I smiled. "Sounds perfect."

She winked. "I'll see you all tonight."

I moved to shake Senior Stonewood's hand. "So good to see you." I emphasized each word and stood tall, letting the mannerisms from family breeding take over because Senior Stonewood scared formalities out of everyone.

His blue eyes held the wisdom and power of one of the most lucrative businessmen in the world. Everyone shrank away under his cold stare. I'd only seen his expression warm for one person and that was Nancy. He was a man of few words which he only chose to speak to Nancy. He was also a man nobody dared say more than a few words to. If Senior Stonewood wasn't enough to make my nervous ticks come out, knowing that the bane of my existence was just feet from me did the trick.

"Pleasure as always, Aubrey." Mr. Stonewood patted my back and stepped away quickly. He nudged Jett forward and latched back onto his wife.

Jett's formalities overpowered any friendship we'd built over the years. He knew who watched and who didn't. He smiled friendly enough as he hugged me. "Account meeting soon? And..." He leaned closer still. His next words started the tremor in me. "Don't crumble. They're watching."

I swallowed hard and avoided looking in Jax's direction, afraid I wouldn't be able to breathe. I didn't say a word, just tightened my grip on Jett.

He squeezed my waist before he pulled back. "You ready?" He searched my eyes while holding a friendly smile. I tried to mimic his grin, attempting to squelch the shaking I could feel creeping out. He gave me a quick nod as if to reassure me that I could face Jax.

I wanted to scream at him to wait. I wasn't ready and never would be. Mostly because if I talked with him, I'd want to yell while I threw whatever was nearby directly at his head. I wanted to claw at him the way he clawed at my heart and ripped it apart.

None of that was for the public.

Instead, I would have to appear calm and collected while I felt the presence of his molten heat burn over my skin as he sauntered toward me.

Formal and polite had been ingrained into me in the most brutal way growing up. My father's insistence that I remain a quiet, well-mannered girl cloaked me like a blanket would on a cold night. The feeling that I was a coward, unable to express myself, made that blanket scratchy and uncomfortable. But it also allowed me to blend in, never cause a stir, and rarely get noticed. It allowed me to survive. So, I snuggled in and resorted back to the formalities like the coward I was.

Avoiding eye contact and looking on at his family, I breathed deeply before I said to him, "Good to see you're all doing well. I'm sure Jay will be happy to see you could make it."

From afar, Jax's presence weakened me. Up close, it just about destroyed me. I tried to ignore the pull to look at him and crossed my arms over my chest. Like a plague, I'd known this greeting was coming and that it had the ability to annihilate me. I'd prepared to just barely make it through, to survive. Instead of getting a quick, polite response from Jax that basically would have amounted to him brushing off the whole greeting like I'd hoped, he stayed silent.

I waited longer.

I watched the Stonewoods talking to my friends, seemingly engaged enough to not be concerned with my turmoil. Or maybe they were pretending to be engaged and hoping I could make it through this.

Probably the latter.

The silence, or maybe just his presence, willed me. No, it taunted me, forced me to look at him. My eyes shifted, slow as molasses dripping from a spoon, toward him. I felt my eyes widen without my permission, betraying me.

He towered over me, even in my heels, and had a smirk on his face that made me weak all over. The wind blew through his dark hair, tousling it just a bit. A dimple stood out while sunglasses hid the blue eyes I remembered so well.

I glanced at Rome and Vick, who were both suddenly by my side, as if sensing my panic, or as if they'd been watching the whole time.

Vick popped forward. "I'm Vick," she practically yelled and stuck her hand out for Jax to shake.

"Always good to meet a friend of yours, Whitfield." He shook her hand but addressed me. Both my knees, and it looked like Vick's too, practically buckled at the sound of his voice. It rumbled out soft and smooth, like a rolling hill meeting the horizon. This voice that made women literally throw their panties on a damn stage.

Jax continued, "I'm sure you've heard a little about me ... "

"Yup. I know who you are." Vick's back straightened and she snapped her hand back as if trying to steel herself. "I've heard *all* about you."

Jax's eyebrows raised for just a second before he smiled. "I hope all good things."

"Not a single good thing, actually." Vick crossed her arms. I smiled at how quickly she'd recovered and dropped her formalities for me.

Rome cleared his throat and introduced himself. "I'm Roman."

Jax slid off his glasses to stare at Rome by my side. I thought I saw jealousy behind those piercing blue eyes that matched the color of the Caribbean Sea. They pulled me in, mesmerizing me like waves on the beach. I blinked to look away, knowing that when anyone basked in the blue sea, reveling in the beauty, those eyes turned ice cold, drowning those locked on them.

When I heard Vick gasp at seeing Jax without glasses, I glared at her. As I turned back, I realized I'd imagined Jax's jealousy. His eyes were calm, light blue, and beautiful.

"Another of Aubrey's friends?"

Rome let loose one of his devilish smiles and I saw the mischief in his eyes like he'd been ready to unleash it all day. "Something like that."

Jax's gaze shifted over to me, and I definitely didn't miss the warning there that time.

I lifted my chin a little, ready for a snide remark.

He ran a hand through his hair, as if knowing now wasn't the place. "You all going to Jay's premiere in a couple days?"

Rome's arm snaked around my shoulder and he pulled me into him. My support and my comfort. I sank into him, knowing he was my anchor, the one who would keep me grounded through this. "Whatever Brey wants, I give her." I don't think the innuendo was lost on any of us as he paused. "She wants Jay happy for the night," he shrugged his shoulders like it was no skin off his nose. "They've been talking about this premiere night for a year. They'll kill us if we don't show. Right, babe?"

Jax's eyes were glued to Rome's arm until Rome called me babe. He looked at me. The relaxing Caribbean Sea turned into the Arctic Ocean. Cold, relentless, hard.

He started backing away toward his family. "And dinner tonight?" We all nodded.

"We'll talk more then," he remarked flippantly. Then he was back to zeroing in on me. "Peaches, you and I have a lot to catch up on." He slid his sunglasses back on and turned to join his family.

Throughout the graduation ceremony, everyone watched the Stonewoods who sat near us. We watched Jay accepting his diploma.

The only eyes that seemed to roam were Jax's and mine. Every now and then, mine would ignore the chant in my head that was supposed to will them not to look at him. Every now and then, I would see Jax's eyes roam over to mine, and then stare at Rome's arm wrapped around my shoulder.

It was the first time I contemplated shrugging out of Rome's hold.

But I didn't.

Instead, I snuggled in closer.

CHAPTER
TEN

JAX

THE RESTAURANT THAT night dimly lit every face in the room and showed that no one was a stranger. Stonewood Enterprises made it very clear to the bouncers outside who could attend.

My parents mingled along with my brothers, and I made my rounds quickly enough. I found myself within listening distance of the one woman I couldn't take my eyes off of since I'd arrived at my brother's graduation.

Her friends surrounded her like she was their queen on a chess board, like she was the most important, and she probably was in that group. She'd always had the uncanny ability to bring people together. I imagined that group wasn't any different.

I watched how she captured their attention and wondered if everyone was as blinded by her radiance as me. She glowed with her dark auburn hair and bright eyes looking as proud as ever when she watched my brother graduate.

Happiness looked good on her. It made me wonder how she looked when she felt every other emotion now. I used to know her every look, and I wasn't happy to admit that I wanted to know all of them again.

There were days I confessed to myself I missed her and I regretted how I'd left. Most days though, I reminded myself it was for the best.

I tried to tell myself that very thing as I eavesdropped on her and her friends.

I listened to Vick—her blonde viper of a friend—ask, "Are these people made of porcelain?"

To which Katie, Aubrey's oldest—and still probably her craziest—friend snorted, "These people probably had makeup artists in their cars on their drive over redoing everything."

Aubrey shushed them and reminded them they were all there for Jay.

I smiled a little to myself at seeing her mind her manners like always. Katie followed up with the truth. "Jay is as ready to go as we are. There's probably a hundred parties going on right now celebrating their graduation. You think he wants to be chumming it up with that?" She made a face and pointed to Jay and an older heavyset man that held his belly while he laughed at whatever Jay said.

Aubrey sighed and let a little smile slip. "Should we save him?"

"He's an actor, isn't he?" Rome said. "Let's see how long he can keep up that interested face."

Katie chimed in, "Two bucks says he ditches the conversation in another minute."

"You guys! We're being rude," Aubrey tried again.

Vick blurted, "I give him longer than three minutes and up the stakes to ten bucks."

Aubrey's eyes met Rome's and he raised his eyebrows as if challenging her. "Sixty seconds and he's done."

She pursed her lips as she looked at him and that's when I made the decision to walk over. The longer she looked at him, the more uncomfortable I felt.

Aubrey glanced at Jay, and I knew she had it figured out as I walked up and saw her tilt her head to say, "He's done in three, two, one."

Katie mumbled, "Unbelievable."

Vick smiled even bigger and clapped her hands. "He literally walked at that exact second!"

Rome didn't say a word because his ass was looking at me approaching.

"The bet isn't in your favor if the winner knows the subject as long as Aubrey has known Jay," I interjected.

Katie balked right away. "I've known him just as long as Brey."

"Pleasure, Katie. It's been a long time." I offered a hand knowing she wouldn't take it.

She stared as Aubrey nudged her, trying to prompt Katie to take my hand. That little devil didn't care about manners though. "The pleasure is *not* mutual."

I let my hand drop. "Fair enough." I turned back to Aubrey. "Come to the bar for a drink with me."

Her feet were already stepping forward to obey but I saw the second Roman's hand slid around her waist. "She just had a drink, but thanks, man."

His dismissal was meant to frustrate me. I knew and still couldn't shake the feeling I had when I saw his hands on her. I ran my tongue over my teeth, trying to settle or ready myself for a fight. I wasn't sure.

Aubrey cleared her throat and stepped toward me though, like she knew she had to diffuse my anger.

"I could use a water, Rome."

I stared at his grip on her waist, saw it tighten and took a step forward. Aubrey turned to him and whispered, "Stand down."

He whispered back, "One wrong move, Brey…"

She rubbed his chest and looked at him with what I could swear was love in her eyes. "I know. I know."

She spun toward me, and I almost wished for that same look to be directed my way.

Her green eyes were dead and empty though.

I didn't say anything to change that. Without a word to each other, we moved to the bar. I ordered an old-fashioned and water for her.

We both waited, not willing to be the first to start any more conversation. She probably did it to grate on my nerves. I did it to gauge hers.

When drinks were set in front of us, I finally remarked, "Interesting friends, Whitfield."

"They're the best kind of friends, Jaxon."

"You look the part. Nice and pretty. I haven't seen you since Jay's last movie premiere."

She glared. "You're here in your normal attire, wearing a tux as always, but I 'look the part'? What's that supposed to mean?"

"You don't normally wear so much makeup, do you?"

"Maybe, I do," she huffed out. "Do you normally dress like you're on the job?"

She'd never been good at lying, and I was embarrassed at how proud I was of myself for being able to read her emotions. I leaned a little nearer to her. "You're lying."

Her doe eyes narrowed, but I didn't elaborate. She stood there stiff in front of me. I'd seen her comfort drain as we'd made our way over the bar. She was as polite with me as she was with her father. Her mannerisms, her stiffness, even her voice.

I wanted to shake her, kiss her, scream at her, and comfort her all at once. I'd known her better than anyone once, and she couldn't hide behind formalities forever.

"Excuse me?" she whispered.

"I've never seen you with that much makeup on." I shrugged. "So, you're lying."

She cleared her throat, glancing around to see if she could sneak away. "You don't see much of me, Jax."

"That's true. But I've seen you in passing over the years with Jay." Why I was admitting it to her, I didn't know. "And, I seem to remember—"

Her glass clanged when she slammed it down. She tried to smooth the napkin on the bar to cover it. "I seem to remember a lot of things, Jax."

I smiled and her eyes widened like she'd been caught. "Well, it's good our memories haven't failed us yet."

"Yes, well, if memory serves me right, you left me high and dry six years ago. Didn't return a call or text. Didn't even send a postcard letting me know we were over. So, forgive me if I don't want to exchange niceties about what you remember about me."

I was surprised she faced the night head-on with me. Normally, people would have danced around it. And she was even more reserved than most. "You want to talk about that night?"

"I never want to talk about that night again." She practically spit the words. "*You* brought me over here. So, what do you want?"

"Well, I figure we're going to be seeing a little more of each other, so we should clear the air." It was the right thing to do. It might have been the reason I took her to the bar with me or it may have had something to do with her friend or "something like that" being near her.

"There's nothing to clear. You had nothing to share with me when you left, and I'm guessing you have nothing to share now."

Her eyes were vivid with determination, and I knew, even without her saying so, she was pushing me to share things about visiting her father.

"If you're looking for an apology—" I started.

She cut me off with a harsh laugh. "I'd never expect an apology from you." Her voice rose before she grabbed her water and gulped some down. "You're trying to get a rise out of me."

I didn't say anything because I wasn't sure if I was or not. For the first time in a long time, I was on unstable ground with someone.

Her face flushed like she'd disappointed herself. "It's Jay's night. Let's just forget about us and be cordial."

"Formalities were never my strong suit, Peaches."

She sighed and her bottom lip pulped out just a little. "Well, lesson number one. It isn't formal to call someone by a childhood nickname at a social function when you haven't talked to them in years. Brey is fine."

"I don't think I ever called you that." I consciously made the effort not to flex my jaw.

She turned toward the crowd but I caught her little smirk. I turned with her to find my brother and her friends trying to act like they weren't watching us like we were their favorite guilty-pleasure TV show. Someone may as well have brought them popcorn.

She leaned her elbows back on the bar as she cradled her drink, and I watched her chest push out just a little. Her strapless dress was barely decent. Damn it, she couldn't have worn a fucking turtleneck? Then again, I'd have found that indecent too. She'd filled out everywhere, and even though most women in the room were showing a lot more skin than her, I wanted to cover her up.

"Well, everyone calls me that now, Jax." She may not have meant it as an insult but her grouping me in with everyone else felt like a sucker punch to the gut. I wasn't supposed to be everyone. I was supposed to be the only one.

As she stared at her friends, I saw her smile at Roman. He watched our movements like a hawk, never taking his eyes off her unless he was staring me down. I stared back, letting him know my place.

What he didn't understand about me was I'd been there before him, and I was starting to think I'd be there after.

Even if Aubrey wanted nothing to do with me.

Even if I told myself I didn't need to have anything to do with her.

Being in her proximity showed me otherwise.

I didn't come here expecting anything with us. The plans I'd made were to come to this town and support my brother while looking into my app launch. If I got to explore the remnants of our relationship in the meantime, that was a bonus. And I needed to make sure she'd be fine through the shit I was about to stir up with her father.

We'd grown apart, I'd hurt her and she'd moved on. I'd moved on. And we were fine. Everything would stay just damn fine too, once I got all this shit straightened out over the summer.

Aubrey was right, we should be cordial. Nothing more, nothing less.

If I decided to fuck her in between to scratch the itch we both had for one another, then it would be nothing more and nothing less.

So, I convinced myself what I was feeling wasn't jealousy when I looked at Roman glaring.

The pain in my chest was just from gulping down the rest of my drink too quickly.

"Well, *Brey*," I emphasized her name as I slid my empty tumbler onto the bar. She looked surprised and then somewhat pleased that she'd gotten me to listen. "Let's get you back to your friends, shall we?"

With that, I nudged the small of her back through the crowd and watched the goose bumps spread across her nape.

I smiled to myself.

We both had an itch to scratch, all right.

CHAPTER
ELEVEN

AUBREY

JAX DISAPPEARED INTO the crowd for the rest of the night, and I was more bothered by that than relieved.

The times in battle where one side retreats without surrendering, there's a sort of confusion and waiting period. I didn't know if Jax had retreated to regroup his army or had given up.

Both of the thoughts terrified me.

When the dinner party began to disperse, I figured I could bail on everyone. I wanted time to myself, alone with my thoughts.

Katie tried to give me the space I wanted but Vick glared from her to Rome to Jay like she would eviscerate them one by one if they didn't follow me home.

So, we headed to my apartment together. When they all had settled in the living room watching some house remodeling show, Vick turned her eyes on me. "Can we please decompress by talking about Jay's family?"

Jay groaned, and I turned toward the oven where I'd been spending my time making brownies. I'll admit it was a diversion tactic. I didn't want to decompress and talk about them. I wanted to forget.

"Please, can we not?" Katie grumbled from the floor where she sat.

Rome's eyes met mine from the rocker he sat on. He took the seat every time like he owned it, spread his legs out, leaned back, and rested his tattooed arms over the armrests. From the corner of the room, he saw everything that went on like he watched over it, like a lion overlooking his kingdom. "You okay over there, baby girl?"

"Just fine," I singsonged as I took the brownies out of the oven and started to cut them into squares. "I'm really proud of Jay graduating. I'm happy we all got to spend it together."

And I'm happy it was over.

Jay got up to grab one of the brownies.

"All right. Remind me to never buy dessert again," Jay said as he popped a whole brownie square in his mouth.

I glared at him and he smiled wide with brownie all in his teeth.

Rome moved in and shouldered Jay out of the way as he took his own brownie square. "Why aren't you baking for the men in your life every night?"

I smiled. "You men don't give me enough motivation to bake every night."

Rome cut me off. "I think I gave you something last night when I—"

"Rome!" I yelled.

Vick yelled, "I knew it!" at the same time.

My eyes snapped to Jay. He didn't know, we'd all kept it from him. He looked around. "What's going on?"

We all looked anywhere but at him. I started to shove a brownie in my mouth. It wasn't that we wanted to hide things from him, it was just that he was the light of our group. His easy going way helped us all to unwind and relax. We couldn't have him uneasy.

"Seriously." He leaned back on his heels and crossed his arms. His muscles bunched under his T-shirt and his jaw ticked. "You guys are hiding something, and I don't want to be shielded like a damn child…"

"Well to be fair,"—Katie started—"you are the baby in your family. You do act like—"

"Don't start your psycho-babble from a class you slept through, Katie." He didn't even crack a smile when he said it.

"Oh, fuck off. I got an A in that class," she mumbled from the floor as I grabbed my glass to take a long swig of the red wine. I figured I was about to need it.

"Rome and Brey are sleeping together," Vick blurted out loud enough for the damn neighbors to hear.

"What?" Jay whispered so quietly the neighbors probably thought no one responded to Vick's outburst.

"Oh God." I rushed to clear the counter and busy my hands.

When no one answered Jay, he roared, "What?" and pounded his fist down on the counter.

Rome crossed his arms over his chest and stood his ground in the kitchen. "We can talk like men or we can yell like children. You want to yell and act out, then we take it outside."

Jay stepped toward him. "I should kill you where you stand." I gasped. "Jay, you don't mean that."

His eyes snapped to mine and they held so much anger, I shrunk back. "I'm fucking pissed at you, Brey."

I set the dishes in the sink and stood between the two men I loved so much. "Jay, let's talk. Rome, give us some time." I sighed and looked at Vick and Katie. "Can we just have some time?"

Vick elbowed Katie and looked remorseful as they headed out of my apartment. Rome stood his ground for another minute, staring at Jay like something more needed to be said between them.

I clenched my fist, trying so hard not to lash out at him. Jay and I were unbreakable, he had to know by now. Rome and I could sleep together, share a bed, wake up and have sex again. He could give me ten million orgasms and make me forget about life over and over again. But he'd never get between Jay and me.

He looked at me one more time and sighed in some sort of defeat before he walked out.

I took a breath, turned to the dishes and started washing. It felt like ages passed before Jay nudged me over so he could manage one side of the sink. "You should have told me," he said barely above a whisper.

I shrugged but couldn't mask the guilt. "I know. Is it too late to apologize?"

"Why didn't you tell me?"

I handed him another soaped up dish. "Because you *are* the baby in your family but the big brother in mine. You're too overprotective and you would have been judgmental and … "

He waved the clean dish through the air. "Excuses, Brey. All I'm hearing are damn excuses. The reason you didn't tell me was because you know that shit's unhealthy."

"To be fair, don't you think it's time for just me to worry about how unhealthy I am?"

Jay set the now dry plate gently down and then dried his hands before he answered me. "It's one thing for me to see you blowing off classes, drinking too much, and dying your hair black like you want to disappear."

"Everyone didn't have a problem with my hair color before," I interrupted.

He just rolled his eyes and crossed his arms over his broad chest. "I can handle those things. We're in college and you're expressing yourself or what the fuck ever. But don't expect me not to worry. You think you can handle all this shit by yourself?"

"What shit?" I snapped back. I stepped up to the plate but hoped he wouldn't throw the pitch.

"I saw you tonight with my brother, Brey, and you looked scared. Back to being as polite and quiet as you were in high school." He waited a beat. "After the fire."

He threw the ball right past me. My eyes probably popped out of my sockets. I started to say something, not sure what, then stuttered to a stop because Jay normally babied me. He didn't bluntly throw his brother or my past in my face.

I stepped back and shrugged. "Yeah. Well, I handled it, and I'm fully capable of handling my own decisions." He tried to cut in but I held up my hand to stop him. "That includes Rome, Jay."

"And are you fully capable of pulling me off him if he breaks your heart because, Brey, I'll fucking kill him. Friend of ours or not."

"Jay, be reasonable." He knew exactly how those words would affect me. As laid-back as he could be, he was also the son of the most brutally lethal businessman in the country. He didn't hesitate when he felt threatened or when he wanted something to stop. Instead, he attacked the situation just as ferociously as any Stonewood.

He targeted my biggest weakness—our group—and endangered it with a pointed attack which made me question everything.

"I'll be reasonable when you start being realistic. Focus on your future. Don't fuck a guy you have no future with."

"You're being an ass."

"And you're being difficult because you know I'm right. You should be mapping out your summer and figuring out what classes you're going to take to graduate."

I walked to the living room, trying to brush off his words. "I told you, I'm taking that investment class you suggested and that's it. I'm busy."

He followed. "You shouldn't be that busy. Those girls are doing fine when you aren't there."

"They do better when I am there though. And helping them with accounting is icing on the cake. I'm getting experience."

Jay sighed. "Investment and accounting aren't the same and you know it."

I didn't argue, just shrugged. "I go there once a week. That's not that much."

"I'm just saying you don't have to take all that on by yourself. You don't owe them—"

I glared at him. "I know I don't owe anyone anything."

He waited a beat. "You want me to go with you next week?"

I sighed. "You have your premiere and need to be in LA. They don't expect to see you."

He leaned toward me, a small smile playing on his lips. "You could come to LA, shack up with me, and leave this shit behind."

I rolled my eyes because he'd made the offer more than once. Jay would keep me under his wing as long as he could if I let him. "Yeah, I think I'll pass."

His jaw ticked and he leaned back on the couch. "I hate I can't be here with you. This shit with Rome and my brother makes it infinitely worse. You could just move to LA for a while."

That was it for him as he grabbed the remote and turned the TV on. He wanted the conversation over, and it could be because we'd shared our thoughts on everything before.

It was the best and worst thing about having a best friend who knew you better than anyone. I knew he was thinking I should avoid them both like the plague. He knew I was thinking about how to overcome everything, how to get along with them and how to move on.

"Jay," I sighed as I grabbed the remote and turned the TV back off. "Rome's always going to be around."

"So." He didn't look at me.

"So, we slept together. We're still good friends and no one is hurt."

Over the years, I'd learned to see past this facade. No one else would notice the way his eyes squinted just a little and his shoulders bunched slightly before he spoke. "Define 'slept,' Brey. Are you still sleeping with him, or is it done?"

"Honestly," I threw my hands up. "I don't know. With your little tantrum tonight, it's probably done."

He sucked in air through his teeth. "We both know that wasn't a tantrum. That was me handling it extremely well."

"Oh, please."

His lopsided smirk was back. "I deserve a damn Academy Award for how well I acted through that one."

"Your acting was subpar. If Matthew McConaughey isn't getting an award for *How to Lose a Guy in Ten Days*, you aren't getting one for tonight either."

Jay's smile turned up a notch. "Have I told you lately that I miss that nice little lady that you were back in high school?"

"I miss the nice little boy who didn't expect Academy Awards for nothing."

He walked around the counter slowly toward me. "You're going to pay for that, Sass Pot."

I jumped up, circling around the couch to put it between us. I made it about two steps before he'd grabbed me around the waist and hauled me back.

I fought him, laughing my butt off. "Let me go, you idiot!"

"Nope. Apologize!" He demanded as he threw me back on the couch and walloped me with a throw pillow.

I ducked and laughed harder, shaking my head no.

He sideswiped me and whacked me again. "I'm the best actor you've ever known. Say it."

I grabbed another throw pillow, scrambled upright and swatted him the best I could before he plowed me with another swing. "Well, since you're the only one I actually know—"

That had him collapsing next to me in laughter, so I took the opportunity to throw one last pillow in his face. He wrapped an arm around me and pulled me close as we both laughed for a minute longer.

My belly hurt from laughing. Then it seemed to hurt for a whole other reason. Jay had graduated and would be moving into a whole new world of acting and fame. He'd already come close to all of it.

He and his brothers had already been named "Most Eligible Bachelors" in magazines. When Vick met us, she'd jokingly named them Brey's Bachelor Boys, and Rome had been an honorary mention in her book. She couldn't believe how down-to-earth Jay still was and it scared me to think he may not be one day.

He was on the cusp of it, just out of their reach, just far enough away from the spotlight that we could still have these moments, still have each other, still be best friends.

I wanted to put him in a damn jar, close it, and never let him out. "I'm going to miss you, Jay."

"Miss me?" He said, his half-smirk back in place, ready to smooth things over right away. "I'm not going anywhere you can't reach me."

"You will," I sighed. "You and I both know it."

He squeezed my shoulder and winked at me. "You can come with me."

"Sure, and I'll just chase women out of your place every day."

"Someone's got to be my watchdog."

"Hire a security team then!"

"Because that'll look good in the tabloids: 'Jay's Bodyguards Carry Another Woman From His Premises.'"

"If it was me, they'd make up something even worse."

He sighed and unwrapped his arm from me. "Most of the tabloids love you, Brey."

"Most of them write totally made-up stories about us, Jay."

"Well, the stories sell."

"Right. So, that makes it okay. I can look like your understanding girlfriend in the tabloids every so often as long as they are nice about it." I sneered.

"I haven't seen you in one in a while."

"Why are you defending them?" I crossed my arms. "Because,"— he stood up and started pacing—"I know you." I blinked at him when he looked at me to respond.

He sighed. "This will be your way of getting out of going to my premiere with me."

Before I could make an excuse, he just waved it off. "I want you there, Brey. This is me making it, me being where I want to be, and I want my best friend there."

I sighed because he was right. I was building to that. We both knew I didn't want to go. "It's not that I don't want to be there to support you, it's just—"

He stopped me, "If you feel like you can't handle it, I get it."

He'd lost his smile and the sparkle he always had in his eyes.

I pursed my lips and smoothed my hair back a little. "I can handle it."

My voice sounded surer than I felt.

AFTER JAY LEFT, I went to lie down, wondering if my decision to sleep with Rome would end up ruining my small circle of friends. I knew that was Jay's intention. I knew he wanted me to think about my actions, to question myself, to second guess my decision. I didn't want to let his words affect me. Yet, I lay there staring at my ceiling and wondering if my self-destruction had bled over into the destruction of our group.

I sighed and stared and stared, hoping the dark sky would lull me to sleep.

Strong arms wrapped around me later that night. Rome's scruff nuzzled into my neck. "You awake, doll?"

"I wish I wasn't."

I heard him sigh behind me. "You know I love you, Brey." I tensed because I knew what was coming.

"Falling in love sneaks up on you. You don't stand at the edge and decide to jump. Someone, probably the person you're about to fall for, pushes you over the edge with a little gesture, a little hint, a subconscious action. Then it's all over. You're falling and humans can't fly. We don't get a shot to catch ourselves mid fall. I don't want to fall for you, and you don't want to fall for me."

"I get it, Rome." I felt my throat close, my eyes tear up. I swallowed hard. "I know we have to stop."

He pulled me closer and said a muffled good night.

I fell asleep crying. It wasn't because I'd lost the casual relationship with Rome. It wasn't because I had more feelings for him than I admitted. It was because I couldn't hide from my emotions anymore, couldn't lie to myself about the real battle my heart and mind always waged.

Truth was, I knew the damn reason I didn't want to date other men. I knew the reason to not get involved.

I hated the reason and the man.

CHAPTER
TWELVE

AUBREY

"YOU GUYS READY?"** Jay asked from my left side. Katie squirmed in her black dress like I squirmed in my red dress. Rome pulled me closer to him in the limo, as if we could shield each other from the screaming outside. The only person who looked prepared was Vick. She looked angelic in a form fitting crystal-blue dress that swung fluidly around her pumps.

"How long do we have to stay?" Katie blurted.

Jay chuckled. "You three look like deer in headlights."

I stomped my red pump. "Shut up, Jay. We're only going because you're making us."

Vick jumped in. "Speak for yourself. I intend to take a selfie with every actor I meet tonight."

I snorted. "I intend to hide in a corner."

"It'll be fun, Sass Pot." Jay poked me in the ribs.

I dropped my head onto Rome's shoulder. "These are your people. Not ours. We don't belong."

Jay's shoulders bunched a little. "You belong anywhere I am, Brey. Always."

Which was why I had succumbed to wearing the form fitting, sequined, designer dress Jay had bought for me. Instead of blending in like I wanted, he pushed me to stand out.

It was why I let Vick, yet again, do my hair and makeup. This was his night, and I couldn't say no to anything.

I had hated cameras ever since the day I'd walked out of the Stonewood house and had been blinded by them. I didn't want to be the center of attention. So, this part of Jay's life, I avoided.

I avoided people who ran up to him for his autograph and asked me if I was his girlfriend.

I avoided tabloids speculating about us. I avoided a lot.

I heard the screaming outside of our limo. My gut clenched. When I looked at Jay, he seemed on top of the world though.

Yes, I hated this part, but I loved the guy on my left with every bone in my camera-shy body.

I turned to him and smiled, trying my damnedest not to tear up. "You did it, Jay."

He took both my hands in his and touched his forehead to mine. "You helped."

Although I hadn't helped much, he made me feel like I had. I remembered the lines I would read back to him and the times I told him he was unstoppable when he doubted himself.

Which reminded me to give him my only advice. "This movie is a romance, which means you're romancing every woman in America. Be charming, be committed. Charming is easy for you."

"Who am I committing myself to?"

I pulled back and looked at Katie, who had a hell-to-the-no look on her face, and Vick, who smiled radiantly. "Your PR team needs to do a better job with these sorts of things," I mumbled.

He and Rome laughed.

I threw my hands up. "Well, it's true!"

Jay sobered enough to say, "My PR doesn't get to tell me who to date. I told them I would have three women in the limo with me, including you. That was enough for them."

I waved that idea away. "I'm not feeding into the tabloids. Vick, you walk with him."

"Well, duh. You and Katie are going to try to *Runaway Bride* this as soon as you can. Rome, be honest, are you the getaway transportation?"

Rome just shrugged, staying quiet but smirking the whole time.

The limo inched forward more and then stopped. Someone tapped on the top of it as if to signal we were next. Jay eyes twinkled at all of us. "Third premiere, and I get to share it with all of you. Vick, you ready to be on my arm?"

"I was made for it," she responded like a true entertainer.

Then he looked at us, a twinkle in his eyes. "You guys got this?"

Did I have it? Could I face a mob of cameras like I had at his last premiere? I loathed the feeling of stepping back into the brightness after it felt like I was hiding. I hated that every camera strobe seemed to glimpse into the deepest, darkest parts of me. Did they remember who I was? Did they want my story?

Did it matter? The answer was always no.

Jay was my rock and my very best friend. My family.

I loved Katie, Vick, and Rome. They were my family too, but Jay was always number one. I'd do anything for him, even if I didn't want to.

"Let's do this with a smile on our faces, all right?" I said, slapping him on the shoulder.

The dimples finally showed on his face, a signal that he'd relaxed and the last of his hesitation fled. His strong jawline and baby-blue eyes paired with dark hair spiked in a crew cut had even me sighing. If there was an eligible bachelor look, he wore it without any flaws.

Beautiful wasn't a word to describe him or any of the other Stonewood brothers. Not even Jay's father could take on that word. These men were hard, fierce, and downright sexy. Every woman vied for their attention. I knew because I'd read, and got to see firsthand, story after story of Jay's reckless behavior with them.

I smoothed the tight red dress down. Versace did form fitting and sparkle like nothing else I'd ever seen. Vick had taken my measurements, Jay opened his wallet, and I ended up in this thing. It didn't fit like his eligible bachelor look fit him. I didn't reek of perfection or class like him either, but it would do.

The limo door swung open. The cameras blinded everyone. I knew I'd lock up if we didn't keep moving.

My heart jumped with each flash. My limbs started to freeze.

But my mind worked overtime.

Would they bring up my past? Would they want to know details? Would they remember?

As my heart jumped with each flash, I searched deep, deep down for my little old friend, Control.

Katie shoved Vick out first. Like a true diva, she lapped up the attention.

The flashes went wild as Jay smiled down at her and she swooned like the actress she was made to play.

Katie mumbled, "What attention whores."

Rome whispered to me, "It's now or never."

Rome slid out of the limo and reached in for me.

I rolled my lips between my teeth, took a deep breath, and stepped out.

No flashes went off.

No one screamed at me.

Katie slid out after me and said, "We look like the reject groupie friends of Jay."

"Fine by me," I whispered as we started to sneak past Jay who smiled so genuinely at the cameras, they practically kissed him when they went off.

When I passed behind him though, his arm shot out. He whispered something in Vick's ear. Then somehow, I was standing in her place. Jay pinned me to his waist and leaned down to whisper into my hair, "Smile, Sass Pot."

I glared at him and saw the determination in his eyes.

He had been made for the limelight and I hadn't. My phobia of it frustrated him. I knew that but I couldn't control it.

I wanted to scream at him for making me confront it so publicly.

Paparazzi screamed at me, "Is he finally committed to just you, Aubrey?"

I held back a snide remark and felt a shake starting to run through my whole body. A few magazines had printed pictures of Jay and me over the years as if our friendship was more. Then, the magazines had gone on to print pictures of Rome splashed with headlines like "Stonewood left for a bartender." The story was wrong, of course. Rome did bartend at the bars he *owned*.

"Remind us, how long have you known each other?"

Since two blue-eyed, dark-haired devils tackled me for my candy right after they'd moved in years ago. Of course, Mrs. Stonewood made them apologize, and we became fast friends. Best friends. Inseparable, really.

Now, if I gave them an answer like that, I'd not only sound extremely committed to him, I'd crush every girl's hopeful dream of ever meaning more to him than I did. So, I held back my answer again.

"How long have you been exclusive? Pictures of you both are everywhere."

I cringed a little. I avoided being out in public as much as I could for that very reason. The cameras, the speculation, the ongoing story were all too much for me. I wanted my best friend without all the crap that came with him. I didn't need to read the magazines saying that I was an idiot because Jay was running around on me. Or they would say I was a genius because I had somehow kept him around.

What they didn't seem to ever want to print was that we were just friends. The Stonewood men, in general, didn't really settle for any one woman. Jett and Senior Stonewood were married to their work. Jax and Jay were married to their noncommittal lifestyle.

The three Stonewood brothers were born into a life of luxury and easy access to women. Their father owned Stonewood Enterprises, one of the largest investment firms in Chicago, and their mother was a soft-hearted beauty from a little town in Wisconsin who fell for the business shark.

They were raised mostly in Chicago, but when business trumped fatherhood for Senior Stonewood, that soft-hearted beauty turned hard and took her children back to Wisconsin to learn a more modest lifestyle. Their separation was amicable, the press wrote.

I knew better. When a man who has conquered the business world begs for a woman to come back, and every paparazzi that asks him about his divorce gets cut off by him correcting them with the word separation, there's more to the story. Every time they saw each other, there was love that couldn't be broken in their eyes.

The girls at our school had love in their eyes for the Stonewood boys too. I didn't think that love could be broken either until one threw her text book at Jax after catching him in the hall with another girl. He apologized, of course, and somehow that love in her eyes came right back. I witnessed the cycle over and over again. I swore to myself that I would never be that pathetic.

At least not ever again.

"Jaydon, are you and Aubrey finally official? We want all the details."

It jolted me into a sort of panic that they already knew my name. How did they always know?

Jay leaned in as we continued to walk. "So, I guess we're back to being a couple?"

I just smiled because I'd started to feel like the crowd was closing in on me. Damn them for getting so close and crowding us like we didn't need oxygen too.

"Relax, Brey. I got you, they are not going to swallow you up. Plus, you need a chauffeur in those six-inch heels. I've seen you fall over before," he smirked as he whispered.

I actually stopped to let out a hard laugh. What a reminder that I didn't belong in this dress, at this event, in these heels, that I couldn't handle the spotlight and luxury like him. "Well, thank you, Jay, but I think I can handle walking on my own," I sneered as I let go of his arm with the intention to walk ahead of him.

Screw him if he thought I couldn't do this. I'd told him I could, I'd made the decision, and I would own it. Damn him if he thought these heels weren't worth the fall. Christian Louboutin bled class out of you. My feet were probably literally bleeding too, but I needed all the help I could get.

I heard his chuckle behind me. I turned to tell him off, but his blue eyes twinkled with mischief and pride. "Look at you, doing everything on your own."

A rush to be bolder and ruder whipped through me. I wanted to knee him in the balls but knew we were on display. Instead, I resigned to mumbling for us to get this over with. Answers to the paparazzi questions were inevitable.

"Jay, give us something. How long is it that you've known each other again?"

"Longer than I've known any of you," he said, looking at me with all the love he could muster. I smiled back like I was in love.

"Is marriage in the cards?" Another screamed and thrust the mic at me.

"Oh, Jay and I wouldn't bind each other to an agreement like that," I said, insinuating what all the ladies wanted an answer to.

"What do you mean? Are you still not exclusive? Are you both still on the market?"

"All I can say is Jay loves women way too much to be tied to just one ... " I looked his way as if a little disappointed. I knew better than to promote the movie. I knew to promote the man because that's what ladies really wanted.

He smiled and finished what I'd started. "But if I were to be tied to one, isn't she just perfect?" The one-liner would charm every woman in America. I could have high fived him right there.

With that, the paparazzi erupted again and the fans did too. We posed for a few more pictures and finally entered the building that promoted *Nights Without You.* The blockbuster would put him on most eligible bachelor list in *People* magazine and land him three more romantic movie lead deals.

He pulled me with him toward his costar in the film, "You have to meet Mila. You'll love her."

"I don't really want to meet anyone, Jay," I grumbled under my breath.

"And yet, you'll be meeting everyone I work with tonight." His smile as he said it was blinding.

As if to emphasize his point, a couple stepped into our path and introduced themselves.

I half-listened but no one noticed. Part of growing up as the daughter of Whitfield Candy's owner meant I needed to know how to keep up appearances and attend events. Manners and small talk were taught at a young age. I'd been quick enough to learn the unspoken lessons too. How to look like you were listening, how to do a quick brush off politely, how to offend without outwardly offending.

I practiced all the lessons as I searched for the only people I wanted to talk to—Katie, Vick, and Rome. They'd been swallowed up by white pillars dancing in different colored lighting, tables set up everywhere with beautiful flower arrangements, and celebrities who mingled among them all.

That's when I saw Jax sauntering toward us. My insides twisted up like they needed him to unwind them. His eyes twinkled in the dim lighting and mesmerized me. When he glanced at Jay, I saw a smile I remembered from a long time ago, a smile from the boy I once knew, the one who saved me, the one who sat with me at a lake and sang sweet songs to me. I remembered a boy who loved me and promised to never leave me.

He didn't love me though. He left.

I considered running to the bathroom but after already making eye contact, I would look like I was avoiding him.

When he reached my side, he leaned toward my ear and whispered, "You having a nice night?"

I leaned away immediately and answered him with a canned response. "Of course. It's a great night."

He smiled down at me and his voice rumbled out for only me to hear, "You're lying."

I hated and loved the way he sounded. That rasp and I had had an ambivalent relationship from the day I realized Jax and I could be more than just friends.

He'd whispered something to a girl in high school and she'd shiver just like I did when I heard it. I'd spun into a jealous silent rage then, realizing every girl in our school was affected in the same way I was. We all wanted him, and he'd shared a piece of himself with everyone but me.

That was until our last summer. Those three glorious months after his senior year, he'd spent only with me. I didn't get just a piece of him, I thought I'd gotten all of him. We jogged down to our lake, away from the world, away from inquiring eyes. He brought his guitar and played just for me. I lost myself in that rasp, in his songs, and in my love for him.

I lost myself altogether when he left.

He looked over at a table and then at Jay who was still talking with the couple. "Mind if I steal your date for a minute?"

Jay couldn't say no. It would have been completely rude. So, before he could even worry about it, I grabbed Jax's arm and he led me to a table.

"Sit with me for a while?" he asked.

"You know, I am actually getting ready to leave ... "

He pulled the chair out for me and I sat down, not wanting to cause a scene.

He sat next to me and asked, "How have you been?"

The question startled me. How could he, after all this time, be that casual?

"Seriously? Do you honestly care about anyone but yourself?"

He flinched at my words. Well, I suppose that came out ruder than I anticipated.

"You're holding onto something from years ago, Sweet Sin. It's no way to live."

"Don't call me that," I whispered as the pain deep in my chest started again.

"All right, sorry, Peaches." He tilted his head to the side and smirked.

Another nickname that shot more pain—reminding me of heartbreak—through my chest.

"I go by Brey. That's it."

"No." He said it firm, low, in command. When he leaned forward just a breath closer to me, I could see his eyes had darkened. "You go by Whitfield, Peaches, or Sweet Sin to me. It will never be anything else."

I'm sure Jax had become accustomed to women, and men for that matter, listening to him, shaken by his demeanor and the power he seemed to hold with just a look. Unfortunately for him, I wasn't one of those people.

"No, Jax." I stood and smoothed the red sequins of my dress. "That's who I was to a sweet boy in high school. He called me those names all the time. But he's gone. I don't have any idea where that boy went."

I felt his eyes brush over me, taking me in. My body reacted in a way I should have been ashamed of. I felt hot, and I knew my eyes showed my reaction to his perusal because he was smiling as he licked his lips like I was his next meal. "Fine. I'll play. Let's talk about where that boy went."

I shook my head, trying to clear out the damn hormones affecting my senses. Half the reason I reacted to him was because I needed to find someone else to hook up with. I also needed to find Rome and smack him for leaving me feeling this needy before I saw my first love who now just happened to be one of *People* magazine's "Hottest Bachelors."

An announcement sounded. "With one Stonewood, you normally find another, ladies and gentlemen. Tonight, Jax is here supporting his brother, Jay. Ladies, you've got to be excited about that one." The spotlight turned directly toward Jax, and I took that as my moment to escape. I moved quickly to find a bathroom where I could pull myself together.

I would have to thank God for making the bathroom a single-person room with a lock on the door.

Silence.

Brilliant, beautiful silence.

I looked in the mirror and tried to muster up some confidence.

"You can handle this. The most uncomfortable situations are what make you stronger."

It was a mantra. Something that got me through the good and bad days. Tonight was definitely turning into a bad night.

I looked like hell too. The mirror reflected a girl with hair that had frizzed. My long, dark curls had lost their luster in the summer heat. My smoky eyeliner somehow made my green eyes seem bigger than they already were.

"Hey, is anyone in there?" A loud knock sounded at the door. "One minute!" I yelled.

They mumbled something but I heard footsteps walking away.

I shrugged my shoulders and smoothed my dress again. My main concern wasn't someone else's bladder issue. There were probably twenty other bathrooms in this humongous place.

As I tried to smooth more flyaways, I whispered one last time, "You can handle this."

I wasn't going to fix much more of my appearance at this point. So with a final sigh, I went to unlock the door. I turned the knob, but it didn't give. I turned it again a little harder and yanked. Didn't budge an inch.

"Come on," I muttered, feeling my control slipping away and the fear seeping in. I jiggled it a few more times as my palms started to sweat.

"Okay. No big deal, just call Jay," I told myself as I pulled my phone out to dial his number.

No signal? No signal!

I tried the door again. I wanted it to magically open. I needed some higher power to give me a break. It didn't work.

Panic and more fear lurked.

"Someone will need the bathroom. Ms. Whatever will be back any minute. Control yourself." It was a command. I wanted to follow my own orders, but knew my panic and fear always stole that control from me.

"Shit!" I slammed my hand on the door. As I did, loud music started on the other side of the door.

That meant people were going to watch the music. They would wait to go to the bathroom. I would be stuck.

"No, no, no," I whispered as I turned my back to the door and slid down to sit.

I couldn't be stuck. It was too small.

"Much too small." I rubbed my forehead, trying to focus on the words, on anything else.

My lovely friend, Control, smiled at me and waved goodbye. He was skipping happily away, and I felt my breath hitch.

"I'm locked in."

I tried the handle again. "Keep calm, Aubrey."

This time it was burning hot. "Stuck. I'm stuck."

I jerked back and stumbled over my heels.

The heat. It meant there was fire. Fire everywhere. I was going to burn. Die of smoke inhalation. There was no oxygen.

Low. I had to get low to the ground. I dropped to the floor quickly and crawled away from the door to the opposite corner.

"Please, please someone come for me."

I heard her voice in the back of my head saying that he would come.

Don't worry, he'll come.

There wasn't enough air to wait. I was suffocating.

Smoke swirled all around. Swirled into my lungs, started to drown me just like water would. I laid down and army-crawled toward the door. I needed help. She needed help. If I didn't try to get out, we'd die in here. We'd burn.

I curled up at the door and tried to yell. With no air, only a whisper came. "Please, please help," I tried to call out as I banged on the door.

The crackle of fire from outside took over. It roared to life like a lion moving in to kill. She whispered from the other side of the room, "He'll come for us, I swear."

I whimpered.

Would he save us if he was the one who'd wanted us to burn?

The question forced Control, my sweet friend, out.

Memory, my sworn enemy, stepped in.

"Sit up straight when you eat at my damn table." My father spit the words at me after he'd caught me slouching.

Women in his household were to have manners. I knew this but hated it all the same. Every time I went over to the Stonewoods, the boys didn't have to sit up straight. They didn't have to keep their elbows off the table or only speak when spoken to. Mrs. Stonewood, or Nancy as she insisted I call her, just told me to relax and have some fun.

Fun in the Whitfield household was unknown.

Mother sat silent. She didn't glance up when my father patronized me. She'd mastered the art of invisibility.

That night, I tried to mirror her, not wanting to aggravate my father's anger. My mother blamed his outbursts on his hard upbringing. She still loved him, said he'd been a sweet man once, that things could always be worse.

I never knew the sweet man. So there was never any love between the two of us.

As for my mother, I saw her sweetness every day. She protected me from him as best she could. She played middle man to the constant hate my father and I had for each other. Somehow, even through his abuse, she remained stoically loyal to him and to me. Maybe he really did love her and that's why he never went after me, knowing that I was my mother's only weakness in her love for him.

"Aubrey, how was school?" he asked, back to trying to have the white picket fence and perfect family that he forced upon us.

"Most students were excited it was Friday, Father. Everyone was happy and … "

"Everyone was acting like animals," he growled.

I started to protest. My mother cut me off. "Your studies are going well still, Brey?"

"Her name is Aubrey. There is a reason we named her that."

My mother's head dropped again. Her long dark hair curtained around her face, hiding her disapproval. Mother always called me Brey when he wasn't around. Just like I called her Mom when he wasn't around. "Just a little secret," she would say with a smile.

So, silence took over our meal, enveloping me in the security that without sound or improper movement, my father couldn't find fault in our actions.

Both my mother and I mirrored each other perfectly. She held her fork in her right hand just an inch into the chicken as she cut into the meat with the knife in her left hand. The knife was never to touch the plate and it didn't after I accidentally did so one night. My mother had stood up for me, saying I was too young to never have an accident. My father turned his anger on her, as he always did. Now, I copied my mother's motions, making sure each slice of chicken was never too large for a woman to properly bite into.

The phone ringing jerked me from my daydream.

"Excuse me," my father said as if we would have objected to him getting up in the first place.

He answered the phone as both my mother and I looked on. The calls to the house were either the Stonewoods or my father's job. My mother didn't have any friends or family left.

"She is eating dinner," he said into the phone. "She will call you back tomorrow."

Silence.

"No. She cannot go out tonight or any night for that matter."

Fear seeped through me. I'd forgotten to tell Jay and Jax not to tell my dad about going out last weekend. My dad had been away and my mother had finally given me permission to go to a party and then sleep at their house.

I didn't drive. I didn't have a cell phone. I didn't do anything other than go over to the Stonewoods every now and then for an hour or two. When I begged my mother, she finally agreed with a warning that my father could never find out.

"What do you mean she did last weekend?"

My mother's eyes snapped up to meet mine. We mirrored each other again. Both of us stared in fear at the other. We sat as still and as straight as possible.

"Well, not tonight," he said, turning slowly to look at my mother. I hated that my eyes were the same color as his. The way his lit up with rage made me wish at night that God would just wipe away every genetic trace of him in me.

"I will have her call you tomorrow." I flinched as he slammed the receiver down on the cradle.

He stared at my mom, waiting.

I watched the clock in the kitchen like seeing the time pass by would help, maybe diffuse the situation.

Tick, tock.

She didn't speak at first.

Tick, tock.

I thought of what I could say.

Tick, tock.

My mom trusted me.

Tick, tock.

He stood with his arms crossed and almost stared through her. He must have been thinking of ways to punish us in those moments.

Tick, tock.

"Frank, please don't overreact." Her voice shook.

He stood there, making her wait for the inevitable punishment. She reminded me of a woman on trial with the Salem witches. She sat up straight, as if with honor, knowing she did nothing wrong, but ready to accept her sentence anyway. In that moment, her strength and beauty overwhelmed me, made me realize how she stood up for me and how I never stood up for her.

"I snuck out," I blurted out.

My father cocked his head as if his attention had wavered just a little from my mother.

So, I hurried on. "Mother told me I couldn't go when I asked, and so I just climbed out of my bedroom window."

My mother started to shake her head, trying to urge me to stop. My father turned on his heels to fully face me.

His emerald-green anger met my emerald-green hate and fear. I didn't avert my eyes this time, didn't try to comfort him by showing my weakness.

I'd had enough and felt just as much rage within me as he showed toward us. "You can't keep me locked in here forever. You think you own me?" My voice rose and I stood up.

I didn't wait for the clock to tick again.

"I won't be here much longer, and I can't wait to leave. I can't wait to be everything you don't want me to be. I'll party and have fun and eat on the couch and study in bed rather than at a desk. I will…"

My mother gasped as he lunged for me. I jumped back but not in time. His fist landed right on my mouth, and I immediately tasted metal.

Blood. Crimson. Red. Blood.

My mother moved to soothe me, but I lifted my hand to stop her and looked at my father again. His face was red with fury which only served to fuel mine. I licked away the droplet of blood running down the corner of my mouth.

My father had hit me hard enough that he was bleeding himself.

I egged him on. "You want to make me bleed, Dad? *You think that's going to stop me from leaving when I graduate?"*

"AUBREY? ARE YOU in there?"

I wanted to answer the voice on the other side but I couldn't. I couldn't breathe, let alone speak.

I could hear the handle of the door rattling just before it flew open and I saw him.

Oh, Jax.

CHAPTER
THIRTEEN

JAX

"**THE FUCK, PEACHES?** Why are you on the ground?" I whispered as I stooped to get close enough for her to hear. Was she drunk? Sick?

I saw her eyes then, the damn eyes that had mesmerized me since I'd met her. The green in them glowed with fear. She grabbed onto my shirt to pull me close. Then she whispered, "Fire."

That one word.

Four letters whispered from her lips was all it took for me to crumble back into wanting to save her. I scooped her up without thinking, without hesitation.

The blonde I'd been thinking about fucking that night picked that moment to scurry up to my side. "What the hell is wrong with *her*?"

"None of your damn business." I tried to brush past her but with Brey in my arms, the narrow hallway wasn't as forgiving.

"Jax," she whined. "Who cares if she's drunk? Just leave her. I want you ... "

"Move," I commanded.

"You *are* an asshole," she mumbled as she sidestepped out of the way.

Old news to me.

I rushed past her and skirted around the corner. I had gotten ready in a secluded area upstairs. I'd have to make it there without gaining any attention. Brey didn't need this shit in the magazines tomorrow. The headlines would read, "Jax Takes Jay's Drunken Fling for a Ride." Or some other stupid shit that none of us needed.

"Peaches, you all right?" I whispered.

She didn't reply and was practically panting. Like that night I'd saved her.

"Hey, I got you, I got you, I'm going to take you upstairs, okay?"

Her emerald eyes widened, shooting up into mine. "No! Jax, we have to get out." Her voice was higher, louder than before.

"You are having a flashback, Whitfield," I drew each word out. "We aren't in a fire, okay?"

"Jax, put me down." Her voice was firmer now and her body tensed. She strained against my grip.

"Settle down."

"Put me down!"

"Fine. I'm setting you down. I want you to realize that you're talking. You're breathing. There is no smoke. Just breathe, baby."

I let her body slide down mine as I said the words slow. The fear in her eyes dissipated, but a passion flared that had me instantly turned on.

Then, her embarrassment took over. As she held onto my arms and looked up at me, she realized what had happened.

"Oh my God. Oh my God." Her trembling started and her eyes turned glassy. "I'm so sorry, Jax."

"Peaches, it's all right." I moved to grab her hand like I used to when she would get embarrassed.

Her hands jerked off my arms and away from my hand as soon as I touched her. "No, it isn't all right. I ... " Her lips pursed as if she wanted to explain but stopped herself. "I apologize, Jax. Believe me, it won't happen again."

"What?" I barked, louder than I wanted to. I'd be damned if she was going to put on a class act for me.

"Lower your voice," she hissed. "I have to get back to Jay. Like I said, I am sorry. I hope you will use discretion if this is the topic of any conversation in the future. I really don't want anyone knowing what just happened."

Ending the conversation abruptly, the woman I'd lusted over for fucking years turned on her heels and started to walk away from me.

"What the ... Whitfield!" I yelled after her but she didn't stop walking.

Fuck that.

Before she rounded the corner back into the hallway, I swept her up over my shoulder and started walking her back toward the stairs. We were having this conversation whether she liked it or not.

"What the hell are you doing, Jax?" she roared, pounding me with her fist.

"You and I need to talk."

"No! Put me down," she said in her best composed tone. Again. I hated that voice and tone.

She only used it when she was uncomfortable and looking for the upper hand. She damn well wasn't getting it this time. I started climbing the stairs, ignoring her.

"Oh my God, Jax. You're going to drop me. I'm going to break my neck." The pitch of her voice climbed as I climbed the stairs.

I couldn't help myself. I started to laugh. "What do you weigh? A hundred and thirty pounds? I'm not gonna drop you."

"I beg your pardon! I weigh one hundred and ten, you ass! And guess what? We aren't at fucking Burger King. You can't have it your way. So, put me the fuck down."

I dropped her onto the wood flooring in the room. Hard. God, the woman wouldn't shut up when she wanted something. I couldn't hold back my laughter. Her sassy mouth was something to be missed, especially when she swore.

She could cut someone off at their knees if she wanted to. Except with me.

And, damn, had I enjoyed it. It was one of the first times I remembered feeling more than just lust for a girl.

Aubrey made me feel a lot of things for the first time, and every time I thought of those memories, I knew why I feared us together. I had those feelings for the first time with her and never again after.

"What are you doing?" she asked, glowering at the closed door as if she could make it disintegrate.

"I want you to tell me what happened down there." I took a step closer to her. I needed to be near her. I wanted to hold her when she let me in, to soothe her. I could protect her. I wanted to protect her from the flashbacks.

She took a step back, staring at me for a minute, then bent over as a full belly laugh burst from her. "You want me to stay up here with you to talk like little girls about our emotions and our problems?"

Just like she used to, Brey built walls and threw stones over them when her feelings were threatened. "Don't give me that. I just hauled your ass out of a bathroom and saved you and Jay a load of publicity." I crossed my arms over my chest. "You owe me."

She slumped a little then, her façade deflating. "Jax, it isn't your concern. I normally have it under control." I barely heard the last part.

"'Normally'?" I boomed. "What the hell do you mean 'normally'? How often does this happen?"

"Never!" Her eyes darted away. "Sometimes. I don't know! Only when I'm in small places or when I feel trapped." She whipped around to pace away from me and then paced back to get right in my face. "Don't you dare tell Jay." Her words held more warning than I was used to, and I'd negotiated with some of the most powerful people in the world.

"You can't breathe on a public bathroom floor. You're having flashbacks of an attempted homicide but you're worried about my fucking brother?"

"Keep your voice down." Her eyes narrowed to slits. "I don't need Jay walking on eggshells around me because you can't keep your damn mouth shut. So, don't open it."

I wasn't used to her commanding me, let alone swearing at me. I wasn't used to anything about her, and that made me fucking livid. "Watch that mouth of yours, Peaches."

"Or what?"

"Or I'll show you how filthy a mouth can really be."

Her eyes widened and shined anger under the dim lights of the small room. She stood a half a head shorter than me, and her heels under that dress had to be at least five-inches tall. Yet, she didn't back down. "You have no idea how filthy I can be nor will you ever get a chance to show me how filthy you are. I want nothing to do with you."

Her comment deflated my anger. "Is that so? Once upon a damn time, you wanted everything to do with me. I was your world, and you were mine."

Her brow furrowed. I moved to rub her shoulder but she flinched away. "Seems like lyrics to an old love song, Jax. Your fans would *love* it." Her tone held sarcasm. "I'm not a fan though. So, save it for your next album."

I sighed and rubbed my hands over my face. "There's not going to be a next album. I don't want to fight with you tonight."

She squinted at me while I studied her.

Even without the height, she'd have been a phenomenal addition on my brother's arm tonight. People were enamored as soon as she stepped out of that limo. Her green eyes and red dress hugging all the right places reminded every man what Christmas was like.

I'd seen her with Jay and instantly wanted to rip my own brother's arm off just so she wouldn't touch another man in front of me.

I tried to chalk my reaction up to the old habit of jealousy. She wasn't mine or a part of my life anymore.

But she used to be *every* part of it.

I lived and breathed for her when I was younger. When I left, I'd wanted to be the bigger person for about a minute by breaking things off and letting us both grow up.

For about a minute.

It took Frank threatening her well-being to realize I didn't want to be any of that. I just wanted to be with her, but it was too late.

I had gotten roped into something I was too immature to handle.

So, I wrote songs about her, named an album after her, and then tried to move on away from her.

And I *had* moved on.

Moved on and up. I surrounded myself with beautiful cityscapes and million-dollar investments. I had beautiful women on each arm and a multi-platinum album in a penthouse that overlooked my world.

I had moved on and up, yet the view up there didn't look half as good as the woman standing in front of me.

I had her up here all to myself and I wasn't sure I would be able to keep my hands off her even if she wasn't mine.

Aubrey sighed in front of me. "You're right. We shouldn't be fighting," she conceded and tried for a nonchalant shrug. "We have nothing to fight about. Let's get back down to the party, okay?" she said just above a whisper.

I nodded but didn't say anything. I'd told her I didn't want to fight but with her telling me that we shouldn't be, it made me want to shake her, rile her up, push her past the façade she'd thrown up for me.

If she thought we had nothing to fight about and that she wanted nothing to do with me, I'd just have to prove her wrong.

CHAPTER
FOURTEEN

AUBREY

TWO WEEKS HAD gone by since my meltdown at the premiere.

Two long weeks of waiting for Jax to leave our little town to go back to his skyscrapers and flashing lights.

Also, two weeks of me moping because Jay would be flying out soon to Los Angeles to find an apartment and start his mentorship.

Vick tried to get me to go out to the clubs with them. She even admitted she'd gone out with them a few nights back. I wanted to accuse her of joining the enemy but I just quietly declined her invites. Every time, she threw her hands in the air and left me in my own misery.

Rome wasn't so willing to accept Jax. He would stare at me like a pitiful puppy and then say he was going out. He didn't go out with Jax though. He went out on his own a lot, probably to drink away his own demons.

Katie showed up and disappeared like she always did, but she never brought up Jax or Jay. They'd been a part of our lives too long, so she was used to my moodiness.

Then, my very small school break came to an end, and my only summer class started. After attending it, I found myself dialing Jay's number. More like pounding his number onto my touch screen phone.

He grumbled something when he picked up, and I laid into him. "You told me this class would be a breeze. That the professor is all Hyde no Jekyll, Jay. Mr. Gremble or something."

He mumbled something else.

I took a breath, trying to calm myself.

"The professor is more like a gremlin!" I screamed the last word, not calming myself at all. "You'd better be ready to teach me everything. You're leaving in a few days, and I can't fail this class."

I sucked in air because if I didn't I would panic.

"Shit, Brey, I didn't know Mr. Gremble would be teaching it. He normally doesn't teach summer classes."

"You didn't know? I told you probably five times. I specifically asked you about the professor. You waved me off and said I would do great and that this class would look wonderful on my—"

He cut me off. "Jesus, it doesn't matter, Brey. You'll be fine. Do we have to do coffee today? My head's going to explode."

I could practically smell the alcohol through the phone. "Fine? Are you serious? I can't do just fine. I need good grades!" He was right, a B wouldn't kill me academically.

Only emotionally.

And mentally.

I got straight A's. Not A minuses or B pluses.

If I got a B, it would make all my work to get the A's totally irrelevant.

I shook my head. "I'm already halfway to the café, and you promised. I can't help that you infuse your blood with liquor every night."

"What the hell time is it?" he asked, sounding unconcerned.

I hesitated on project rant-until-I-one-hundred-percen t-find-blame-in-Jay. It wasn't his fault that I made the horrible mistake of picking up an accelerated investment class for the summer or that the class started at seven in the morning. This class was supposed to add to my business major but the more I looked over the material, the more I dreaded it.

"Nine. You said coffee shop at nine thirty on Tuesday. Not me. I need your help on this or I will fail. Not just C or D grade but fail…"

I heard a rumble of laughter that seemed all too familiar. At first, I was shocked, then furious.

"Do you have me on speaker phone while Jax is with you, you jerk?" I said far too loudly.

"Damn, Brey. Too loud. Seriously, I can't talk about this right now…" I heard rustling like he might be getting out of bed.

"Peaches…" The voice I dreaded and looked forward to all at once rumbled through the phone. It sounded so close that it caused goose bumps to form along my neckline.

I didn't answer him. Instead, I continued to walk to campus and tried to focus on how ghostly it had become. No students bustled or basked on the grassy hill. There weren't bikes speeding by when I made it to the crosswalk either. The breeze rustled through the trees and through my black maxi dress.

He breathed a sigh into the phone, and I just knew he was running his hands through his hair. How was it that after all this time I could still know that, still see him doing it perfectly?

"You know, normally people talk when they are on the phone with each other."

"Normally, people talk to the person they called. Not with the person who hijacked the phone."

"Jay handed me the phone. He's dead to the world." I heard the smirk in his voice.

"If you didn't drag him out every night to party—"

He cut me off. "Pause what you're about to say, babe. Think about Jay. He parties harder than anyone I've ever met. And I've met a lot of people. His ass keeps dragging *me* out."

"Doubtful." Why did I sound so childish? I sighed. "Look, could you just make sure Jay meets me at The Corner sometime this morning. I need help studying for this investment class."

"No problem, Peaches."

I started to tell him not to call me that but heard him click the phone off before I could.

I stomped the rest of the way to the cafe. When I walked in, The Corner mirrored the ghost town outside. Normally, the bustle of college students made for a ten-minute wait.

Instead, Jackie, my favorite barista, waved me over right away. "Brey! Thank God you're here. I'm about to fall asleep."

I laughed as I dropped my book bag on a chair and made my way over to the counter. "Oh please. You probably don't ever sleep. You're like a cheetah on speed."

Her laugh boomed through the empty shop. "You're right. I have permanent insomnia or some shit. I was up all night trying out this new idea I have for lattes. It will literally blow your mind." She turned and started up the espresso machine. "You have to try it. Tell me what else it needs. It's missing something."

"I probably should just have a coffee, Jackie," I said half-heartedly.

"Black coffee is boring," she said over the machine.

She was right and we both knew it. I loved trying out her new inventions. "How's the new manager like your concoctions?"

"Well, since he didn't show up again this morning and I had to open, who the hell knows?"

I sighed. "Have you complained? Can't you just take over?"

She smiled as she started to pour the frothed milk over something she'd mixed. "I wish. I'm too disorganized. Want to come manage us?"

I laughed at her plea and pulled a barstool over to the side counter. The eclectic style of the café allowed customers to sit at a sidebar and watch their coffees being made.

"I'm serious! Don't laugh. We would be awesome together. You make a damn good cup of coffee already." She talked like a cheetah on speed too. "You could help me with concoctions. I'd teach you all the rest behind the counter, and you could teach me the business side of it."

I waved off her idea as she slid the drink over to me to try. Jackie didn't know I had my sights set on a different business to run.

My mother had given so much back to a little home on the reservation. I avoided it when she passed away but finally pushed myself to go visit after they consistently reached out. I thought I would just go one time, it would be a formal, quick trip. The home was a safe haven for those who didn't have anywhere else to go a lot of the time. And for me, it became that and more. A way for me to keep my mother's dreams alive, a way for me to connect to her, a way for me to move toward my future while still connecting with my past.

I wanted to invest well enough to expand that home and help those kids always.

I took a sip, closed my eyes and let the flavors take over. Hints of caramel and pecans accented the bold flavor of cinnamon. The sweet milk reminded me of a chai latte on steroids. I moaned as memories of Christmases and Jax washed over me. The drink was literally a trigger.

When I'd finally swallowed, I opened my eyes. "This is fucking orgasmic, Jackie."

She beamed. "I made you swear and say 'orgasmic' in the same sentence. I knew it was a winner!"

We both jumped when we heard from behind me somewhat of a growl and then, "Sounds good. I'll take whatever she's drinking."

His voice heated my face. Then it heated my body, my core, and my stupid toes too. I looked toward the sky and silently cursed.

I started to stand when I realized that Jackie appeared to be in shock.

"Jackie, you okay?" I asked, leaning over the counter concerned. "Oh my God. Jax Stonewood is in my shop." She shook her head. "I mean, oh my God."

I rolled my eyes as I heard him approach and say, "So, I guess Aubrey can skip that part of the introduction. And you are?"

Her eyes got even wider. "Wait. You're meeting Jax Stonewood here this morning and you didn't tell me beforehand?" Her voice rose to a higher octave.

I shook my head, backing away from the counter and from Jax who had come to stand right next to me. "Actually, I was supposed to meet Jay here." I turned to shoot a glare at Jax and braced for impact.

His appearance, seeing him standing right in front of me as lethal as ever, still hit me like a freight train. He dressed casually in jeans and a black shirt as if he was just out for a stroll.

As if he wasn't upending my whole world by being in this town.

The man was a stark difference from the boy I used to know. Now, his jawline looked like a sculptor had spent a day perfecting the angles. He had age lines on his face that extenuated those angles and made him even more appealing. He crossed his arms, and I watched as his biceps bunched bigger than they ever had before. His hair was mussed as if some girl had run her hands through it before he'd gotten out of bed this morning. Somehow, that made him more attractive.

And more dangerous.

He smirked and stepped toward me. I stumbled back and tripped over a stool.

A laugh rumbled out of him as he caught my elbow and righted me before I could catch myself. As his hand touched my elbow, I held back the gasp from feeling his skin on mine again.

I silently willed myself to calm down and tried to hide the goose bumps that popped up over my skin.

"Thank you," I mumbled, looking at his hand on my elbow, and then I slipped out of his grasp.

I felt him looking at me, questioning me. When I looked back at him, he stared like he needed to know me again, and he stood in that cafe like he owned it.

He didn't.

This was my town, my safe space, and my café.

I hardened my gaze, not giving him a window into my thoughts.

Jackie still eyed both of us in some kind of stupefied celebrity shock. "Jackie, thank you for the latte. I should run since Jay won't be showing. How much do I owe you?"

That sort of snapped her out of it. She scoffed at the notion of my paying, like always. "You can pay me *later*." I knew that meant I would be paying her in details about Jax. "I'll get one made for your *friend*, also." She spun around and started working extra quickly.

She was now on speed for real.

I moved to pick up my bag and get the hell away from Jax. I felt rather than saw him behind me. His goddamn presence still sent shivers down my body.

"Peaches, we need to talk," he rumbled behind me, close to my ear.

Too close. "You can't avoid me forever."

He'd avoided me for years, and now after two weeks of trying to talk to me, he thought I should just cave?

I smoothed my hair and pulled my lips between my teeth, trying to stay calm.

Truth was, I hadn't avoided talking to him, anyway. Avoidance meant I went out of my way to consciously not talk to him. I hadn't. My way, since the day he'd left, had been to move on. I was simply carrying on with my normal daily routine. In that routine, I didn't *want* or *need* to talk to him, so I didn't.

He would sit me down and spew some nonsense about how he regretted that summer. Or he'd make a lie up about how he regretted leaving me but his father had needed him.

Something ridiculous, belittling, or condescending to the fact our relationship had been the most real, intense part of life I'd ever experienced.

Things I didn't want to hear.

Jax would say anything to make the woman in front of him happy. I saw right through it though. He didn't require a tell like most people when they lied to me. All I had to do was look at him and remind myself that although everything he said sounded sincere, it was complete and utter bullshit.

I sighed and turned around, my bag now on my shoulder. "There really isn't anything we need to discuss."

I started to walk away, but Jax stepped in front of me.

His chest flared out like he was daring me to push past him. My body warmed, adrenaline kicking up a notch.

We'd done this dance before, and even though my mind repeated that I shouldn't engage in it, I never listened.

Control played such a huge role in my life. I could tone down my feelings, my appearance, my life in general so that I lived the most normal life possible. I craved that normalcy.

Yet with Jax, my control fled.

He overpowered it.

He was the man who made me love men. I learned how much I craved the soft touch of a man from him, the caress of a man who loved rather than hurt. To have a man so full of power, so capable and able to harm me, touch me without injuring me. Well, quite frankly, that touch became my addiction. The touch that derailed everything.

"Nothing we need to discuss? Don't act like you don't remember the other night." Jax stepped close to me, his hand hovering near my cheek but not touching it, as if he knew something had shifted within me, as if he knew exactly how I was feeling. I stared into his ocean eyes and remembered my downfall with him.

I ripped my gaze away. "I have to go, Jax."

"You have to or you want to?"

I just sighed and looked out the window of the café. "Jay is your best friend, right?"

I shrugged. "So what?"

"I'm his brother, Aubrey." He put his hand behind his neck and pulled on it as he looked toward the ceiling. "I don't regret much, but I do regret not being closer to him. We lost years, and I don't intend to lose anymore. You're really going to make him pick who to hang out with while I'm in town?"

I crossed my arms over my chest. "Well, I'm not too concerned. You aren't one to ever stick around…"

Below the belt? I didn't care. I was ready to *kick* him below the belt if necessary.

"I'm here for my app launch, which could last most of the summer, babe."

My mouth dropped open. I attempted to form a rude retort, but I felt like a damn guppy that had been left out of water. Mouth open, mouth closed. Mouth open, mouth closed. I shook my head and stepped back. "No. That's not possible. I mean, you can't think that staying in this town is good PR. Don't you need to promote your new app where you plan to launch it or something? Don't you need to work on your investments at Stonewood Enterprises? You can't possibly … I mean … Jay won't even be here."

"He asked me to stay at his place while he's in LA."

"Did he now?" I would have believed him, his lies fell just that good off his tongue, except my friend wouldn't have kept that from me.

He narrowed his gaze just a bit and resigned. "He *will* ask me."

"Or you'll beg him," I retorted. "You'd be surprised how little he cares about that house. He might care a little more about the whole freaking town you'll be wreaking havoc on while he's away though."

My town. My whole freaking town.

"Fair." He leaned back like he needed to relax. "Let's cut the shit though, Whitfield. The app I'm rolling out needs to be tested on college campuses. What better college than one so close to Stonewood Enterprises? I also have investments that need attention in this region. And … " He took a sip of his drink and let the word linger in the air.

"And what?"

"You're right about this drink being orgasmic." His eyebrows lifted like he was trying to lighten the mood.

I rolled my eyes. Not just a little. I rolled them so dramatically I wondered if Jackie could see from the other room.

I motioned for him to continue. "And what, Jax?"

"You're here, Peaches. And you're much better than this drink." He growled the last part while he stared at my lips, and his gaze shot through me all the way down to my core. My body heated, and I clenched my fists trying to stave off my reaction to him.

"Just because I'm here doesn't mean I want anything to do with you." The words sounded meek and hollow even to me.

He smiled. "I don't want anything to do with you, either." My stomach dropped, like it couldn't handle him throwing back my words. "Doesn't necessarily mean we get a choice. I think we can agree what we have isn't healthy."

"We don't have anything."

"We did, we do, and we always will if we don't try to work it out together."

At that moment, my legs gave out. It was like they—along with the rest of my body—gave up their struggle with fate.

I couldn't blame my legs. Who in their right mind would want their job to consistently fight against gravity to keep my body away from the ground? They couldn't win all the time.

Nor could I win my fight to get Jax out of my life. Somehow, his gravitational pull on my world had become too strong.

I didn't realize then, I should have fought harder.

CHAPTER
FIFTEEN

JAX

AUBREY MIGHT HAVE been in shock. Her mouth opened to say something but nothing came out.

I nodded to her plopping down in the chair and gave her a moment to digest the situation while I scoped out the little café.

The barista had put a bell on the counter in case someone stopped in for coffee and then disappeared behind the coffee bar's door midway through our conversation. I'd read her like a book while she did it. I knew she'd just given the illusion of privacy because her eyes had widened as Aubrey and I discussed everything. Really, she was probably listening right behind that door.

The woman cared about Aubrey too much to not listen. I didn't know how close the two of them were, but there was something unspoken that passed between them when I got here. From that, I was sure the barista wouldn't sell my location in the next few minutes.

For that very reason, I liked the eclectic little café. It made my life easier and that was what I cared about most. Selfish bastard that I was.

I didn't even know if this was the right place to launch my app.

Sure, it was a soft launch and wouldn't matter too much. Isabel pitched it that way and I knew she usually didn't steer me wrong.

Mostly I was here for her and to finish what I'd started with Frank. Fuck. I was losing it if I was basing decisions off them.

I prided myself on putting my work first. I'd gone down the road of putting emotions above all else with my music, but I'd hung that hat up. I studied her while she studied me back quietly. One thing we hadn't lost after all that time was our silence. Most people would fold under the awkwardness of it, give in to social practices and offer up small talk. With anyone else, Aubrey would have done that. She had etiquette pounded into her from birth.

She would have been a perfect nature-versus-nurture experiment though. Her eyes were wild and rebellious always. The etiquette and formalities locked her up most of the time, but they had to stomp out a shit ton of wildfires, especially with me around.

Sitting with her, watching her wrestle out the formalities only to meet me with silence, felt fucking good.

Like I was playing with fire and for once, I *wasn't* winning.

Her gaze woke me up. Made me feel more alive than I had in years. She was meeting me head-on while wrestling with her own thoughts. I saw the wheels turning, saw her starting to plan and make sense of the situation. I just couldn't see the plan.

"Look, besides me and you figuring out our shit," I said, trying to ease into the conversation. "Jay's got a lot going on right now."

"I know that," she snapped. "You think I don't know that?"

"All right." Different approach. "He's flying out soon, and I think us being cordial is better than putting more on his plate right now. He doesn't need to feel guilty about not having enough time—"

"How do you know he feels guilty?" Good. We were getting somewhere.

"He starts to talk about you and then looks guilty, like he can't talk about you to me. Then says he should call you, then looks all fucked in the head."

She sighed and looked down at the table. "He doesn't need to worry about me."

"Of course, he doesn't need to worry about you."

She held up a finger. "Okay, to be fair, friends worry about friends, but ... "

"But he worries an exorbitant amount. If I didn't know both of you, I'd think he was fucking you."

"Excuse me?"

"Let's save that conversation for another day."

"Let's save it for never."

I shook my head, tabling her attitude and getting back to the real matter. "He can't worry about that this summer. If he can't concentrate on acting in this new movie ... "

"He'll concentrate on that movie. Jay might play hard—"

I finished for her. "But he also works hard. I know, Whitfield. You don't have to tell me about my brother. But for his sake, we should make this work."

She glared at me, brows furrowing. Some part of her wanted to throw it in my face that she knew him better than me and dredge up all the past. She waged a war with herself. I saw her trying not to bring it all up, and I hoped that part of her won. I didn't want to dive back into that time in my life.

The green in her eyes turned mossy as she sat up straighter. The part of her ready for answers danced with a victory sign in her eyes. "Make what work exactly? Make you being an ass work? You think you can guilt me into making shit work with you for Jay's sake after all these years?"

I'd trained myself to look unaffected when it came to dealing with people's emotions face-to-face. It was part of the Stonewood Enterprises business. If someone approached with emotion, you sidelined it with apathy. If someone hit you with more money for a deal, you stayed neutral. Someone could have bled out and begged for their life and I wouldn't have blinked any type of emotion their way.

For her though, I caved almost every time.

"That mouth of yours is a lot filthier than I remember."

Some stupid part of me wanted to bend more and talk about just how much I remembered her mouth.

I knew it shouldn't matter. I wasn't a part of her life anymore. She'd wiped me out of it like a weed that had terrorized her garden.

"This isn't a guilt trip, Peaches. It is simply two people agreeing to get along for the benefit of a person they care about. We can work our shit out for him."

She chewed on her lip, then closed her eyes as she breathed in deep. When her eyes opened again, I saw the mask that Aubrey had created better than even I could. "Jaydon is and always has been the biggest part of my family. I would never jeopardize that, especially not for you. Friends?" Her tone was cold.

I smiled and shook her hand. The shock jackhammered through me so fast I almost jerked back.

Our chemistry should have faded by now. It should have fallen apart when I shattered that little glass house we'd built for ourselves so many years ago.

Yet, it was stronger than ever. At least for me.

From where I sat, it looked like she hadn't felt the effect at all.

I didn't let go of her hand when she started to pull back. "Just friends?"

"What else could we possibly be, Jax?"

"Well, once upon a time, we weren't *just* friends." I shouldn't have goaded her.

"Once upon a time is for fairy tales, and that's not what this is."

"Peaches." I emphasized the nickname to reprimand her.

"L.P." She brought that stupid nickname back in the same tone.

"I wonder, do all your friends know how you sound when you're coming?" The question was a low blow, meant to shake her from that cold, hardened tone she used with me.

Her pupils dilated as she froze, and a flush surfaced on her skin. Good.

If I couldn't forget about being with her, I needed to make sure she thought about it too.

She snatched her hand back. "Fuck you, Jax."

I crossed my arms, wanting to smile at the fact that she was swearing. "Unfortunately, we haven't gotten that far lately, Peaches."

"Thank God for that." She pushed away from the table, making the chair screech. "For someone who never wants to discuss the past, you sure as hell like to bring up specific parts of it."

I shrugged. "Some parts of the past are better than others."

"Yeah and some parts remind us just how painful life can be if you aren't careful."

"You avoid those parts, Peaches, and you won't remember how to live."

Her eyes narrowed, trying to hear all the words I hadn't said between the ones I had.

I sat back, pulling the tension back away from her and us. "It was just a bad joke, okay?" I hurried on before she could respond. "What's with this class Jay needs to help you with? You're smart enough to get by, aren't you?" She sighed and let the moment go. "It's difficult, okay? I'm pretty sure every student left and checked their schedule to make sure they were in the right one. We all could've sworn we didn't sign up for a foreign language study, yet when we walked out of there, no one understood a word of what the professor had said."

I smiled. "Let's see the textbook. I'll help you."

My smile died abruptly. What the hell was I doing?

"I … you … I really don't think … " Aubrey stuttered.

"Speechless? Really?" Normally, she could fill any moment with small talk if she needed to. "Get your damn book out, Whitfield. Jay's not going to have time to help you when he's in LA anyway."

"When was the last time you took a class, Jax?" she said with all the sass she could muster while she reached in her bag to pull out her book, laptop, and phone.

"Doesn't being part owner of Stonewood Enterprises qualify me as a good tutor?" I grabbed her phone to put in my number.

She shrugged like she used to always do when she knew I was right but didn't want to admit it. "What are you doing with my phone?"

I flashed her the screen. "Now, you have my number. Let me know what times work best for you to study. And we'll probably have to find a more secluded place than this café."

We both looked toward the window and then the back room. I was sure Jackie was still listening.

WE SPENT TWO hours going over material that I'll admit was as boring as shit.

But I'd be damned if I didn't enjoy working through it with her.

CHAPTER
SIXTEEN

JAX

WHEN I GOT back to my brother's apartment, he was still passed out face down on his couch. I was wound so tight from having to sit across from a girl I used to want to give the world to that I could barely focus on putting one foot in front of the other.

I hit him in the back of the head. "Wake the fuck up."

He mumbled into the cushion. So, I shoved his legs off the couch and sat next to him.

He glared over at me through groggy, sunken eyes. "What the hell, man?"

"I just did your chores and studied with Aubrey. You owe me."

He shot up off the couch. "You what? What time is it?"

I let him work through it.

He paced toward the clock in the kitchen, squinted, and paced back. "It's noon? I told your ass to wake me up at eight!" he yelled.

He stomped into the kitchen and back again. "You saw her? Is she pissed?"

I chuckled while he swore under his breath.

When he started to search for his cell, I said, "Calm down. She's taken care of. I helped her with her class like I said."

"You helped her?" He eyed me. "You *helped* her? Ha!"

He went back to shuffling through the cushions looking for his phone. I wondered whether or not that had to do with him not trusting me with her. "You act like I can't be cordial to your high-and-mighty princess."

"Damn right you can't be cordial. She can barely stand to be in the same room as you!" He threw his hands in the air. "Where the fuck is my phone?"

I pointed to the table in the dining room. Jay couldn't compose himself for the life of him. Made him a great actor, able to display every emotion, but a terrible businessman.

Before he dialed her number, I walked over and leaned on the table. "We talked, Jay. We can stand to be in the same room, all right?"

He studied me for a beat and then said, "You apologized?"

I glanced toward the ceiling. I knew that's what everyone wanted. My family had said their piece more than once regarding Aubrey. "The past is the past. She doesn't need apologies. I'm going to help her through the rest of the class."

He started to say something.

I held up a hand to cut him off. "Thank me for it later. You're off the hook, and this will give Aubrey and me a chance to put the past behind us."

He tapped his finger on the dark wood of the table. "That's impossible, man. You don't know what you—"

"We're adults, Jay. What we had when we were kids is irrelevant."

"Irrelevant?" he spit back at me, taking a step toward me.

"You want to do this now?"

His eyes narrowed. "No better time for it."

I sighed, knowing the look in his eye. The tabloids used to say my brothers and I looked exactly alike. Sure, there was a resemblance but not the way they described it. There were times like these though when I saw it all too clearly. This look was the exact look I had when my anger boiled over and I couldn't control a damn move I made.

I cracked my neck, trying to release the tension and stay calm. "She's fine, and we're fine. She doesn't need anyone to coddle her."

"How the hell would you know?"

"Because I was there that night, and no one's coddling me." I crossed my arms.

That deflated him a little. "You were able to disappear after that summer and do what you wanted. You got to follow your dreams."

"Oh, fuck off. Those weren't all my dreams. I went and made a life for myself. It wasn't all rainbows and fluffy shit, Jay." I ran my hands through my hair down to my neck.

He just shook his head at me. "She had to go back to school, Jax. You know what that did to her?"

"She's fine," I shot off loudly, surprised at how quick I retaliated.

I didn't want to hear how much she'd suffered because I'd suffered too. I realized too late he wasn't in the mood to be tested. His eyes widened before he reared back and threw a punch across my face.

"Fuck!" I roared as I bent over. I went straight for him, rushing my shoulder into his stomach and slamming him to the ground.

We rolled around the living room like idiots. I can admit to the stupidity, but damn I was pissed. Truth was, I couldn't honestly remember the last time I'd been this immature since being out of my mother's home. The only time I sparred was at a training facility to keep in shape.

Getting this physical because of emotions was a regular occurence when we were growing up but Jay and I had been too distant for too long to engage. I hadn't tested my brother in a long time, and I was surprised to find that I couldn't tell who had the upper hand.

Back in high school, we'd been close enough to know exactly what buttons to push. Jett had beat me to a pulp more than once and I had done the same to Jay. He was the youngest and had never even gotten a punch in. Now, for every punch and headlock I got him in, he got me in one.

"You're losing it," he grumbled when I'd subdued him in a head-lock he couldn't break.

"Shut the fuck up or I'll choke you out."

He shoved at my arm as we both laid there, him struggling to get out of the hold and me seriously considering watching him pass out.

"You would have ducked that punch a couple years ago," he wheezed.

I squeezed him tighter, "I let you get one good one in." Then, I shoved him away as he gasped in air.

"You know you deserve to get your ass beat," he managed.

"Maybe," I sighed and we laid there, both out of breath for a minute.

"She had to face everyone and tell them why you left, why she wasn't good enough for you to stay, why you visited the guy who burned her house to the ground and almost killed her. I had to listen to her cry at night and try to explain why you left. She might not act like it, but she's still broken."

I kept my eyes on the ceiling, not wanting to have this conversation anymore. "That was years ago."

"But you're here now, bringing up the memories from those years ago."

"Maybe I should go back to Chicago." For some damn reason, that made my chest hurt.

"Fuck, man. I don't know. I don't know what's best." He looked defeated.

I felt just how he looked. The next question out of my mouth I didn't plan for. "Is she really with him?"

Jay didn't say anything, just shook his head.

I waited him out, not willing to take the question back. "If you stayed just to figure that out…"

"You know I stayed for my app launch and because I need a break from everything."

"I'm not giving you details about her love life, man."

"Supposedly, it's your love life." I smiled. But only a little. My neck always tightened when I saw a magazine with Aubrey looking longingly at Jay. Even if I knew it was just the perfect photo at just the right time at just the right angle.

Jay laughed. "At least for once they said she was leaving me for someone and not the other way around."

What the media didn't realize was that Aubrey was really leaving me behind. They never photographed Aubrey with anyone but my brother. I never worried about them, knew Aubrey and Jay were just friends. Then Rome was in the picture and suddenly I was damn close to buying the magazines just to figure it out.

"Jay, he was all over her at your graduation ceremony."

"Man, that's none of your business and you know it."

"Fine. Do you trust him with her though?"

He sighed. "She's like my baby sister. I don't trust anyone with her. She trusts him though." I grunted.

"Jax," he said in warning. "It's taken this long for her to trust anyone. Katie and I have been the only ones she confided in. You know how fucking lonely that must have been, to only have us?"

"Well, I don't know why she picked you two. Katie is…" I trailed off. There weren't words to describe her.

"Brutal." Our eyes met. I could see there was an unspoken agreement there. Katie was a fierce best friend, the only one I would want for Aubrey.

I nodded and we both chuckled. The anger toward each other from over the years seemingly diffused.

We turned our heads and exchanged a knowing glance. His smile toward me was genuine for the first time in years.

CHAPTER
SEVENTEEN

AUBREY

"**B**REY, I JUST** think it's a fucking bad idea." Katie followed me in as I unlocked the door to my apartment.

"What's a bad idea?" Rome said from my couch.

I eyed him and Vick who were watching TV and eating some of the food I'd saved in the fridge for myself. "You two do know that you don't live here, right?"

Rome shrugged and Vick smiled innocently before she said, "We were really hungry, Brey."

I wanted to tell them to order their own food or ask if they wanted to eat mine. But I couldn't bring myself to. It wouldn't have been polite.

"Go get your own damn food, you freeloaders," Katie said for me when she saw my face.

Rome waved her off. "That's rich coming from you. What's your latest sugar daddy's name?"

She rolled her eyes. "Just 'cause the men I'm with can provide for me and you can't provide for any woman ... "

Katie had a type she always looked for. None of us agreed with it because those types were ones who could provide extravagant gifts for her.

"You got it wrong, Kate-Bait. I provide something other than money and gifts to the women I'm with."

"Gross, Rome." Vick shoved him. She looked at us. "Come on, fill us in. What's a bad idea?"

Katie spoke for me again. "Brey's having Jax help her with this last class she needs to pass to graduate."

Rome jumped off the couch. "What? What the hell do you mean he's helping you with this class?" Rome paced my small living room, his muscles rippling.

I shrugged, and went to sit down next to Vick. We watched Rome pace toward Katie, united for the first time. She followed his lead. "Yeah! That's what I said," she practically seethed.

Vick leaned in and whispered, "I, for one, am totally on board with you doing this even if it is just to see these two like this. They. Are. Fierce."

"Vick, the whole damn world can hear you even when you whisper," Rome growled, crossing his arms over his chest as if accusing her of conspiring with the devil.

Katie aligned with him and crossed her arms too. The two of them stood on display. *Tomb Raider* and the darkest version of *Gladiator*.

I smiled at them both glaring at me. "You two would be kind of cute together."

Katie's eyes bulged before she spit, "Fuck you, Brey. Get your shit together. This is a fucking bad idea, and if Rome is the only one who agrees with me, so be it. Jax is a bad toxicology report waiting to happen. You were addicted once and the next time you get addicted, you won't survive it."

I wanted to argue, wanted to say she was wrong. Every person who survives heartbreak wants to believe they could survive it again. No one is ready to agree that the first break nearly killed them and that one more crushing blow could be the end of their heart.

I wanted to argue. But I couldn't.

Vick shot up, facing Rome and Katie. Her blonde hair swayed like usual, this time with warning. "You two need to back off! She needs this. Either of you heard of closure?"

Rome opened his mouth to argue.

She stepped up in his face and shoved her finger into his chest. "No. You don't get to answer the question about closure." She poked his chest again. "You don't have closure. You used Brey as a distraction. You keep using every woman you sleep with as a temporary closure that just leaves a larger, gaping hole afterward—"

Katie cut her off. "Hey, that's a little harsh. Rome and Brey had an understanding. No one got hurt."

I nodded my head because it was the truth.

Katie continued on, "He does what he has to do. Everyone has their demons."

"Oh really, Katie?" Vick cranked her neck so slowly she could have got the lead role in *The Exorcist*. Even Katie backed up a step. "Do you really think you want to justify Rome's actions here?"

Katie's mouth snapped shut, and I suddenly felt like I was trying to understand what large elephant was in the room. I cleared my throat. All of their heads snapped to me like three children caught with their hands in the cookie jar. "Does someone want to explain what is going on?"

After a beat of silence, Rome grumbled, "I just don't want to see you hurt."

"And Jax will hurt you," Katie quickly added.

"Or maybe he won't because he's realized what he lost," Vick finished.

Rome balked at that. "He shouldn't need to realize. He should've known."

With all three of them standing over me looking down with complete concern while I sat cross-legged on the couch, I really did try to contain my laughter. I mean, they all meant well. But it was silly. I even looked toward the ceiling, willing myself to hold it in. As I took in the scene one last time though, the loud cackle couldn't be held back.

Katie threw up her hands, mumbling something along the lines of me losing it, and Rome just stared while Vick smiled.

I sucked in a breath and started to explain but it just came out in another laugh. I slid onto my side to hold my belly from laughing. I wheezed and blurted out through giggles, "It's just a study session, guys. I didn't say I was sleeping with him."

Vick's smile was full blown at that point and then she started to giggle when she added, "Can you imagine their faces if you'd told them that?"

I cracked up again. Vick joined in, falling to my side on the couch.

Katie looked on like she was totally disgusted. "How I continue hanging out with you two is completely a mystery to me."

With that, she turned and stomped out of the apartment with me yelling after her from the couch that I love her. Who wouldn't, right?

Rome wasn't as easy. I just didn't know it then. He swept in and brushed the back of his hand across my cheek. "Be careful, babe." Then he turned to Vick and shoved her hair around on the top of her head, messing up her ponytail. "You'd better be right, Vick."

His eyes held mine a moment longer, and in them I saw real anxiety. It hit me harder than I wanted it to.

Rome and I, we'd been a team, blocking out the world for a long time together. I was going against that, and I knew letting the world in—letting my heartbreaker back in—didn't sit well with him.

I wanted Vick to be right as much as Rome did.

Except a part of me knew she wasn't the one who was right that day.

Love was an addiction and overdosing on it left bad toxicology reports, destruction, and fatalities.

CHAPTER
EIGHTEEN

AUBREY

MY PHONE VIBRATED as I laid out my notes and book on the library table.

When "Winner" popped up, I smiled at his stupid way of trying to get rid of the old nickname I'd given him. I took a breath to calm my racing heart. "Hello?"

"Where are you?" His voice sounded soft, quiet. "The librarian is trying to kill me with her glare. Seems phones are frowned upon here."

"Third floor, to your right."

He didn't waste time talking, just hung up.

I grumbled about how rude he was and went about setting up my laptop. The low battery had me crawling underneath the table to find an outlet. My hips did not want to wedge themselves between the chair and table leg as I reached further to get the plug in.

"I've got to get into better shape." I grumbled more complaints to myself, now in a sour mood.

That's, of course, when Jax's head appeared at the edge of the table. "View looks great from where I'm standing."

"Crap!" I jerked upward and my head banged into the table, causing my whole body to ricochet just enough to put me off balance. My hip rammed into the table, and I swore again.

Scrambling out from underneath the hazardous area, I glared at Jax. "What is wrong with you? You can't just sneak up on people like that."

"Hardly sneaking, Peaches. I was just on the phone with you, and now I'm enjoying what I see." He chuckled, looking at me like I was pitiful while I rubbed my hip and my head.

He shoved a coffee cup with a lid on it into my hand. "Here, I got you some chai tea."

I made a face. "I don't really like chai tea anymore."

He just nodded like he expected that response. "Sure, Peaches. Just humor me and sip on it, okay?"

Part of me wanted to throw it at him. "Fine, but next time you decide to arrive with tea, try to do it without scaring people into injury."

He barked out a laugh that overtook him long enough for me to drink him in. Like the first bite of my favorite dessert, pleasure shot all the way through my bloodstream. I'd feel guilty later, but I indulged anyway. My eyes scanned him from head to toe, taking in everything from his messy hair to his casual running shoes. My indulging crossed the line into memories when I saw he wore dark jeans and a fitted light-blue T-shirt.

"You're not wearing a suit," I murmured more to myself than to him.

He quirked an eyebrow at me as if I was being silly. "It's a library, not a conference center. You're not wearing a dress. Don't get me wrong, your black jeans looked great from where I stood."

I should've let it go and gotten past it easily but something about being around him, with not another soul on the third floor and him looking just like he used to, wouldn't let me.

I lost myself in the indulgence and couldn't seem to find my way out. He reminded me of how we used to be. The sparkle in his ocean-blue eyes slammed into me harder than one his facewash snowballs ever had. And the memory of him smirking at me just like this years ago as he flirted with me knocked the wind out of me.

I shook my head, rubbing it again. "You always wear suits now."

The corners of his mouth lifted just a bit. Then somehow, he was right in front of me, like he'd silently crept up to me and maneuvered his way into being only an inch away. He brushed my hands away, replacing them with his. First, he inspected my head. One arm wrapped around my lower back where he slid his hand under my shirt to shift it up enough for his other hand to rub the sore spot on my hip.

As he looked at the reddened spot, he grumbled, "I'm not on TV or in a magazine right now, so I think jeans are fine. I'm sure you don't always wear black."

I didn't answer because nothing mattered but his hand rubbing my hip slowly.

Soothingly. Nicely.

Just like he used to do.

Each circle would dip under my shirt and then cause my jeans to ride a little lower.

"Peaches, your hip okay?"

My breath picked up, and I licked my lips, trying and failing to not clench my thighs together. With him so close, I was losing myself in his smell, in his eyes, in the way my breath seemed to sync up to his.

When his eyes locked on mine, they dilated, and I was pulled in. The Caribbean Sea now looked dark, stormy, ready to devour. His hands shifted, both under my shirt now, wrapping around the small of my waist, almost encircling me.

As he leaned in, I parted my lips.

The loud vibration and ring jerked me back to reality.

Jax swore and tried to hold my gaze. "Ignore it," he commanded. My body screamed at me to listen but I sidestepped.

He growled and pulled his phone out. "This better be good."

Even the menace in his voice had my knees shaking and weak. I smoothed my hair back and tried to take in slow breaths, tried to calm the ache in me to have him again. I sat and shuffled the papers around, trying to forget what just happened.

I needed to remember who we were today rather than who we were years ago.

He eyed me while listening to his phone call and something in him seemed to snap. "I can't talk about this right now. I hired you to handle it, so handle it."

He ended the call and looked down at me. I just moved my textbook to the middle of the table and opened a few windows on my laptop. Clearing my throat, I said, "So, I already reviewed the lesson plan. The professor wants us to create an investment plan and track it for six weeks. I studied some stats, and I figure if—"

"Sweet Sin," he harshly whispered, planting his hands on the table as if trying to steady himself.

I flinched because I knew what that name signified, what it meant, how much weight it held when he called me by it. "Jax, I wish you'd stop calling me that," I sighed.

He exhaled, and then his intoxicating voice rumbled out, "When I get as close to you as I did a second ago and I'm tempted beyond reason, it'll *always* be what I call you."

To say I was embarrassed by the fact that I vibrated in my seat across from him just from his confession would be an understatement. I was embarrassed and so angry that I still wasn't immune to him. I tried to roll my eyes and look uninterested, but I heard the snark in my voice when I replied, "Or what you call me and every other girl you bring up on stage."

I admit, some sort of sick hope festered in me when I glanced up at him. I wanted to see some sort of guilt, some sort of remorse, or maybe even a sliver of regret.

The evil half-grin on his face didn't show any shame though. "You want to talk about my *Sweet Sin* album and tour, I'm happy to, babe. Calling women on my tour 'Sweet Sin' is basically a damn memorial to you anyway. I named my album and my tour after you."

"It's a memorial to me when you call them a name you once called me and then make out with them in front of millions of people watching on TV?"

He had to be kidding.

"They obviously never meant anything." He shrugged.

His nonchalance grated at every nerve that had been hurt every time I saw those concerts on TV. That sick feeling in the pit of my stomach intensified as I thought about it. "It meant a little something to me when my ex called other women a name he'd only used when he couldn't resist me the night before he left. Not only did you use it with them, you used it the same way."

He balked at that. "I didn't use it the same way," he almost growled. "It was a gimmick, good PR, and like I said, it's a sort of memorial to us."

"So, if the roles were reversed ... "

"What? If you called some guy L.P.?" He smiled. "I'd let them take that nickname any day."

"If I called them L.P. and then started sucking their face, you'd be just fine with that?"

His gaze narrowed. "Aren't you already doing that exclusively with *Roman*?" He sneered the name. "You want to talk about my album and tour? Why don't we talk about you and him and what you've been doing for the last couple of years?"

My eyebrows raised because I knew he was trying to accuse me of something. "I have nothing to hide. If we're going to talk about that, let's just add in what happened when you left and why you still go to see the man everyone calls my father?"

An article in *Rolling Stone* had claimed the man who stood a foot away from me couldn't be read, that his walls were so high they couldn't be penetrated, and that he didn't have a tell known to man. So, the music he wrote was even more unique, giving people a window into the mind of a man so calculated and so elusive the world would never really know what he was thinking.

They called him cold and unconquerable.

I remembered that article because it captured what he hit me with right then. His blue eyes froze over like an arctic storm.

I donned a smile that hopefully looked to him like it was keeping me as warm as a polar bear's fur under his icy gaze. "Ah, not so talkative now, are we?"

He sat down across from me, ready for war. His gaze drilled into me so brutally, I nearly backed down.

Nearly.

His voice was low when he spoke. "Sometimes, I wonder how your manners and formalities elude you when you say shit like that. I don't discuss that part of the past with you because it doesn't change the present."

I didn't shrink away from his anger. I just glared back with what I hoped were drills of my own. "Then there's no reason to discuss what I've been doing, right? We're friends in the present, trying to work things out 'for Jay.'" I air quoted as my tone turned condescending. "So, the past can be swept neatly under a very large, very thick rug. Right, *L.P.*?" I sneered the old nickname like a weapon.

He sighed and rubbed his hand over his face. "Jesus Christ, Peaches. Do you want help with this class or not?"

I hummed low at his stubbornness before I shoved my lesson over to him. "I already completed this portion of the investment plan. If you think it works, we can call it a day."

Really, the help I needed was much more than him skimming over my investment plan but pride and frustration coursed through me.

If he wanted answers, I deserved them too. While he looked over my homework, I secretly tried willing pain into him, willing guilt into him. I literally started hoping for some voodoo or hypnosis power so that I could just get through to him.

"Aubrey, before you know it,"—he didn't even make the effort to glance up from my work for the reprimand—"you're going to hurt that pretty face of yours by glaring at me. So, stop it."

I sighed and repressed my childish retort.

A few more minutes of him studying my work passed. I sipped the chai tea and suppressed a moan when I tasted how good it was.

He didn't look up or say anything else as time passed. I started to fidget. My work wasn't bad. It was sufficient, and maybe even good.

I'd spent a tremendous amount of time researching to make sure I made all the right decisions. I wouldn't admit that I spent extra time on it to make sure he couldn't insult my intelligence when he looked it over.

So, his lack of positive reinforcement had me trying to distract myself by texting Jay the update he requested.

> **AUBREY:** Studying with your brother and I haven't killed him yet.
> **JAY:** I'm surprised…contemplated it every day since he's been here. :-P Seriously, u OK?
> **AUBREY:** Of course

Even if I wasn't so sure, Jay didn't need to know that. He didn't need to know that I already sparred about the past with Jax and pushed for answers I knew I probably wouldn't get. He definitely didn't need to know that Jax still got a rise out of me.

Jax cleared his throat loudly. "You can text later."

I set my phone down and glared at him.

He slid my papers back over to me. "This is all wrong."

I waited to see if he would elaborate. I even stared at him with wide eyes. Instead, he had the audacity to pull out *his* phone and check it.

"Jax, you do realize you can't just say it's wrong, right?"

He looked up and gave me a blank stare. "You want a good investment plan. That isn't one. Start over."

If I could've thrown my papers and laptop in his face without hearing about it from Jay, I would have. "That is not how you tutor someone." I enunciated each word. "You walk them through it."

"I *am* walking you through it. Start over," he enunciated back.

"This is your problem, you know that?" I tried to rein myself in. I even mentally counted backward from ten to one while I smoothed my hair.

It didn't work.

"You just think because you're so damn brilliant that everyone else is too. Then, when they can't see your logic, you can't be bothered. Your logic is so obvious to you that you can't *fathom* anyone else having another opinion or idea. *Rolling Stone* thinks you're so lethal and dominating and blah, blah, blah."

Stopping my rant was impossible. He tried to cut me off by saying my name.

I didn't stop, wasn't going to stop until I was done. I needed this like I needed a thousand-pound weight lifted off my shoulders. "You're not any of those things. You're just an arrogant ass who can't see past his own views, who can't *help* anyone else to understand. I mean, would it kill you to elaborate for once in your life? To answer one godforsaken question? I mean, really—"

"Whitfield!" he shouted.

In the middle of a library. Like it was his right. Startled, my mouth snapped shut.

He pushed me and I let him. Somehow, he irked me just enough to get under my skin, to move past my manners and let the raw, unhinged side out of me.

To my surprise, he started laughing. "I love your sass, woman, I actually miss it. Can you believe that?" His eyes twinkled. "But give me a chance to defend myself."

His hand slid over to take back my plan. I sighed, knowing I'd overreacted. He didn't owe me anything anymore, and even if he did, it didn't matter. I started to apologize, "Look, Jax—"

He stopped me with a look. "Same goes from years ago, Peaches. Don't apologize for letting me see you."

His words brought back memories from that day on the lake. I shook my head because I didn't want him to continue, didn't want to remember how hard I'd fallen for him that day. Remembering meant this wouldn't be just us here trying to shake each other from our systems.

"It's still one of the sexiest things I've ever seen in this world and one of the only things I can't seem to live without. No matter how fucking hard I try."

CHAPTER
NINETEEN

AUBREY

I WALKED HOME IN a daze after studying that day. He'd shifted gears completely, walking me through every step of an investment plan, telling me the only reason I wasn't getting it was because I wasn't taking risks.

He'd looked at me and said, "Let yourself fly a little. Playing it safe won't get you anywhere in this class or in life."

His words rang over and over in my head that night and the next day.

They knocked around in my head until the next time I saw him.

He brought me chai tea again, and I grumbled about not drinking it again.

He just repeated as he sat down, "Humor me."

I made an effort to look somewhat disgusted as he passed it over.

He looked me up and down. "Black and gray today, I see. So, I guess you don't wear black everywhere you go."

It'd become our little thing to comment on each other's wardrobe. A smirk slipped out when I replied, "And no suit again, I see. Guess I'm just not good enough for those TV clothes."

A genuine laugh rumbled from him.

I took him in and smiled behind the cup of chai tea. The way he relaxed when he laughed made him look a little younger and a little less dominating. He was just as beautiful but in a boyish, carefree way. I found myself wanting to see him like that more, like I cared about his well-being.

That thought scared me enough to snap my attention to the tea. I took a huge gulp and practically moaned. He'd had Jackie make it, I was sure. The woman was a magician, and chai tea was my favorite even if I wasn't going to admit it to him.

It tasted of memories, sweet and so painful, and I normally avoided it.

When I looked up, his eyes were trained on my lips, dilated and pulling me in. I rubbed my thighs together and tried not to act aware of him.

Clearing my throat, I began walking him through my investment plan again.

This time, he responded so well that someone might have thought he'd been teaching his whole life.

The man was an easy study. He could be good at just about anything.

FOR ANOTHER TWO WEEKS, we met and discussed investments every other day.

It wasn't enough and too much at the same time.

Every time I saw him, I wanted him but knew I couldn't handle having him again. My heart would warm even though it should have cooled.

Falling back into friendship with Jax proved to be even more difficult.

We danced around the serious topics. He didn't discuss the past with me, didn't divulge why he still visited my father.

I didn't discuss my past with him. I didn't share anything about my past relationships or other friendships.

He didn't really talk about his life at all back in the city. I knew he had one there but was too afraid to ask him questions I wasn't sure I wanted the answers to.

Did he like the city he chose over his family and me?

Did he have as much fun as the magazines showed him having?

Why wouldn't he just make another album? His fans begged and begged him to. Instead, he would just repeat to any inquiry that investing was his true passion and he wanted a quiet life.

I don't think the world believed him.

I didn't either.

Was he still with the woman all the magazines said he was with? Were they exclusive?

Did he love her like he loved me? Had he ever really even loved me?

The stupid voice mail I'd saved played over in my head, and I found myself going home and listening to it after studying with him.

I heard the hitch in his voice when he said those three words. I rewound it to hear it again. And then again.

The words echoed in my room, echoed in my head, echoed in my heart. Over and over again they played, making my heart skip a beat each and every time.

I slammed my laptop shut. I needed to do something other than study with Jax that day. My body was shaking with a pent-up emotion I couldn't quite put my finger on and seeing him wouldn't make it go away.

> **WINNER:** Library at 1?
> **AUBREY:** I think I got this assignment handled. Going to take a rain check and work on it alone today.
> **WINNER:** I guess I'll go into the city to work then.

I silenced my phone, trying not to feel guilty about my lie. I jumped up to survey my closet and took in my wardrobe. Mostly black, some grays, some creams and whites.

Neutral. A way to blend. A way to stay off people's radar, which was hard enough when I was seen with Jay on a normal basis. Now with Jax in town, I'd probably have to lurk in the shadows if I didn't want people talking.

I grabbed a sports bra and black capris. One of the small splurges I'd made for myself was in the exercise department. Hell would freeze over too before I felt guilty about spending extra on my bright Nikes and a Lululemon sports bra. When a person has enough incentive to take care of their body, they should feel good doing it.

I tied my hair up in a messy bun and breezed out of my room, ready to go for a jog.

Vick and Katie halted me in the apartment hallway and Vick groaned when she saw my outfit. "We were just coming to get you. Day drinking, not jogging!"

I sighed. "You guys know I will once I'm done with this class. I can't afford a hangover tomorrow though."

Katie, now a redhead with black highlights, squinted at me. "Day drinking with Vick and Rome isn't going to be any fun."

Vick balked at that. "Whatever. It's going to be fun because Rome will let us drink free at his new Heathens Bar. And my God, Brey, the guys he hired are drop-dead gorgeous."

Katie laughed, and I sidestepped them. "I'll take a rain check. Tell Rome I said hi."

"Tell me yourself," he said as he came out of his apartment and locked the door.

He wore all black and looked lethal with his hair mussed just the right way. I smiled at him. "Hi, Rome."

He looked me up and down. "Not coming out with us?"

I shrugged, and Katie piped up, "Running instead." She crossed her arms. "I just wonder why she's choosing to do that instead."

"I just told you why."

"I know what you said, I'm just trying to figure out the real reason." Rome put his arm around my shoulders and leaned in to whisper loud enough for everyone to hear. "You don't have to answer to this little redheaded devil."

Katie glowered as she ran her fingers through her hair. "Oh get fucked, Rome. Your bartender liked my hair last night. He probably will again today."

I needed to jog and clear my thoughts, not worry about their constant bickering. I backed away and waved. "See you all later." Then I spun around and left.

I ran near a lake and then veered off to run up a large hill.

The sun warmed my skin and the breeze cooled it as I worked up a sweat. With the trees rustling and people sprinkled throughout campus, the stress that had built in me eased out.

My lungs took in the life around me, mixing scents of lilacs and maple trees. It reminded me what I loved so much about just taking time to enjoy running and the changing of seasons. Those seasons pushed you to take advantage of the short summers because winter was always lingering in the back of your mind.

Lost in my own thoughts, I found myself stopped in Jay's driveway. I knocked on the door, taking in his house as I always did when I stood there waiting. Sleek, contemporary, and manly described it. With its intimidating size and lakefront location, I knew how expensive it was.

Yet, it suited Jaydon more than any other place we'd shopped around for. I smiled, remembering how he'd asked me to look for a house and then move in with him when he bought this one. I rolled my eyes at how mad he'd been when I'd said no and moved down the hall from Rome instead.

The door swung open and I jerked back, shocked to find a more dangerous Stonewood holding open the door.

Jax leaned onto the door and looked me up and down. He did it as slow as the Big Bad Wolf had when he'd looked over Red Riding Hood.

Instinct had me wanting to shrink back. I never paid attention to the looks I got when working out. I didn't care whether or not people accepted my wardrobe, just that I felt good in it. Now though, I snapped my head down to look. Sweat dripped from everywhere, and I could bet every part of my body glistened in the sun.

Every one of my curves shined more brightly. Jax dated stick-thin models. I knew that when I snapped my head back up to look at him, he wouldn't be devouring my body with his eyes. Instead, he was looking over my shoulder with a muscle in his jaw ticking.

He was probably that disgusted and wanted to check to see who'd seen me at his brother's door.

I huffed and put my hands on my hips. Whether or not my instinct told me to curl into myself, I stood taller on display.

I was real. No plastic surgery, no lipo, nothing. He'd appreciated me once before, so I let him take in reality for a second.

Instead of him dwelling on my stance a second longer though, he grabbed my elbow and yanked me in. "Did you jog all the way from your place?"

"Yes." Was he insinuating that I wasn't in good shape?

Jerk.

I crossed my arms and stared him down as he scanned outside, probably looking for paparazzi. So what if one actually caught him standing with a woman who looked a little bigger than his type? Right?

"And I looped near the lake." I'd make sure to set him straight regarding how in shape I really was. "Anyway, where's Jay? I only have a little more time to spend with him before he's off to LA."

He ignored my question as he slammed the door and spun around to face me. "What the hell are you thinking running around like that?"

"Excuse me?" I paused to lift my eyebrows at him. "Like what?"

"Like that!" He motioned to my sports bra and I realized he was actually stupid enough to comment on my body type.

Even so, I'll admit I crossed my arms over my bra to hide what I normally felt comfortable in.

Bastard.

"You're an ass."

I went to find Jay and left him standing in the entrance. He belonged in there with its two staircases and statue of Venus. The foyer and him—both perfect, pristine, and completely pompous.

"Brey, that you?" Jay yelled over the clanking of pans.

I walked into the kitchen of stainless steel, granite counters, and windows the size of the walls. The kitchen, although not exactly how I would have decorated it, always made my heart ache for a home. I wanted to learn to cook, make my chai tea in the morning, and overlook something other than apartment buildings.

This kitchen in particular made my heart stop though, because one beautiful blue-eyed man was smiling so big at me that I couldn't shake missing him already.

"Sass Pot, you want a burger?"

I went and hugged him from behind as he worked on his indoor grill. "Not after jogging over here."

"Come on. No one's judging here. Jax is having one too, right?"

"No judging from this side of the room," Jax grumbled as he walked in behind me and sat down at the barstool near the marble island.

I huffed into Jay's back and squeezed him a little tighter before I let go and went to the fridge to find something a little healthier.

"Come on," Jax goaded me. "Just relax and let him cook for us."

I turned and glared at him over my shoulder.

He raised his hands up in surrender. "Truce, all right? Come sit down. I won't bite." He patted the barstool next to him. "Brey,"—he said with a deeper voice—"come sit down." He enunciated the words as if that would help my decision.

When I saw Jay tense though, I gave in because I didn't want to make him uncomfortable. "I can only stay for a little bit. I have to get back, and really I just want a salad." Jax put his hand on the small of my back and rubbed while he leaned in and said, "Jay will be hurt if you don't eat his burger. It's a new meal he's trying."

"Don't lie." I straightened to try to deter the rubbing that sent sparks to areas I didn't need them sent. "He makes this all the time."

While Jay threw more spices on the grill, Jax whispered in my ear. "You told me you were reviewing your assignment alone this afternoon. *You* lied."

"And you told me you were going back into the city," I hissed leaning away from him.

"Only because you canceled on me." He waited a beat. "Now, I'm wondering the real reason you canceled."

I looked away. I wasn't going to tell him it was because I wasn't sure us hanging out was helping me to get closure. I wasn't even sure I could find a way to call him just my friend.

Especially with him sitting there rubbing my back.

"Stop that." I shoved his hand away, and he laughed.

I wanted to scream at him.

"And burgers are served," Jay said turning around with a pile of plates and burgers. "You guys get started. I'm going to go change. Got grease on this shirt."

He disappeared from the room and I felt the walls closing in. I could swear Jax felt it also, because he got up from his stool to move in closer to me.

"Why did you cancel today?"

I rolled my lips between my teeth and didn't answer. I couldn't. Not with him so close. Not with him holding my gaze like he wanted the world from me and was willing to take it. Jax never settled for less, and I was sure I couldn't give him any of it.

Not even an answer to his question.

So, I shrugged. He grunted as he took a step closer. "Whitfield, there's a reason."

He was right. There was a reason I wasn't willing to share.

He gripped my thighs and my eyes shot to his hands. Then, he started to rub circles.

It was automatic for him. It had to be muscle memory. Or something he did with most women.

My body didn't think so though. Heat flooded my veins, and my heart echoed those three words I'd heard him say on the voice mail.

When he stepped closer still, my legs spread willingly to let him push up against me. He leaned down, and I looked up at him.

The man couldn't be denied what he wanted. Not when he looked like that. The sun shone from the window onto him like a god, and he smirked at me like he knew I'd be fine with him right up against me, close enough to kiss me.

We'd been this close before, closer six years before, but right then, I teetered on the brink of insanity. So off balance and unsure.

Yet, I'd been on solid ground for a long enough time without him. I'd played it completely safe.

With him looking at me like he used to, I wondered if we needed to fall over the edge into insanity, to get lost in each other to find ourselves again.

At the moment our lips would have touched, Jax turned his head and smelled my hair.

"Cinnamon. I swear, I am addicted to it." He ran his hand through my hair on the other side of my face and I felt him fiddling behind my head. My hair fell out of its bun in waves. "Come to dinner with me tonight. I'll take you anywhere you want."

That snapped me back to reality. Anywhere? He couldn't take me anywhere.

We went to the library just to stay secluded enough from the local media and paparazzi.

Beyond that, he'd had the chance to take me to dinner years ago, to go anywhere with me years ago, and he hadn't even picked up the phone.

Now, we were two very different people, getting along for the sake of me passing my class and for Jay.

I shook my head and shoved him back to stand up. "I don't want to go to dinner with you, Jax. I'm busy."

"Busy doing what? Working on the assignment you're supposedly working on now?" he said, stepping toward me again. My anger slipped as his eyes twinkled. "Just dinner, Brey."

"Don't you have a girl to go to dinner with in the city?" I hated that I'd whispered it, like I should feel guilty for finally pushing us past the small talk we'd done for weeks now.

I'd seen the magazines though. I'd seen the life he lived back home, the woman he was with back home. The one in magazines, the woman at his concerts on TV too.

Isabel. Beautiful. Smart. Perfect.

"You want me to dump her?" He drawled the questions as if it was all a joke. "So, you want this to be a date? Not just working through things and being friends anymore?"

Maybe he was joking with me. Maybe this was all a joke to him and a way to pass the time.

Maybe none of this meant anything to him. And how could I be sure, really? He'd left me once like I'd been nothing. The only other proof I had o the contrary was a stupid little voice mail clanging around in my head every so often.

"No," I said maybe a little too loudly as I leaned back to create a little distance between us. "I just mean, I don't think she would like you going to dinner with anyone other than her. You guys can't see a lot of each other with you being here, and I don't trust the media to not spin something ludicrous about us."

"Launch is almost over. She won't mind if the media spins it that we went on a date."

I didn't care whether she would mind or not.

Because I did. That was the real problem.

I was starting to care about a lot of things when it came to him. Or maybe I'd never stopped caring.

I brushed past him and let out a breath.

I bustled around a little, grabbing silverware and went to set the dining room table. He followed silently, bringing in the food.

We moved around each other, comfortable enough to know where the other would go, careful enough to not get in one another's way. We needed space, we needed to get ourselves in check before something we couldn't take back happened.

Jay waltzed back in. "Why the hell do we have to eat at the dining room table?" he whined.

"Seriously, Jay, we spent forever picking this table out." The man wanted to avoid eating like an adult at all costs.

"You might have spent forever picking it out. I spent forever flirting with that nice little lady selling it," he mumbled around a bite of the burger.

I leaned over to grab some salad that Jax must have found in the fridge.

"You're serious?" I already knew the answer.

"She was worth it, I promise," he snickered.

"Ew."

Jay's chuckle turned into a full belly laugh when he saw my face.

"Can't you give it a rest or find just one girl to be serious with?"

"Only girl I'm serious about is you, Sass Pot." He grabbed his burger and took a bite while I tried to hide my smile.

"You gonna eat or what, man?" Jay said through a bite of his burger.

"Yeah, just thinking." Jax stared at me.

"What?" I moved my hand over my mouth. He dragged his eyes over my face again and then dug into his burger, without answering.

My cell beeped, and I grabbed it to check the message.

> **ROME:** Just left a married woman's house. You don't want to know…Can we reconsider not hooking up anymore? :-P
>
> **AUBREY:** Throw me to the curb and get served. You're on your own.
>
> **ROME:** Cold, woman, real cold.

"Aubrey." Jax's voice was sharp. "You gonna eat?"

"Like I said, I am not that hungry," I replied, looking back down at my phone just to irritate him.

"Is the person texting you that important?"

"My friends are always important."

"Is that *just* a friend?" he asked.

I harrumphed. It wasn't a question he had a right to ask.

He pointed one of his utensils at me. "You'll be skin and bones if you don't eat something."

I glared. "And what am I now?"

Jax looked to Jay for help but Jay was shaking his head smirking into his food. He wasn't getting involved. "You know exactly what I mean, Peaches. I don't want … I mean, no man wants you to be … " Jax stumbled over what to say. "Well, they want you to be healthy. It's a figure of speech."

I raised my eyebrows. "You sure about that? The men I hang around seem to really like models."

He choked and then coughed.

Jay silently laughed over on his side of the table.

"What's so funny, Jay? Your ass has been dating models since your first movie."

Jay didn't miss a beat. "I don't date anyone. They know it, and I know it."

I rolled my eyes. "Can we save this for your guy talk later when I'm gone?"

Jay shrugged and changed the subject. "I gotta conference call about the movie in a few. If I'd have known you were coming over … "

I waved him off. "I didn't call or tell you. It's fine."

He still looked remorseful. "I fly out to LA in a few days. You want to come to the airport with me?"

I nodded. "Of course." My eyes flicked to Jax's. "Rome can probably drive us."

Jax grunted but Jay responded, "I got a driver but just come see me off."

When he winked at me, my throat started closing and my eyes started to water just thinking about him leaving.

I jumped up and started grabbing plates to clean up. "I should get back home."

Jay nodded toward the plates. "Leave it. I'll have Jax do the dishes later since he's crashing here."

I waved him off. "Go get ready for your call. And let's have dinner before you fly out."

He nodded and stared at me and Jax a beat before leaving the room. It was his way of giving his brother space.

Space I didn't want or need.

Jax glanced at my phone that pinged again. "Something got you in a rush to get back?"

I shook my head and wondered if he would be jealous that Rome was the one texting me. "I just need to get back."

"You didn't eat anything."

"I'm not going to eat and then jog back home, Jax."

"I'll drive you."

"If I don't run home, I'll be too wired later." Not that I needed an excuse to not drive with him. I could barely be in the same room alone with him without feeling something. The same car was out of the question.

He stood, walking toward Jay's bedrooms. "Wait a minute. I'll go with you, all right?"

"Um…" He was already out of the room when I asked, "Why?"

Throwing my hands up, I decided I wasn't waiting for an answer.

Beelining for Jay's front door, I figured I could text Jay later about my abrupt departure.

I was halfway down the street when Jax yelled, "You were supposed to wait."

"I never said I would," I managed between breaths.

His footsteps gained on me and before I knew it, his step was in sync just behind mine.

I looked over and he was just behind me, keeping pace. It dredged up memories of us years ago. Like a predator, he'd always kept me so close, just within his sight and grasp. I wondered if he was hungry enough to take another bite.

Our proximity was dangerous. I smelled him, and it was just like I remembered. Mint and sandalwood shaving cream was all around me. Every one of his footsteps had me imagining how much of a perfect machine he was when he worked out. It was like some gym gurus came together and built his muscles for advertising. His fitted T-shirt showed off his chest, his abs, and his muscular shoulders.

As his tennis shoes hit the pavement, his calf muscles took the impact gracefully. Every stride was fluid. His muscles stretched and bunched, drawing my eyes to them along with every other part of my body. The way he ran reminded me of how he moved doing other things. Things I shouldn't be remembering.

I didn't take any side routes. I needed to get home, away from him. The next two miles, we ran in silence with stolen glances. Every time I looked over at him, my body remembered another something. No sort of memory suppression can last when your first love is running alongside you, sweat dripping from his face, his neck, his arms.

Everywhere.

My heart was racing, and I was sweating.

It wasn't from the run.

I willed myself to stop drooling over him and make it home without trying to jump my silent running partner. Instead, I figured I needed to push myself harder. I picked up speed, sprinting the last block to the apartments.

He matched my stride effortlessly.

I wanted to curse him out loud for it.

As we slowed at my apartment building, I turned to face him, totally out of breath. His thin sheen of sweat had me wondering just what I must look like now. Without being able to even muster up a quick wave, I bent over and put my hands on my knees.

He chuckled as he stood over me. I'm not too proud to say I didn't care that he was mocking my exhaustion. I was just happy his shadow blocked the sunlight.

The breeze cooled me quickly enough, and I attempted to gather myself as I straightened. Smoothing my hair back and then resorting to pulling out my ponytail to tie it all back more tightly, I eyed him. "I'm not sure why you decided to jog with me but you can go now."

His mouth kicked up to smirk at me. "I missed you, Peaches."

I squinted at him, not sure my exhaustion had me imagining it. "What?"

He crossed his arms over his chest. "I missed you."

Something in the way he said it, standing there so full of confidence and being so candid had me wanting to jump over the big hurdle that was our past.

If he could be open and transparent, what reason did we have to hold on to things that caused us pain before?

Running made me honest. It made me see reality clearly. "I missed you too."

As I said it, his mouth dropped a little and then he snapped it back up.

He backed away as if what I'd said was enough for him. "Let me know the next time you're going to run outside looking that good. Can't have you going alone."

It was my turn to be surprised. I glanced down at myself.

When I glanced back up, he was jogging away from me but turned to wink.

My heartbeat picked up and that, I told myself, was the reason I had to hold on to the pain we had been through before. If I didn't, I'd fall headfirst in love with the person who'd made me scared of it in the first place.

CHAPTER
TWENTY

AUBREY

EVERY DAY AFTER THAT, I'd get a text from him in the morning.

> **WINNER:** Going for a run today?

The first morning I got it, my phone became a sort of grenade, one I wasn't sure I wanted to hold. I stared at it for way longer than I wanted to admit, thumb hovering over the screen to type a response.

It stayed glued to my side as I ate a light breakfast and put on my bright purple camo leggings with a purple sports bra.

As I tied my shoes, it alerted me to another text.

> **WINNER:** Quit ignoring me, Whitfield. I'm going with you on your run.

I smirked and before I could talk myself out of it, I texted back.

AUBREY: You have twenty minutes to meet me in front of my apartment.

I threw my phone onto the couch, knowing I'd just pulled the pin and thrown the grenade that might cause me to self-destruct.

The rush of adrenaline from communicating with him surged through my veins. It shouldn't be something I got addicted to.

Every day that I wanted to go for a run, I'd text him that same message. Every time, he didn't answer but was there twenty minutes later.

For the next two weeks, we studied and jogged together. In between, I sent Jay off to LA and cried like a baby on Jax's shoulder when he asked how I took him leaving.

On days Jax went back to the city, I went to visit my girls at the reservation.

We formed a routine.

One I liked to think was a friend routine but Katie, Vick, and Rome seemed to think otherwise.

I argued that I would have run and studied with all of them. They thought I was full of shit.

I told myself that being close to Jax came naturally. We grew up together, and I missed Jay.

Jax was a decent substitute.

When we ran, he didn't say much. His breathing was methodical, steady, and rhythmic as if because he was a musical genius, he could make the damn necessary action of life a song.

It infuriated me, soothed me, and hypnotized me all at the same time.

With the summer heat and quick pace, I always reached a point where my muscles just took over. My mind turned itself off, and I just ran while I listened to our feet hit the ground.

That was the part I was addicted to, with or without Jax. It was freedom. No control, no worries, no thoughts.

That day, I can also say there was no direction or preservation of life in me because one second I was running up the hill and the next I was being tackled onto the grass.

Screaming, my reflexes kicked in and stuck my hands out to catch my fall.

"Goddamn it!" Jax yelled as he landed on top of me.

"What the hell, Jax!"

"Motherfuck..." he yelled looking over his shoulder.

I glanced that way and saw a large man barreling down the hill on a bicycle.

Jax whipped back around to me where I was caged underneath him. "Are you fucking blind?"

"What... of course not... excuse me?" I stammered.

He pounded his hand down into the grass and then leaned closer. "You heard me, Whitfield. That bicyclist almost took you out."

"So, instead *you* took me out?" I screamed back at him and shoved him in the shoulder. My hand connecting with him shot pain up my arm and I winced.

His hardened gaze shifted to my hand, and somehow, he gripped my wrist and examined me before I could even examine it myself. "Shit, you tried to catch your fall on the cement before we hit the grass."

It wasn't a question so I didn't answer. Instead, I huffed and tried to pull my wrist back but of course we were doing this the Stonewood way.

"We need to clean this up, Peaches." His voice was soft and his eyes were back on mine, vivid blue with concern laced in them.

That look—the one he reserved for reading people and seeing into their soul—had me shivering under him.

I tried to move and get up, to get away, to put some distance between us. "I'll be fine."

His body on top of mine was stone, immovable.

"Whitfield," he growled. Then, he ran his tongue over his teeth and I just knew.

"Jax, we should get up," I whispered.

I just knew.

He gave me that calculating look and then mumbled, "Fuck it."

I. Just. Knew.

His lips crashed down onto mine. As I gasped, he shot his tongue in my mouth, reclaiming it as his like he'd never lost the title. He staked his flag on the territory and not even I could fight the war and win. We weren't equal opponents here. It was predator meets prey. I couldn't survive because he'd already ripped me open.

He kissed me like he was ravenous, like I was his first meal ever, like he'd consume all of me. I would never be able to outrun him.

I wish I could say I shoved him back right away. That I thought about jeopardizing my friendship with Jay or who was waiting for him back in the city.

I didn't.

I held onto him for dear life because he might have ripped me open and fed on me like he was ravenous but I needed his kiss just as much. It was the blood in my veins, the oxygen in my lungs, and the water in my body.

He tasted like he used to and of so much more than he used to. This was Jax grown-up, primed, and aged perfectly.

His hand snaked up my shirt, and finally I realized where we were and what we were doing.

I shoved him back. "This isn't right."

He just looked at me. "We're always right."

He said it like we had our own reality and nothing before it mattered.

I cleared my throat and looked away from him, waiting, hoping he'd move because I wasn't sure I could keep pushing him away.

He sighed and rolled off me.

We both stared up at the sky for a beat. Then his lethal control was back in place, the one that looked effortless, like I couldn't cause even the smallest reaction in him.

He smirked his signature smile at me and said, "I asked you before. I'll ask you again. Want to have dinner with me?"

"I don't think you asked last time."

"And yet, dinner still didn't happen."

I sighed. "I don't think dinner's a good idea."

He conceded for about a second. "Fine. Why don't you walk me around, show me some of the best of this college town? First stop can be a drugstore to clean you up."

"I don't think..."

His brow furrowed like he couldn't take another rejection from me. "Humor me, huh?"

The words rolled off his tongue the exact way they did when he'd bring me tea, and I found myself nodding the way I did when he'd hand it over.

We walked in the direction of a drugstore as I tried to clear my head.

Nothing could shake the kiss. Nothing could move it from my memory.

He pulled me over by my waist in the Walgreens, and the same charge as that of his kiss shot exactly where he touched me. I glanced at him to see if he felt it, too, but he was looking at the Band-Aids.

When his fingers wrapped around my wrist, I eyed him warily. He just nodded at my closed hand. "Open."

I did.

Then he nodded again and went back to looking at the first aid items on the shelves. Instead of letting go of my wrist though, he pulled my hand to his lips and brushed more than one kiss over the back of it.

It was probably muscle memory to him.

He'd always taken his time with me. Years ago, I'd have expected it.

Now, my whole body seized up. We were too close, and I was too weak.

I snatched my hand back.

He didn't look over at me. He just smiled to himself and grabbed some bandage wrap.

When I pulled a small cardholder out of my sports bra while we stood in line, his smirk turned wolfish, "What else are you hiding in there?"

I glanced around. "Shut up."

He sidled closer to me. "Come on. Let me see." He peered down my cleavage.

I shoved him. "Grow up, perv."

"Name calling now, are we?" His eyebrows raised a little but he kept peering where he wasn't supposed to.

When I pursed my lips, he shrugged. "Can't knock a guy for trying."

Then, he pivoted in front of me to pay for the bandaging. There was no point in arguing, I mumbled a thank you. No Stonewood man had ever let me pay for a thing.

Once outside, he led us over to a cement wall that came up a little past my hips. He set down the bandaging and I went to open it. "I don't think I even need this."

"Right, Whitfield. Do everything by the book except when it comes to you getting an infection."

I stopped opening the bandaging and glared at him. "I don't do everything by the book."

He tilted his head slightly. "Really?" He leaned his hip onto the fence. "Enlighten me then. What are you doing that isn't by the book?"

My heart skipped realizing that his opinion of my life still mattered too much to me. I went to smooth my hair back and hated that he caught my nervous move immediately.

His expression softened. He rubbed the back of his hand over my cheek, "Never mind, Peaches."

I closed my eyes and leaned into his touch. He moved closer still and then I felt his hands slide around my hips to hoist me up onto the wall. My hands slammed into his shoulders to steady myself, and the pain from the scrapes seared as I sucked air in through my teeth.

He gripped both of my wrists and moved closer to me. Right in between my legs. "Shit, sorry."

I didn't feel the pain of my scrapes anymore, just the pain of him up against me. It hurt more than any scrape could, yet I relished in it. I wanted to roll in it, bask in it, and lose myself in it. His proximity was every type of pain I knew I didn't need.

"Jax," I breathed and it sounded like a plea. I just didn't know if I was pleading with him to move back or lean in more.

Nothing made sense anymore and I needed time to think, to organize my thoughts and feelings. Then, I'd have more control of them.

I pushed him back but he didn't move like he should have.

Instead, he rustled around in the bag and found the wipes. He didn't warn me and maybe it was partially to punish me for pushing him away. He took the wipe and smeared it over my hand. When he did, I hissed and his eyes glared up at me. He was baiting me to yell at him and start the fight.

He wanted to war with me, I saw that hunger in his eyes. I clenched my jaw, lifting my chin.

"I like you stubborn just as much as I like you fighting me, Whitfield," he ground out, his voice low as he threw the wipes into the plastic bag.

I bit the insides of my cheeks to hold back the smile that worked out of me. If he knew how close he was to breaking me down, he'd push our friend boundaries even further.

Friends didn't admit what he just had. Friends didn't move in this close, and friends didn't put their hands all over me like he did.

Mostly though, friends didn't like all of this closeness as much as I did.

So, when he pulled the bag up to his elbow and then put his hands above my knees so he could lean in, I didn't back away. I should have. I should have done a lot of things in that moment but I was saved when I heard a girl screaming behind him.

"Oh my God! Oh my God! Are you Jax Stonewood?!"

His hands clamped down tight on my upper thighs and he shut his eyes hard as if trying to calm down. When he opened them again, he'd transformed from brooding to megawatt-smiling, lovable singer-songwriter Jax.

He turned to greet a peppy blonde girl about my age. "You caught me."

"Oh my God!" It seemed to be the only thing she knew how to say. "Keep my location to yourself and take a picture with me?" he offered, but more people were already turning our way.

I felt more and more eyes on us, and I wanted to disappear into the shadows. Jax must have felt it too, because after he snapped a quick photo with her, he grabbed my wrist and moved so fast, I had to jog to keep up.

He didn't say anything.

I didn't say anything.

We moved together.

In sync. Connected.

When the crowd started closing in, my breathing picked up.

I could feel the air getting thinner, my window of sanity getting smaller.

Would they get a photo? Would they recognize me?

I tried so hard to ignore the panic creeping in.

He yanked me onto a side street just as I started to wheeze. His eyes snapped to me. "Peaches, focus on me, okay?"

I looked back instead. The first paparazzi camera was as blinding as it had been that day on his mother's porch. The crowd faded to black as my mind focused on the one paparazzi who snapped blinding photo after photo of me.

I wheezed again and Jax stepped between me and the huge camera. "Move, Whitfield."

My gaze jumped to him. His eyes were assessing me, calculating something.

I didn't have time to figure him out.

Couldn't he see I was panicking? Couldn't he hear me wheezing?

I couldn't breathe. I couldn't think. And there was definitely no way I could move.

His gaze hardened. He didn't wait for me to gather myself. He shoved me backward instead. "Move your ass."

"Seriously?" I stumbled backward and used the momentum to pivot away from the crowd down the alley. "You're pushing me?!"

He didn't say anything from behind me.

Great, because I had more to say anyway. "I couldn't breathe back there! Do you know how that feels?"

The only answer I got was the pounding of his footsteps behind me.

Of course, he didn't sound at all winded back there either.

"You know, those people wanted nothing to do with me. It's your fault they were taking our pictures in the first place, yet you have the audacity to shove me when I'm having a meltdown, nervous they might dig up my past or something. I could have fallen and scraped my hand again!"

I heard him scoff. So, I did it right back.

I wasn't wasting my breath on him anymore.

I focused on weaving through more alleys to get back to my place as quickly as I could, on the route. Not on the fact that I could be in the spotlight again, that someone really could dig up my past if they wanted to.

I sighed when I got to the apartment complex and was able to get through the lobby.

I reminded myself that no one could follow us any farther, but my hands still shook when I tried to unlock my door.

Jax didn't say anything. He just took the keys from my hand quickly and looked at me with pursed lips and worried eyes as he unlocked it for me.

When I rushed inside, he stepped in behind me and shut it.

He followed so close. So close, I could smell the mint mixed with just him.

My body wanted to lunge for him and rip his clothes off. How ridiculous that just his scent could erase all the panic and make some part of me want him again.

I cleared my throat, not sure where to start and not sure I wanted to turn around to see him standing there with that same worried look. Did I tell him to leave because people were gathering outside? Did I tell him to stay because I'd just had too good of a day with him?

"Sorry, I shouldn't have pushed you," he blurted from behind me.

I was pretty sure my eyes almost bugged out as I turned around to face him. Never had he ever apologized to me. Not when we were together and definitely not when he had left.

"But you needed me to push you metaphorically and literally. It got you moving."

There it was. Somehow, I was the wrong one. I nodded and rolled my eyes. "What a great apology..."

He brought his hands to his face and scrubbed them over it. "Look, as much as I would love to work you up into a fit, this is too serious. This is a fucked-up situation. I know you don't like attention and publicity. I don't like it either. This might make the news, and I know it scares you and—"

"I'm not scared of it." My response was a knee-jerk reaction.

"Whitfield, you're still shaking."

CHAPTER
TWENTY-ONE

AURREY

"SHAKING FROM WHAT?"** Rome asked a little too casually as he ambled down my hallway and took a seat at my kitchen island. He must have seen my questioning look because he returned it with one of his own and then shrugged. "Stopped over to eat, babe. My cabinets are empty."

"Okay," I mumbled.

I heard a low grumble from Jax.

Being in the same room with the only two people I'd ever had relations with made me feel like a little prairie dog wanting to duck into a hole. Then maybe after a couple minutes, peek my head out to see how everyone was doing.

"Rome, um, Jax was just stopping in for some water." I cleared my throat. "There may also be some paparazzi outside."

Rome's back stiffened. I didn't have to turn around to know that Jax stiffened behind me too. Glares were being thrown over my head between the two of them. When Rome turned in his stool, I figured if I was a prairie dog, I probably just would have stayed in the hole.

Rome's dark eyes filled with anger. "Why the fuck would you steer paparazzi back to her place?"

"Rome…" I started but Jax cut me off.

"Would you rather me let her run home with paparazzi on her tail alone?"

"You could have taken her anywhere. Now they know where she lives."

"Yes, because that woman is so easy to persuade when she's hyperventilating."

Rome's eyes snapped to me. "He's exaggerating. I wasn't hyperventilating."

Both Jax and Rome glared at me.

I moved fast toward the cupboards. "You want something to drink, Rome?"

He didn't answer. So, I grabbed another water bottle.

When I went to hand it to him, I noticed both men were in some sort of staring contest. Rome didn't even glance over as he mumbled a thank you and took the bottle from me.

"That run was brutal." I opened the freezer door wide like I was in a Broadway play, trying to get both men's attention.

They looked ready to kill each other and when their gazes lasered in on me, I almost fell into the freezer from the sheer anger they unleashed in just their stares.

I fanned my face and slumped in front of the freezer, keeping the theatrics going. "I seriously might stand in the freezer door all day."

Relief washed over me when Rome finally cracked a smile as he stepped into the kitchen. He moved closer to me and said, "Looks like you worked up a sweat."

I laughed a little. "More like I worked out a bucketful of sweat."

Rome studied me for a second. Then, without the slightest bit of hesitation, he slid between me and the freezer, spread his hand over my bare stomach and nudged my back to his front. I let out a little gasp as I glanced up at him over my shoulder, but he was smirking directly at Jax.

He leaned down and dragged his tongue across the most sensitive part of my neck. "Mmm, a Brey-sicle, just what I wanted. I could lick your sweat all day. I'll text you and Vick later to see if you want to hit a few bars."

With that, he smacked my ass and I yelped.

He made his way to the door, nodding toward Jax. "Jax," he said curtly.

Jax and I stood there, taking one another in after the front door slammed.

The only movement in the room was the clock ticking.

His glacial eyes bored into me so much that the freezer seemed to warm my back. It was the stare people talked about, the one no one could read, the one where you knew, deep down in your core, that he either didn't give a crap about you or cared so much he might rip your head off.

I can honestly say I didn't know which emotion I wanted from him.

Goose bumps skittered up my arms, and I willed myself to take a breath in and a breath out.

Somehow, my living room and kitchen seemed so much smaller once Rome was out of it. Jax took up all the damn space. His stance dominated every square foot of the room as he stood there in his workout clothes and let the sweat run down his temple.

He didn't move or even seem to breath. I only knew he was alive because he held that water glass so tight, I saw his knuckles turning white.

I had to be the bigger person. I couldn't succumb to rubbing my relationship in his face because Rome and I hadn't truly moved on from our broken hearts. We'd just bandaged them.

I turned to close the freezer, trying to dispel the moment. "So, are you hungry?"

He grunted out a sort of laugh and mumbled, "Are you kidding me?"

I turned back to him, crossing my arms over the sports bra that was drenched in my now cold sweat, "I have a pizza I could heat … "

"Are you fucking him?" he asked so matter-of-factly I almost questioned whether I'd heard him right.

"What?"

"You heard me, Whitfield. Are you fucking him?"

"I don't think this is an appropriate conversation between friends, Jax."

"Well, when he touches you like that in front of your *friend*, I think it's perfectly appropriate to ask."

Did it really matter? He left me, and he was definitely fucking someone else. It was all over the news. I contemplated screaming it at him.

Who did he think he was asking something like that as if he had a right? Did he really think I was going to tell him?

He slammed the water down on the counter and some of it spilled over. Then, he stalked toward me in the kitchen and I backed up. When I bumped into the edge of the counter, he caged me in with his arms.

This look in his eyes I knew. It was the one I dreamt about and cried out his name for. His eyes would turn the bluest blue before he'd take me as if all of me was his.

"Answer the question, Whitfield."

"I don't think it's fair of you to ask."

"Answer the fucking question."

"No, I'm not." Then, I mumbled, "At the moment."

I realized my mistake when he shoved back from the counter, spun around to pace and roared, "She says *at the moment*. Fuck!" Then his hands were pulling his hair up. "How many times?"

I slumped against the counter. "Jax, really?"

He whipped back around to pace up to me again. "Yes, really."

"Does it matter?" I whispered.

He touched his forehead to mine and searched my eyes as if he could gaze the answer out of me. "Yes, baby, it matters."

"Why?"

"Because I need to know how long it's going to take me to erase every time you were with him from your memory."

I shook my head. "That's not what friends do. Friends actually encourage friends to go get some wherever they can so they aren't drooling over some unattainable man that has the ability to ruin them."

The words slipped so quickly out of my mouth, I barely realized I had just admitted to drooling over him. To wanting him even though he was unattainable. I'd blurted out my biggest fear too, which was him ruining me again.

I could have curled up and died from embarrassment.

His jaw locked into the place where I knew he was trying to contain some emotion, trying to leave my ridiculous comments alone. Suddenly, he pressed himself against me. I should have shoved him away, but instead, I gasped. I felt how hard he was, and my body seemed to know he belonged between my legs. Every part of me was magnetized toward him.

He must have seen his opening because he grabbed both of my legs to lift me up onto the counter. I automatically wrapped them around him.

"Do I feel unattainable?"

I bit my lip to stop from gasping again and rocked into him.

He pulled back just a little to run one of his hands up my thigh. We both watched that hand as goose bumps trailed its path.

I wouldn't ask him to stop. My breath came too fast, my mind too hazy with his scent all around me, and my body too languid after the run. An inch further and he slid under the leg of my shorts, dipping his fingers into my panties.

"This, Sweet Sin, doesn't feel like we're friends. This feels like you're wet for me."

I whimpered and he didn't stop. Anyone else who cared about me would have stopped in that moment. Rome always stopped to make sure I was okay with this or okay with that. My friends walked on egg shells to maintain my well-being. They always watched and padded any sharp edges for me, made sure that even if I wasn't protecting myself, someone was.

Jax didn't do that. He plunged headfirst with me into the sharpest object called oblivion. Then, we'd each swim around in a lust-filled wonder, holding our breath because the second we gulped for air, the toxicity of our past would fill our lungs. He didn't protect me at all. He let me risk drowning in the heartbreak that would inevitably ensue again.

He rubbed my slickness up onto my clit with his thumb and jammed two fingers inside me. My head fell back as the climax that normally took so long to build started to rush faster than ever to the finish line.

He dragged his other hand across my collarbone and then wrapped his fingers around my neck, bending it to one side. That sensitive part that Rome had licked was now exposed to him. "He touches you like he knows every sensitive spot on your body."

"Jax," I whimpered.

"Didn't you tell him all of those spots are mine?" he asked as he languidly stroked me.

I couldn't control how quickly I climbed toward my climax. My emotions got involved, and they pulsed through me more than they ever had with Rome.

Before I could answer, he devoured my neck. He'd bite it and then lick it better and then suck on it so hard, I moaned from the pain and the pleasure.

My mind spun and spun as I rode the hand that fingered me faster and faster.

The way Jax touched me and made me feel shot through my blood and reached all the way to the tips of my fingers and my toes. I tingled all over, shivered and trembled at his touch. Every flick of tongue and every movement of his body on mine set off sparks in me. He set off a reaction in me everywhere, even in the one place he should have never been able to set off a reaction again: my heart.

When he dipped another finger inside me and squeezed my neck just enough to demonstrate his control over me, my body erupted in stars and fireworks.

Spiraling toward my finish should have been exhilarating. It should have been rewarding. I should have felt satisfied and relaxed. But coming down from it, watching him watch me, seeing his cerulean eyes searching mine as though they lapped up all my secrets, I felt exposed.

I shoved him back from me. "You need to leave."

"Peaches," he said low, as he stood there, still aroused and ready for me. That thin sheen of sweat was back, and I wanted to rip his shirt off and lick it from the chest that was heaving.

"L.P.," I threw back, singsonging the nickname to lash out at him. "We're supposed to be friends. And we aren't really even that."

He grumbled something I couldn't make out but I didn't care.

I was done playing nice and tiptoeing around the subject. "Are you still going to visit him?"

I didn't look away when I asked. I watched his every movement. The way his body stilled, then his muscles bunched and his breathing evened out.

His eyes turned cold when he answered with one word. "Yes." It was all I needed to hear. I shoved off the counter. "When?" His lips thinned, "This weekend."

"Will you explain why?"

He pulled at his hair, "There's nothing to explain."

"Then this ... "—I waved between us—"there's nothing to it and you need to leave."

He took a step forward and I found that although he maintained his look, I could see the anger underneath that he hid from others so well. It was like my body was now fully aware of him after he got me off.

I absolutely hated it.

"I'm not leaving just because I visit your father, Whitfield. You can't deny what just happened between us."

I matched his stance and took a step forward. "Nothing really happened. Me getting off isn't out of the norm, L.P."

"Don't act like that was a common occurrence, Whitfield," he warned.

"Get out of my apartment." I kept my voice even, trying like hell to get him out before I did something stupid like agree with him.

He ran his tongue between his lips and teeth, contemplating and calculating.

I didn't have time for it. I wanted him out. "Get out!" I yelled right in his face, too drained to question my control or sanity.

He licked his lips and I made the stupid mistake of flicking my gaze down to watch rather than holding his stare. Just the tip of that tongue, I knew, held so much talent, and suddenly I was aching between my legs all over again.

The mouth I stared at relaxed into a half-smirk. "You sure you want me to leave?"

I snapped my eyes away from his mouth, realizing I'd been caught. "I am fully capable of finding someone else and pointing out all of *my* sensitive spots to them, Jax. I don't need you here to get me off."

His eyes bulged and mine probably did also. I couldn't believe I'd just blurted that out.

He shook his head and backed away like I'd gone too far. "You'll pay for that."

Was it bad that later that night, I couldn't control fantasizing about paying for it while I laid in bed all by myself?

CHAPTER
TWENTY-TWO

JAX

LEAVING THAT DAMN woman's apartment was like leaving a song unfinished. Aubrey spoke to me like the perfect melody, a harmony that wrapped you up and stuck on you for days. When I got that close to her, she was that damn hook in the song that made me forget any other song existed.

I would rather have climbed through barbed wire than her doorway at that moment. Because whether she wanted to admit it or not, we made the perfect song together. No other man could get her off like I did.

At least I fucking hoped so.

That hope had me spiraling. I got back to Jay's empty house and figured focusing on the algorithms for my new app would help.

Instead, I tried to break down her facial expressions. I couldn't read her as well anymore and didn't know if she meant everything she'd said.

Did she think learning about the bullshit Frank and I talked about would help, would allow her to forgive me for leaving her?

Hell, I could barely forgive myself.

Add to it the shit I did for him while he rotted in prison, not even the devil would forgive me. Probability was not in my favor, and I wasn't willing to risk her never talking to me again.

I'm not proud to say I spent hours working over a single glitch in the app and it amounted to nothing. I couldn't focus on how we were going to swing the PR. I couldn't focus on when the best dates were to maximize profits on the launch concert. I could barely focus on what music should be put into the app first.

Walking down to the lake finally cleared my head. Any lake was an old friend of mine, ready to bring clarity where it was needed.

Mostly because every lake reminded me of her. The calmness, when everything was quiet at night, lapped quietly at my soul and soothed every nerve just like she could. When the winds picked up and the waves crashed into the rocks nearby, I remembered her wild and free near the lake that night so many years ago, begging me to let go with her. Her dark hair caught in the wind, whipping away at the world, her eyes a vivid green, and her soul so lit up, it battled out all the darkness around her. She'd finally become herself, and there was no way I would ever let someone take that independence from her.

All of this was for her. She may never know it but protecting her from her father was about the only thing I was willing to give her up for.

I DIDN'T WASTE more time there but jetted back to the city to work out more details.

My flight took longer than expected. It allowed me to map out the investments I wanted to make, calculate the stocks with just the right amount of risk, and discover that the app would generate more success than Stonewood Enterprises had ever expected.

My driver was waiting for me when we finally landed. He mumbled something about Isabel instructing him to tell me to call her. I grunted and as I slid into the black SUV, my shoulders relaxed like a damn weight had been lifted.

Here, I was comfortable. I was a Stonewood and that held the most weight in this city. My instant fame from one album didn't matter in the city where my name overpowered it. People feared and respected us here. It reminded me of why I left in the first place.

Here, I could hide away from my demons and could make something of myself so I didn't have to focus on selling my soul to the devil.

I remember distinctly the day the news broke of my visit to see Aubrey's dad in prison. Tabloids everywhere captured me striding into the building and variations of "Jax Betrays Family by Visiting Whitfield" were the headlines. Walking into Stonewood Enterprises that day to let my dad know the news wasn't something to look forward to.

He mirrored an older version of me, a version that had been around the block, had calculated his every move, and had learned everything the hard way.

He was a better man and a scarier one. Before I walked into his office, I almost turned around and fled back to my mother, thinking nothing could be worse than disappointing and facing him.

Walking through the doors and seeing the look he had on his face made me realize two things that day. My father wasn't just a ruthless businessman, he was also a ruthless father.

"You all right, son?" he asked quietly, his eyes working over my face as if he could find the answer before I opened my mouth.

I nodded and let him scrutinize me more.

He nodded back at me as if he'd come to the conclusion that day that I was a man, a Stonewood man. "You want me to handle this with Frank and the tabloids?"

"I've got it taken care of."

"Your mom loves Frank's girl like her own, Jax," he warned.

"Yeah, and I love her more than I do my music, my life, and my damn soul combined," I answered back.

He sighed and ran a hand over his face. "I figured that. Be careful, then."

"Always am when it comes to what's mine."

My father rubbed the side of his mouth before saying, "I thought that once too. Don't make the same mistakes I did. This city is a good place to find yourself and lose yourself all at once," he whispered almost to himself more than me. He looked down at a picture on his desk, one I knew was of my mother.

"She's still waiting for you whenever you're ready to give up this life, Dad," I mumbled.

He grunted, and I left him to his own thoughts because I had my own thoughts to sift through that day. I had to come up with a plan to cut ties with Frank, fulfill his requests, and protect the damn spitfire that had me wrapped around her finger.

***

CHICAGO HELD SO many memories, but I found comfort in knowing I was doing the same thing as my father. I was able to hide from my true self, the one that felt fucking pain every time I saw a glimpse of a woman who looked like Aubrey or a magazine that captured her hanging out with Jay or Roman.

People either go to the big city to be a star or to disappear into the masses. No one cares what anyone else does there unless they are doing something phenomenal. The beauty of the cityscape is that a person can either change it by creating their own empire or get lost in it without anyone noticing they ever existed.

I accomplished both of those things by moving there.

My cell rang, and I scrubbed my hands down my face as I glanced at the screen.

Isabel.

Because the damn woman couldn't give me a second to breathe once I was back. I ignored it, knowing I needed a good night's sleep and barked at my driver to take me home.

That night, I dreamt of Aubrey wrapped around me, in her neutral-colored clothes and all.

Going to see Frank in prison the next morning would make the headlines. I knew when I saw two SUVs following. They'd snap a picture and build a story on anything they could right now. With the app set to launch in just a few weeks, anything was more than nothing to them.

"Want me to lose them, boss?" My driver asked.

"No use, really. Others will be waiting when we get there."

My phone rang, and I saw that Isabel was calling again.

My driver chuckled to himself.

I shot him a look and he outright laughed at me. Probably the only man who would. "I told you to call her last night, boss."

"Shut the fuck up," I said as I pushed the privacy window button.

"Isabel, I'm busy," I answered.

"You're on your way to that god-awful prison. You can't be that busy."

"News already?"

"Yup. They've got your SUV on live TV. Now that leaves me to clean up the PR mess before your launch, and honestly, we don't have time for this shit, Jax."

"This shit is what I pay you to make time for."

"Then maybe you should answer your phone when I call so you can prepare me for making time for it."

I sighed. "Isabel, I'm not in the mood. You know what I'm doing. What do you want?"

"Well, I want a call when you're back in town, Jax." She sounded a little hurt but I'd become immune to people feeling hurt when they worked for me. "We could have gotten dinner or something."

"Like you said, I have this launch coming up. I don't need to remind you that it is a multimillion-dollar launch that needs my time and attention more than you need it at dinner."

"I've never wasted your time, have I?"

I smiled. "No, you haven't. Yet. You are a pain in my ass though."

"Sweet talk from the boss," she purred. "I love it. Does my boss want to scratch an itch tonight with me? I haven't been fucked since you've been gone."

Just like her to cut straight to the point. "That's not my problem. You can sleep with whomever you want."

"Right. Well, I recall having to make out with you for every one of your launch concerts, which somewhat limits my little black book, considering no guy is willing to step on your toes. And let's be honest, you're easier than most men I sleep with. Might I remind you, we seem to work, Mr. Stonewood."

I grunted because, normally, she was right. The woman had an uncanny knack for knowing how to do well in the PR industry, which included manipulating our relationship in the press just the way she wanted. It had always served in both of our favors, in more ways than one.

I just wasn't so sure it would serve me well in the future. "How are we trending? Is our launch date still looking good?"

"Of course."

"Then that's all I need from you now." I hung up, not willing to discuss anything else with her, as we pulled up to see Frank.

Over the years, the jitteriness of facing him had subsided. It'll make a damn man out of you walking into a prison and facing a monster. I used to hope I'd become like Jett or my dad, but they lacked one thing I learned by coming to visit Frank for all these years.

I learned that power doesn't just come from doing everything right, from calculating and stepping in all the right directions.

Sometimes, power comes from fear. Facing the fear over and over again until you are manipulating it and breathing the fear onto everyone else. What most people couldn't do though, was learn to calculate the fear and unleash it at just the right second.

The time drew near with him, it would be only a few more visits, then I'd never have to see him again.

CHAPTER
TWENTY-THREE

AUBREY

THE REST OF the week I didn't call any of the Stonewood men. I needed a break. I focused on studying by myself and jogging closer to home.

Katie and Vick plowed into my apartment with their spare keys on Saturday as I got ready to go visit the kids for a second time that week to pass the time.

Vick animatedly tossed keys up and down as I pulled on a black cardigan. "Rome loaned his truck to us."

I glanced back at Katie who rolled her eyes and Vick who smiled cautiously. "So? Are you going grocery shopping or something?"

"No." Vick waited a beat and then in one breath said, "Katie told me you have a charity that you support forty-five minutes from here and I want to go with you two to help volunteer. I like kids too, and so what if I've never volunteered, right? I can be a volunteer. My parents always donated to charities but never let me be involved. I was too young, and they thought it was dangerous, which now I know is ridiculous a–"

"Vick," Katie cut her off. "You don't need our permission to come along. You got a truck so we don't have to bus anyway. Works for all of us. She's coming, Brey."

Like a mother protecting her child, I wanted to protest to introducing anyone new to something so precious in my life. "Sure." My response was lackluster at best.

Vick face scrunched up. "Oh my God, Brey! Could you sound any less excited?"

I straightened up and painted on a smile. "Anyone who helps is appreciated."

"'Anyone who helps is appreciated,'" she air quoted back in a nasally voice. Then, she put her hands on her hips. "Don't look so nervous. I promise I will be extremely helpful. I can do whatever."

"I know, Vick." I smoothed my hair back and wondered how I could put it nicely to her. "These children don't have a lot of contact with figures in their lives who stick around though. My mom gave a lot to this home. It took me a long time to understand how much she did and how much I was capable of doing too. I only just started going when she passed away, and they really appreciate us being there every week. I know some would be crushed if we didn't show. It's a real commitment."

"Okay, I hate when you act all professional and uptight." She turned to Katie. "Think we could beat it out of her?"

Katie smiled. "Not a chance. That's Whitfield-ingrained manners." My hands went to my hips too. "Hey, that's rude!"

"That's true, bitch," Katie retorted.

Vick stayed on target. "It'll be good for you, and it'll be good for me. It'll mostly be great for the kids. They need good people around them, and I'll be committed, I promise," she blurted quickly.

I glared at Katie because her logic seemed too logical, like she'd been prepped.

"She's committed to annoying both of us." Katie shrugged like she didn't care. "She can be committed to the little minions too."

"I know." My heart beat way too fast. It was a reminder that I was much too invested in the organization. "It isn't my home. I mean, anyone who wants to go can go. I just think everyone should understand that once the kids meet you, they're hurt if you don't show up again. I've seen it happen in this last year already way too many times."

Vick nodded her head vigorously. "I totally get it."

"Okay." I struggled with the social norm of allowing this to happen easily and my protectiveness that was probably not necessary. "Let's get going before Rome changes his mind."

Vick squealed and I gave in to her excitement, laughing a little as we piled into Rome's pickup truck.

"This is going to be so fun." Vick clapped her hands in the backseat. "The drive is boring as hell," Katie corrected.

"At least Rome let us use his truck." Vick started and then turned to me. "Brey, remember to tell Rome you drove the whole way, OK?"

I rolled my eyes, "I'm guessing he only gave me permission to drive."

Katie's gray eyes met mine, and they weren't filled with guilt. "Obviously."

"No wonder he doesn't like you." Vick laughed along with her. "Can we leave a Katie memento in here too? Let's aggravate the hell out of him by dousing his truck in Katie's perfume?"

"I don't wear perfume, you freak. That idea is borderline crazy, by the way."

"No, it isn't! I did it when I was dating this one guy. He absolutely loved it," Vick said, totally proud of herself. "For you, well, you always smell like vanilla and Rome's gotta know it. He probably smells vanilla and runs the other way to avoid interacting with you."

"Feeling's mutual." Katie gave me a she's-crazy look.

I turned to Vick in the back, "You and Katie aren't being very grateful that he is letting us use the truck."

"Grateful for what?" Katie snorted. "He has another one. It's not like we are putting him in some bind."

"Actually, I'm pretty sure he has three vehicles now," Vick pointed out and then turned contemplative. "Remind me why you haven't exclusively claimed that man, Brey. He's hot and totally ... "

"Annoying as fuck," Katie finished.

I rolled my eyes and smiled as they filled the silence with their bickering.

When we arrived, Vick looked a little disappointed and I knew why. Where I volunteered wasn't a large, beautiful building or a fancy facility. Instead what looked like a little farm house sat on one of the green hills that rolled on and on until they finally met the bright blue sky on the horizon.

"They're waiting inside." I motioned to Vick and she straightened her T-shirt as if she was preparing for the worst. I sighed and led both my friends toward the front porch.

Before we even made it there, a scrawny little girl with brown hair down to her waist came running out in her signature purple shoes. The shoes were worn down and didn't match her blue T-shirt and jean shorts.

Yet, not one of us could talk her out of wearing those shoes ever.

Ollie had a stubborn side. One that, I would guess, had come from a few years of being surrounded by other children here at the home. That, and probably having to deal with a mother not many of us understood. That woman let men through her house like her doorway was a merry go round. She worked unknown jobs and unknown hours. It was always hell getting a hold of her.

Yet, Ollie showed up on her own at the home everyday. Her mother had done something right to raise such a responsible kid.

The little seven-year-old flew at me like a bullet and didn't slow down at all when she jumped into my arms.

"You're here!" she exclaimed.

I laughed. "Of course. I told you I was coming again this week."

She beamed at me, then turned her little brown eyes on Katie and Vick.

"Hey, you little tyrant," Katie said, hands on her hips.

That little ball of energy extended her arms out to Katie, ready for her next hug, and Katie showed her rarest side by snuggling the little one right out of my arms. "Katie! Jasmine wants hair like yours but her momma said no."

"Probably for the best, Ollie," Katie responded.

Ollie dropped the subject as she eyed Vick. She leaned back over with her arms out toward me. I sat her on my hip and started toward the porch again, knowing the group was waiting for us.

Vick didn't say a word as Ollie whispered to me, "Who is that?"

Neither of them were great at introducing themselves to one another. Ollie was nervous around new faces and Vick could talk to just about anyone her age. She didn't know how to talk to children at all though.

I sighed as we reached the front porch, set Ollie on her feet, and turned her toward Vick. She hid behind my leg but peeked out. "Ollie, this is Vick. She's a really good friend of mine and wanted to hang out with all of you today."

Vick fidgeted in her designer skinny jeans and looked ready to bolt. Instead, she stuck out her hand and practically yelled, "Hi, Ollie. I'm Vick."

Ollie jumped and gripped my leg tighter. She looked up at me and whispered, "Why is she yelling?"

I tried not to laugh as I glanced at Katie who had her hand over her mouth as she tried to keep her snickers quiet. "She does that when she's nervous," I said, trying to warm Ollie up to the idea of Vick. "Why don't you ask her why she is nervous?"

Ollie's eyes narrowed as if she was trying to figure out if I was lying, then they swung towards Vick's hand. She stepped up and took it, shaking it vigorously. "Why are you so nervous, Vick?"

Vick glanced at both of us, eyes pleading for help but I let her answer honestly. These children needed honesty most. "Well, um, I've never been here before. I want you all to like me, but I don't know if I'll be someone you'll like."

Ollie let go of her hand and studied her longer. "Well, Jasmine likes the color pink, so she will probably like you and your shirt. If you don't yell at everyone, they will probably like you too."

With that, Ollie turned on her purple-shoed heel and opened the porch door to go find the others. I smiled and nodded at Vick before following Ollie inside.

Margie, the group's leader, opened the door wider and welcomed us in with a clipboard ready. "Katie, Brey, you made it." She looked over at Vick. "I haven't met you, so you will have to fill out a few forms."

Vick nodded and took the clipboard from her. "I'm Vick. I wanted to start volunteering with Katie and Brey."

While Vick filled out the forms, Ollie reappeared holding the hand of Jasmine. "Margie's mad because Rodney didn't come to the house today." She leaned in to whisper to us three, "His mom is sick again."

Katie and I glanced at one another. 'Sick' was code for something else. All the children had one thing in common. Their parents struggled and when they didn't show up to the house, we could usually guess the reason. Margie prided herself on taking care of all the children she could during the day on the reservation. Instead of having those seven kids today, she had one less. The frustration I felt was nothing in comparison to what she must have.

"Why don't we go find the others and we can pick some veggies while Margie makes some calls to Rodney's mom and friends, okay?"

Jasmine took Katie's hand as we walked out. "I like the red in your hair."

The air hit us like a humid summer wave, and after an hour of picking vegetables out in the fields, Vick announced she was going to get sunscreen for all of us.

Jasmine piped up, "I don't wear sunscreen."

Brenda, who was a few years older than Jasmine and Ollie, added, "I don't either. You only need it because your skin burns."

Walter, the youngest of them all, stopped dusting off a carrot. "I wear sunscreen because my mom does too. She says I'll get an owie if I don't."

Walter's mother definitely was right about that. He had blonde hair and blue eyes with skin the color of porcelain. The other children though had been graced with the same skin I had. It was olive toned or darker like their Native American heritage.

Vick seemed to take their comments in stride. "Well, Walter, we are just a little special, huh?" she replied to them all, winking to us as she headed toward the car.

Ollie jumped on the opportunity to gossip. "I think I like her, but her hair isn't as pretty as Brey's hair and doesn't have as many colors as Katie's. What do you think, Jasmine?"

"I like her shirt, and she said she would get us sunscreen if we needed it. She's nice."

Walter chimed in, "I want to marry her."

I laughed as my worries about bringing Vick were officially squashed.

Every time I visited the kids, the muscles that usually bunched between my shoulders relaxed. The anxiety that normally tightened in my stomach loosened. We were free here, no one judged us on anything but how well we got along.

Instead of focusing on a tabloid or what the media might be saying about Jax and my father, I focused on them.

CHAPTER
TWENTY-FOUR

AUBREY

THE KIDS WENT to get cleaned up when Margie informed us that Rodney may not be coming back because his mother wanted to move out of state with her boyfriend. We talked over different scenarios but knew that ultimately it would be the mother's choice.

The situation weighed on our minds the whole ride home.

When we got back to my apartment, Katie and I let Vick turn on the TV and indulge in her favorite guilty pleasure—celebrity gossip. She turned up *Entertainment Tonight*, but I barely listened as the host droned on and on.

That was until the screen showed the same dark vehicle I always saw on the same damn road in my nightmares. They showed a scene that had my stomach twisting in knots, bottoming out, and then rolling down a hill collecting more and more anger.

I blinked and then blinked again. Surely, I was imagining that damn SUV.

I tried to rationalize that maybe Jax hadn't meant what he said, and he really wouldn't have gone.

Not after kissing me.

Not after helping me with my class.

Not after he'd been nice enough to get me tea.

I blinked, slower this time. So slow that I commended myself on the control of the movement.

Me. That is who I can control.

I sighed and let the anger roll on in. As the truth washed over me, I rolled my lips between my teeth and tried not to scream. I coiled control around the truth and the anger and the hurt. I wrapped it up tight and double knotted it, hoping it would hold.

When they cut to commercial, after promising to reveal who was in the SUV and where he was going when they returned, Vick turned to me. "Do you think … "

"Don't ask the obvious, Vick," Katie sighed. "Maybe it's someone else," she tried.

The coils strained a little at her comment.

I normally welcomed Vick's unwavering optimism of love or at least ignored it. She nudged Jax and I together ever since she'd heard my story. "He was your hero," she would say or, "He has to still love you," or "Just see where it goes."

I always rolled my eyes, but now, I realized I had secretly wanted to believe her.

I'd walked out onto the battlefield wearing a target, waving for him to take his shot. I'd opened my arms to it and let my damn guard down.

The coils tightened even more. "It isn't someone else," I stated. Katie grabbed the remote to turn it off.

Was she serious? She, of all people, wanted to shield me now?

I lunged for it. "Oh no! I'm going to watch every minute. You should want me to considering… " I stopped, trying so hard not to let my friends have it. My anger wasn't for them.

"Considering what?" Katie asked, her eyes narrowing a little.

I looked up at the ceiling and imagined that ceiling coming down on my anger. It was all part of controlling it and keeping it bottled up.

"Nothing. Nothing," I sighed. "It's the SUV, you guys. And it's the road."

Vick squinted at the screen as if willing it to show us something better. "If that's true, I'm sorry, Brey."

My jaw clenched. I hated that he'd done this. I was that dumb little bug, always drawn to the light that zapped and stung when touched.

Jax was my light.

And he'd burned me again.

God, I kissed him, let him get me off.

"You what?" Vick screeched.

Katie's eyes popped open wide in disbelief.

"I what?" I jumped.

"You just said you kissed him."

"Shoot," I mumbled, realizing I had thought out loud.

Neither of my friends knew what to say. Even Vick, who knew what to say to everything, couldn't come up with a comment.

I turned up the volume and paced as the commercials ended. "I mean, he can exercise with me, act like we're getting to know each other again, help me study, and … "

"And kiss you?" Katie added.

I waved her off. "And go visit him again."

The host smiled like he was about to share America's biggest secret with us. "Jax Stonewood, on his way to visit his one and only prisoner friend. We've seen it before, guys. Now, we have a bigger scoop. We asked sources to share with us why Jax would have any contact with someone behind bars. Turns out he is still visiting the infamous Frank Whitfield, his former next door neighbor. It has been speculated that Jax now believes Mr. Whitfield may be innocent and he looks up to the former businessman and investor. We're told they now have investments together. Or maybe, he's visiting him because he's been spending time with someone new."

Suddenly a picture of us flashed on the screen. We looked like we were enjoying a jog together when we'd really been running to get away from the paparazzi.

"Is that Frank Whitfield's daughter? Jay's on-and-off-again girlfriend? You decide!"

The ringing in my ears started soft as I saw the percent of people voting.

As the numbers rose, the ringing raged, and my vision blurred with a tinge of red.

The coils dug in hard to the anger, trying desperately to hold the beast it had become.

Katie stood in front of me, calling him names while Vick's melodic voice sounded like it was trying to soothe me.

I didn't hear their words though. This had happened before.

They tried the same words to soothe me, but this time was different.

This time, Jax had woven himself into my life again.

I didn't need to hear what Vick and Katie were saying. I knew the dialogue. I knew exactly how their faces would look. I knew they would run out and get me wine and ice cream. I knew my friends were here for me.

I just didn't know how to keep my rage coiled and compress it enough so that I could control the fireball it had become since seeing him.

I could have screamed. I could have thrown a fit. I could have gone off the deep end and called him to confront him immediately.

Instead, the fireball choked me as it bubbled up into my throat. It burned and clawed its way up, trying to make its way out of me in a scream. I shut my eyes so hard, I saw spots behind my lids. When I opened them, they were wetter than before, but I told myself this wasn't crying. It was just my eyes watering from holding in the fireball.

Vick rushed forward while Katie raged for me, "Where is your phone? That motherfucker is going to answer our questions."

I didn't answer her, I just let Vick hug me and rub my back. I didn't respond to either of them. I didn't think I could respond to anything right now.

Katie found my phone, and I could see her scrolling through the contacts.

"It isn't worth it, Katie," I grabbed my phone and she handed it over, not willing to fight me on calling him.

"Good. You shouldn't ask him questions. You shouldn't ever talk to him again! I knew this would happen, I absolutely knew…"

Vick cut her off. "We don't know why he was there yet. We have to give him a chance to explain."

"No, we don't," Katie blurted. "What the fuck is wrong with him?"

There was a better question to be asked. One that started to eat at me after I went to my bedroom, telling my friends I just needed time to think.

I stewed on the reason why he would go there, I thought about what the fuck was wrong with him like Katie asked.

Ultimately, the better question was what was wrong with me? I'd been so careful about letting people in. Why was I never careful enough with him?

CHAPTER
TWENTY-FIVE

AUBREY

FOR THE REST of the weekend, I stayed in my room. Not because I was mad or moping.

I had a great reason. I decided my room needed a face-lift. I looked around and saw its neutrality, how lackluster and void of life it was. I remembered my room with my mother and father.

I used to hang a picture and my mother would see it before anyone else. "Aubrey," she would sigh in that tone that I was so used to hearing. Like a balloon being deflated of all its air, she sounded defeated. I could still hear the fatigue in it and surrender. I hated it so much every time I heard her say it.

Yet, it was the only word I could still imagine her saying perfectly in my head. Maybe she had just said it that often, or maybe I'd hated it so much, it imprinted itself on my memory.

Either way, I could hear it now.

Not because I was considering changing my room, but because I hadn't changed it yet. I imagined her walking in, hair longer than my father would have ever allowed and sighing like she always would. Then she would say, "Aubrey." The tone wouldn't be any different but the reason would be. She'd smile like we both knew it wasn't his choice to make anymore.

The white dresser and the grey bedspread stuck out more than ever before. She would roll her eyes at them. Then, she'd put her hands on her hips seeing the white walls that mocked my independence.

I loved imagining her there like that. We'd dictate how the room should look together.

He'd kept our house so empty and pristine.

My room looked just like that house, just how he would have wanted it.

After the fire he started, I let the fear of standing out in the spotlight dictate how I dressed, how I decorated, and how I acted.

Everything—especially me—needed to blend in, and my room ended up the same. Bland.

Just the way my father would have wanted, with me in the shadows, not fussing or calling attention to myself.

Now, my father dictated my relationship with Jax even from behind bars. He still reached out to control my life.

Changing my room let my mother and I take back some independence, pushing back against the life we had to live for so long with him, even if she wasn't there to enjoy it with me.

I threw myself into it and didn't think about anything else. I never touched the trust fund my mother set up for me other than to donate to the kids I visited every week. That day though, I spared no expense and overnighted everything I wanted for my home makeover.

I needed the change immediately. So much so that after ordering everything, I jumped up and ripped off my bedspread and sheets. Bundling them into a ball, I put them up to my face and screamed in them. Screamed for my mother, for me. For the life we lost, the dreams he cut away from us.

I jetted straight out of my apartment, down to the lobby, and outside straight to the dumpster.

"Aubrey!"

"Ahh!" I screamed and threw up the huge pile of fabric as I jumped.

Rome stalked toward me from the building. "What the hell are you doing out here this late?"

He looked a bit mad and a lot confused.

I glanced down and realized I was wearing very short shorts and no shoes. I looked up and was startled to see the moon in the dark sky. "What time is it?" I asked.

Once he reached me and looked at my bedspread, his brows scrunched together. "I don't even want to know," he mumbled.

I licked my lips and started to bundle my hair into a ponytail. "Probably for the best."

I moved to grab the bedspread but he snatched everything up for me. I opened my mouth to explain that I needed to throw everything away but he seemed to already read my mind because he stood next to the dumpster and nodded toward the lid. "Lift."

I did and he dropped it all in.

"It's past midnight. Can we dump whatever else you need to tomorrow?"

I rolled my lips between my teeth because I felt something in my throat again. This time it felt like sadness and regret. So deep and dark that it would swallow me whole.

I swore my tears were because I was grateful Rome didn't ask me anything. He just put one arm under my knees and one around my neck as he lifted me up and carried me back to his apartment.

I cried the whole way.

CHAPTER
TWENTY-SIX

JAX

WHEN MY SUNDAY night redeye landed in our home-
town, I expected there would be bridges I would have
to mend. The walls I'd torn down and destroyed with
Aubrey were probably fucking resurrected the moment the media
leaked coverage of my visit to the prison.

I called her again and again on my way back.

When I didn't get an answer, I tried to call Jay.

He ignored the call and texted me.

> **JAY:** It's midnight. I don't have time for your shit and don't
> use me to get to her. That shit's unhealthy and we both
> know it.

I pocketed my cell, deciding he could fuck off. He was just
reinforcing her resurrected wall by not helping me get to her.

I needed to call Isabel to figure out how to spin the media with Aubrey in it. Yet, for the first time in a long time, I didn't feel right calling her. The more I thought about our relationship, the more I realized she'd been a stand-in girlfriend for me along with a PR agent over the years.

Not that I had to answer to anyone about my relationships, but if I didn't want Aubrey sleeping with her friends, I damn sure couldn't be sleeping with mine.

I should have resorted to working on my app or trying to get the sleep I was sure wouldn't come but the damn woman permeated my every thought. I could barely think of anything else.

I called her again, knowing it was too late.

When she didn't answer, I told myself that she probably shouldn't. It was for the best. Reaching her would be toxic and most likely end in both of our destruction.

I knew it then just like I'd known it when I'd left her that summer after high school.

So, I didn't call or text her again but let the idea of her haunt me.

I changed into some shorts and put on my running shoes to go for a midnight jog.

When I hit the pavement, I tried to focus on exercise even though the thought of her consumed me.

Kissing her in her kitchen had taken me right back to the days of wanting to write about her, muse about her, yearn for her, and sing for her. She ignited those raw feelings of jealousy and hate and love within me. With her, my emotions ran wild and let me make my only real music.

I couldn't let that happen now. I'd left the music industry for that reason. The emotion and intensity of it all nearly consumed me. I'd exposed myself, and the world looked at all my emotions with a kaleidoscope, dissecting each one, changing and distorting it.

There was a damn good reason musicians walked away from the industry or built fortresses around themselves to disappear. I'd done the same thing, sort of. I'd turned my attention to investments and apps. I still utilized my old music for it, but I didn't have it in me to get lost in the emotions of my music all over again.

Getting lost in her and in writing the music surrounding those emotions without knowing whether I would have her again or if I wanted her again was like taking a bullet wound to the stomach. It penetrated my insides in a hot flash, the trauma acute enough to trick my mind into feeling no pain at first, just long enough to believe I might make it; then, as my brain adjusted to reality, I'd be left unable to ever forget the scorching, searing pain inflicted by my own reckless abandon.

For some damn reason, my body didn't shy from the pain. I'd seen her in that kitchen with a man I knew was playing games with me and jumped at the chance to use it.

I pushed myself harder as I jogged, trying to burn off my frustration.

My mind knew indulging in her wasn't the smart thing to do. I prided myself on making those types of deductions and calculating the most likely of the outcomes.

The end for her and me should have been when I walked out on her a long time ago. Unfortunately, both of us were tied to the man that had set our lives aflame. He'd held a trump card for so long, I couldn't back away until I'd beaten him at his own game and taken every card he held, including the one he held over my head and hers.

I still couldn't figure out if I was doing that for her or for myself.

So when I stopped in front of her apartment, out of breath from my run, I didn't immediately knock on her door.

I didn't have a good reason to keep seeing her or to run here in the middle of the night to bother her.

She would ask me why I visited her father and I wouldn't give her an answer. Part of me wanted to knock on her door for that reason alone. So I could see her light up with anger and lose herself a little. She needed that. Without unraveling a little, she would wind herself up so tight, she'd continue to have panic attacks like she'd had at Jay's premiere.

Immediately after I knocked, the door swung wide open and the bane of my existence stood there.

Katie's smile looked a little like a maniac's when she said, "You here to see someone?"

I just stared at her.

She scoffed, "She's not here, and I don't think she'll be back tonight."

I felt my jaw tick before I could catch it. Her smile widened. "Where is she?" I said, practically growling. I knew the answer. Katie just laughed and started to swing the door shut.

I wedged my running shoe between the door and the wall before she could fully slam it though. "Answer me."

Katie's eyes narrowed and her smile turned so saccharine, it was evident she was out for blood. Looking as if she was about to storm away, she stomped her heel so far into my big toe I'm certain my guttural cry could be heard through the whole complex.

"What in the flying fuck, Katie?" I yelled.

She didn't even turn back around, just said over her shoulder, "Do not fuck with her anymore." Then, she slammed the door.

I pushed off the wall and bent down to rub my foot through my sneaker. "Jesus Christ," I muttered.

"She got you with one of those heels, huh?" Rome leaned against the doorframe of what I assumed was his apartment.

I nodded and stood up, trying to bite the bullet and talk to the man I knew had been fucking my girl. "Roman."

His mouth stretched into a smile, "You can just call me Rome."

I sucked on my teeth. "You happen to know where I might find Aubrey?"

The full blown smile told me all I needed to know. "She know I'm out here?"

"I wasn't going to wake her."

If we'd been back in high school, when I considered her mine, I would have broken his jaw.

I wasn't proud to admit I still considered it.

"She wouldn't be happy," he stated as if he could read my mind. I raised my eyebrows in question.

From the looks of him—his wide frame and stance, the way his muscles bunched under all the tattoos, and the way his eyes watched my fists—he could probably read when a man was ready to come at him.

He'd put up a good fight, that was for sure.

He nodded at my hands like he knew I wanted them to connect with his face. "Brey's never liked fighting."

"Your point?"

"You'd make her more unhappy than you've already made her." I crossed my arms over my chest and let him continue.

"You're here looking for forgiveness, and she's not going to give it to you if you break my nose."

"I was thinking jaw."

His dark eyes sparked with a little life, like he might enjoy it, but he didn't move toward me. Instead, he rocked back on his heels. "I know that look you have."

"What look is that?"

"It's the same one I had for a girl I thought was mine, who I thought I had under my control. Turns out, she owned me and the chaos surrounding us couldn't be controlled at all."

"Well, there's the difference. I've always been able to control even the most fucked-up chaos."

"Might be true, Jax. But I know Brey, and she'll never choose to come anywhere near you if you keep talking to her father."

I pushed off the wall and looked at his door one last time. Then I directed my gaze toward him, making sure he heard me very clearly. "You might know her, but you don't know her with me. You assume she has the choice of coming near me in the first place."

It was his turn to raise his eyebrows in question, looking like he may be ready to fight me finally.

I held up my hand to stop him and explain. "You assume I have a choice in keeping away from her too? She and I have never had a choice. We're drawn to each other whether we like it or not."

He scoffed but there was no reason to indulge in the conversation any further. "You want to tell her I'm here or you want me to break down your door?"

He contemplated it for about five seconds.

It was long enough for us to size each other up again. The man stood to just about the same height as me. I commanded attention in a room but he did too. I could see why he might appeal to Aubrey but couldn't see her with anyone but me.

He smiled wide like he'd come to some conclusion. "If you hurt her again, I won't have to break your neck."

I shrugged, not promising him anything.

He continued. "Katie and Jay will skin you alive before I find you. You better believe I'll help hide the body though."

With that, he headed toward the exit door of the complex and said over his shoulder, "Just try calling or knocking to wake her up instead of breaking down my damn door and ice that toe of yours. Katie's heels are mean motherfuckers."

I should have broken down the door just to make a point, but he was being relatively helpful under the circumstances.

I'd learned over the years that I could make a point pretty clearly by navigating my social relationships the right way. I'd be navigating him the fuck out of her life and her into my bed soon enough.

Instead of knocking, I leaned against the hall wall, stared at Roman's door and called her cell.

I heard it ring on the other side and imagined her groggily reaching for it. She'd never been one to wake up happy, so I didn't expect her to answer on the first call.

It went to her voice mail. I hung up just to dial her number again.

It would have been rude to ignore a second call and I knew some of the politeness she'd been taught as a child was still there. She cleared her throat before speaking, but her hello was still full of sleep and sounded a lot like how I remembered it sounding after I'd slept next to her years ago.

"Polite of you to answer a call this late, Peaches."

"Impolite of you to call this late, L.P." she said back, using my nickname to grate on my nerves.

I heard rustling and even though I knew she was in another man's bed, my body wanted to be right beside her.

Normally she and I would battle with each other, but tonight I battled with myself. I should have walked away from every damn feeling. She had me angry as hell that she wasn't mine. The memories of us had me longing to be next to her again. And hearing her over the phone had me walking right up to Roman's door wanting to be next to her.

"Can I see you?"

She stuttered, "Why?"

"Because we should talk."

"We have nothing to talk about."

"We do," I corrected. "Can I see you right now? Are you busy?"

She hesitated. "It's really late, Jax."

"But you're up."

"What time is it?"

"Late. I'm outside your door. Let me in." It was a cheap way to make her forget our real issues and worry about the fact that she wasn't in her apartment.

I heard more rustling and it made me wonder if she was putting her clothes on.

Did she sleep naked with him? Did she let herself unwind that much or had that only been with me a long time ago?

She sounded a little out of breath when she responded with, "Jax, it's three in the morning."

I smiled a little because I recognized the tone she used when she wanted to be nice but was getting rubbed the wrong way. The girl I used to know couldn't keep up a front that long. Her annoyance and emotion bled through.

I had lived for those moments. "Yeah, it's late."

"Look. We don't have anything to talk about, but I can do coffee tomorrow if you want. Would you like to do that?"

"Would you like to open Roman's door?" She sucked in a breath.

"On his way out he mentioned where you were sleeping."

"Great," she said. Then she hung up.

I promised myself I would only wait about another minute before I walked away but I knew if it took her longer than that, I'd probably break the door down. I had invested too much of my night to not see her now.

When the door swung open only seconds later, I took in the woman I'd fought like hell to make just another notch on my bedpost. Her dark hair laid on her shoulders and spilled down her chest in messy enough curls that she'd either been sleeping or rolling around in bed.

The idea made me want to toss her curvy little ass into a box that only I had the key to. Then, when I wanted to explore all the shit she made me feel, I'd let her out to play. She was my toy, not anyone else's.

"You're wearing gray again, I see," I started.

"Yep. It's a nice, bland look. You know I don't like to draw attention even if I was on the news earlier today."

I crossed my arms, ignoring her attempt to rile me and tsked as I looked her up and down. "Peaches, anything you wear that is that short and tight on your ass is going to draw attention."

She rolled her lips between her teeth, and it was like my enemy showing me their weakness. It egged me the hell on.

"Did Roman tell you he was only looking in a nice, *friendly* manner?"

Her green eyes narrowed just a little. "I'm tired, Jax. So, if you don't have anything important to say..."

Damn, she'd gotten so much better at holding that temper.

I wondered how much longer it would take to light her up and get a rise out of her.

I also wondered why I was here in the first place.

That had me holding back, knowing we had to figure out this pull between us.

"Let's talk."

She stared at me like I'd morphed into a creature she didn't understand.

"Peaches, let me in so we can talk, okay?" She rubbed her eyes and stepped back.

I walked in and closed the door behind me.

When I turned to her again, she didn't look up from her phone and typed away to someone else.

"Something important happening on there?"

"Rome said he won't be back for a while and ... "—she cleared her throat again, showing another nervous habit of hers—"that he hopes we can work through some things."

"How *friendly* and thoughtful of him."

She set her phone down on the table a little harder than I'd seen her do in the past. "Well, Jax, he is a good friend."

"Hmm." I stepped toward her. "You sleep in all your friend's beds?"

When she rolled her eyes, I saw a little heat from her temper seeping through that quiet façade.

"How do I get to that friend level?"

Her hands went to her hips. And then, she unleashed. "I just can't. It is the middle of the night and you, what?" She looked me up and down. Then she motioned to my running attire. "Jog over here to annoy me after you spent the weekend having conversations with my father? Are you completely out of your mind or just a total fucking asshole?"

"Watch that mouth, Whitfield. You used to hold that tongue a lot better. It's new you can't do that."

"'New'?" Her eyes shone so bright I saw only green fury swimming all around me. "You think me swearing is new! News flash, Jax, everything about me is new to you! I'm a totally new person. The girl you knew years ago broke down and died after a summer of hell and a summer with you. Although, hmm ... " She tapped her chin dramatically. "That was pretty much one and the same."

This anger, this raw emotion was what moved me, moved us, made us who we were. I tried to step up to her, I wanted to experience this outburst as closely as I could.

She stepped back and moved to stand on the other side of the apartment's small kitchen island. "You think that helping with some class, taking a few little jogs, and trying to make me feel good on a kitchen counter one day is going to change the fact that you and I are oil and water? Or worse yet! We're like two chemicals that when mixed together create a bomb."

"Ammonia and chloride."

She waved her hands at me. "Whatever. I don't want to be woken up at three in the morning by you after you went and did stuff you knew would bother me all weekend."

I crossed my arms over my chest and nodded. "Fair enough."

Her eyebrows went up in confusion. She wanted a fight. I did too. My body buzzed for another battle with her but seeing her let go like this reinforced what I already knew.

"We need to come to some conclusions tonight, Whitfield."

Her head tilted to the side a little. "I am coming to some conclusions."

"Are you now?"

She held up a finger. "One, I don't want you bothering me outside of studying."

I leaned into the counter, letting her ramble on while I used one foot to slide off one sneaker.

"Two." She held up another finger but looked at my feet like they were letting out all her steam. "Once this class is over, we don't talk unless you want to talk about my father. Because quite frankly, until you do, I have nothing to say to you."

I pushed the other shoe off and shoved them both aside as I started toward her, ready to be done with the counting.

"Three … "

"The only conclusion is you and I are going to keep bumping heads until we get each other out of our systems, Peaches." I kept my voice soft, trying to coax her into understanding as I cornered her in another kitchen that reminded me very much of the one we were in just a few days ago.

"What?" Her question was a whisper on her lips, so quiet I barely heard it.

"It's been years but my body still remembers exactly how your skin feels up against mine."

She licked her lips, "Jax ... "

"I'm not saying you're the best I've ever had." The fire lit up in her eyes again. "Are you ser—"

"And I'm not saying I'm the best you've ever had. But our bodies connect. When I see you, I want to be inside you. I want to fucking own you. Nothing else."

Her breathing picked up.

"It's more of a primal instinct. Maybe it's something about what we went through together or maybe I just cut that summer too short."

She looked over my shoulder like she wanted someone to run in and break this up, like making any more eye contact with me would pain her. "You leaving me that summer wasn't my fault. You did that."

"Peaches, I know that. We both needed to move on."

"Move on to this?" she yelled and threw her hands up. "This, right here between us? We've moved on to what? The connection neither of us can shake?"

I boxed her in by putting both my hands on either side of her hips on the counter. I made sure my lips were only an inch from hers when I said, "We can shake this. Let me shake it from you from here on out. No strings. When I'm here, helping you with your class and getting ready for my app launch, you let me get you out of my system and allow yourself to let go enough to get me out of yours."

I saw her mind working as she slid her hand over her hair. "And when you go back to the city and visit my dad? You expect me to just wait here for you?"

She framed her question to drill home a point and with it, she struck one of my nerves. Before I could hold my tongue, I shot back, "You obviously have a comforting system here. How many times did you fuck Roman while I was gone?"

"Are you kidding me?"

"It doesn't matter," I shook my head, attempting to shake off the jealousy I finally had to admit I was feeling. "Let yourself go with me, Whitfield. Get me out of your system."

"I don't have you in my system, Jax."

She stood tall, her head tilted up at me, like she meant every word she said.

I knew different.

I knew this stance better than any. She wanted to run. She wanted to wave a white flag and go back to some comfort zone where she could lick her wounds, build her wall back up.

"If you don't, prove it."

"How?"

"Play along for two minutes. If you want me to stop, just say so, and I'll walk away."

The fire in those emerald eyes of hers burned with fear.

If she walked, I'd find someone else to be with, I reminded myself. Something in me screamed I would never find someone like her.

I silenced that scream as best I could and stared at her like I'd walk away right then if she asked me to.

I knew better. I just hoped she didn't.

CHAPTER
TWENTY-SEVEN

AUBREY

MY LIFE FOR the past couple of years had been stationary, stagnant, filled with general content but no amazement. And monotonous. So awfully dull.

I loved my friends, I loved volunteering, but I was bored.

Bored was better than scared though. After all the publicity my family stirred up over the years, attention made me jumpy, cautious, and gave me those panic attacks.

I had hidden the abuse of my childhood for so long, I didn't know what to do when the blinding light had shined down on all my father's wrongdoings. I was clueless on how to react because the person who did know what to do had been taken by him.

Or rather, she'd let him take her.

I struggled with that idea every day, that she'd chosen to give her life for the man who had been willing to take it.

I was standing in front of the man who had been willing to risk his own life all those years ago to save mine.

The irony of it all was that he also chose to make my life hell and not share the reason why with me.

Was I willing to give up my comfortable lifestyle to get someone out of my system? To get my life back? Or to ruin my life all over again? I couldn't decide which question made the most sense.

This glorious specimen of a man stood in front of me, knowing he wreaked havoc on my body and attracted the whole female population, asking for two minutes.

Could I hold out for two minutes?

I honestly took time to think about it as I stared at him. I took him in again, looking him up and down.

His shirt stretched over his muscles as he towered over me. I knew he felt my stare because his body shifted with my perusal, as if my gaze affected him. That was our chemistry though. The one thing I couldn't deny. He and I were connected in a way I didn't want to be anymore. I wanted to cleanse myself of him but didn't know how.

Maybe he had a point. Maybe he needed to get me out of his system but I needed him as well if I was going to overcome what I'd turned into.

I could use him as my closure and he could use me in whatever way he needed.

Did I even really want to hold out for two minutes?

I thought of my room and of my mother as I gazed into his blue, determined stare again.

"Two minutes…"

I didn't get to finish my sentence because he lunged to devour my lips, like he'd been coiled and waiting, like he'd prepared years for the moment.

The second his tongue touched mine and I tasted that familiar mint, I moaned.

His hands dove under my waistband and he groaned when he squeezed my butt. "Goddamn. Tell me you wear these shorts every night."

I started to pull away to come up for air and to let him know my nightwear wouldn't matter in the future.

He leaned forward into me immediately and grumbled, "My two minutes, Whitfield."

My heart beat as fast as a bomb that was about to go off while his determined blue gaze stole the breath out of my lungs. "Jax, maybe this isn't such a good ... "

He murmured into my neck, "I've got a minute thirty, then you can finish that sentence."

He bit into my neck, and I clenched my thighs as he sucked on one of my most sensitive spots. His hands slid to my hips, rubbing his thumb up and down, dipping in and out of my panty line to the same rhythm of his tongue on my neck.

My skin dampened as my core shook with need.

I started to pant, to sweat, to lean into him. All parts of my body responded to him just like he wanted. Except my mind. It balled up with every concern and doubt about our situation. It screamed to be rational and conservative, to protect myself.

Control, my sweet, dear friend, wrapped my fingers around the counter's edge and helped me white-knuckle it like it was the last strand of hope I had at saving myself from imminent heartbreak.

Jax pulled back for a second, his time too valuable to waste and glanced at my hands.

That jaw of his ticked a bit and he smirked. "Peaches, I've got one minute."

I swallowed hard and licked my lips.

"And if you're barely restraining yourself now, you'll be writhing under me, begging and moaning when I slide my fingers across that wet pussy of yours soon."

His fingers hooked on to either side of my shorts and panties. He kneeled and ripped them down in one fast jerk. Then, he stared. "Still perfect," he whispered almost to himself.

This was the way I needed to be handled, like he wasn't worried. Like I could step up to any challenge he threw at me because he knew I was strong enough.

His right hand went to my inner thigh, and goose bumps popped up all over my skin as my eyes followed his hand sliding up my thigh.

Without warning, he plunged two fingers into me and leaned forward to suck on my clit. The explosion of ecstasy buckled my knees.

My control slipped as I let go of the counter. As he sucked me harder, my hands migrated to his hair, and he used his other hand to guide one of my legs up over his shoulder.

He nipped me and I whimpered, wanting all of him and more of the same at once.

His fingers worked methodically inside me, bringing me just to the brink, hovering right on the edge.

I rocked into him, trying to get more of something, more of him, more of what he was doing—anything.

He held back though.

I gripped his hair and pushed him further into me, moaning.

He pulled back instead, taking his mouth from my clit but leaving his fingers in me, working. "Two minutes are up, Whitfield. What's it going to be?"

His words splashed over me like a bucket of ice cold water. I almost pulled away but he slid a third finger in and twisted within me, speeding up the pace.

I whimpered, "You're an asshole."

He flicked his thumb over my clit and responded with, "Beg me to fuck you, baby. I'll make sure you get off here and in Roman's bed over and over again."

I rocked on his hand, not saying anything but trying so hard to get there.

My body wouldn't listen to my mind. Wouldn't stop chasing the orgasm it so desperately needed from the one man who knew everything it loved.

He tsked and slowed the pace of his fingers. He leaned forward and blew on me before looking up at me again. "Beg, Whitfield."

I whispered it so quietly, I hoped my mind and old friend, Control, didn't hear. "Please, Jax."

"Louder." He sped up the pace a little. I rocked with it. "Please."

He rubbed his thumb over my clit. "Keep it coming. Louder, babe." I did as I was told, rocking and chanting "Please," like he wanted. He licked my clit and fingered me like I wanted.

My first orgasm rolled through me fast. Bright spots blurred my vision, and I almost collapsed on him.

He didn't let up though. He continued to work me, not giving me a break to recoup.

When I thought I couldn't take anymore, he grabbed my other thigh, wrapped it around his neck, held my ass, and swung me up in the air to the other wall where my back slammed hard against it.

His face buried deeper into my core and he ate me out so good, I slammed my head back into the wall over and over again as I came, trying to dispel some of the nuclear orgasmic bomb that exploded within me.

As I slumped over him, he let me slide down his body and then carried me to Rome's room, ready to throw me into his bed.

"I should probably wait to fuck you in my own bed."

I smiled. "Like I said, Rome texted and said he was giving me time to work it out with you. He won't be back tonight."

Jax didn't smile back. He just turned and headed back the way he came.

I wriggled against him. "Hey, you're going the wrong way!"

"Nope." He set me down a little harder than I expected he would and started throwing my clothes my way. "Put your clothes back on. We're going to my place."

I caught my shorts. "Are you kidding me right now?"

He laced up his shoes, "Do I look like I'm fucking kidding?"

"You are being ridiculous," I practically yelled, frustrated that he was stopping our momentum. "I'm not going to your place."

I shot my legs into my shorts and wiggled them up over my body as his head snapped up. "Don't be difficult, Whitfield."

I sighed up to the ceiling. "Jax, how can you possibly think I am being the difficult one right now? You literally have an empty bed and a willing woman to fuck you. Yet, you want to trek all the way back to your house?"

His whole body tightened at my words. "Just a 'willing woman to fuck,' huh? That all it is to you?"

"Isn't that the way you just described this? Getting this out of our systems?"

He stepped toward me, taut, ready for a fight. "You fuck Roman in that bed." He pointed toward the bedroom furiously. "You've probably fucked him all through this goddamn place."

I didn't deny it. I wasn't about to go into specifics about how I'd cried to Rome over the weekend but hadn't slept with him. I just passed out at his place.

Without giving any detail, I practically saw Jax's blood pressure rise as his face reddened.

"I might blow your mind in his kitchen and mark you where he touched you,"—he slid his hand over my neck—"and I damn sure will make you forget every moment you thought he got you off. But when I take you again, it will be in my bed, on my terms, and without him giving us permission to work it out."

"Why?" I whispered, hoping with all my heart that his words meant that he wanted something more than just getting each other out of our systems. My mind told me to be smarter.

"If I knew the answer to that, I'd tell you."

I crossed my arms across my chest, trying to stand tall but knowing it came off as a protective mechanism. "Maybe we should wait until you have the answer."

He sighed, ran his hands through his hair, and squinted at me like he was trying to read my every thought.

I stared back, wanting to tell him this was all bullshit, that he should have never left, that him visiting my dad was bullshit, and we could have made it if he had stayed.

His squint turned into a stare I thought looked a little too close to sympathy.

I squeezed my eyes shut and in the next second, he'd swooped in and kissed me so hard that all the air whooshed out of me. He held my face as he devoured my lips like he was starved, and I met him with equal fervor.

Then, just as quickly as he'd moved in, he jerked back. I was gulping for air as he backed up toward the door, swung it open, and said, "My bed is coming. Until then, stay the fuck out of his."

CHAPTER
TWENTY-EIGHT

AUBREY

THE SOUND OF the door slamming behind Jax ricocheted through Rome's apartment.

I almost screamed. He infuriated me so much that I wanted to text Rome to come home and screw me in his bed where Jax wouldn't. I trudged back to my apartment so tired of following rules and fitting myself into the stupid box I imagined my father must have somehow psychologically built for me.

When I opened the door to our apartment and saw Katie sitting to the left on the living room couch with wine in both her hands, I sighed.

"I figured we could start with the wine and move to something stronger if needed."

I closed the door behind me and leaned into it. "How'd you know I'd be home?"

"After I stiletto stomped his ass and insinuated that you were sleeping with Rome, I figured he would be heading next door. When I didn't hear a fight break out, I was pretty disappointed."

I scoffed.

"What? Like Rome and Jax fighting wouldn't be epic?" She waved off her question. "Anyway, Rome texted me that you might be back and you might not. I figured Jax is a dick and you'd be back."

I grabbed a glass from her and joined her on the couch. "I just want him to tell me why he continues to go. What is it they could possibly be discussing after all these years when they never had anything to discuss before?"

"Nothing, Brey," she replied casually as she took the remote and started surfing through channels. "We've gone over this again and again. People are just fucked in the head when they lead a cushy life and get thrown into a fucked-up situation. Maybe he has guilt, maybe he doesn't. Maybe he's just psychotic. Who cares? It doesn't matter."

I slumped into the couch, knowing I needed one of her reality checks. "Tell me why it doesn't matter again?"

"Because he should have bucked the hell up and chose you. He should have told you why he was going or *stopped* fucking going. He did neither. Instead, he left you high and dry. So, fuck him."

I gulped my wine. "Ugh. You are right. I know you are so right."

She stopped channel surfing and turned to smile at me. "I know I am, but you are too damn nice, and you love too damn hard to listen to me. So, I'll say this only once, and I'll never repeat it again."

I squinted a little at her, wondering what my best friend could possibly say that she hadn't said in all these years.

"Shit." She looked disgusted with herself as she launched off the couch. "I need something stronger than wine if I am going to say this."

"Should I have something stronger too?" My question sounded meek.

She jumped up on the counter to dig in the cabinets and grabbed the long lost Macallan that I hadn't touched in weeks. After hopping down and pouring four shots, she looked up at me. Her dark eyes held no humor and were all business when she said, "Come drink up. You're going to need it."

I hesitated, not sure I needed to hear what she was going to say.

Katie was my best friend, the one who'd always stuck by my side. Her compass needle pointed directly to making me happy and the other end of the needle was the total bitch who protected that happiness.

If she was going to say something I couldn't handle, I needed more than two shots of liquor.

I downed the first one with her without saying another word.

She nodded at the next two shots and we downed those also.

I breathed out the burn of it and let it travel down into my stomach.

I sighed. "Maybe another?"

She nodded and poured, "God, I hate this whiskey, you know that?"

Her admission surprised me. "You always used to drink it with me."

"I drank it with you because every time you brought it out, I knew something was wrong. It's like the punishment drink."

I rolled my lips between my teeth. "Maybe."

"Remember when you told me your dad drank only this?" She held up the bottle.

I nodded.

"It's some real circle-of-angry life shit to drink it too, when you're mad at the world."

"I know." I sighed. "I get lost sometimes and it ... I don't know ... it helps bring me back and get even more lost at the same time."

Her brow furrowed as if she didn't understand.

"We all deal with our pasts differently, Katie. For example, you blaze through life like this is it and shit just happens to everyone for no reason. Someone could run over me with a car tomorrow and you'd probably shrug your shoulders, agree that it sucks, give me a kick-ass funeral and move on. You don't dwell. At. All."

Katie looked a little wide-eyed, like she didn't exactly enjoy my perception of her. "I dwell sometimes."

I laughed at the fact that she didn't deny she'd move on quickly from my death. "You've been in countless relationships, and I don't even keep track of them anymore because you're never hurt when they end or happy when they begin."

"Well…" She shrugged like my neglect as a friend didn't matter. "I don't care about those relationships. They provide me something and I provide them something. When they want more or less, we end it. There's no reason to dwell on them. Quite frankly, there's no reason to dwell on a lot of shit."

I sighed because I hated that she put herself in those relationships. Most men she was with had money and were old enough to be her father, but it wasn't my place to judge her when I dealt with my demons in a way she didn't necessarily approve of. "It's what I love about you. You know that. But it's also what people hate about you."

She shrugged. "Whatever you say, honey. I'm still not sure what this has to do with the bottle of whiskey I'm holding."

I sighed. "My dad controlled everything in my family. I was too young to drink and he never let my mom touch the liquor cabinet. When I think of him locked up, not able to drink, and me free, completely able to drink his favorite whiskey whenever I want, I get a sick sort of pleasure from it. Then, I'm indulging in it and the smell brings back these awful memories and I get angry. *So* angry."

Katie waited, letting me work it all out.

I continued. "I start to lose myself in it. I drink and lose control, you know…whatever. But he always had the control. It was his to lose, not mine. So, even in that way, I'm happy about it."

Katie was nodding and smirking a little. "You're even more fucked up than me."

I rolled my eyes. "That's so rude."

"Whatev." She nodded to the next shot. "Bottoms up, you sick bitch."

I downed the shot and winced.

"Okay, we are done now, for real." She shuddered, trying to shake off the burn. "Hopefully, what I have to say, you will just forget tomorrow, anyway."

"Ha, probably not after this type of build up." I hiccupped a little.

"He's a dick, always has been and always will be. That's my main point, always, okay?"

"Okay?" I dragged out the syllables, trying to figure out what she was trying to say before she said it.

"And he's probably psychotic or sociopathic or something."

I raised my eyebrows.

"I'm not kidding you, Brey." She shoved away from the counter and went to turn off the TV to busy herself. "Have you ever watched the way he stares at people. Like he's reading them, calculating them. It's fucking creepy."

I shrugged. I knew exactly what she meant, except I thought it was hot.

"Okay, fine. We all know he's hot, so the way he studies you can be too, but it's still creepy. Especially considering that every time he does it, he knows exactly what to say to get what he wants from you. He reads everyone right."

I folded my arms over my chest. "Not us."

She fist pumped in the air, probably because she was pretty much drunk at this point. "Damn right, not us." Then she winced. "Kinda."

"What do you mean 'kinda'?" I walked over to the couch where she stood and plopped down into it when she did.

"Well, he pretty much reads me right all the time."

"No, he doesn't!" I retorted. "You snap at him every time he says something to you."

She sighed and slumped into the couch. "That's the thing. I think he meets me toe-to-toe on purpose. He lets me snap at him, but never really takes the bait. I see him testing me, making sure I'm still ready to bite his head off because of what he did to you, and he likes it."

I scrunched up my face, confused.

"It sounds stupid, I know, which is why I'll never repeat this, but I know I'm right. He's testing me to make sure I'm being your best friend and busting his balls still. And it kinda makes me *not* hate him."

I felt my eyes widen.

She must have seen them too. "Only a little! I only don't hate him a little!"

"What?" I practically yelled.

"I know." She put her hands up to her face. "I still think you should boot his ass out of your life but … "

"But what?"

Her hands fell to her lap and her eyes bored into mine. "Maybe you should boot him after you give him a shot to make it right."

I didn't realize how much her opinion of Jax really meant until that moment. She was the last one on the seesaw with me, shifting toward not giving him another chance. My world that had been so stable, so level and smooth, shifted. I gripped the armrest of the couch as if trying to find my balance.

"You can't be serious," I wheezed.

Katie never looked apologetic, so when I saw that exact look in her eye, I almost screamed. "You told me this whole time he wasn't worth anything!"

"He's not," she placated softly.

Katie didn't use a soft voice or try to calm anyone. That only made the world shift under me more.

"Oh, shut up," I blurted before my hand flew over my face as her eyes bulged. "Oh, my gosh. I didn't mean … "

She cut me off. "Yes, you did." Her accusation came out with a smile.

"Katie, no I didn't. That's so rude. You're my best friend and I don't ever want you to not … "

"Exactly." She poked her finger into my shoulder. "I'm your best friend and you're mine. You can be rude to me, Brey. God knows you aren't rude to anyone else."

I rolled my eyes a little. "I think the alcohol is getting to me because I sort of want to call you a few names at this point too."

Katie sunk into the couch and started laughing. I chuckled a little. "Let's be honest, okay? Just fuck Jax's brains out and see what happens. Maybe it'll work it out, maybe it won't. Either way, you'll get answers."

I elbowed her. "I don't just want to hook up with him. I need closure or answers or I don't know."

She wiggled her eyebrows at me. "But you do totally want to hook up with him along with all those things, right?"

"Ugh." I put my face into my hands. "I want to screw him so bad."

She cackled when I finally admitted it.

I let her have the laugh while I looked up at the ceiling, trying to squelch the desire I had to call him right then and find a way to be with him. I wanted his hands on me again. I wanted his lips grazing my neck. I wanted the taste of mint ... and him.

I shuddered thinking about it.

I didn't feel centered without him and that scared me.

Katie nudged me. "Tell me what's going on."

So, I told her. I told her everything from the summer I loved him until now. I told her how he walked away tonight and how I didn't know if I could do what he asked.

"Can I just sleep with him and try to figure it out?"

Clearing her throat and reaching for more wine, she said, "I doubt it."

I winced a little. "I know."

"No. You don't know. You're stronger than you think, girl. I don't doubt that you can handle it. I know you can. I doubt that you can walk away without caring. You can't detach from your emotions like that. Most people can't."

I nodded. "So, how do I avoid caring? Teach me."

She laughed again, her colorful hair swaying with her shaking her head. "Brey, you can't learn that. I'm detached because it's all I've ever known. It's also what I want. My detachment is my survival. Your love is yours. You love. I don't. And it's okay to love. It's why we balance each other so well."

"What?" I whispered.

"You only got to where you are because you loved your momma so much. You and your dad would have killed each other much earlier if it hadn't been for that love. When she passed, you shifted your love to the Stonewoods. Now, you love all of us."

I cocked my head. "Huh. I think we've had way too much to drink because you're kind of making sense."

"I know, right? I'm a fucking genius psychologist when I've had enough whiskey."

The night regressed into nonsense after that.

The next morning, my phone went off like a siren, so loud and jarring I wasn't sure which direction it was coming from. When I shot out of bed to turn it off, my whole body swayed in excruciating pain.

Hungover didn't begin to describe what I felt.

I swiped the screen automatically, just needing the sound to stop. "Hello?" I croaked.

"You're not outside," Jax said matter-of-factly.

"What?" I tried to play catch-up.

"Are you asleep?" He sounded surprised and a little disgusted.

"I was," I retorted back, wincing because I should have been whispering. Any sound louder than a whisper wasn't helping.

"Well, let's go. I don't have all day."

Did he sound pissy or was it just me?

"I can't go today, Jax."

"We go every Monday, Whitfield."

"Not today," I stated with finality.

"Why?" He breathed the question with an edge.

"Because I don't feel up to it." I didn't owe him an explanation. He ran with me. Half the time we ran, we didn't talk anyway. I never called him to run either. He just showed up. It was my time that he invaded and pushed himself into like everything else in my life.

"Is this about last night?"

"No, it's not."

"Hmm." He waited a beat. "Then humor me."

I sighed. The way he said those two words all the time, like we didn't have all the history in the world to worry about. Like our feelings weren't involved and this was just another day.

He thought I could handle it all and anything together. Like I should just listen to him because he knew best.

No part of me wanted to admit that maybe he did know best, or maybe he knew me as well as I knew myself.

So, I hung up on him and threw on a sports bra and yoga pants.

I piled my wavy hair into a messy bun and started to tie my shoes. Katie popped up from the couch. "What in the actual fuck are you doing?" she croaked.

"Going for a run, apparently," I said more to my shoes than her.

"What?" She shook her head like her own voice was too loud for her. Then she whispered, "I seriously feel like a boulder rolled over me. Indiana Jones's boulder." She groaned and threw her arm over her face as she plopped back down on the couch. "You are a masochist, you know that?"

I didn't reply because she was more right about that now than ever before.

The sun blinded me when I stepped outside. The hot, humid air reminded me that summer in the Midwest packed a punch every single day. Winter would come and steal most of the year. So of course, summer had to make a mark.

Today, it made the mark of pure, unforgiving heat.

Instead of talking to him and trying to figure out what the hell we were doing, I started my jog immediately.

I thought I heard him sigh before he fell into step behind me like always.

Each step I took at first, felt like a hammer to the head.

The feeling reminded me of a time not too long ago when I'd drink way more than I should have without anyone around.

I ran harder, wanting to feel physical pain rather than the emotional pain I was in because of him and my father.

All because of them.

I pushed harder as I corrected myself. It wasn't just because of them. I was unhappy with myself.

Unhappy with my life. How had I gotten there?

Katie was right. I loved my friends, but what else did I love?

I avoided everything that I could get attached to. I let my room go unpainted and undecorated, avoiding anything of meaning for years.

I avoided relationships by attaching myself to Rome.

I sidestepped attention by dressing plainly and falling back into the shadows.

I'd succeeded in making myself unhappy. It was me. Not him. Not my father.

Not anyone else.

I ran to try to escape myself, hating that I'd somehow built something all on my own that I couldn't stand. I had the control, and maybe I'd always had the control, to make my life better, but I couldn't see past the misery I'd inflicted on myself to do something about it.

When I tried to push myself even harder, I was jerked back by him, grabbing my elbow and bringing me to a halt.

"Whitfield, slow the fuck down or you'll end up..."

Before he could finish, I bent over and vomited all over the sidewalk.

CHAPTER
TWENTY-NINE

JAX

AUBREY WAS NORMALLY a creature of habit. It suited her upbringing. Less could go wrong when you understood the schedule, organized it thoroughly, and executed it perfectly. In a lot of ways, I admired that about her.

In high school, she stood her ground when friends pushed her to do something she didn't want to. She'd never wavered, never did anything outside of her comfort zone.

I realized her routine was unshakeable because it protected her and her mother. Frank didn't allow for mistakes. Had Aubrey deviated from her normal schedule, the inevitable most likely would have happened sooner.

Now, her day-to-day centered around her friends, her studies, and her health. I could count on her to show up to a tutoring session, completely prepared with her homework done. I knew she'd unfailingly be available to Jay, Vick, Katie, or fucking Roman if they needed her.

And running. Running was her thing. It kept her healthy and grounded.

I used that to my advantage when I called her. When she stepped out, didn't look at me, and went right into a jog, I figured it was for the best.

We never talked much when we ran.

I never pushed her on it because, for some reason, it felt like our bodies synced up in the silence of a jog.

Today was no different.

She needed the exercise to burn off the anger toward me, and I just fucking needed her at that point.

The night before had been like taking a burning stake to my libido all on my own. Why I couldn't take her in Roman's place still made me livid with myself. The whole fucking point of us sleeping together was to shake each other from our systems. I'd led with that, wanted that. I just wasn't sure I still believed that.

Because I couldn't follow through with it.

When she told me that Roman had given us permission, I wanted to break her phone, tell her she could never text him again, and go find him to bust his face up like I should have done before in the hall. It didn't matter that he probably wasn't trying to goad me.

Didn't he know that she was mine? Whether she actually was or wasn't.

We owned one another. Our souls were burned together, welded and molded by so much molten emotion that no one—not him, not Jay, not even fucking Frank—could split us up. I knew, because I had tried to split that bond myself.

So lost in my own thoughts, I didn't realize how much our bodies moved together until I found myself in a full-out run behind her to just keep up.

I heard her wheezing ahead of me and knew something was off.

She was pushing herself too hard, like she was trying to escape.

Aubrey was a creature of habit. She didn't veer off that course for anything or anyone.

Or so I'd thought. I miscalculated.

I forgot to factor in her temper or how quickly she swerved when something provoked her well-built fortress of walls.

I grabbed her elbow and yanked her back. "Whitfield, slow the fuck down or you'll end up..."

I didn't have to say 'sick' because she puked all over the goddamn place.

I crossed my arms over my chest and let her dry heave. The smell of alcohol was more than potent. "You drink enough last night?"

"Please, be quiet," she said with her hands on her knees.

I scowled at her. She made me crazy. "We both know drinking that much never ends well."

The second I said it, I realized what I'd insinuated.

Her eyes snapped up to mine, "Really, Jax?" Her tone was hard and accusing.

It didn't matter. The green-eyed stare that she'd hid pummeled me so hard, I almost took a step back. Eyes the color of a forest, so deep and so penetrating, I got lost in them and wondered how I'd ever find my way out.

Scanning the street, I broke eye contact with her. "No one has made us yet." I saw her body tense and immediately had to restrain the fucked up need I had to shield her from anything and everything. "Can you walk or do you want me to call a driver?"

She scoffed but straightened. When I saw her wobble, I started walking toward the road while I pulled out my phone.

"What are you doing?" she said from behind me.

I waved her off and stared down the street. "I need you to pick me up." I looked at the street name and rattled off our location.

When I ended the call and turned to her, a blush had crept into her cheeks and her nostrils flared a little as she said, "I don't need a driver."

"You need food, toothpaste, and a bed, Whitfield."

"I need nothing of the sort."

I just chuckled when the SUV pulled up and opened the door for her.

She glared the whole way to the house.

As I opened the door and she hesitated, I smiled a little to myself. Aubrey was weighing the situation. Her mind worked a lot like mine, she calculated more than she consciously knew. Our night had ended with me wanting to fuck her on my own terms.

I still did.

It wasn't going to be today though. We needed better ground to start on, as much as I hated to admit it. I worked through my fucking rage from the night before and chalked it up to the fact that I wanted her to respect our history just like I did.

Our history wouldn't allow me to just take her wherever.

I wouldn't fuck her on another man's bed for the first time in years out of respect for our history. In return, for the future, history would go the fuck to bed and we'd get closure when this was all said and done.

I worked it all out. Or so I thought.

She didn't know my theory or that I looked to form a better base between us, and that made her jumpy. I could see the goosebumps on her skin when she passed me in the foyer. Her breath hitched when I looked at her lips.

I loved her like this.

I wanted her guessing, needing, and hopefully at some point, begging.

"There's toothpaste in the … "

"I know where Jay keeps his toothpaste."

"You know where he keeps other things too?" My tone shouldn't have been accusing. I knew their relationship was platonic.

"You're such a child, even when you know there isn't a reason for it." With that, she disappeared down the hall.

My apology was the Advil and water I put on the granite counter when she turned the corner into the foyer that opened to the kitchen. "I'm toasting some bread for you."

She leaned on the counter and slid the Advil to the edge with one delicate hand. Over the edge it went into the other and then right into her mouth. She eyed the water and then mumbled, "You know where Jay's liquor cabinet is?"

I raised my eyebrows.

She sighed. "You know as well as I do a shot the day after cures a hangover."

I turned toward the liquor cabinet so she wouldn't see my jaw pop. "What's your poison?"

"He should still have Macallan in there," she murmured close enough that I knew she was looking over my shoulder.

I blamed our history again as I felt my stomach get yanked to my throat. I grabbed the bottle and spun around to crowd her fast enough so she didn't back away. "This is a big drink for a small girl."

She stepped into my chest, reached those light as a feather fingers to the bottle to unscrew it, and then chugged.

Her bright green eyes bored into mine as she took her time with each gulp. Her pouted lips hugged the rim and her throat craned back. The gulps were small but each one was there to taunt me and with her gaze on me, she did a good fucking job.

"Enough," I snatched it from her.

She smirked and her pink tongue slid out slowly to wipe the whiskey from her upper lip. "I know how much liquor I can handle, Jax."

"I know how much liquor you should be handling."

"Really? And how much is that?"

"None. At. All."

She scoffed and turned to grab the bread out of the toaster. As she buttered it, she mumbled, "You don't make the rules for me."

I leaned on the counter and crossed my arms. "Peaches, you follow rules before there are ever any rules that have been made."

The butter knife shook a little in her hand. She kept her head down and said, "I wanted to fuck you in my fuck-buddy's apartment and then proceeded to spend the night drinking the liquor my homicidal father used to drink. You would be surprised with my lack of rules, L.P."

My jaw tightened at her swearing but I let it go. "Macallan was his drink of choice?"

The butter knife flew into the sink and emerald eyes sent beams of pain my way. "What? You want to ask him about it next time you visit? I'm surprised you've never discussed with him the alcohol he used to get so drunk on. God, the way it just sits on your tongue and in the air like stagnant filth…"

When she took a breath in, I heard the shakiness. I heard the pain.

The problem with me being so close to her was I remembered every fucking feeling I'd tried to bury. I remembered and felt the war she waged in herself because it was the same war inside me.

We hated to love each other. It meant we had to dredge up the memories and the past. We had to be reminded of our demons because we triggered them in each other. It made us the enemy for one another and we fought like hell to tell ourselves we couldn't love that enemy. And we ended up hating ourselves for doing just that.

I couldn't blame that on history. That shit was solely on me.

Ignoring the boundaries I wanted to set, I took her face in my hands.

"Your eyes are the exact same color as his."

She squeezed them shut like what I said physically pained her. "And the difference in them is fucking staggering."

They shot open, curious.

I continued. "His eyes are empty, dead. Your eyes burn with the fire of life, baby. They're wild, sometimes, like a caged animal when you want to break free of some shit standard you've set for yourself."

"Jax…" she whispered like she wanted me to stop.

I just shook my head and kept going. "They sizzle when I touch you, like I'm heating you up. I get lost in every damn feeling you hold in them."

"I can't do this." She started to back out of the kitchen. "Can't do what?"

"This!" She motioned between us. "You and I aren't meant to be anywhere near each other. We can't be friends, and we can't work through whatever is between us. No one is supposed to go through what we did and then be able to live in sync with each other, especially when you add my father, the arsonist, to the mix."

"Isn't that what specifically makes it so we can live in sync? We're the only ones who know what it's like to go through that trauma and survive."

Her shoulders slumped, her little mouth turning down just enough so that her bottom lip jutted out even more. She stared out the kitchen window as if hoping to find some spark of hope there.

She wouldn't.

"How can you honestly think that what we have is healthy or right?"

"I don't think us being together is any of those things, Peaches." Her eyes snapped to me.

"It's just inevitable."

She straightened. "Help me to understand, Jax. If I can understand, I can move forward. I can shake this thing we have or accept it. Or something."

"No." Maybe she wanted me to sugarcoat something but that had never worked before with us. I wouldn't lie to her and tell her we could be healthy and perfect now.

We were a fucking mess, and I wouldn't be able to fix it with the shit I was doing. I knew that, and I had a pretty damn good feeling she knew it too.

Her jaw set. And before I could steel myself, she closed the distance between us, placed her hand on my chest, and slid it up to my neck. Her finger went to my pulse point as she stared up into my eyes. Every emotion I saw in her swirled and collided.

I glanced at her parted lips as she stretched onto her tiptoes to be closer to me. My hands moved to her hips to pull her closer and she came so naturally that I couldn't see past the face that her small body seemed to mold perfectly to mine.

"Why not?" she whispered, her breath on my lips and I could swear I tasted her. Her desperation, her heartache, her desire to be over this hurdle so she could be with me. I had it all there, mesmerizing me.

"Because this is one thing I need to do for you, Peaches. You don't control it and you don't meddle in it. I want you out of it until it's done."

She recoiled from me faster than a rattlesnake that had bitten someone. Our connection broke and so did the damn spell she had just cast on me. "So, this is an elaborate plan of some kind?"

I looked down at my hands, still in the air from holding her hips, and clenched them. I stalked toward her as she backed up toward the entrance of the house. "So, you're using your body to fucking bait me now?"

"Are you calling me bait?" she practically spit.

I stopped directly in front of her in the foyer of Jay's home, her hand on the front door, ready to leave. I let her look up at me to make sure she understood who was calling the shots. "I'm calling it like I see it. You wanted me vulnerable."

"Well guess what, Jax? I'm always vulnerable in this situation because you don't tell me anything about your visits with my father. I talked to him years ago, you know that?"

I knew but I didn't say anything.

"Of course, you knew." She shut her eyes for a second like she couldn't bear the conversation. "I asked him what you visited him for. And you know what he did? He laughed. He laughed so hard, I almost hung up right then. But I asked again, hoping he'd tell me. Can you believe that? I saw hope in the person I hate most in this world because the person I loved the most had left me with no hope at all."

She waited a beat for me to say something.

I didn't. I couldn't. I wanted to console her but knew it wouldn't matter. She would take no consolation except the truth of my visits, and I couldn't give her that.

She sighed. "He didn't tell me anything. He just told me to never ask again and if I did, he'd ignore me. I wrote a few letters, all asking the same question again and again. He didn't answer. When I'd call him, he wouldn't take my calls. When I tried to visit him, he wouldn't come to see me. I find it hard to believe that he'd pull out all those stops unless you were behind it."

I wanted to scream at her for trying any of those things. I knew they'd happened. Frank was candid about her trying to get answers. This wasn't her fight though.

It was mine. And I meant to keep it that way. "Let it go, Peaches."

"You don't get it, L.P." She shook her head as she opened Jay's front door. "I've tried to forget. If we could forget everything…" She looked down and sighed. "I've tried to let it go. To let it go means I have to let you go too. And for some reason, I just can't seem to do that."

She walked out and slammed the door.

CHAPTER
THIRTY

AUBREY

THE CONVERSATION WITH Jax tipped my world onto a different axis. How could I fight him when he'd taken a different direction?

It was like the enemy brought a gun to sword fight. Then, with that gun he said, "Wait, you thought we were going to duel here? Silly girl, we'll be fighting in quicksand where you'll never gain your footing."

There weren't any rules or outlines, I found myself stumbling over what to do, how to act, who to tell, and who to trust.

I acted like structure wasn't something I needed, but I found myself feeling more than a little ashamed that I wanted rules, outlines, and structure for this.

"Baby girl?" Rome's voice broke through my thoughts.

He sat across from me at his Heathen's Bar where we shared lunch while he took a break.

"Sorry. My mind's on something else."

"Yeah, and I'm telling you to talk with me about it."

I hesitated, eating another French fry from our almost cleared plate of food.

"You slept with me for a reason."

I squinted across the table at him with question. "What's that supposed to mean?"

"You know I won't judge you."

"That's what you got from me sleeping with you?"

"Well, a whole lot of good ass too," he said loud enough that the waitress who had served us heard and glared my way.

"Loud enough?"

He shrugged. "I'm not trying to hide it."

"Well, what about me?" I whisper-yelled at him. " And your waitress … "

"Let's not worry about my waitress." He steered me back. "Now, you slept with me."

I started to cut him off.

"More than once, I might add. I didn't judge you then, won't judge you now."

I gulped. He was right. I'd been lost, and he'd let me be lost with him in a maze of crazy pleasure and pain. We got off on knowing neither one of us was falling. Instead, we were spiraling in misery, and it felt so good not to be spiraling alone.

I closed my eyes for a second and rolled my lips between my teeth. Then, I whispered, "Do you think he could be worth it all or that maybe there's some justifiable reason he's doing all this?"

"Worth hurting your pretty face? No, baby girl." His dark eyes held mine so fiercely, I knew there was no argument. "Justifiable? Not in my book."

I sighed and slumped a little in my booth.

"It's not my book you should be worried about though. You need to take a hard look to see if you have enough forgiveness in your book for him."

I twirled a French fry between my fingers. "Maybe if I knew what I was forgiving." Because not one other person knew what happened within those prison walls except for Frank and Jax.

"I've said it to you before, and I'll say it again. As a businessman, I have always kept my enemies close enough to know their game. That's all I got for advice, baby girl."

"Ugh, I know!" I'd mulled over a million different reasons why he would visit my father in my head. So many times. So many different ways. Rome had been subject to said mullings for years.

He'd lay next to me, listening to constant rambling until he'd found other ways to shut me up. I'd be forever thankful that he lent an ear when I needed someone to listen and for other things when I'd needed someone to stop listening. "Change the topic, please," I blurted because my mind was going in the wrong direction, a direction that was easier and much more comfortable.

"Yes, please change the topic," Katie announced from behind me.

I smiled as I got up to hug her. "You don't even know what we're discussing."

"I know you two never discuss anything worth shit."

She motioned me back into the booth and slid in as Rome nodded at her. "Kate-Bait."

She rolled her eyes. "Asshole," she responded in the same tone.

Then she eyed our empty plate and whined, "You two already ate?"

"I invited Brey for lunch, not you."

"Brey invited me when I texted her and she expressed extreme boredom at being alone here with you."

"Not true," I chimed in. They just continued death staring each other. I sighed. "Rome can't you just put in another order?"

"No. It's fine. I'm going to eat later ... "

"Mindy! Put in another order for Kate-Bait. She'll do the avocado burger. Medium rare. Extra fries." Mindy glared more laser beams full of hate at Katie while I eyed her for a whole different reason. Normally, Rome wouldn't have ordered her exactly what she wanted.

She hid her look of surprise by snapping at him, of course. "I just said I'm eating later."

"And you'll eat now too," Rome retorted.

"Thanks for the food, Rome. We both appreciate it." Used to their rudeness toward one another, I opted for placating them rather than asking questions. "You finish your errands?"

"Enough of them. Still need groceries and to drop by a friend's." Rome scoffed, but I didn't ask. Katie had a lot of friends. Most of them we'd never met and most we probably didn't want to. She was socially accepted in circles I didn't understand and did things socially I could never do.

Her life was hers. No one judged her. She didn't allow it. But Rome tried.

Her gaze snapped to his when he scoffed. "Speaking of, can I use your truck today?" Her tone was just a little saccharine. "Brey and I will be going to see the kids in a day or two anyway. I'll just keep it till then ... "

"Not happening."

Just then, Mindy not so gently placed Katie's food in front of her and beelined back to the bar without saying a word.

"What's up her ass?" Katie mumbled, already digging into her food.

Then she glanced up at Rome who looked like he'd been caught red-handed. Katie's smirk didn't reach her eyes. "Say no more, Casanova."

My jaw dropped. "Really, Rome? Your waitress?" I whispered. "You could get in trouble."

"Vick and my lawyers made sure I never would when I opened this place. My contracts and handbooks make it very clear ... "

"You used Vick's law education so you could come to work, be the boss, and dip your di—"

"Katie," I practically whined. "I am pulling the middle-ground card. Don't finish that sentence."

She took another bite and squinted at me. With her mouth full, she said, "I hate your manners sometimes, best friend." Then she turned to Rome, "Let me use your truck."

"Just said that's not happening."

"Why?"

"I don't want you driving it. You're a maniac."

"It was returned fine last time, wasn't it?"

I eyeballed her.

"Yeah. Brey drove it last…" He shifted his body to fully face me with a glare. "You let her drive, didn't you?"

"She's weirdly persuasive," I shrugged and grinned.

He looked her up and down. He took his time with her, raked his gaze over every inch of her and if I hadn't known them better, I'd have thought there was more to their story. The sexual tension was so thick, I wondered if I'd missed something. "Yes, she is very weirdly persuasive."

As she took another bite and glared at him, he slid his hand in his coat jacket and retracted it with a set of keys. "I want it back by Sunday—in one piece, Kate-Bait—and my seat better not smell like it was doused in your lotion this time."

Katie coughed on her burger as he got up from his side of the booth.

"Gotta get back to work, baby girl. Stay out of trouble."

"I find it kind of weird that he knows exactly how your lotion smells." Katie knew my tone. The accusation hovered in the air.

"I find it weird too," she said without meeting my eyes.

I let it go because I couldn't begin to imagine what type of relationship my best friends might have under the surface of their mutual hatred toward one another.

CHAPTER
THIRTY-ONE

AUBREY

STAYED OUT OF trouble by studying on my own for the next couple of days. I went to class on Tuesday with my assignment finished, handed it in, and smiled to myself, proud to have completed a full week on my own. I listened avidly as my professor droned on and on. I took precise notes, confident that I could handle it.

That night, I ate dinner with Vick and Katie, one I'd whipped up for all three of us, and smiled as we chatted about what we would do with the kids during our next visit.

"We could cook for them!" Vick exclaimed. She had taken volunteering to a whole new level and was visiting them even more than I had been in the past few weeks.

"Um, they have dinner every night, girl," Katie deadpanned. "That's legit the worst idea ever. They want to have fun when we visit."

"Cooking can be fun. We can make something really nice and then make dessert and decorate it." Her voice rose. "They will love it."

I nodded. "It would be teaching them skills, and we could make it fun."

Katie rolled her eyes. "Fine. But I hate cooking." I laughed and moved to take my empty plate to the sink while my friends made more plans.

This was nice. This was what my summer was supposed to be. Relaxing. Easy. Lighthearted.

We watched a show before I excused myself to get an hour of studying in before I went to sleep.

Rereading my notes for the day reaffirmed that I remembered the material and could apply it without anyone's help.

I was independent and at peace with it. I didn't need Jax.

I didn't need drama.

I needed distance and space to enjoy the rest of my summer.

So, when my phone beeped signaling a text, I thought I knew exactly how the conversation would happen.

> **WINNER:** See you tomorrow at 9. I have 2 hours.
> **AUBREY:** I actually have a pretty good handle on the material this week. I appreciate all your help but I don't think we need to meet tomorrow.
> **WINNER:** Real convenient Whitfield.

I could almost hear the low rumble in his voice when I read my name. I wiggled deeper into my blankets as chills ran up my spine.

Trying my best to hold on to the peace I was feeling that evening and not let him get under my skin, I replied as nice as I could again.

> **AUBREY:** I know we had a rough conversation the other day but this isn't about that. It really has nothing to do with convenience. I just would rather not take up your time when I understand the material.

WINNER: Is that so?

AUBREY: Yes. Thank you for helping me get to this point.

I waited to see if he would respond and after a minute, I smiled when he didn't. We handled that well.

I placed my phone on the nightstand and turned out the light.

A minute later, my phone buzzed. With it, my body zinged with anticipation.

I'd have to work on getting over that, I noted to myself.

I reached over and grabbed my phone. Laying back on my pillow, I stared at the screen.

WINNER: Glad I could be of service. Any other services I could offer you tonight?

Instantly, my day flashed before my eyes. Nice, sweet, at peace. I needed these days. I was in control of them.

I set my phone back on the nightstand, resolving to just ignore him.

I needed to just act like I never read it, continue with my day of bliss.

The more I pushed myself to do that though, the more I considered the text.

What else could he offer me? Especially tonight? I knew he was just trying to get under my skin and make some ridiculous sexual advance but could he have really meant it? Would he follow through if I asked him to?

Not that I ever would. I hated everything he was doing. Hated his secrets, his lies and the way he made me feel out of control.

But I loved it too. So much so that I felt the wetness between my thighs.

Maybe I could keep control and see what he meant. I didn't have to see him. I didn't have to indulge in the emotional rollercoaster of being near him. Just a simple texting conversation. I rationalized.

I snatched my phone back up and typed a response quickly.

> **AUBREY:** What exactly are you talking about, Jax?
> **WINNER:** I got a response. So, you're interested. I
> never label shit between me and you. So, let's just
> start with you telling me where you are and what
> you're wearing.

My stomach flipped. This was wrong, still I didn't hesitate to reply.

> **AUBREY:** In bed. My tank and shorts.
> **WINNER:** Black?

I smiled.

> **AUBREY:** Lucky guess.
> **WINNER:** Have you slipped your hand down those
> shorts yet?

My breath hitched. He was seriously going to do this. I'd never sexted or had phone sex before. Anticipation zinged through me. I slid my hand in slow.

> **AUBREY:** I just did.
> **WINNER:** Bad girl.

My nipples tightened as I imagined him saying just that softly in my ear. My eyes fluttered shut as I brushed my finger over myself with one hand. As my phone vibrated with another text, my body responded to just knowing more of his words came in. I moaned and cracked one eye to read it.

> **WINNER:** Take it slow.

I bit my lower lip, knowing I should slow down but not wanting to.

I rotated my hips into my hand, rubbing myself faster.

I jumped when my phone rang. I swiped the screen when I saw it was him.

"What the hell, Jax?" I answered.

"You're supposed to be taking it slow, Peaches." His voice was gravelly, like he was lying next to me, ready.

"I could not be taking this anywhere," I retorted. "Is that why you sound breathless?"

I didn't answer. I couldn't.

My body hijacked control, took over steering my common sense in the right direction. I veered into enemy territory, not worrying about each emotional landmine we could set off.

My skin tingled as I imagined him touching me everywhere, his hands where mine were, running between my legs in perfect rhythm.

"Tell me you want this, Peaches."

I hummed into my phone, pulling my roaming hand out of my shorts. "I have to go."

"You have to go or you have to come?"

Lashing out wouldn't do me any good. I knew that. So, I tried to grab the steering wheel from my body and veer it back to sanity.

"Stop thinking, Whitfield. Slide your hand back down your shorts."

"Jax, the moment…"

"Just started. I make the moments and rules with us, baby."

"No, you don't." The words sounded weak even to me. My body held the reins and all it wanted was to turn toward Pleasure Road with Jax.

Jax chuckled at my sorry excuse for a denial. "Spread your legs and feel how wet you are. Rub back and forth just like I would for you, baby."

He hypnotized me with his voice like a melody rocking away all my thoughts.

"I want to be around you, next to you, touching you, in you," he breathed. "It feel like I'm making a moment for you yet?"

My fingers slid over my clit and inside myself again. I didn't even contemplate admitting how slick I was.

"That's okay, Peaches. The next time we do this, I'll make sure you answer every question." He stopped for a second and then growled, "I'll make you beg for it, and believe me, you'll like it."

I should have stopped, hung up the phone, and gone to sleep.

Instead, I hummed, "Jax," as my fingers picked up speed.

"Keep it moving. Almost there. You need to unravel tonight, baby, just let it take you. Feel me with you."

My body let go of the steering wheel. I let go of my perfectly planned, relaxing day. I unleashed the ball of unknown in me and just let it roll spontaneously through me.

My orgasm hit so unexpectedly I practically screamed into the phone. It was feral, unhinged, and more ferocious than I'd felt in a long time.

As I came down from its high, my body shook when I realized Jax was breathing heavily on the phone.

"Jax, you okay?" I hesitated to say more. I didn't know where to start. Should I thank him for the phone sex? Ask what he was doing?

"You felt me with you, Sweet Sin. Next time, I sure as fuck will be." I wanted to tell him there wouldn't be a next time, tell him how wrong this was and that we shouldn't do things like that anymore. But he hung up by the time I'd gathered myself enough to respond.

I searched for the feeling of guilt for going that far with him over the phone. I'd never done anything like that in my life. Never even ventured into that type of territory and instead of testing the waters, I'd thrown caution to the wind and dove all the way in.

I should have felt bad, I knew that. This wasn't what a proper girl who followed the rules did. This wasn't what a girl who wanted to blend in and relax through her summer did either.

The idea that I wasn't proper made me smile a little though. I stared at the new décor with pops of color in my room and reveled in post-orgasm bliss.

This wasn't proper maybe, but I needed to be me. If me was inviting the enemy back into my sheets through just a phone call, then so be it.

The sleep that came after shouldn't have been so peaceful but I slept so soundly, I woke up later than usual and wasn't prepared for class.

I especially wasn't prepared for the firing of questions and impossible assignments that came my way. "Ms. Whitfield, you chose to invest in a stock that tanked this week. You have a theory behind that?"

"The market, in general, didn't do well this week. I realize my investments took a hit but—"

"Do you intend to tell your clients that?"

I cleared my throat, not really knowing how to answer. "I, of course, want to be honest ... "

"Honestly, no one cares how the market is doing. They care about what's theirs."

The other students' eyes ping ponged between us. Mr. Gremble— the gremlin—had chosen to target me today. Everyone knew it and everyone was secretly happy it wasn't them.

Trying to get away only mildly embarrassed, I sank a little lower into my seat and glanced around.

So many eyes were on me, staring, prying, making assumptions. My mind started to swirl.

Panic filled my bones while sweat dampened my hands.

Normally, I would have been prepared for an anxiety attack. Normally, I had a very perfectly laid out routine in the morning that prepared me for everything.

Today, I jumped up to just the stupid birds outside my window because I'd fallen into a post-orgasm coma so quickly I hadn't set my alarm.

Normally, I washed my face, brushed my teeth, and picked out comfortable, loose-fitting clothes that didn't draw attention.

Today, I threw on a bright pink tank that I'm pretty sure Vick left in my room because I didn't have time to grab anything else.

Normally, I had a cup of water with toast.

Today, I'd grabbed a cup of steaming coffee that Vick held out as I ran out the door.

My hands shook from either everyone staring or from the amount of caffeine flowing through my blood.

They were waiting for me to reply.

I was waiting for the floor to open up and swallow me up.

I responded with a meek, "I understand," hoping he would just move on. The sweat beading on my forehead told me I might be losing enough oxygen to cause a scene if everyone's eyes didn't shift from me soon.

He didn't move on and the students' eyes didn't shift. Instead, his eyes turned as evil as those little gremlin creatures from the nineties movie. "Do you really understand? Because I'm looking here at your assignment,"—he gestured down at my paper—"and I can only see error upon error. I thought you were going in the right direction, but now I'm sure you're not cut out for this."

I'd never been a victim of word vomit. I actually believed it wasn't a reality until that moment. A ripple of some foreign body surged through me though, and spilled out of my mouth. "If I'm not cut out for it, then why are you wasting your time on me? You want me to do the assignment again? I'm happy to. This exchange though, is a waste of my and the class's time. And, quite frankly, we're your clients at the moment."

His mouth snapped shut, like I'd jostled him out of his evil rage.

Maybe my lashing out had woken him from his evil hibernation.

A few students' mouths dropped. Mine did too.

I knew better. I'd been taught from a very young age not to talk back. As I shut my eyes and moved to start packing up my bag, I waited for the wave of guilt for talking back to sink in. I waited for the panic and hyperventilation to start.

Every single person was staring at me so wide-eyed, I could just imagine what they were thinking.

But the oddest thing happened. I didn't imagine it, didn't even really care to think about it. And when I gasped for a breath of fresh air, it flowed into my lungs so clear and crisp, I actually smiled.

"Ms. Whitfield!" The professor snapped.

I looked up to face him as I slid my backpack on my shoulder. "Yes?"

"Where do you think you're going?"

My spine straightened with a newfound spirit. "I figured you were going to kick me out of class. I'm happy to go."

He humphed. "You're all dismissed. You can thank your classmate here,"—he pointed to me—"for the early day and for the new assignment I'm giving you all."

Everyone started to groan. He held up his hand. "Now, hold on. You all got below a C on your last one. I'm giving you the option, because Ms. Whitfield thinks she can do better, to redo it. Your choice."

As students filed out, some grumbled thanks a lot as they passed but I stood there, still staring at our professor. As he sat down at his desk, he didn't look up but slumped over the papers almost like I'd defeated him.

Every class, he looked menacing walking back and forth in front of us all, like an old bull pacing back and forth, ready to headbutt anyone who challenged him.

Sitting behind the desk though, he looked tired.

I walked up, bewildered with myself for even approaching and said, "Professor?"

He sighed and looked up over the glasses that sat on the rim of his nose. His eyebrows were too bushy for his face and his mouth pursed before he responded. "Yes, Ms. Whitfield?"

"Why did you do that?"

He smiled a little more to himself than me. "You're right. You're my client. You pay to go to school, and you pay to be in my class. I get carried away because I want all of you to actually get something from the transaction. You pay me, and I give you the knowledge to survive in the investment world."

I nodded. "I appreciate the chance to redo my assignment."

He nodded back. "I've enjoyed some of your assignments and your strategy. Don't let me down with this one."

I walked out of the classroom questioning whether or not I should pinch myself. With my morning routine destroyed, and word vomit coming out to play, nothing should have panned out well for me.

I hovered over Jay's name because he would have been the first person I should have wanted to call. I thought about each of those Stonewood boys as I leaned against the hallway wall. They each evoked such a different emotion in me.

Jay was home, my anchor, my foundation. He lifted me up just as much as I did him. He'd celebrate the moment with me but he'd also worry about my panic.

Jett didn't know much about me, yet he knew everything about everyone. I'd never shared anything about my life with him other than my finances he controlled, and then every time I talked to him, there was no doubt in my mind that he was somehow omniscient. If I called him, he'd listen, but I'd never called him for something so trivial like my monumental life moments.

I scrolled to find "Winner" at the bottom of my contacts. Although he was at the bottom, he was at the top, ruling every-thing in my life even when I wanted him to be a mere afterthought.

I highlighted his name and hit the green call button.

It rang twice before he picked up. "Peaches, you told me we weren't meeting today."

His voice sounded detached and far away.

"I know. And we aren't." I clarified.

He hummed like he wasn't paying much attention.

"Jax, what are you doing?"

"Working…"

"Working on your investments or songwriting?"

I heard rustling, typing, and a sigh. "I retired from music. I'm writing code for my app launch."

The word retirement sounded so final on his lips, I wanted to ask why and pry from him the reason.

I ignored the need though. He wasn't mine to figure out anymore. "You don't hire someone for that?" I stopped walking to wait for traffic to pass before I crossed the street.

He chuckled. "I would if I could find anyone I trusted to do it better than me."

There it was again. Jax being king of everything without even trying. "Well, I might need your help with something I thought I could do better than you." My voice was a little more breathless as I picked up my pace to cross the street. I blamed it on that, although I admit the night before crossed my mind. Begging, even asking him for something, ignited a small fire in me.

It must have done the same in him because I heard a grunt before he said, "Ask me and say please, Sweet Sin."

I licked my lips. "I should tell you that you are being inappropriate. But today, I've decided I don't care about appropriateness. Want to know why?"

"You sound like you might tell me even if I say no."

"Yes, I will because today, I overcame a panic attack all on my own by just being me, Jax."

"You had an attack?"

"Yes, well, almost. I was—"

"Where are you?" His voice boomed over the phone loud enough to have me stopping mid stride on my street.

"I'm about to be home."

"I'm coming over."

"What? No! Why?" I stuttered.

"You had an attack! Last time you could barely breathe…"

"You're not listening, Jax!" I nearly yelled back. "You, of all people, know not to freak out and baby me."

I heard his breath, in and out. Then, "Okay, I'm listening."

I let the smile slip from my lips as I relayed the story to him. I unlocked the door to my apartment and went straight to my room. "I probably seemed a little unhinged. And I think I was. It was like I was dealing with…"

You.

Catching myself, I cleared my throat.

He pushed me. "Like you were dealing with? Me?" I cleared my throat again. "Not necessarily ... "

"Why can't you admit it, Whitfield? I make you the kind of crazy you want to be."

"You make me crazy, that's for sure."

He chuckled. "I'll take it. So, it sounds like you still need my help investing."

"I think I can handle—"

"We can study tonight if you want to." His voice, normally so full of confidence, carried a hint of vulnerability. I almost invited him with us.

"I can't tonight. I have plans."

The silence that stretched over the line scraped at my nerves. It would have been polite to fill it with small talk, to delve into my plans, to share more. I sacrificed my most precious formalities for those kids though.

So, my mouth stayed shut long enough for him to concede. I expected a harsh response or a question. Instead, he sighed. "Tomorrow I'm going back to Chicago. We'll have to plan for early next week."

Now, the tables turned. I wanted to ask the questions and pry for information.

Why this weekend?

Was it for work? For play? For visiting purposes? I cleared my throat. "See you next week then."

True to himself, he hung up before a goodbye could be exchanged. I stared at the colors of the pictures I'd hung on my wall for a long while after the call. I teetered on the edge of calling him back and inviting him to go with me to see the kids.

CHAPTER
THIRTY-TWO

AUBREY

THE HARMONY THAT surrounded me when I visited them shouldn't have been anything I wanted to share with him. I shared that with Vick, Katie, and the kids.

Yet, the young girl I'd tried to leave behind, who was so scared of the reservation and embracing her own heritage after my mother died, still lived on here.

He knew that girl and knew my fears. I was conquering them; I'd found a way to love where I came from, even if my parents never exposed me to it, and I enjoyed being a part of it.

He, more than anyone, would understand the gravity of that.

I dressed in jeans and a black button-down. I left my makeup behind. I was going to the place where I was most myself, where happiness met fear and triumphed.

Katie, Vick, and I drove to pick up groceries for dinner. We argued over whether our meal should be healthy or delicious.

Vick, believer in all fairy tales, argued we could accomplish both. We ended up buying chicken, pasta, and broccoli with cabbage. Katie eyed the broccoli and I eyed the pasta.

As we walked into Margie's, Katie insisted, "If we give them broccoli for their first cooking experience, they'll quit on the whole idea."

"Or, they'll be thankful they have energy and aren't feeling bloated," I replied.

Margie swung open the door where Ollie, Rodney, Jasmine, and two kids we'd never seen before waited behind her. "You're early."

"Early's a good thing," Vick pointed out. She'd been back a few times without me, and I could see Margie was warming up to her from the little smirk she hid.

I lifted the grocery bags. "We brought dinner."

Rodney, just shy of ten years old, stood tall. "I can take those bags and carry them into the kitchen."

Katie gave him one bag to take.

Ollie danced from purple shoe to purple shoe. "What's for dinner?"

We all moved toward the kitchen. "Well, let's lay it all out on the counter." I started to grab everything. "You can help us make it."

Margie grabbed some more vegetables from the refrigerator. "Whip these up too."

Katie looked offended along with the children. Ollie blurted, "I don't really like vegetables."

Another boy who seemed her age agreed with her. "Simon and I were hoping for Chinese," Ollie announced.

I moved to start washing veggies and ignored their pessimism. "Ollie, you and Jasmine will help me wash and cut the veggies. And maybe if we work really hard at it, they'll taste good."

Both Katie and Ollie rolled their eyes.

For the next half an hour, we all fluttered around the kitchen in complete chaos.

Ollie and Jasmine were frustrated I wouldn't let them hold the knife to cut vegetables.

Rodney claimed he should be in charge of the stove because he was the oldest.

Vick had to talk with the newest member of the home about not crying when she had to share and Katie almost screamed at Jasmine for barreling into her while she held boiling pasta.

The chaos of cooking with five small children helping was probably close to experiencing a panic attack. I literally thought I was going to die more than once. Yet, when we finally wrangled them all in to sit at the table, the accomplishment was beyond worth it.

"Holy shit. This broccoli is good," Rodney announced with his mouth full.

Katie snickered while Margie laid into him. "Boy, you use that language in my house again, you'll be eating that broccoli outside. And finish what's in your mouth before you open it. You think a lady wants to see that?"

Rodney hung his head for all of one minute.

Jasmine nudged the little girl she sat next to who's name we'd learned was Willow. "You like it?"

Willow nodded but didn't speak. She'd said only a few words since we'd been there, shier than most who'd come through the home.

Katie wrinkled her nose and pointed to the cabbage mixed in with the broccoli. "Be honest, Willow, that isn't really that good."

Willow smiled a little and looked up at Katie. "It's okay."

"Nuh-uh. Vick steamed it until it was too mushy," Katie said back.

Ollie jumped in. "Hey! I helped and I think it's,"—she took a bite and made a face—"just fine."

"Oh really? Take another bite then," Katie egged her on, noticing that Ollie had finished most of the stuff on her plate.

Too stubborn to admit it, she took another bite and tried to say yum but it came out like more of a grunt.

Margie snickered, and Simon chimed in, "The cabbage is terrible!"

Vick started laughing too, and I couldn't hold it in either.

Ollie glared at the whole table. "These vegetables are good, and you all better clear your plate."

Willow looked a little horrified, but Margie corrected Ollie. "Ollie, you know you get to eat as much as you want here. What do I always say?"

Ollie looked to the sky and grumbled, "We don't force-feed. If you want it, eat it. If you don't, leave it."

Margie eyed me seriously. Her little lesson was a reminder that these children came here for refuge, not fun.

"Brey, come sit with me in the living room for a bit."

"She's in trouble," Rodney whispered.

Katie grabbed the children's attention. "You're about to be in trouble too, if you don't help me clear this table. And the faster we clear it, the longer we can play Hot Lava in the basement."

Margie and I walked to the next room and sat on the couch together. She took the long coarse hair of her braid and flipped it casually over her shoulder while she smirked a little. "Well, should we celebrate?"

"Celebrate what?" I squinted at her.

"Don't act like you don't know!" she exclaimed. "Know what?"

"Well, I'm building out the kitchen to four different work stations for the children and adding on an Education Wing to my home."

I almost sprung off the couch. "What? That's amazing!"

She practically vibrated with energy. "It should be done in six months and the contractors are going to work around the children. So, no shutting down for the remodel."

I wanted to ask how it was all possible. Since my mother passed, I'd given annual donations, but there was no way that money could have covered an expansion. I knew my contribution only helped Margie keep things running. I hoped soon enough I would be able to do more, but it seemed someone else already had.

I grabbed her hand and squeezed. "I know you've been hoping for something like this for a long time. The kids will really benefit from it. I'm so happy for you all."

"Well, we have you to thank."

"Me?"

"Well, we will thank that pretty boy, Jay, one day when he comes back to visit but he wouldn't even know we were here if it weren't for you."

My heart stopped and then restarted. "Jay did this?" I whispered.

"Of course, he did. I'm convinced he thinks that Ollie is his long-lost spirit child."

A laugh bubbled out of me. "I'm so glad he did this."

Margie slapped her hand onto her thigh. "Well, me too. With everything, I'll have to have you look at some numbers, but I might be able to expand further in a few years."

"Why more expansion, Margie? You keep saying you can't handle much more."

Her omens for the future scared me and probably the children even more. Without Margie, they had no place to sleep sometimes, no meals in their bellies other times, and no safe haven to rely on.

"Remember the first day I started showing you each child's file?"

My gut clenched at the memory. Like a Rolodex, each child's file flipped through my head—abuse, addiction, neglect.

I nodded my head, too full of emotion to speak. "Children are resilient. Your mom was too."

"She tried her best." I looked away as I said it. Her best would have been leaving my father behind, trying to escape that fire without him.

Margie studied me. "Your mother was one of the strongest girls I've ever met."

I rolled my lips between my teeth to stop from contradicting her but she must have seen the disbelief in my eyes.

"She came to this little house one morning hurt pretty bad."

I squinted at her, not knowing this story and curious about what Margie knew.

"She didn't talk about it with me, but she'd been beaten and the blood on her pants, well…" Margie sighed and shrugged as the wrinkles on her face deepened. "Your mother helped clean her own clothes that very day, and we went on as if nothing had happened."

Each word landed like a brick in my stomach, weighing it down with the gravity they held.

Memories of pleading with my mother to go back to her childhood home jackhammered into my thoughts. I'd cried more than once, telling her nothing could be worse than staying with my father.

My mother stood firm, saying we couldn't just leave my father and go back to where she grew up. She told me things could always be worse.

I shook my head, not wanting it to be true. "Why are you telling me this?"

Margie shrugged. "This place is for kids. I need to expand so there can be room for women too. Everyone should have a place they feel safe."

I didn't say anything after that. I couldn't. My mind raced, trying to reevaluate everything my mother had gone through, how she'd stayed with my father, how she'd never gone back to her childhood home. I wondered if, for her, he was the only safe haven she'd known.

Afterwards, we sat in the living room listening to the kids in the basement. The giggles and screams about hot lava reinforced their resilience and their ability to stay innocent.

***

THAT NIGHT, I stared at the colors I had added to my room. I tried to imagine my mother standing there, smiling. I wondered what she would be had the world not been so cruel to her. Would she have let her long hair dance in the wind? Would she have spoken the words of her heritage and shared stories of what it was like to grow up on the reservation? Would she have really lived, bold and bright like the colors in my room?

I tried to imagine her like that. But I couldn't. The tears that fell for her disappeared into my pillowcase and I wanted the weight of Margie's words to disappear that way too.

I called Jay and told him everything. He listened but didn't know what to say.

I didn't know what to say either. I just knew I needed to tell someone about my mother.

When he couldn't find a way to cheer me up, he persuaded me to drive with Rome and the girls to Chicago that weekend where he'd be ironing out some financials with Jett.

"We'll go out. I'll take you to my new favorite restaurant."

I nodded like this was what I needed. "That sounds great. I definitely need to see Jett while I'm there too." I cleared the anxiety from my throat. "I could see Jax too."

"You *could* see him or you *want* to, Brey?"

"I know I should define this for you," I said.

"You shouldn't do anything for me, babe. You should do it for yourself."

I sighed. There wasn't an easy way to define the barreling heartbreak that I saw coming from a mile away. It was wrapped in a tall, beautiful package that made me want to melt with pleasure half the time and scream with rage the other half.

I saw insanity written across my head in the mirror each morning and still couldn't define the relationship I was getting into.

"What if I said I am trying to be honest with myself?" And I had to be because for the first time ever, I started to realize my mom hadn't been honest with me about so much. For so long, I based my feelings on that dishonesty. My past, my views of my mother, my idea on how I was raised had to be rewritten, and I had to start with honesty.

"Sounds like we need to talk over a drink, not over the phone."

"Can you be easygoing, fun-loving Jay without worrying while I'm there, please?"

"After we have this talk over that drink." I smiled. "I miss you."

When we arrived the next day, Jay had rented hotel rooms for each of us.

As I unpacked in my suite and looked out over Chicago, the city pulsed with life.

In the distance, the Stonewood Tower's rippling glass windows resembled waves reaching into the sky. It dwarfed other towers and stood as tall as the Sears, like a guardian watching over everyone—a king, reminding them all who ruled.

I shivered, thinking of how Jax emulated the same reaction in this city. This was his territory, and I hadn't let him know I'd walked into it.

When Jay sent a car for me so I could meet Jett at Stonewood Tower, I weighed my options. Jax would be there too. I didn't think I should ambush him and show up in his office, but what if he didn't see me at all or what if he wasn't in? Then, there was no point in burdening him.

On the other hand, Jay could have told him I was coming, although Jay never really got around to telling people half the things that were going on.

I opted to let it play out. We were friends. Friends in a gray area leaning towards something more but, if anything, that was casual.

Casual. A word I never thought I'd end up hating.

CHAPTER
THIRTY-THREE

JAX

THE ALGORITHMS DROVE me through the roof of my office, to the damn edge of my building, and nearly off to the crowded street below as I worked on them.

I was missing shit.

I knew it, and I couldn't reformulate it well enough to fix it.

I shoved away from my desk and grabbed my phone, frustrated enough to want to lash out at someone. That usually meant calling some woman I could rage fuck and leave, but after running circles around Aubrey for the past month, I could only picture her.

I dialed her number, wanting to hear her voice and grate on her nerves a little. She didn't answer though.

Jay popped his head into my office just as I was rolling my chair back to switch gears to look at my stocks. "Hey, you know where Jett is?"

I looked at my calendar. "He's in a meeting with marketing for another hour. And what the hell are you doing here?"

"Got a few days off and had to run some moves past Jett. Plus, I miss my girl."

"You're dating someone here?" I was half listening to him as I read through some of the financial gains we'd made over the past month.

"Only girl I've ever had is Brey."

When he said her name, my body jumped to attention a little too quickly. He knew he'd pushed the wrong button because he was smiling like a son of a bitch when I glared at him. "Fuck you, Jay."

He laughed.

I shook off the way he was trying to rile me. "You flying to see her after you talk with Jett?"

"Nope." The word popped out of him like he was excited to answer me. "She needs to get out more. My driver should be bringing her to the building in an hour or two to see Jett."

"Your driver? What do you mean your fucking driver is…"

He backed out of the office, smiling, and slammed the door before I could finish.

"His driver?" I repeated, muddling through it all again and feeling something a lot like jealousy stirring in my gut.

Why the hell hadn't she answered and why the fuck was she getting picked up by his driver?

As if on cue, I received a vague text from her.

> **PEACHES:** In town to see Jay. Maybe we'll run into each other.

Maybe? She barely acknowledged that she was in my town, and now she thought that maybe we would run into each other?

"Maybe," I grunted and shoved back from my desk dramatically.

I undid my suit jacket and whipped it onto the chair. Unfastening my sleeves, I rolled them to my elbows as I made my way to the elevators.

The elevators had been an extreme addition of this tower a few years back. I'd been a year into investing with my father when we remodeled.

My father pushed for conservative, I pushed for innovation, domination, and perfection. He and Jett had given me control of the look and feel of the lobby and elevator, knowing investors wanted something sleek and young.

The waterfall that cascaded around the elevator created an illusion of moving through water. The clear view out of the elevators was only one way as the elevator appeared like a dark bullet flowing through the water faster than most did.

It represented our strategy.

I thought it represented my lifestyle too. I thought I flowed through each of my experiences efficiently, smoothly, fluidly and stealthy. I detected those around me from within those elevator doors. I had access to what I needed–always. My FOB gave me access to floors in this building that not even my father had access to.

I entered the lobby and the crowd near the elevator fell silent. They knew not to continue a private conversation in front of me. Young, driven, and very aware, our staff represented the best in the industry. This hustle and bustle of Stonewood Enterprises, I loved. It always vibrated with ideas and people so determined to implement them, you could almost taste their drive. I should have nodded politely to put them at ease but Aubrey and her "maybes" made me feel every damn thing but polite.

I sat down in the leather chair much too expensive for the lobby and angled my stare toward the door.

I waited for what I was sure was hours and tried to focus on the atmosphere I'd helped create. Here, I wasn't regarded as a celebrity. Here, I was the boss who made everyone enough money to implement their dreams.

So, witnessing how they all shifted, knowing their boss sat in the lobby waiting for something or someone interested me. Some looked nervous, others amused that they were seeing me as a human rather than their elusive boss who waited for no one.

And I was human enough to admit time dragged and scraped along, almost making me bleed with impatience while I waited for her.

Time screeched to a complete stop when she finally walked through the revolving glass doors. Wearing a white dress that cut close to being revealing at so many different angles, I saw her stop to crane her neck upward as if she was measuring how big Stonewood Enterprises really was.

Sky's the limit, Whitfield.

I took in every inch of her from afar. Her hair was down in waves. Men and women looked her way. She drew attention in that stark-white dress, especially with the plunging neckline that cut pointedly down her chest, showing off her cleavage. The material was snug over her entire body, accentuating everything I wanted. I was sure men looked, contemplated, hoped they could have a word with her.

Her stilettos clicked across the floor as she made her way toward the elevators but they stopped when I stood. Her eyes widened as she looked at me looking at her.

"White dress today?"

She shrugged, not making an effort to say a thing as she raked her eyes over my collared shirt and slacks.

I placed my hand on the small of her back and felt the tension there, like she wasn't sure she wanted to see me. It shouldn't have bothered me so much. I should have accepted she had her issues and I had mine, we were separate people leading separate lives.

Instead, I slid my hand to her upper elbow and steered her to the elevator. When I stepped on with her by my side and turned to see a few of my employees starting to follow, I stepped closer to the door and waved my FOB over the light.

Each of them stopped. Eyes shot to one another, they looked away, down, anywhere but toward me.

When the door slid shut to move to the designated floor the FOB signaled, Aubrey mumbled in a small voice, "Nice party trick. They all that scared of you?"

"Whitfield, it's respect, not fear."

"Hmm."

"What's that mean?"

She looked up at the glass ceiling of the elevator and around her until her eyes fell to me. "Back in your work attire, I see."

I smiled, watching the numbers count floors as quickly as they were supposed to.

When the doors opened, I didn't turn to enter my penthouse, just backed up as I watched her taking it all in.

She moved her line of sight to the floor-to-ceiling windows and her jaw dropped. Mesmerized by the city skyline and lake, she flowed into my living space. When she reached the window overlooking the city, she sighed like it was a masterpiece.

I came up beside her, smoothed my hand down and up her back to rest right on her neck. I pushed my thumb into one tendon where I knew most of her tension gathered and massaged as her eyes darted from building to building and then to the lake.

She tilted her head to give my hand better access. "Jax, I can't take my eyes off it."

"Hypnotic, I know."

Her neck tensed again because she knew damn well I wasn't talking about her view, I was talking about mine. My eyes only saw her, alone in my penthouse.

I buried my fingers further into her neck to chase that tension away. "How do you look away?" Her brow was furrowed like she thought she would be lost in the view forever.

Stepping in behind her, I whispered into her ear, "I put something in front of me that's better."

My hands slid over her hips as I pushed up against her ass.

She gasped when she felt how hard I was. "I have to meet Jett at one, Jax."

"And I finally have you near a bed that's mine, Whitfield."

She started to turn to face me but I grabbed her wrists and shoved her hands up above her onto the window.

I bit her ear. "This is nonnegotiable, Sweet Sin."

Her ass ground into my dick before she whispered, "We don't have a lot of time and this isn't us getting over anything or being friends. It shouldn't be happening."

I chuckled. "You sounded like you were ready for it to happen the other night on the phone."

She groaned and wiggled her hips again. "Keep your hands on that glass, Whitfield."

She nodded and I let go of her wrists to explore her body. "This fucking dress…"

"It's terrible, isn't it?"

"Terrible because every man wants to fuck you in it."

The slit in the back of the skirt gave me enough access to slide it up just enough that she didn't have much space to move freely but I could slide my hand between her thighs.

"Why the fuck aren't you wearing panties?"

"Jax…" she sighed as I rubbed her clit and felt how wet she was for me.

"Answer me, Whitfield."

I rolled her clit between two fingers and pinched. "Oh, God," she moaned.

I smiled, liking how out of control she got right when I touched her, how I could draw her attention to her lack of it. "If you can't answer the fucking question, I'm happy to stop."

She panted and blurted out, "Panty lines. The dress is tight and…"

"Too fucking tight," I ground out and whipped the zipper down her back with the other hand. It loosened enough for me to wrap my arms around her shoulder and slide my hand into her bra.

When I pinched her nipple, she shook like she might combust. I pulled away.

"Jax!" she yelled and snapped her eyes from the view to me. They were so fucking green in that moment, I could have written a song about the damn vividness of the color.

I almost stopped everything to try to capture that damn look, this woman, with words in a song. That scared me enough to shake me into commanding what I knew would be a moment I'd never forget.

"Take the dress off so I can see what I do to you."

Her lips rolled between her teeth and her hair slid over her shoulders as she grabbed the sides of the dress and slid it down over her hips. It fell to the floor and she was left with a white lace bra and her black heels.

"Leave the shoes on, lose the bra." She didn't move. "What about you?"

I unbuckled my belt, unzipped my fly and took my dick in my hand to stroke it in front of her. "That's all you get, Sweet Sin. If I want to take my clothes off, then I will. You, on the other hand, will do what I say."

She glared at me but I saw her eyes flick to my cock and her nipples pucker. When I glanced down at them and arched a brow, she crossed her arms over her chest. "Is this what you mean by putting something better in front of your view? You bring women here and just command them around like you own everything in this city?"

I smiled and stepped up to her, knowing this was her attempt to throttle the conversation enough to get some control back.

I reached around her and unsnapped her bra.

Before she could say more, I crashed my lips into hers and my hands flew everywhere. I wanted to touch and taste every part of her. I yanked her hair back so I could get better access to her mouth and she arched into me, letting me have the control she'd wanted.

Deep down, we worked in sync like this.

We were two chemicals that bonded perfectly—my control and her surrender.

I yanked myself back, wanting this to last as long as it could. I spun her again to look at the view and placed her hands up on the window again.

This time, she resisted with a tremulous plea, "People can see us, Jax. I'm naked."

"And you're mine. You do what I say if you want to come."

When she whipped her head around like she wanted to accuse me of something, I just glared back and snaked my arm to her front where I slid my hand between her legs again. "You're so wet. You want to stop just because someone might catch a glance of you out the window?"

She moaned but rolled her hips as I slid one finger into her and wrapped my other arm around her to pinched her nipple just hard enough that it pebbled.

"This is wrong, Jax. We should be in a bed."

I let my dick slide back and forth between her ass cheeks and then over her wetness. "Does it feel wrong?"

She choked on whatever she was about to say and gasped as I slid two more fingers in. I pumped them against her G-spot while rolling my thumb over her clit.

"Mmm, it sounds like you like wrong."

Her pussy pulsed as I said it, and I licked her neck.

"Tell me, Whitfield, do you like people seeing you come? You like me finger fucking you here?"

"Jax, please."

I still loved hearing her beg as much as I used to. So, I kept the same rhythm, knowing she wanted just a bit more. She met my cock with a roll of her hips and arched her back so much, I almost lost what little control I had left.

When she moaned like she'd reached her limit, I bit down on her neck and picked up the pace, rubbing her harder and twisting her nipples close to the point of pain.

Her body convulsed, pushing back into me as she screamed. I let her ride my hand long enough for her to come down off her orgasm and felt her muscles relaxing all around.

When her hands began to slide from the window, I slid my hand from the small of her back all the way to the nape of her neck and leaned in to tell her we weren't finished yet.

I was starting to realize we would never be.

CHAPTER
THIRTY-FOUR

AUBREY

"**W**E'RE NOT FINISHED YET**," he said low into my ear from behind me.

My whole body, and probably even my spirit and soul, shivered in anticipation. Even if I'd just experienced the best orgasm and quite possibly the most passionate moment of my life, my body wanted more.

I needed more.

Somewhere along the way, my body parted from my mind and decided Jax was the ally, and common sense was the enemy.

Now, it seemed to be in survival mode, ready to tap into energy reserves just to keep him close, to keep experiencing him over and over again.

My body rebelled and aligned with the enemy. I was an addict, feeding off Jax as if he were a drug.

The situation went from bad to worse when I spread my legs further apart, like I wanted him to continue.

His hand slid up my thigh and rubbed the inside of it with his thumb. Back and forth. Back and forth. Like he used to do so many years ago.

The touch triggered me. "Jax, if you want to fuck me, just do it."

His hand left my thigh and before I could ask what he was doing, his whole body overtook me when he wrapped a hand around my neck.

While I gasped for air, he thrust so hard into me, I just barely caught myself before slamming into the window.

He didn't pull out but rolled his hips as he tightened his grip on my neck and used his other hand to push my back further down. "Fuck you like this? That what you wanted?"

His cock stretched me so much, I almost whimpered. If someone were watching, I knew it would look bad. He had me bent to nearly a ninety degree angle in front of a window, while he just barely let me breathe, fucking me just the way he wanted.

I had no control in the situation, I was at his mercy and his disposal. Yet, it was the most liberated and alive I'd felt in so long. My heart pumped blood under his thumb on my neck, and I swore it pumped stronger than it ever had before. My skin tingled where he pushed at my back, and I could feel his breath on my shoulder, the air around us shook with tension.

I could feel every little thing.

The colors of the cityscape and lake vibrated to life in front of me.

The world was brighter, louder, and so freaking beautiful.

When he pulled back and loosened his grip on my neck, I sucked in deep and it made me feel even more alive.

When he slammed his cock into me even further this time, I swear I felt the blood rushing all the way down to my toes in my pumps.

Together, we lived and burned brighter than my life could ever be without him.

He rolled into me harder but loosened his grip to get an answer, "You like this don't you, Peaches?"

"Yes, yes, God, yes."

He pulled out of me and spun me around to face him.

I leaned against the window and took every inch of him in. The man, whether he would ruin me or not, was the perfect specimen.

He'd trumped every other male in the world with just the way he looked at me. The dominance and hunger in that stare was enough to make me sacrifice everything.

His breathing had picked up enough that his chest expanded under his dress shirt over and over. His cock hung from his pants, bigger than I could remember it being and so hard I licked my lips. I knew firsthand that wrapping my mouth around it wasn't a chore.

He grabbed it and pumped it once in front of me. "Keep staring and I'll make you do more than just that."

"I want to do more," I said, without even thinking. He moaned. "You're starting to drive me crazy."

"Just starting to?" I questioned as he stepped close again, smoothing some of my hair behind my shoulder.

He grunted. "You know I'm already crazy fucking insane when it comes to you." He gripped the back of my thighs as he lifted me.

I wrapped my legs around him. When he thrust into me this time, he spun so that his back was against the window and I could take in the view while he ravaged my neck and pounded into me.

The lake constantly shifted from each wave and the skyline stood tall with little movements all around it. I lost myself in it, got swallowed up by how enormous it all was and how small I must have looked in it.

He'd choose this over me and over anyone. Anybody would. With that thought, he pushed me over the edge again as his hands gripped my ass when he came in me.

My world spiraled down deep into a place where only Jax and I mattered, where I lost my ability to talk sense into myself or think logically.

Jax nestled into my neck. "Bed?"

I closed my eyes and wrapped my limbs tighter around him. "Mm-hmm."

He carried me, without removing himself from me for a second to his bed. As he did, I took in the sleek lines of the penthouse, the granite countertops, the marble tiles. I noted every black-and-white picture, meticulously hung symmetrically throughout. "Did you decorate?"

He stopped mid-stride and glanced around. "What? You don't like it?"

"Well, it's beautiful, of course."

He chuckled and bounced me a little on his hips by squeezing my butt. "You choosing to be polite when my cock's still in you, Whitfield?"

I left one arm around his shoulders but moved the other to poke him in the chest. "I'm being nice, you ass!"

"Nice?" He surprised me by slapping my butt cheek and continuing to walk to the bedroom. "I'm going to start punishing you for being nice."

He threw me on the bed and that was the moment we both realized the mistake we'd made.

His cock stood to attention in front of us both like we hadn't just had sex. As I stared, I was ashamed to admit I got wet all over again even knowing what I did.

"Shit, Peaches, I'm clean. I swear…"

I closed my eyes to shield my embarrassment as I scrambled to sit up and gather what pride I had left. "Have you been tested since you slept with Isabel or whoever?"

He buckled his pants back up and I scrambled to wrap the gray quilt he had over his bed around me. "Are you kidding me?"

"It's a legitimate question, Jax. Just last week, I saw a magazine at Walgreens that—"

He stepped up and grabbed the sheet I'd tied at my chest to undo my tie. "You know damn well those magazines don't mean anything."

"What are you doing?" I practically yelled over him and scrambled to retie the quilt.

"And I could ask you the same question about your dear friend, Roman, but I'm not." He grabbed both of my wrists to hold them hostage under one hand while he untied the quilt with the other.

I struggled, but it was no use.

He looked at me pointedly. "I'm not asking because, either way, you belong here with me." He ripped the quilt from my body. "Naked, in my bed."

The cool air against my bare skin felt like vulnerability as goose bumps formed all over. I didn't shiver or shrink into myself though.

Standing in my heels before, he drank in every inch of me, and my body discovered a new addiction. Jax couldn't pull his eyes away to dominate or calculate his moves. He looked ravenous and starved, and I knew his appetite was just for me.

I slid my hands to my hips and his eyes trailed my exact movements, when I cleared my throat, his eyes met mine in a tumultuous sea of blue. "We have to lay ground rules if we are going to keep doing this, Jax."

He took a step back like he needed the space to operate. "Fine. You have a minute to lay out whatever the fuck you want."

His tone had my thighs rubbing together. "If we sleep with someone else, we need to at least get tested before—"

"Not happening. You with someone else while we're doing this…" He growled and ran his hands through his hair. "Don't do it, Whitfield. I don't handle jealousy well when it comes to you."

"Jax, be logical," I tried.

He stepped up to me so his dress shirt lightly rubbed against my breasts. "Fine. Logically, I'm territorial of you. Even though it was six years ago since you were exclusively mine." He unbuttoned his shirt standing against me, his knuckles rubbing my torso.

I shivered.

Then, he pulled the shirt from his shoulders, and I got a look at the expansive, muscled chest I'd spent so many nights laying on so long ago. "Logically, I only want to fuck you even in the midst of fucking someone else ... "

I gasped at his admission but he kept stripping, unzipping his pants again.

"Logically, the idea of you fucking someone even if you are thinking of me makes me see red, Sweet Sin." He dropped his pants and pushed his body against mine to walk me back into his bed. "Logically, you're mine and I don't share."

"Jax, that's not logical at all."

He hovered over me and smirked. "Are you on birth control, baby?"

"Yes, and I'm clean but—"

"Minute of ground rules is up." He plunged into me again.

The aftershocks of what we'd done hit hard minutes after coming down from another explosive orgasm solely because a ringing sounded throughout his house. When I looked at him, he just shrugged and said, "Answer the phone, Alice."

"Okay, it's your brother calling most likely about your last text," a woman's voice responded.

I eyed him with questions. He whispered, "New app we're trying." Then louder, he asked toward the ceiling, "What do you need, Jett?"

"I need you to release my client so she can come work over her investment portfolio with me."

I shot up in bed, feeling exposed and embarrassed all at the same time. I couldn't figure out if his voice was coming from the ceiling, the walls, or some device. Jax's hand went to my hips to steady me and he pointed to a little speaker installed into the wall.

"Jett, she needs to reschedule."

My eyes bulged. I couldn't possibly cancel on Jett. I knew how busy he was. Clients waited months for a meeting with him, he was highly sought after.

I glared at Jax but he didn't glare back. His eyes held a look that didn't waiver, didn't bend, and the look was so serious, I knew I would crack.

"Aubrey, you there with my brother?"

I scrunched my nose and squeezed my eyes shut wanting to die from embarrassment. "Yes, I'm here," I basically whispered and then wondered if he could hear me mumbling into the pillows.

"You want to reschedule?"

Well that answered the question of how much he could hear. I tried not to rustle the sheets at all when I replied, "I think I will have to. I am so sorry for the in—"

Another voice cut in. "You rescheduling our dinner and night too?" Jay's voice sounded somewhat dejected, but also like a warning.

I could feel my cheeks turning red. I jumped from the bed and started looking for clothes. "Of course not! I am just on my way out of here. Jax and I were just talking about my investment project. Time got away from me. I can meet you both in five minutes."

Jett answered this time. "I'll fit you in later this afternoon. Just come to my office when you get a chance. You can talk with Jay later about the relationship you have with Jax. He seems to look like he needs an explanation. Anyway, I have to go, I have another meeting." With that, Alice announced that the call had ended.

"How can he possibly have another meeting when he was supposed to ... " I trailed off somewhat baffled.

"You'd be surprised how often Jett double books."

I found my dress and started zipping it up. "Seems unhealthy."

"Or driven."

I didn't argue because no one could argue work ethic with Stonewood men.

Instead, I gave him a look that I hoped conveyed exactly what I felt. They all needed rest, to be healthy, to be taking care of themselves.

"I don't work half as much as him."

I shrugged, "Okay."

"I haven't seen you disagree with me like that in years."

"I didn't disagree."

"No, you placated me without sharing your true feelings."

I sighed and looked over at his view again. "It's a beautiful place to work a lot if you're going to do it."

He stood and came to look at the view with me. "If I worked less, would you come to see me more often?"

I raked my hands through hair, feeling guilty that I'd ditched my meeting and was condemning myself for not feeling worse when I eyed Jax, still bare chested next to me. "I didn't come to see you. I should be meeting with your brother."

He smiled. "Next time, you'll come to see *only* me."

I groaned because his voice sounded so damn gravelly, I almost leaned into him. "No, this should stay casual, Jax. I know we said things a moment ago…"

"Things I meant."

"You mean them right now, at this moment, but later it won't be the same," I said it, hoping it wasn't true, and knowing it needed to be all the same.

Talking to Jett and Jay had burst our little bubble.

We couldn't do this, not again. Not with what he did, where he lived, who he was, who I was. We were so far apart from compatible, it seemed ridiculous to even consider it.

"I could have said those things to you a year ago, in high school, today, tomorrow. The time wouldn't matter." His voice shook me from my thoughts.

"The timing always matters, Jax. Our timing will never be right. This could be perfect for us. You and me, getting over each other by keeping it casual and—"

"I'm already starting to hate that word," he groaned.

I wrung my hands. "You have your demons, and I have mine. We couldn't possibly do well tied to each other exclusively. You have to know that, considering all your relationships."

"What relationships are you referring to?"

"Well, Isabel is a perfect example." I turned away and started for the door, not really wanting to talk about her at all. Thinking of him with someone else struck something feral in me that I wasn't proud of.

"She works my PR and knows me having a girlfriend works well for the media. We've never been exclusive and no feelings are involved. We're nothing." He grabbed my elbow to turn me and stop my beeline for the door.

I glared, weighing his words, wanting them to be true and knowing it didn't matter at the same time.

I'd never be able to deal with the PR. Or the media. Or him visiting my father. "It's fine if it's something. That's what I am saying. What we have is nothing."

He stepped back as if struck with the finality of my words.

I continued trying to convey my point. "What we should have is a casual, no-strings relationship and beyond that, hopefully, we're friends and getting over whatever we were under in the past."

He flexed that chiseled jaw like he was grinding steel between his teeth. I almost winced.

"If you think this is casual—" He trailed off as he stared into my eyes.

We let the silence take over, he knew our chemistry didn't need him defining anything more.

Everyone wants to believe they can overcome that type of chemistry, that they can listen to reason. I physically felt nauseous as I tried to do just that. My body just rebelled as if it knew the only thing it needed to survive was Jax.

"Why are you fighting this so damn much?" He ran his hands through his hair and left it sticking up as he took a step closer to me. "Just stop thinking about it and see where we go." His last word was a whisper. "Please."

I whispered back, "How? How can I see where we'd go when where it went before wrecked me? You go to see him still, Jax. And every time you go, it nearly kills me. There are so many unknowns and so many questions."

"Then ask what you want to know. The wheels turning in your head never help. So ask, Whitfield."

"You've never been willing to answer … "

"Try me," he replied.

Even I was surprised when I retorted, "I don't want to." His eyes narrowed, "Why?"

I closed my eyes, embarrassed. Honesty was difficult. I was starting to understand why my mother never shared some parts of her childhood with me.

When faced with the ugly reality, it was hard to admit that I'd lied to myself for so long. I'd acted like I wanted to know what he was doing with my father but that wasn't the truth.

When I looked at him, I knew I had to be honest. "Because I'm afraid of the answers. Or afraid you won't answer at all, and then I'll be stuck imagining the worst like I have for years."

"What if I said it's almost over?"

I sighed. "Then, maybe us being casual will last until then."

"Then what?" he pushed.

I shrugged. "Are you doing something illegal with him? Will I hate you after it's done?" My question was a whisper.

"It's not illegal." He held my gaze. "And, I don't know."

I nodded but didn't attempt to respond because my throat closed and my eyes watered. I'd thought of talking to him about this for so long, and for some reason it felt wrong and crushing.

He sighed and the fight in his eyes was there again, warring with itself. "Peaches, you had this childhood where you met the enemy of your life early on. You overcame that monster."

I shook my head. "I didn't."

He reached out to touch my cheek. "You did. You overcame him every day by surviving him and being there for your mom. I met my worst fear and that monster when I was eighteen, running into that fire. Before that, I'd only been scared to let my dad down or scared my mom would ground me for some shit. One day I was living an easy life, the next I was standing between you and death."

I nodded like I understood but I couldn't understand that struggle because mine was so different. I was still struggling, trying to figure out if I'd been there for my mother or made it worse.

"I chose to save you." He hesitated for only a second. "I chose to let him die too. It just ended up being your mother who we lost instead."

I shook my head, trying to relieve him of the guilt. "No, you just acted in an emergency, Jax. You told everyone how you—"

"I lied." He drew out those two words to make sure I heard them. He didn't stutter or hesitate.

I shrugged, "So what?"

When he realized he wasn't going to get more of a reaction from me, his eyes widened. "I lied, Whitfield!" he practically shouted. "I left Frank to die in that room. I did it on purpose."

"I know."

He stumbled back. "You don't know. I'm saying I *decided* he didn't need to live. I fucking *wanted* to kill him."

His admission was one the cops and my father's lawyer had looked for but had never received from him. He never, ever admitted to anything when called to the stand or asked by the press.

I placed my hand on his chest and felt his heart thundering. "Father always kept the keys on him, and you've never—not once—done something without calculating the odds. I knew, Jax."

"But that summer, you never said anything."

"I didn't care." I corrected myself, "I don't care."

He narrowed his eyes at me. "Part of me is fucked up from that."

I rubbed his chest wanting to soothe him but not having the right words.

"Fucked up not because I was capable of it but because I didn't accomplish it."

"Does it make me fucked up that I still want him to die too? That I still want to conquer him in some way after all these years?" I whispered.

He sighed. "You don't have to conquer him, Peaches. I don't want you fucking near him. I want you to forget he exists."

It was my turn to sigh. This Jax I rarely saw anymore. He was calculated when it came to his emotions, so much so that people thought he didn't have any. I knew though, he wanted to protect what he loved, not thinking of anything more or less. "I never asked you to do that. I didn't want that from you ever. I just wanted—"

"I know," he whispered, like it pained him. "It wasn't just about knowing you could move on without facing him because I couldn't. It started out like it was about you, and now, it's an addiction to bring him to his knees, to leave him with nothing."

His words spiraled around me. My mind spun too fast to keep up with all the emotions, yet the one I could ultimately decipher out of the mix was doubt. "Jax, that's not possible."

His eyes snapped to mine, and in them, I saw a fire so blue and so cold, it would burn whoever looked long enough at it. "Yes, it is."

I wanted to push more, argue more, be consumed by him more. I just wanted more.

I grappled to find the control I needed though. The look in his eyes told me I wasn't getting more and I needed to digest what he'd given me anyway.

As I zipped my dress, I heard him from behind, "You always hated fitted dresses like this."

I sucked in a bit of breath. "You remember that?"

"You were so stiff at that charity event back in high school. I couldn't understand why. I thought you were scared to disappoint your parents. Turns out, you were just uncomfortable in the dress."

I hid my smile as I grabbed the last of my belongings. "I'm sure I was a little scared too."

"Were you scared to come here today?"

"I'm always a little scared to face you." It was an admission I wouldn't have given him before.

He grunted. "The dress is lethal. It somehow hides and shows everything."

I smiled outright this time. "Mission accomplished."

"One day, when this is more than just casual, I'll burn it." Casual rolled like acid off his tongue.

"*If* we become more than casual, Jax, and that's a big if." With that, I walked out, knowing his jaw was ticking behind me.

CHAPTER
THIRTY-FIVE

AUBREY

JAY WAS THREE beers in, and I was sure Rome had just as many when we met up with them later that evening at a Korean Barbeque restaurant. With the atmosphere, I knew someone had moved something around to get us reservations. Not one person eyed Jay like he was a celebrity which meant most people who dined here were either always in the company of them or were themselves celebrities.

I normally would have felt uneasy and out of place but Vick and Katie started our celebrations back at the hotel.

While we'd gotten ready, I'd told them how I'd ironed out my finances well enough that I could make a sizable donation to Margie's too. Although Jett had outright disagreed with the substantial figure in our earlier meeting, calling it a terrible investment that would never pay off, I wanted to celebrate. It wasn't meant to be an investment, it was meant to take care of those kids.

Katie and Vick wanted to celebrate too. Or they were just happy to be in a big city, getting ready for a night out.

I let Vick blow out my hair, so it looked somewhat untamed and wavy as it fell down my back. She'd done my makeup while Katie worked on cutting the back of a shirt so her outfit looked ravaged.

Vick's dress glittered and shined just like she wanted.

I opted for an all-black halter top that essentially only had two ties holding it together in the back. My front was covered but my back was bare. Paired with a tight skirt and heels, I could blend but still look a bit sexy.

When Jay saw us, he whistled and Katie plopped down by him to kiss him right on the lips. "I missed your obnoxious ass."

Jay looked affronted. "Kiss me again and I'll forgive you for calling me obnoxious."

Rome rolled his eyes and sipped his beer like he couldn't stand either of them.

I sat between Rome and Jay at the round table. Jay put his arm around me and I said, "We all missed you."

Vick clapped her hands together as she looked around the table, "How does this work? Do we get to grill the food ourselves?"

Jay chuckled at her excitement. "Yes, but we have to order it first."

The waitress beelined for our table, and Jay put in for a round of drinks and enough food for all of us.

When she left, Rome asked what I'd been wondering, "Your brothers meeting us out?"

Jay's eyes snapped to mine like he had questions. "Neither are coming to dinner. Jax wanted to know where we would be later." I must have tensed a little because he followed up with, "I don't have to tell him where we're going though."

I shook my head as all my friends' stares landed on me. "We're fine! The more, the merrier."

I took a huge gulp of the wine the waitress had brought over. No one said anything. They all just watched me.

"What?" I caved.

"You're blushing," Katie pointed out.

"Blushing like you do when someone would catch us—" Rome started.

I held up my finger. "Do not finish that sentence, Rome."

"Or I'll punch your dumb ass," Jay finished, glaring at him.

I wanted to roll my eyes. Instead, I shrugged Jay's arm off me and glanced around the table. I took a deep breath and gave them all the confession they were waiting for. "I might have ... probably ... slept with Jax again."

Vick jumped up and screamed while she pointed at me, "I knew it! You love each other!"

Jay started coughing on whatever he was drinking and Katie shushed Vick for me.

"We don't love each other, Vick." I denied and meant it. The word was reserved only for what I'd felt for Jax a long time ago back in high school. Now, thinking I could ever love him again culminated a fear so stifling, I could barely take my next breath.

Jay massaged my neck like he knew I needed comfort. He leaned in. "We should talk someplace more private."

"Fuck that," Katie blurted. "She put this out on the table for all of us. We're discussing it together."

Then, she looked at Rome who hadn't said a word. She elbowed him and said, "Right, Rome?"

He glared at her. "There's nothing to discuss."

Katie's eyes widened. "Are you kidding? You slept with her for over a year and you don't have an opinion about her sleeping with the guy that wrecked her?"

The left side of his mouth turned up but he didn't look happy. "Sleeping with someone doesn't mean I have an emotional investment in who else they sleep with, Kate-Bait."

She glared and didn't say anything.

Vick broke up their silent-glaring conversation. "Okay, aside from the mess happening between those two,"—she gestured between Katie and Rome—"can we focus on what Brey is going to do to keep Jax around?"

Katie started to respond but I slammed my hand on the table. "Stop."

Jay's hand fell from my neck as he eyed me warily.

"Rome is right," I announced as Katie blew a raspberry. "There's nothing to discuss."

Jay started to object.

I cut him off. "No. I'm serious. We're keeping it casual. You're all right. I never got over him. I didn't get closure. So, I need this."

They were all silent, none making eye contact.

Vick was the only one brave enough to ask the question. "Is closure really what you want? To keep it casual and let him go?"

"I think it's what I'm capable of right now."

Jay sighed and I think that sigh was how the table universally felt.

He raised his glass. "I guess we'll toast to you getting closure and us getting seriously fucked up tonight."

Rome lifted his beer bottle, fully on board. "To that last part." We all lifted our glasses and downed our drinks.

Jay took over then, salvaging the night by announcing we all had to do a round of shots. We drank probably the same amount we ate before we left for the club. The decisions didn't get any better as the night continued on.

The club Jay took us to couldn't compare to a small-town bar or even a college town's best night spot. It radiated money, luxury, and a loss of inhibitions. The crowd of clubgoers moved in waves to the beat of the music. They let the music consume them, flow through them, it owned their bodies. With alcohol in my veins, I felt myself move with them rather than shrink away.

Once we made it to the stairway to get to the VIP section, security took over pushing away some fans of Jay's. We entered a room that was wall-to-wall glass panels, giving us a perfect view of the crowd. We felt a part of it but were above it, literally and figuratively.

People in the VIP area were recognizable figures in one way or another. Jay waved us over to introduce two tall, gorgeous men, both with dark curly hair and brown eyes.

"Caden, Bastian, meet my crew from back home." He lifted his chin to introduce all of us. When he got to me, his arm wrapped around my shoulders, "Brey's my on-and-off lover according to tabloids."

I tried not to roll my eyes as I reached my hand out to shake both of theirs. "I'm a childhood friend. Probably the only one he'll have left soon enough with his personality."

Bastian's hand held mine while he searched my eyes for something. I wasn't sure what. "It's a pleasure to meet someone who knocks Jay, or any Stonewood, down a notch for a change."

Rome snorted near me and grumbled, "Or all Stonewood men."

I glared at him and glanced back at Bastian who still inquisitively looked at me like I had the answer to a question he hadn't bothered to ask me. I smiled and pulled my hand away, his gaze remained on me as we moved on to meet others and get a drink.

Vick and Katie immersed themselves in conversations, but I found myself staring out at the waves of strangers, moving, flowing, partying together.

Bastian walked up behind me. "A sight when we're up here and they're down there, huh?"

I didn't answer at first. He was right, but I hated the feeling that I wasn't a part of it. I didn't want to be separate from the crowd or hide for once. I wanted to feel the energy they all had and lose concern for everything else.

Maybe it was taking a leap with Jax or maybe it was the idea that my mother never took a leap away from my father, but I wanted to push my limits. I wanted to lose my control a little.

I turned to Bastian, wanting an escape. "Why are we up here?" He squinted a little at me. "You mean why aren't we down there?"

I glanced back at my friends who were all enjoying themselves. "Sure," I shrugged. "Shouldn't we get lost in the crowd like everyone else?"

His lips lifted slowly, like warmed molasses, as a smile formed across his face, and just like that molasses, my body warmed to him. "Finally, someone who's speaking my language."

He turned to yell to Jay, "I'm taking this girl down to the real party."

Caden groaned from the seat he was sharing with some blonde. "Do you always have to do the opposite of what our security asks?"

Bastian chuckled and told me to ignore him.

Jay walked over. "Bastian, my man, I told you she was my girl. He trying to steal you, Brey?"

"More like saving me. I want to go." He eyed me curiously. "You sure?" I held his gaze. "Sure."

He nodded at Bastian and we moved around him. Bastian whispered into my ear as we walked toward the steps, "That was easier than I thought."

Reading Jay was my specialty though. I looked up at Bastian, held up my fingers, and whispered back, "Three, two, one."

On cue, Jay appeared in front of us again. "I know all your secrets, Bastian. Remember that when you're with her. And, Vick!" he yelled, searching our tables. She popped up from Caden's other side, smiling wide. "Go with Brey to dance for a while."

She glared for a second, and I protested by saying I already was going with Bastian, she rolled her eyes like she knew this dance by heart. "Got it," she singsonged and wove her way toward us.

Bastian was laughing at this point, so I decided not to make more of a scene by rolling my eyes.

When Vick met us at the stairs, he swung both his arms around both of our shoulders and proclaimed, "I'm not going to complain in the least about having you both here with me."

Adopting his carefree attitude worked for both of us as we laughed at his blatant flirtation.

Security eyed Bastian more than once as we passed, like they weren't sure they wanted him to move into the crowd with us. As the beat hit, the lights strobed faster, fast enough that making out each other's faces got more and more difficult.

We moved with the wave of people and Vick grabbed each of our hands to throw them up in the air. She whipped her hair and immediately a guy was next to her while Bastian moved to wrap an arm around my waist.

The next beat hit, and we smiled, jumping into the frenzy that it was.

He spun me. He dipped me. He lifted me. He danced and danced with me.

Vick leaned in to say, "Jay would tell me to save you and rip you away from him, but no one wants to be saved from that. He's to die for."

On one slower song, Bastian leaned in, "Okay, I concede. You could dance forever, and I need a break. Come to the bar with me."

He pulled me through the crowd and people's eyes shifted as they moved toward him. It registered then that he probably wanted off the dance floor for a very different reason. When someone yelled his name, I saw it register on his face.

He was well-known in some circle I wasn't aware of. His fame caught up with us, and I hadn't realized we weren't as protected as we should have been. When he made a sharp turn into the crowd again, I followed quickly at his side. We got lost in the anonymity of the masses long enough to get to the bar where he placed me right on a stool. He wedged himself between me and a man who didn't seem at all interested in him.

The bartender appeared in front of him immediately. "Bastian, you braving the masses already?"

He waved off the bartender's comment and ordered a beer while I looked at him. His forehead had just the slightest sheen, his dark curly hair was disheveled but his eyes danced like he'd been ready to play in the crowd all day. "What'll it be, little dancer?"

The crowd closing in brought it all back, and the drink I didn't ever want slipped from my lips instinctually, "Macallan on the rocks."

The same look he'd given me in VIP, he gave me again. "I've decided something about you."

As the bartender walked away to make our drinks, I replied, "Really? What is it you've decided?"

He put his hand on the back of my stool and leaned in close enough for me to smell some subtle mix of soap and cologne. "You don't belong in Chicago."

I smiled but it was a sad one. His words walloped a firm reality back into place for me.

I didn't belong there, I didn't belong in the middle of a crowd, losing myself. Instead, I lived a tightly-wound, lockstep life that didn't push me from my comfort zone at all. I turned my head to see where my drink was. "You're right. I don't belong here."

He stayed close. "Where do you belong then? I want to know so I can be there."

Butterflies erupted in my stomach and the hair on the back of my neck stood up. My reaction should have been to his words.

I didn't react to other men though.

I felt his cold blue eyes on me from afar and knew if I turned, he'd be heading our way.

Suddenly, mint and sandalwood surrounded me. I felt his abs up against my back as he pressed right into me and leaned far enough forward that his arms enclosed me as he set his hands on the bar.

By doing so, he'd nudged Bastian back, and they stared each other down, neither willing to speak at first.

Bastian, like most, conceded first. "It's never a pleasure, Jax."

Jax didn't respond, and I turned a little to elbow him back and away from me.

His body, hard as steel, just leaned in closer. "Where's your security, Bastian?" His voice barely registered it was so low.

Bastian sort of shrugged off the question. The bartender took that exact moment to deliver our drinks.

Jax eyed mine and connected the dots as fast as only he could. He whispered into my ear, "You all right?"

I nodded and tried to hide my drink. "Of course." I sat up straight and looked at Bastian. "We're all just trying to have a good night out, Jax."

Bastian smirked at me and looked over at the bartender to hand him some cash for our drinks.

Before he could though, Jax spoke loudly across the bar, "The drinks are on the house, Ricky."

Our now named bartender smiled and shrugged at Bastian before he nodded toward Jax and walked away.

I saw Bastian tweak his neck a little one way as if trying to rid himself of irritation. "Leave it to Jax Stonewood to always one up a man even when it comes to buying a girl a drink."

"She's not a girl. She's *the* girl. *My* girl." His words should have embarrassed me but goosebumps flew up my arms and my heartbeat picked up speed.

"Come on, man. I saw you walk in with Isabel."

Bastian's words snapped my eyes to Jax's to see if his statement was true. When he visibly flinched, I tried to stand up but his hand flew from the bar to my thigh and held me down.

Bastian sighed like he didn't want the drama. "What's your angle? As Brey said, we're having fun."

I nodded and started to say I agreed with him, but Jax cut me off. "Go have fun with someone else."

"There isn't anyone else I'd rather be having fun with." Bastian's eyes were on me, and I felt his attraction. If Jax hadn't been there, magnetizing all the attraction I could have in one lifetime, I probably would have felt something more for him.

With that, I knocked back some of the drink and let it burn all the way down. I must have swayed a little on my stool because his arms flexed to keep me steady. Bastian tried again, "Jay introduced Brey and me. I got the rundown on you all being childhood friends."

"Not just friends." Jay enunciated each word and looked at me like I'd disappointed him. "Never were we just friends."

His voice, his stare. Everything drew me to him. And I just knew, us together, we were this magnetic force that repelled anyone else. Jax alone was a force to be reckoned with, but our energy was impenetrable.

Bastian stepped back after a second. "You have my number, little dancer. Call me when this ends."

I gulped, not knowing what to say. My meek, "Sorry," didn't seem good enough.

I reached for my drink but Jax reached quicker and set it two feet from me. "You've had enough."

I glared over my shoulder at him. "How do you know? I could just be getting started."

"Fine. I've had enough of seeing you drink. So, now you're done."

His eyes were a blue so brittle, I thought they might shatter into a million pieces. "I don't answer to you."

He smiled and his teeth looked bigger, meaner, ready to devour. That smile ran shivers down my spine all the way to my toes.

"I didn't come here tonight for you to test and bait me, *little dancer*," he sneered at the name.

"I'm not baiting you, Jax. I'm being honest. I don't answer to you or anyone."

He hummed against my neck as he moved so close to me, I felt swallowed up by him.

His hand on my thigh slid higher, and I sucked in a breath when I felt his tongue touch my collarbone.

When his hand slid even higher, my breathing got shallow. "Jax, this isn't the place."

He bit my neck and whispered, "Humor me."

With those words skittering over my skin, I shivered and didn't think twice about parting my thighs just enough to give him access.

Never one to hesitate, his fingers slid right to my center.

"Fuck, Peaches," he swore swiftly in my ear when he found I wasn't wearing any underwear again.

I rushed out, "The dress didn't allow for it."

"Bullshit," he spit out as his thumb rubbed me back and forth. "You this wet for me or for him?"

I didn't answer, just looked right and left but the dark club lighting hid mostly everything. Jax's figure stood between me and the world, blocking anyone from seeing anything.

My body listened to Jax more than it listened to me. I let myself indulge. My heart raced to the beat of the up-tempo music, and I forgot about my fear of the crowd around me. Jax stole an orgasm from me like an experienced art thief stealing a painting from a museum. No alarm sounded, no one knew anything happened, no one even took a second glance.

I sat there like the hollow statue an art thief would have replaced a priceless solid-gold piece of art with. He'd depleted me of every feeling except ecstasy. When I came down from my explosive high, he was already whispering in my ear, "Go clean up. We're leaving."

I turned to disagree but he'd already disappeared into the crowd.

Without the shield of Jax, I knew I looked disheveled. As the music and the crowd faded back into my view, I saw the bartender wink at me. I loosened my white-knuckle grip on the bar enough to push myself up. I straightened my skirt and tried to smooth away the wrinkles and my embarrassment.

In the bathroom, I patted down my hair. Staring hard at my reflection, I tried not to chastise myself too much. I wasn't a child, and people probably did this sort of thing all the time.

I thought about his hands between my legs in the crowd again though, and the flush on my cheeks, the sparkle in my eye gave just a bit too much away.

Smirking a little to myself, I washed my hands and was about to leave the bathroom when Isabel walked in. Women like her aren't born that way. She had spent copious amounts of hours perfecting her look, her wardrobe, and her character. When she smiled at me, the calculation was evident.

"So, you're the reason for his little speech that he had with me tonight," Isabel stated.

I replied with the truth. "I don't know what you're talking about."

She leaned over the sink and smoothed her hair as if this conversation meant nothing to her. "He reminded me that we're casual and convenient. That I'm only here tonight for the media." She looked out of the side of her eye and smirked at me again. "We've always had a relationship of convenience. I guess it's casual now too, considering he wants to make your history a part of his present life."

Casual.

The word I repeated over and over to him. Casual.

It was what I wanted our relationship to be before I left this afternoon.

Casual.

It was what I couldn't fathom him having with somebody else.

When she said the word now, directly from her lips, it was like pouring acid into my ears. For the first time in a long time, I wanted to tell Jax that he was mine and only mine.

Pride and fear stopped me. I guess my mother had a point in not always being honest.

CHAPTER
THIRTY-SIX

JAX

TELLING AUBREY WE were leaving may have been a little too direct. Asking her to leave though, would not have been an efficient use of anyone's time. She had no other option. I wasn't letting her leave with anyone else.

Decisions had to be made, and I was going to make them for both of us.

When I looked in her eyes, I thought she understood that. If she couldn't avoid me feeling her up in a bar with a crowd of people around her that would normally make her panic, there was no way in hell she could avoid going home with me.

Or so I thought.

The thing about a stubborn woman is she almost always fails to see it the right way. She will fight the inevitable until the bitter end, hoping the pendulum will swing in her favor at one point or another.

Our relationship wasn't structured like a fucking pendulum though. It was a circle, always leading us back to the same point at which we belonged.

We belonged together.

In a bed, if I had anything to say about it.

So, when she avoided looking my way as she entered the VIP area again, I contemplated throwing her over my shoulder and leaving the bar with her that way. Fuck what the paparazzi would say.

Fuck what my brother and Roman would do.

I just wasn't sure the damn skirt she wore would cover her perfect ass if I did just that.

Instead, I watched her disregard our whole encounter as she sidled up to Bastian and Jay. I reasoned that she might be saying goodbye to them at first and I told myself not to get frustrated.

Then, they were ordering more drinks and Jay was spinning her around to the beat of a song. Katie and Vick jumped in for another drink. And another ten minutes passed.

Isabel came to sit next to me. We didn't talk. She just leaned into me as she checked her phone. When Vick approached us, I was hoping she would say the night was wrapping up. Instead, she shouted, "We're getting another round of shots. You want one?"

Isabel looked at me with a bored expression on her face. My face, I know, didn't hide my rage very well as I glared back at Vick.

Vick stuttered, "We're just trying to have a good time. We're trying to make the most out of the situation."

The situation? The situation was that Aubrey needed to stop drinking and come home with me. The situation was very straightforward.

Instead of explaining that to her, I grunted and Isabel waved her away.

"She seems to be a lot of extra work for a man who is so efficient, don't you think?"

She had a point. For anyone else, I would have moved on. Aubrey wasn't anyone else though. She'd been the girl I grew up with, the girl I wrote songs about, and the only one I ever loved.

She wasn't anyone else, she was everyone else to me.

"Do you think I want to discuss this with you?" I glared at Isabel, knowing most people withered under my stare. She was no different.

Her eyes jumped away from mine and tried to focus on anything but the attention that I knew Aubrey and I created in VIP.

No one was immune to that force. I witnessed the glances as eyes jumped between us.

When Rome's stare met mine, neither of us looked away. The silent understanding that we had come to ping-ponged between us. He loved her, maybe not in the way that I did, but it was there. Its presence boiled my blood. My infatuation with Aubrey swirled around in a cloudy, thick mist, mixing with jealousy.

As Jay put his arm around her, it got even cloudier. I didn't want anyone's hands on her, not even my brother's in a platonic way.

I kept watching them until Aubrey finally looked over. No guilt or remorse hid behind her forest-green gaze. When she saw Isabel planted next to me, all I saw was fire burning that forest down.

A stubborn woman shouldn't be attractive. Yet they're fiercely beautiful when they set their mind to something. Aubrey owned me, and probably every other man that could see her.

She stood tall and flipped her dark wavy hair over her shoulder before she took long strides that accentuated her legs over to Isabel and me. When her black stilettos stopped inches from my own shoes, I took my time dragging my gaze up her body.

Her skin glowed under the strobe lights, and her black skirt shifted every time she moved like it was made to mesmerize men. Knowing she didn't have anything on under it, and that it was the only damn barrier between her and every other man that wanted her in the club, had my neck tighter than it had been in years.

"You ready now, little dancer?" I sneered.

She knew she should have never danced with him or even let him have his hands on her.

She squinted her eyes at me and unknowingly swayed to the music. When she replied, her voice was laced with alcohol and a loss of inhibition. "What should I be ready for, Jax?"

I shook my head. "Do you think I normally waste my time on issuing commands that don't get followed? When I said we were leaving, I thought it was clear that I didn't want to wait for you to socialize for half an hour."

She glanced at Isabel. "Isn't it obvious to you that I'm not going home with you? I haven't looked your way or talked to you for thirty minutes."

"That's never fucking obvious anymore, Whitfield. From now on, the expectation is that we'll always leave together." I realized too late that my voice boomed out louder than I had intended it to.

My brother and Rome showed up at her side almost immediately. Katie and Vick weren't far behind as she crossed her arms like a petulant child.

She'd created a family, an army, some sort of cavalry that would have been intimidating to everyone else. Probably formidable, and almost impenetrable in most circumstances.

They just didn't know they were dealing with a nuclear bomb of a force so strong not even I could overcome it.

One minute she stood with them and in the next, she flowed like a siren up to my chair to lean over me. I caught a hint of alcohol with the sweet smell of cinnamon I always longed for.

"This may be casual but it is not a relationship of convenience." She practically spit the last word and as she said it, her eyes were so frustrated that even I, the man who loved seeing her lose control, wanted to soothe her back to calm.

Both our eyes held one another's until hers snapped to Isabel's as if to lay the culprit of her anger out on the table.

Isabel didn't back down. She protected her image and mine at all costs.

"This night is over, Whitfield." I let my steely gaze run over each and every one of her soldiers behind her.

Vick took a step back immediately, but the others stood their ground.

I pushed off from my chair to stand, and Aubrey stumbled

back. The alcohol caused her to wobble a little more than she had intended it to.

Katie righted her immediately.

"If you're night is over, go home." Aubrey shrugged like her statement wouldn't feel like sandpaper on an open wound for me.

I was sick of the bullshit and drunk or not, she damn well knew it. "Don't make me carry you out of here."

"I'd love to see you try." She lifted her chin, so emboldened by the alcohol in her veins that she didn't realize it would only take my one arm wrapped around her to carry her out.

When I took a step forward, Rome started to move but Jay moved faster. Stone-faced, he stood toe to toe with me.

"Don't make me go through you, little brother." Isabel grabbed my bicep. "Hey, not here."

Jay didn't say a word and he didn't move.

Aubrey leaned to the side to peer around Jay. Her eyes seemed to focus for a minute and they widened at the scene. She stepped around to Jay's side and whispered, "Maybe I should just go. No one needs a scene."

"Jay," I tried to use my most consoling voice. "You know this is unavoidable. I'll take care of her."

His jaw worked and his muscles flexed. It pained me to see this struggle he had just because I might be interested in his best friend.

Aubrey patted his arm while glaring at me. "We'll call you when we get home."

Still holding his ground, he commanded, "Breakfast with me tomorrow morning. I'm not taking no for an answer."

She nodded with a love and trust in her eyes I would have bled for as she looked at him. "Okay."

He backed off and nodded to the others for them to back off too. He led the forces that protected her, I guess, because they all turned to leave.

Isabel squeezed my bicep again, reminding me that she'd be another problem of mine soon enough. "So, I guess I should leave with you both." Her voice was resigned like it was the only option. "I'm fine with a threesome but it won't be the best PR."

Aubrey had moved close enough to hear Isabel's words and her skin paled to a porcelain white as she blurted, "I think I'm going to be sick."

I swore and shook Isabel off while wrapping my arm around Aubrey. She curled into me, fitting right where she belonged. I started weaving through the crowd and waved Isabel off to go home.

She knew the drill and probably wouldn't be irritated other than with the fact that she would have to deal with the media questions regarding me coming with her and leaving with another woman. My driver pulled up at the side of the club just in time for Aubrey to slump so far into me that I didn't think she'd be able to walk.

I scooped her up and carried her the last ten steps to the SUV. No paparazzi caught us, thanks to my driver's maneuvering, and we endured a half silent drive while he made his way back to my penthouse.

Out of the darkness, her little voice floated over to me, "He used to drink so much, Jax."

I tensed, knowing exactly who she was talking about.

"How?" Her question shot out angrily. "How could anyone drown in it so much and know they had everything? She gave him every single thing. And for what?"

Tears streamed down her face as she looked at the city lights and they danced over her features, accentuating each slant and curve I had memorized.

I put my hand on her thigh and rubbed circles, soothing her the only way I knew how. She sighed like it was enough for me to just touch her, hold her, be with her.

"I thought she ran back into the fire for him, you know? All this time I didn't realize he was her saving grace." Her whispers didn't make sense. I didn't ask. She'd drank too much and was haunted by a day that had changed us all.

So haunted and drunk that, just as we pulled up to my building, she opened her door and vomited most of the alcohol she'd consumed into the street.

CHAPTER
THIRTY-SEVEN

AUBREY

SLEEPING IN WITH a hangover never worked for me. The sun had just crossed over the horizon right as I cracked my eyes open. Immediately, I tried to take in more of my surroundings. My body verged on being smothered with heat because another body was wrapped tightly around mine.

My back to his front, he spooned me with his large arm curled around my waist and his leg even enveloped my thigh. I turned my head over so slowly to take in the tanned skin of his bicep. Licking my lips and squirming a bit under the blankets, I reveled in each muscle before I inched my gaze up to his face.

Terrible man he was, his smile and eyes were as bright as the stupid sun.

I groaned and tried to roll away, knowing his chipper attitude would grate all the wrong hungover nerves.

He gripped my hipbone to stop me from moving from his side. "The moment you sit up to get out of this bed, that headache is going to hit you like a semi-truck."

Part of me wanted to jump up and fake completely good health.

My stomach and brain wrenched in pain at the idea though. "I have to get up sooner or later, Jax."

"Sure. Just wait a minute." He pulled me close and ran his hand up my bare hip. I looked down and saw that I was wearing only a baggy shirt of his. His hand roamed around under it while he nestled into my neck from behind. "You smell like me."

I huffed, knowing I probably smelled like booze. And other things.

"Oh, God," I mumbled and winced. He ran circles on my ribs like he did my thigh and some of the embarrassment melted away before I asked quietly, "Did I vomit in your car?"

He chuckled, slid his hand down to my butt and smacked it lightly before he rolled away from me and got out of bed. "You just missed. Of course, you got some on your top and in your hair."

I looked at my hair, confused.

"Baby, I washed you up before we went to bed."

Warmth spread through me. So much so, I contemplated how it would look if I succumbed to spreading my legs for him that very minute. "You took care of me after how we acted in the club last night?"

"Yeah," he answered with a sort of confused look on his face. Then, his chin tipped down. "And I always will no matter how we act anywhere."

I swallowed and pushed the blankets off me. The room was heating up, and I had to get out of here to clear my head. To figure things out.

I froze when I felt his eyes tearing up my skin, making invisible marks like he wanted to devour every inch of me.

"If I could, Whitfield, I'd tattoo my name on every inch of your skin."

I gulped and slowly got up, knowing the headache I had was about to get worse. When I stood, I grabbed the nightstand and winced. "It's probably more like an airplane hitting me, a big one. Not a semi-truck."

He grabbed some water and Advil for me.

"Now,"—he said as I hydrated by emptying the whole glass—"we run."

"Oh, no." I started to back away but he grabbed my elbow and pulled me toward his closet.

"Oh, yes. We have breakfast with my brother in an hour or two and you have to shake some of this hangover."

I glared at his back while he went through a massive closet where everything seemed lit perfectly and organized conveniently. When he pulled out running shoes and work out clothing my size, I glared harder. "I'm not wearing some other women's workout clothes." He smirked, and I said, "Are those Isabel's? Because they won't even fit me."

He grunted away my pettiness and shoved the clothes into my chest. "They're your clothes."

"I never left any here."

"I had some brought here this morning."

"Who would…how?" I asked. "Money," he responded.

"How convenient." I didn't mean to drag out the word but it just rolled off my tongue that way.

He ran his hand through his hair and sighed. "I shouldn't have brought Isabel last night. I did it to rile you and ended up riling everyone."

I narrowed my eyes at his confession because Jax never really admitted to being wrong. I snatched the clothes from him, waiting a couple beats.

"You did say this was casual though."

"Hmm. There it is. Your reasoning."

Instead of responding, he started to strip in front of me. I'm not proud to say I stared for a little too long.

He caught me and grumbled, "Put on the damn clothes before I decide to take advantage of you in my shirt instead, Whitfield."

I looked down, somewhat appalled. "You're kidding, right? This is the worst look ever."

"You're in my clothes." He took a step closer. "You smell like me."

I clung to the clothes he'd pushed into my chest as he moved in enough that I had to crank my neck to look up at him.

"And I bathed you last night." He wrapped his arm around my waist so we were close enough that I could feel his excitement. It was long and hard enough that my body, although hungover, shivered at his touch.

Embarrassment swept swiftly through me. I looked down at my hands gripping the clothes. "Can we never talk about that again?"

"Oh, we're talking about that night again."

I succumbed to the need to roll my eyes even if it was rude. "I don't see why. It was terrible." I pulled away from him. "Can you turn around or leave the closet?"

He smiled at me like I was an idiot. "Why?"

"You know why! I need to change."

He scoffed. "I'm not turning around or leaving. I've never let you hide from me. I'm not starting that shit now."

My foot itched to stomp. "Jax, I was an embarrassment last night. I need some privacy to get myself looking presentable again."

This time he snorted. "You always look too damn presentable, if we're being honest here. And the privacy you can expect to get from this point forward with me is zero."

I wanted to throw the clothes in his face but figured it wasn't worth the battle. I ripped off the shirt quickly and I pulled on the panties and sports bra that somehow fit perfectly. Then yanked up the black yoga capris. I threw the workout shirt at him for good measure and said, "I don't need that."

His laugh boomed around the closet and echoed its way into my heart. "All right. Suit yourself," he replied as he pulled on a long sleeve shirt. We both put on shoes and moved together like we were made to do just that.

He looked so happy here with me that I thought somehow, some way, maybe we could work.

That scared my heart into making my mind not think for the first part of our run. I pushed myself hard to keep up with him but halfway through I grabbed his arm to stop him and bent over.

I didn't have to say anything when I vomited into a nearby trash can.

I groaned before going to push my hair out of my face only to find Jax already held it out of the way.

I glanced his way and mumbled, "Thanks."

He nodded. "Happy our runs are starting to have a pattern of you purging your mistakes from the night before."

I shoved a little at his chest and took in the park we'd run through. The morning was cooler than I'd anticipated as I walked ahead of him.

He moved in right behind me, rubbing up and down my arms. "You're cold now, aren't you?"

I hated that he was right. I should have worn that dumb shirt. I wasn't admitting a thing though.

I shrugged and kept walking. When I turned to find the culprit of the rustling behind me, I saw Jax in glistening glory without a T-shirt on. His abs were more defined every time I looked at them, and the sweat exaggerated the V that dove into his pants.

Suddenly, he shoved the shirt over my head. "Oh my God, Jax. I can put on a shirt."

"Might be true, but I'll maul you in the park if you keep looking at me like that."

My laugh burst out around us, and I found my heart absorbing that echo so much that it couldn't silence any thoughts anymore.

"I wanted to be casual with you because I figured that was all I could handle," I blurted out.

He eyed me with surprise.

"I'm trying to be open and honest. I found out not too long ago that my mom wasn't always open about important things.

Finding that out now has me realizing I need to be better about not repeating the same mistake."

I waited for his response while the wind rustled around us and the sun spilled through some of the leaves. One little sparrow hopped across the pavement in front of us and I focused on how it pecked at the ground for just a little food.

He nodded. "It's something we both need to do. We can't forget. Whatever force there is between us, it'll destroy the fucking world, Whitfield, before it lets us forget about it or be casual." His words rumbled out of him. "We're inevitable."

Inevitable.

He'd said it before in describing us. And so had I.

Inevitable.

It used to scare me with its finality. It used to be the end for me.

Inevitable.

Now it seemed solid, concrete, reliable. It signaled an end but also a beginning.

"I guess I agree, even if that means overcoming all of our history and the baggage we're carrying with it," I replied.

He stopped walking and turned me to face him. "You mean that?"

I cleared my throat and looked down at my hands. "Whatever we are, even if it's a casual thing, I don't want you being casual with anyone else. That force you talk about, it will destroy whoever you're casual with in the future if it's not me."

His eyes twinkled. "If another man calls you 'little dancer' or touches you the way Bastian did in front of me again, Whitfield, there won't be any force needed for me to dismember him slowly and deliberately."

We finished our run and I got ready with Jax doing work I didn't care enough about to listen to. Every step I took in his home lifted me up until I was walking on clouds.

We had issues bigger than mountains, but being high up in those clouds, I thought we could overcome them.

CHAPTER
THIRTY-EIGHT

AUBREY

JAX'S DRIVER DROPPED us off at a little café to meet Jay. I'd asked Jax to let Jay and me have time alone but he knew it meant we'd just be discussing our relationship. So, we walked in together and even as I tried to speed up my walk, he grabbed my hand, not letting go.

Jay's eyes lingered on our hands laced together like it was monumental and people took notice. Or they took notice of their Chicago royalty in the café.

I wanted to curl up under the table and hide. I was thankful Jax had his stylist bring me a flowy black top and skinny jeans that made my legs look great because I wanted to blend in as much as I could while being in their attention-grabbing presence.

Jay crooked one of his large arms around my neck to hug me. He didn't try to hide the anger or contempt rolling off of him when he looked at his brother. "Your ass wasn't invited."

I started to reprimand him but Jax cut me off. "A lot of time has been wasted and I'm not willing to waste anymore. You see her, you'll be seeing me."

He still held my hand and pulled it back just enough that I took a step out of Jay's hold to stand with Jax.

Jay smiled, "So, you'll be spending the whole day with us?"

"If that's what it takes," Jax replied flatly.

Genuine excitement spread across Jay's face. "Great. I intend to take Brey to Navy Pier today." He leaned toward me like we were sharing a secret. "Let's get some food in you, Brey, so your hangover doesn't win today."

I scoffed and wiggled out of Jax's grip to an open table while telling Jay, "I already went for a run today."

Jax and Jay followed me to the table where we fought over what I wanted to drink. Jay ordered a coffee for me first and Jax corrected him to a chai tea.

I corrected them both, knowing that my stomach couldn't handle any caffeine. I opted for water, realizing these two men could suffocate anyone's independence if given the chance. Most women would happily let them, but I found I didn't want to be most women, and I didn't want to blend in so much that I lost myself. Especially when I was just finding out who I really was.

We made small talk until our food arrived piping hot from the wood-fire grill the café boasted. The chic rustic decor mixed well with the lively crowd and made me want everyone to get along.

Surprisingly though, Jay was the one to cut off pleasantries. "So, we all leave tonight. Jax, you have meetings in Chicago tomorrow," he ticked off matter-of-factly. "Brey you'll go back to school, and I'll be back in LA."

I nodded and knew his one-two punch and follow up were coming. I could have counted it down and had people bet me on it. Jax knew it too because he sat there stone-faced with his jaw clenched. All three of us had such a history that the point we were leading up to never really had to be said. It was a courtesy that we even let him finish.

"The problem with me being in LA is that I'll worry Brey will get lost chasing you." He zeroed in on Jax. "And this time, she won't be able to find her way back. I am not fucking Alice in Wonderland and I can't navigate her world well enough to bring her back one more time."

Although his words were true, they hurt when I heard them out loud. Jay had been the trampoline that saved me when I was falling headfirst out a window in my own self-pity. He had babied me back to some sort of life.

Even so, I wanted him to trust that I knew what I was doing and it hurt that he couldn't.

He wanted reassurance that everything would be okay but no one ever got that with love. I knew Jay really did want me to stay safe but he'd wrap me in cellophane and never let me live if he could.

"Jay," I smoothed my hand over his. "Life without really living at all isn't any way to live."

Jax slid his fingers to the inside of my thigh where he rubbed circles. Then, he said the words that seared into my soul, burning away more of my doubts. "Jay, if we could have forgotten each other, maybe we would have. But she wasn't ever okay without me. Just like I wasn't okay without her."

Jay started to say something, but Jax cut him off.

"Everything she does without me is an act, a fucking way to get through the day. I know it because I do the exact same thing. You want your best friend, you get me along with her. And you damn well know it."

Jay pushed his plate away. "You think I don't know that I only get half of Brey when she's mourning the loss of you after you can't fucking pick up the phone and call her? You think I don't know her pain when you go visit that fucking guy in prison with no explanation?"

A couple of people's heads turned our way and I leaned forward to whisper to them both, "I don't think this is the place for us to discuss this. You both need to keep your voices down."

Jax's fingers kept rubbing my inner thigh, yet I felt the tension throughout the whole rest of his body. His voice was low as he completely ignored me and answered Jay, "You never asked for a reason or wanted to know why."

He sounded almost remorseful and resigned as he looked right through Jay. His fingers stopped their circles, like we'd lost him to his thoughts. Maybe I was the only one who could relate or find him again, because the look he had on his face was one I had only seen on one other person. Myself.

His eyes lost their sparkle, their depth, their life. He disappeared as we sat there. Some memory had robbed him of his humanity and his reason for existence. I knew it because I felt the same every time I thought about that night.

Maybe I should have given Jay and myself the satisfaction of waiting him out and making him answer. Maybe we deserved it.

But my soul was intertwined with his, and I didn't want to lose them both. We had to come to each reason in our own time and his reasons haunted him just enough for me to stop the conversation.

"Jay shouldn't have ever asked the reason because …" I turned to Jay. "Jay, it's not your place. I don't need either of you making decisions for me." I threw my hands up, frustrated with it all. "I don't need you discussing me like I'm not here, either. I'm not a fucking fly on the wall. I'm a woman, or maybe still a girl, but I get to be as reckless or conservative as I want because it's my life." I stared both of them down. "Mine. No one else's."

Jay cleared his throat and, with a bit of a sheepish smirk, side-eyed Jax. "So much for the Sass Pot keeping her voice down."

Jax's smile reached all the way to his eyes as he chuckled. "Never fails to amaze me how quickly you can put us in our place, Peaches."

I took a quick sip and ignored both of them patronizing me.

Our conversation came easily after that. Questions weren't answered and reasons weren't given. Our histories weren't explained and our futures weren't mapped out.

I accepted that recklessness. I accepted the pain that would come with it.

For the first time in a long time, I started to believe I could handle it.

CHAPTER
THIRTY-NINE

AUBREY

NAVY PIER EXTENDED over Lake Michigan looking like a proud sort of carnival all lit up and full of fun. It boasted beautiful views of the water and the cityscape, along with rides and shops that provided entertainment for days. With the sun out on a Sunday, tourists flocked there, excited to enjoy the few months of great weather the Midwest had to offer.

Jax glared at Jay the whole time we walked toward the Pier. "This is a terrible idea."

"Get over yourself, man. No one cares about us here."

"I saw two paparazzi on our walk over already," he blurted and then slid his hand in mine like it was the most natural thing to do.

"They're probably just here for the fun too," Jay said, glancing at me.

I mouthed to him that I was fine. He nodded and moved ahead of us to get us through the entrance.

Then, we were off into the chaos. Jay was right, most everyone was too involved in their own day to care that two celebrities were among them—especially the Stonewoods, as they were a normal Chicago sighting.

My best friend stole me away from Jax to ride the big carousel more than once. I giggled uncontrollably when he posed with each of the hand-painted animals he rode. He made me ride the same horse as him until we were scolded, and then we giggled more.

Jax stood a ways off, making calls. The man was working, I was sure, but he smiled our way every now and then.

Jay and I ran on to some of the stands where he made me try on a ridiculous hat and necklace that he insisted I needed. He probably just felt bad that we'd bothered the vendor. So, he bought it and handed it to Jax for him to carry.

We bounced around like kids with no responsibilities and no plans for the day.

As the sun began to set, I found myself at the very end of the pier. Looking back at it, I realized I hadn't worried through my whole time out there. The people, the happiness, the buzz of it all. I found myself enjoying it rather than being scared of it.

Had I missed all this by laying out my life and trying to blend in? Was my relationship with Jax a hyped up version of this chaos? Did I need to dive in and swim through what it might turn out to be?

Jax leaned on the pier's railing, and the wind flowed through his hair just enough to mess it up and make him look like he belonged on the cover of *GQ Magazine*. "We going to ride the damn Ferris wheel?"

We'd avoided it because of the crowd and line.

Jay looked affronted. "Of course, Brey and I are going to ride it. I was saving it for last."

Jax rolled his eyes. "We're all riding it." He looked at his phone and then motioned for us to start making our way there. "Everyone's there. So, let's go."

"Who's 'everyone'?" I asked as I followed him.

He glanced back with a twinkle in his ocean blues. "Just who you want everyone to be."

We didn't wait in a line when we filed up to the Ferris wheel.

Instead, we were ushered over to a waiting area where Katie, Vick, Jett, and Rome waited.

Vick ran over when she saw me and hugged me like she hadn't just seen me last night. "Oh my God! I love this. You're coming in my cart, right?"

A man explained to Jay that we could all go on the gondola together, but Jax had requested that the women have their own. I looked over at him, "Why?"

He just pulled me close and whispered in my ear, "Go enjoy a ride with your friends. After, you're all mine."

I absorbed that look he gave me, like he revolved around me, like I was his center. I took in how my friends buzzed around us and how the sun set on each of their faces. He'd orchestrated this moment like I meant more to him than being just a girl he left behind years ago.

I leaned into him further. "Thank you."

His grin came fast and wicked. "You'll thank me later."

Vick pulled me away from him to step onto our gondola. Katie shooed the guys away and told them to enjoy their sausage fest. None of them fought her too hard though, making me wonder if there would be small talk or talk of me.

I shook off that anxiety as soon as I stepped onto the gondola and looked down to find another worry was the glass floor we walked onto.

"Oh, God!" I exclaimed and grabbed Katie to balance myself against the wave of fear that took hold. "Can this glass hold us?"

"No. They make these gondolas for a drop-through experience where you could fall to your death once you reach the tip top of the wheel," Katie deadpanned.

Vick laughed a little nervously as the gondola started to move. "Seriously, isn't this amazing? We are going to see all of Chicago from above."

Katie laughed a little. "You sound very convincing with that tremor in your voice."

Vick huffed and pulled a little at her white knitted dress. "I'm a little afraid of heights."

I watched as we started to ascend over the pier and agreed. "We stepped on though, so we're committed."

Each of them stared at me rather than the sunshine glinting off the water. Katie asked the big question. "Are you committed?"

"Committed to what?" And she just scoffed because we all knew what she was asking. The ride, all of a sudden, with just them made more sense. Jax was giving them their chance to talk with me privately. Maybe he was doing the same with his brothers and Rome.

Maybe this was his final step.

My blood ran a little cold and shook fear into my veins. "I want to be committed and move forward with him. I'm not sure if we can though."

"Why?" Vick asked immediately. "You two are perfect together. He looks at you like the sun on the water."

The view outside the gondola, the sun shining down on the water, showed what she meant. The sun danced on the surface, making the water gleam like they mingled perfectly with one another, forming a masterpiece that was too extravagant to capture in one shot.

I turned to Katie and she looked out past my shoulder at the city. "You know I've said it before, I wish I could say something different. I don't know if it will work out. But if you avoid trying, you've chosen to fail miserably by default and then you will never move on. Life is brutal when you live with all those regrets."

Vick lightened the somber thought by adding, "Plus, he's gotta be phenomenal in bed. For that alone, give the happily ever after a go for even the story of it."

I must have blushed because she pushed the subject, "Give us details already!"

Katie grumbled that she didn't need details, to which Vick said she did and jumped a little with excitement.

Our gondola wobbled just a tad and all three of us immediately looked down. Katie's wide gray eyes glared up at us like she was blaming her fear on us. I moved to hold onto something.

The staggering height of being on a pier, hanging from a cart two hundred feet in the sky could humble anyone in the right circumstance.

"So, this is really fun," I whispered like my voice would keep us afloat. "How many times do we go around?"

Katie licked her lips and replied, "One more."

That one, we enjoyed in complete silence. Vick took some pictures while Katie reluctantly helped her pose in a few selfies. I stared at the skyline, reminded of Jax and how he'd added to it.

I could see Stonewood Tower, tall and striking as it stood proudly among the other buildings. I wondered what other buildings they had influenced and as we reached the end of the ride, I wondered how I could influence a man who'd altered something so great.

When the guys met us after the ride, their solemn expressions couldn't be ignored. "Do I want to know what happened up there on that gondola?" I asked.

Jay tried to lighten the mood. "Jax got scared and yelled at everyone the whole time."

Most of our group laughed but Jax's stare bored into me enough that I hung back to walk next to him. "Is everything all right?"

He grunted but didn't answer the question. "I'm heading back to my penthouse. Come with me, and I'll take you home tomorrow."

It wasn't a question but I tried to argue it anyway. "Rome's driving us tonight."

He shrugged and turned to the group. "Whitfield's going back to my place for the night. I'll get her home tomorrow."

I glared and waited for one of my friends to jump in to say he wasn't my keeper but they all happily said their goodbyes. Each of them either hugged or shook Jax's hand as they left us on the pier.

I stood there stunned, realizing that Rome, the most protective of them all, didn't even toss a backward glance my way as he left.

Jax seemed rather pleased with the turn of events and started to walk toward the sidewalk where an SUV idled.

When I didn't follow immediately, he yelled over his shoulder, "I'm not in the mood to drag you to this car, Whitfield. Especially after traipsing all over Chicago for you today. Move your ass."

I stumbled a little to catch up with him. "What did you do to my friends? Why do they trust you all of a sudden?"

He opened the back door of the SUV and folded himself in after me. "Do you really want to talk about your friends right now?"

I stared at him, trying to figure out his angle. When he looked me up and down, I knew exactly the approach he was taking.

I scooted back away from him and crossed my arms. "Yes, I do want to discuss them. Don't change the—"

He leaned forward and covered my mouth with his. I opened for him immediately, not that he gave me any room to back away. I inhaled every part of him that I could. He smelled like damp lake air mixed with mint and everything I craved all the time.

We took advantage of each other for the rest of the night.

The next morning, Alice ruined everything as I tried to tiptoe to his closet. "Jax, Aubrey Whitfield is up and starting her day. Also, Isabel continues to call and won't be ignored for much longer. She overrode your previous command to block all information."

By the time Alice had finished her report, Jax was groaning and stretching. He rubbed his eyes as I stared at the sheet that was dangerously low on his hips, "Whitfield, come back to bed." He patted the empty spot next to him.

Blush rose to my cheeks and goosebumps spread across my arms at hearing his voice.

He sat up. "Peaches," his voice, gravelly with sleep, scraped every nerve of mine in just the right way. "You look cold. Let me warm you up."

As his eyes rolled leisurely down my body, he took in every inch of me as if he owned it.

I wasn't fooling anybody, he did own it.

My body lit up everywhere his gaze roamed. He focused on my neck and I remembered the way he'd licked every inch of it after he bit it. He looked at my lips and they immediately tingled as I recalled how his felt pressed against mine. When his eyes dragged lower, I shook with need. Until I looked down and practically jumped as I realized I didn't have a shred of clothing on.

My hands flew up to hide my face as I backed away into his closet. "Stop looking at me, Jax!"

He chuckled and I heard him moving closer. I whipped around to find something to wear, but he was on me before I could take another step. His arms wrapped around my waist and his length pressed into my butt. "I'll never stop looking at you, Sweet Sin."

I groaned. "Don't you have calls to make?"

He nipped my ear to reprimand me. "I don't have anything to do when I'm with you except doing you. Alice shouldn't have been overrun by anything. I told her to hold all the work calls."

"Well, Isabel isn't always work, I guess." I tried to mask my tone as understanding, but it came out bitter.

"Jealousy suits you, especially when you're naked."

Then, he was sucking on my neck and I was leaning into it like I didn't have anywhere to be.

His hands moved to grab my breasts, and I couldn't tell him to stop.

I wanted him everywhere.

I wanted him on me, in me, around me, and with me all the time.

CHAPTER
FORTY

JAX

PICKED AUBREY UP and put her back in bed. Her dark hair splayed out across my white sheets and her olive skin, tanned from the sun, brilliantly contrasted against the fabric.

One day soon, I'd have to ravish her for hours here. I fantasized about tying her up on this very bedpost and taking her in for hours. Completely owning her, the way she owned me.

Today, I'd settle for just one hour with her before we left. I'd take advantage of her body's willingness to succumb to me even if she was a little irritated that Isabel kept calling.

I took my time kissing her, then inched my way down her neck, nipping at the spot I felt her heartbeat fast.

She yanked at my hair to stop me even though she was flush with need and panting. "I need to get going, and you should probably call Isabel."

My dick twitched at the little green fire of jealousy in her eyes. I held her gaze and slid my hand down her stomach. She hissed when I slid it lower to see how wet she was.

When I easily slid two fingers in her, she gasped.

"You sure you need to go?"

As I rubbed her clit and fingered her, those emerald greens got a little more hazy. Her muscles became a little more languid too, and when she rolled her pussy in my hand, I smiled.

When I moved to take her lips in mine, she turned away. "Jax, it's my impression that Isabel still thinks you have a relationship of convenience with her. We shouldn't be doing anything if that's the case."

"What you've never understood, Peaches, is that I've never had a relationship of any sort with any woman other than you. Everyone I've been with has been you. She'd have your hair or your eyes or say something like you."

She narrowed her eyes.

"They were a way to pass the time, a means to an end. A way for me to feel you even if you weren't there with me." Admitting it out loud jarred the shit out of me but it also made sense.

And now with her writhing underneath me, I knew I wasn't wasting any more damn time. "Alice," I slid another finger into Aubrey as I continued with my command, "Call Isabel immediately."

Aubrey gasped, but the desire for her orgasm overpowered the anger and shock I could see on her face. I felt her tighten. As much as the woman didn't want to admit it, she loved the forbidden, the taboo, and the unapologetic edge this scenario put her into.

Isabel answered on the first ring. "Ignoring me never works, Jax."

"I'm ignoring everything work related right now, Isabel."

"Well, Alice was obviously confused by that, considering I was able to override her programming." The snark in her voice allowed some of her hurt to seep through, and I knew then what I was doing was right.

"She won't be confused any longer." I hovered over Aubrey and stared right into her eyes as I said my next words. "My girlfriend doesn't want me to have any relationship of convenience and I can't imagine her working with someone she's fucked. So, you're fired."

Aubrey gasped and Isabel's voice came through my house speakers loudly as she squeaked out, "What?"

I repeated claiming Aubrey so that she and Isabel knew how serious I was. "My girl is done with our arrangement. I will be sure to provide you with great references."

Isabel started scrambling, talking about the huge aspect of publicity and how she had worked for me and only me for years.

I wasn't listening and neither was Aubrey. I was taking in how Aubrey's cheeks hollowed just a little as she sucked in each rapid breath. When I picked up my pace, she hissed.

I sucked her bottom lip into my mouth and tasted something as sweet as honey on her tongue.

Making out with her, fingering her, bringing her to the brink wasn't nearly enough. I ripped my mouth from hers and licked my way down her body. When I got to her chest, I growled, knowing I'd have to fuck her again before the morning was over. I sucked one of her nipples into my mouth and looked up at her as she tried to muffle a moan.

Isabel yelled over the line, "Jax, are you even listening to me or is your *girlfriend's* pleasure worth making this big of a mistake?"

Aubrey's eyes got wide like she wasn't ready for Isabel to call her out on being there.

I, on the other hand, didn't give a fuck. I curled my three fingers in her pussy and she tightened around them. I lapped at her nipples again, and her body responded to me like always.

She gyrated in my hand, her eyes rolling back as she breathed out, "Oh, God."

I whispered for her sake, "Tell Alice to end the call if you don't want Isabel to hear you."

When I turned my head, her eyes were bold. Somewhere along the way, Aubrey succumbed to us together for everyone and anyone to hear.

I swear my dick got harder than it had ever been in my life, and I refrained from bringing her to a quick orgasm. Instead, I pulled my hand away as I maneuvered my way out of her and off the bed to stand before her, showing her how ready I was to dominate her while anyone listened.

Isabel's voice came over the speakers to remind us that she could hear everything, "I can hear Aubrey just about to get off, and Jax, I know exactly how you look with your clothes off. I can picture everything. So, I suggest you both stop to discuss this."

"Isabel, no one gives a fuck what you hear." I grabbed Aubrey's ankle and dragged her to the edge of the bed. I took my time sliding my hands up her calves, her knees, her soft thighs.

I bent to suck on the inside spot I circled my fingers over all the time. She shuddered and moaned loudly, finally unleashing uninhibited sounds.

I smoothed my hand up her back and then dragged my finger back down her spine.

I leaned forward to ask, "Are you ready?"

Her body purred under me like an engine ready to go. My words only revved the engine more. She nodded her head and some of her long hair fell to the side of her shoulder.

She was going to give me more because we were past holding back. I grabbed her hips and lifted her to turn her around on the bed. I yanked her hips back so that her ass was right in front of me where I wanted it.

I positioned my cock right at her entrance and combed my fingers through her hair before I started to wind it around my knuckles. I gripped the strands and pulled.

"Oh, God." She arched her back and pushed back into me.

Her pussy wept for me to fuck her, but I wanted to hear the words. "Tell me what you're ready for."

She just rolled her hips and moaned louder.

"Whitfield, you want to fuck, then you'd better beg for it."

Her pussy tightened so much, I felt it even at her entrance. I shifted about an inch away, trying to maintain some semblance of self-control. She tried to turn her head to glare at me but I tightened my hold on her hair.

"Jesus, please. Please. Please," she chanted. "Please what?"

"Please, fuck me. Please. Please. Please." She was rolling her back, shoving her tits further into my hand and her ass further into the air.

"On second thought, tell me exactly what you need to come, Sweet Sin."

Aubrey knew what I was pushing her to do. She knew she could either stop what we were doing or completely let go of everything she'd been taught.

Every day Aubrey stepped closer to the line that read unapologetic.

Here and now, with me, was where she crossed it.

As she white-knuckled the sheets, she begged through clenched teeth, "Please stop with the foreplay, I want all of you in me."

I took my other hand off of her breast to give myself some relief. I stroked my dick and told her to look back at me.

The woman submitted immediately, her eyes wide and glassy. I let go of her hair and slid my hand back to finger her more. Her pleading and chanting got louder. She warned me she was going to come with my fingers fucking her and I continued to stroke myself. She was so close, on the brink.

I took a step back right as I knew she would have hit her high.

She swore profusely and whipped around to face me while kneeling on the bed. Her dark hair cascaded over her chest and her eyes burned with an angry fire.

She looked ready to kill me and I would have smiled while she did if that's what she wanted.

"What the hell, Jax? If you want to play games, I'll get myself off."

I leaned forward so my dick was against her clit as I stroked it. I grabbed her hand and wrapped it around me, smiling. "You're frustrated. Squeeze my dick hard and make me feel just how mad you are."

She glared but did just as I told her.

"You want to get off?"

"Obviously," she hissed but kept working me.

"Let's ask Isabel if she thinks it's time."

Aubrey's wide-eyed expression told me she'd forgotten Isabel was still listening but I heard her breathing get faster. She got off on this whether she wanted to admit it or not.

"Isabel, is it time for me to fuck her?"

Isabel responded, "Please. I think it's well past time for us all to get off."

Aubrey nodded enthusiastically and slid my dick closer to her entrance. I stopped holding back as I grabbed her leg to lift it over my shoulder so I could get better access as I shoved my dick hard into her.

Sliding all the way in and filling her up to the hilt.

We fell backward together onto the bed from the force.

She screamed and swore and clawed at my back as I continued to pound into her, not letting up at all. I kissed her everywhere, she bit my ear. She begged me to go faster, and I told her to calm down, to make the moment last.

"Jax, I'm so close," she whispered, and her eyes held mine like I could be her world.

I stopped everything I was doing to her. "Alice, end call."

She gazed up at me and questioned, "I thought you wanted an audience?"

"I want what turns you on, and thinking someone is listening, makes you fucking crazy."

She smiled.

"But you only come for me." With that, I plunged back into her so deep she hissed like she was in pain. When I pulled back though, she commanded that I do it again and again and again.

We clung to each other like we'd been separated for too long. Her pussy tightened around me while she orgasmed and I hit an uncontrollable high.

Getting off with her was like walking through the gates of Heaven, but I didn't see bright white light. I saw that deep, emerald green. It got so dark, I thought it'd swallow me up.

She had that look from years ago, it was her surrendering and taking control of me at the same time.

By giving into me, she was taking my heart all over again.

CHAPTER
FORTY-ONE

JAX

WE MADE OUR way back to her little town.

She worked on her class, and I worked tirelessly to slot everything into place. After my talk on the Ferris wheel with my brothers and Rome, I had allies to help put everything into motion. Pieces moved fast but with the four of us working together, we predicted each movement correctly.

Aubrey didn't pay much attention to my working in her apartment other than asking about my music app. I think she genuinely cared about my music career, so I told her it would revolutionize the way people listened to music and how artists could share it with them. Artists would have the ability to release their own hand-picked music to whichever followers they wanted, share private locations to specific followers for an intimate concert, and give artists more ability to control their careers with their followers in general.

I was prouder from her smile and praise than I had been when Stonewood Enterprises agreed the launch would be a huge financial success.

I helped her with her class too. She had my tutoring advice on hand whenever she liked. Every now and then, she'd saunter over with a question about her investment project.

Admittedly, the answers I gave were incoherent because her short-ass shorts we're just way too damn enticing. After a particularly good phone call, I decided to dominate her just like I was dominating the workforce.

I took her against her countertop. Another time, I took her against the table. I took her all around that apartment.

We enjoyed each other and fell back into that comfortable place we'd been in so many years ago.

So that night, when Aubrey's anxiety crept in, I didn't know if it was because of her class tomorrow or something else.

It couldn't be us. We worked too fucking well together.

Maybe it was the fact that Rome had stopped over and instead of us fighting, we'd sat down and talked business over a beer.

Whatever it was, I took my time fucking away her anxiety instead of dwelling on it.

I found that taking my time was more difficult than expected though. I had wanted to own her for so long, and damn, my body had missed hers. She had always said we were at war with each other or whispered things like, "I can't keep fighting you."

My girl didn't understand she had just been fighting herself. She wanted to keep that recklessness of being with me bottled up in a neat little color-neutral package.

Her vibrance needed to shine though, and I made sure it would.

The next afternoon, Aubrey buzzed around her kitchen, not making eye contact with me and barely responding to my touch.

After only about two minutes, I found my anxiety rising so much that when she tried to open their refrigerator, I shot my hand out to hold it closed from behind her.

She looked over her shoulder, "Excuse me?"

"I'm not moving my hand until you tell me what's going on. You're jumpy as hell and it's making me jumpy. I don't do jumpy, Whitfield. This is supposed to be a vacation before my app launch this weekend."

She scrunched up her face. "A vacation for you? You've been working this whole time!"

"I'm working much less here than I normally do. I consider this a vacation."

"You should probably reevaluate your work habits. You work too much and this app launch isn't going to give you any more time to yourself—"

I grabbed her by the waist and yanked her up against me. "You're changing the subject. Answer my damn question."

She huffed out a breath and looked toward the ceiling. "I'm still trying to figure out how much we can trust each other."

I wanted to tell her she could trust me with every bone in her body but words didn't bring that type of trust. We'd had it before, and I'd broken it. I'd broken both of us.

I was ready to put us back together, fix what was broken, earn back that trust, and have her as mine forever, but I knew my plans over the next couple of weeks would test everything we'd ever built. We had to get through that first.

So, I stayed silent.

She sighed and ran her hand through her hair. "Right. I get it. We can't promise each other anything, but this isn't about me and you. I have plans tonight and—"

"If you think you're leaving to go do something without me while I'm here visiting you, you're mistaken, Whitfield."

She glared at me. "I was going to give you the choice of coming with me or staying here while I took Rome's truck to go—"

"We'll take my car."

She looked out the window. "You have a car here?"

"I store one at Jay's. I'll have my drivers bring it over."

"We can just take Rome's—"

If I had to hear that guy's name again. "I'll drive."

"You don't know where we're going."

"So, tell me."

She looked down at her hands that were folded tightly together. "I visit this house out near the reservation sometimes. I'm sure you know. Jay's gone with me before, and he's probably mentioned it."

I nodded, a little dazed from the impact of her actually confiding in me about it all. I'd miscalculated her again.

I expected her to keep her visits tucked away quietly in a box of secrets from me for much longer.

"It's just…" She cleared her throat before continuing. "The kids there can handle just about anything. Okay? But they can't handle having a celebrity come in and make empty promises or anything like that. If you come with me, you have to remember that. And…just…they mean a lot to me."

"I get it."

"They should mean a lot to everyone, really. They're kids. Kids are the next generation, and they have so much to offer. They just haven't been given a chance. And plus, they're still growing…" she rambled.

I nodded and squeezed her waist to get her attention. "I get it, Peaches."

"You don't. Not many do, but I'm going to try to show you."

We fell into a tense silence after that while she got ready to go. I wondered how the hell I was going to get through the next few hours. I liked kids, but I didn't know how to act around them.

Aubrey eyed my car when we made our way to her parking lot. "A little much?"

I scoffed. "You grew up with nice cars."

She pursed her lips. Then said, "This is an Aston Martin, right?" I nodded and smiled as I opened the door for her. "Let's go."

She might have wanted to act like the car wasn't impressive but an Aston Martin Rapide impressed just about everyone. I saw her drag her hand on the leather before she sat down and her gaze lingered on the sleek black lines of the metal.

Our drive there passed faster than I could have imagined once Aubrey's admiration for my car faded. She had more important things to discuss, like briefing me on every child. She also went through a list of rules she said were crucial to a successful visit.

As we drove up to the house, a squad car's lights spun round and round. Aubrey barely waited for my car to pull to a stop before she muttered, "What the hell?" and jumped out.

I followed her into the house where I noted about a half a dozen children huddled in the living room, sitting on shabby furniture. They looked nervous and alert, not watching the TV that blared in the room. Instead, they listened as closely as they could to what the policeman was saying to Aubrey and the older woman wringing her hands in front of him.

"I'm confused. She specifically said she would be here two hours ago. You don't want to send out a search party and you haven't tried to go to her mother's?" Aubrey's voice shook as she questioned him.

The older woman glared at me as I walked up. "You're exactly right, Brey. Seems this policeman here doesn't want to do his job. I tried to call you before. It isn't a good day for Mr. Fancy Pants, here."

"I'm Jax Stonewood." I eyed her, knowing she wouldn't take my hand if it was offered. So, I offered it to the officer who stood just a bit taller.

"I'm Sheriff Jim Nacotee." His handshake crushed mine.

I read men like this every day. They wanted empty praise for their title and recognition, for doing something they hadn't done yet. Men like this I handled every single day.

While the older woman scoffed and Aubrey tried to jump in, I spoke over them both, maintaining my presence and steering control of the situation. "Jim, you know how to do your job. It sounds like someone's missing from the lineup today."

He smiled, happy to be talking to someone he thought would side with him. "Happens all the time around here, Mr. Stonewood. These girls aren't well disciplined. They run away or go off with a group of friends…"

Aubrey cut in, her voice low. "That's not the case with Ollie. She's not even a teenager. Do your job and set up a search party. We need to get ahold of her mom too."

Jim rolled his eyes and winked at me. "Honey, we know how to handle these situations. If she doesn't turn up by tomorrow and her mom calls, we'll file a missing persons report, all right?"

The older woman took a step closer to him. "Thousands of reports of missing Native American women and girls have been documented. Thousands *more* aren't being documented at all. You want to be a part of that number climbing? A little girl is missing. You want her blood on your hands?"

He rolled his eyes again. "You're overreacting." He pivoted pointedly toward me. "Mr. Stonewood, this girl's mother has had issues with the law before. Drugs."

I let him continue without responding to his explanation.

He eyed me and shrugged, his whole body moving with the motion. "She probably got caught up in something and just forgot to bring Ollie here."

Aubrey crossed her arms. "Ollie walks here every day, rain or shine. You've had the ability to issue an Amber Alert since 2017 according to the Indian Country Act. If you don't, I will utilize all of my resources to make it public knowledge that you're not doing anything to improve the national statistics of women and children going missing under your watch."

Jim squinted at her and shifted on his feet before jutting out his gut. "You think anyone is gonna believe you, Ms. Whitfield? I don't mean much disrespect but you and your mom shunned the reservation years ago when you took up with men outside of it." He waved my way. "I'm doing my job the way I see fit. You don't get to tell me how to do it."

Aubrey took a step toward him, but I grabbed her arm. She tried to yank free while I held her close, grabbing her waist and drawing a circle into her bicep, trying to calm her.

When she glanced up at me, nothing was calm though. Ruthlessness, empty and dark and violent, swirled in her eyes. Aubrey resembled her father for the first time ever. Her stare was motivated and lethal.

That look had me pulling her behind me and taking over. "Jim, let's agree to disagree here."

"You disagree with me?"

"I'm saying some of us disagree with you. I think we should start with a drop by the mother's, huh? Let's do that. Get some answers. Go from there."

"Sure, sure. I'm going to get to that. We gotta do our due diligence. I'm just preparing you all for what the outcome will be. And if we'd give it a few hours, we probably wouldn't have to waste our time going over there."

I wanted to punch his teeth down his throat. I knew every minute counted here and his lack of enthusiasm might cost a little girl her life.

Jim wouldn't respond well to my candidness though, and I needed him to move. "Let's just take a ride now. Tell you what, Aubrey and I will take you in my car. Not every day I get to drive over the speed limit in that thing."

Jim's eyes lit up and both Aubrey and the older woman looked at me in disgust. "Ma'am, Aubrey and I will call you as soon as we know more." I pressed a button on my key FOB and nodded at Jim, "After you, man."

I followed him out as Aubrey hugged the older woman and murmured a few encouraging words before she turned to the children. She told them she'd be back soon, and that there was nothing to worry about.

As she caught up to me, she whisper-yelled, "What the fuck are you doing?"

"Getting answers and making him move. He's only going to listen to what he thinks is another man's reason."

She was vibrating near me with rage as she walked quickly toward my car. "You better be right, Jax. I swear to God, she's only seven and if we can't find her..."

"I'll tear apart this whole fucking reservation if we can't, Whitfield, starting with that man sitting in my car."

She nodded and whispered before she went to get in, "I've never been so close to wanting to leave someone for dead than I was with him."

I didn't look away from her. "I have. And I'll do it again and again for you if I have to."

Her eyes glassed over, and I saw her shiver before she looked away.

Lines were blurring, walls were falling, barriers were toppling and I think we both knew in that moment we would break down everything between us even if it meant others would be hurt in the process.

It was a dangerous thought, one that chilled me to the bone but brought me more comfort than I'd had in a long time.

Driving to the little girl's house was all a show for the police officer. I chummed it up while speeding as fast as I could to cut down on minutes wasted. Aubrey stayed quiet in the back but the force of her silence spoke louder than words could have.

When we pulled up to the small house, a tiny wind chime moved in the breeze as we hurried to the porch. As we banged on the door, I took in the kid's shoes lined up below the wind chime. They were worn in but lined up with care.

We heard a scramble and then a very thin woman who looked depleted of life answered the door.

She squinted into the sun and pushed her dark hair from her face, "Yes?"

Aubrey folded her hands together, as she let the officer ask questions about Ollie.

The mom was defensive. She kept the door between herself and us as if we were there to hurt her. "I don't know where she is. She was supposed to go over to Margie's."

The officer nodded like he believed her. "I know. She's young and probably ran off, right? She do this before?"

The mom's dark eyes skittered across the lawn behind us, avoiding meeting any of ours. She answered with a whisper, "I don't know, I was asleep for a little while."

I saw Aubrey's knuckles turning white, her nails dug into her skin. We both knew the mother was lying, but it was a matter of getting the truth. The truth from a skittish, abused individual was earned by staying completely composed.

Aubrey had learned that well.

My hand slid into hers, and I rubbed circles over the half-moons that marked her skin where her nails had been.

She breathed in deep and stepped closer to the woman. The woman immediately moved back and pushed the door to just a crack open. "Ollie doesn't miss days. We document it. She's always there. She tells us how sweet you are to let her come all the time. We're just here to make sure we find her alive and well, no other questions asked."

The woman assessed her for a long time, so long I thought she'd slam the door on us. Finally, she sighed. "Jerry came by." She cleared her throat and glanced back at me and the cop before she whispered to Aubrey, "He wanted me to go with him somewhere. I told him to leave. He didn't want to, so I left him in my living room to go lie down."

Aubrey nodded, her whole body tensing. "Okay. Was Jerry here with Ollie while you were sleeping?"

"I told him to leave and ... " Realization dawned finally on the woman's face. "I ... do you think he would have ... oh, no. He wouldn't have taken her?"

The officer took down his address and called it in. He was all business now that he knew the situation was being documented. He stayed behind with the mother to make sure she could talk to authorities.

When we arrived at Jerry's, Aubrey instantly recognized purple sneakers on the front porch, and I held her back as officers arrived and entered the premises.

"She's going to be okay." For once though, I had no idea of the outcome. We'd made it there quickly but criminals had an uncanny ability to be quicker.

She stared at the house. "You've never been a liar, Jax. Don't start now."

I nodded and let my hand fall to her thigh so my fingers could trace the soft spot I knew soothed her.

We'd been here before, in front of a house where devastation probably had occurred, waiting for an outcome we probably didn't want.

It felt the exact same.

Time slowed.

Sounds faded away.

The red-and-blue lights from the squad car lost their color.

I heard her breathing, mine synced to it.

Her tension vibrated through the air, and the hair on my arms stood up like the vibrations commanded them to.

The difference this time, I kept rubbing circles and kept her close. I knew, this time, nothing would stop me from helping her through the outcome. I'd pick her up wherever she fell.

It was what I was meant to do.

The screen door, tattered and rusted, opened with a drawn out screech. Aubrey was up and running toward it just as I saw a policeman come out holding a stricken little girl's hand.

The little girl shook her head full of long, dark hair yes and no as they asked her questions. She never opened her mouth, like she'd gone completely mute.

When an officer leaned in to her, she jerked away quickly and glanced around. Aubrey reached her then, and the little girl's body practically lunged for her.

Her arms went around Aubrey's neck as Aubrey caught her and fell back into the gravel. Aubrey hugged her so tightly, no one would have been able to separate them even if they tried.

When the officer stepped toward them, Aubrey grew two sizes, ready to envelop the little girl with her body as a shield of indestructible love. No one was allowed in that shield she'd built around her and the girl, not even me.

When she lifted her head to take in those around her, glistening emeralds with so much determination stared back at us all.

I was wrong to think her eyes shone like her father's. They were both vicious, but hers were more threatening. They held the look of a mother protecting her child. Dangerous. Fierce. Merciless. It was the first time I saw her ready to lose everything.

It made me want to have children with her. Want to protect her protecting others, and it made us both more dangerous than we'd ever been before.

CHAPTER
FORTY-TWO

AUBREY

WHEN SHE JUMPED into my arms and wrapped her shaking little body tightly around me, I swear the beat of my heart stuttered. Some part of me died holding her, seeing the red marks on her arms and face. A kind, understanding part of me. One that would have held back and rationalized what I could.

It all died along with some of her innocence.

I sat on the gravel, rocking her, soothing her, trying to absorb her fear and pain. Trying to rid myself of the fear I'd felt. Her disappearance evoked a new sort of panic in me. It made me realize all my panic before about crowds and social norms and spaces was irrational.

This panic and fear was real. Rational. Ferocious. And completely catastrophic.

I stayed quiet on the ride over because my mind wouldn't stop thinking of the what ifs, the already had beens, and the sure to comes. Women and girls were taken advantage of everywhere, and Ollie didn't have the luxury of money or status behind her. She only had us.

And what if? What if we hadn't come today? What if Jax hadn't schmoozed the cop? What if her mom didn't remember what had happened?

What if Ollie really was gone and we couldn't ever find her again?

The questions bounced around in my head, banging and clanking enough that no one could blame me if a craziness swept through me as a policeman approached us.

"Her mother is on her way. We should get going on some questions here."

"She's in no state to answer questions right now," I responded, looking up at him and continuing to rock Ollie from the gravel.

"Ma'am, let me do my job." He knelt down. "Ollie can handle some questions. Can't you, honey?"

She gripped me tighter and shook her head into my neck. The red marks on her arm and face should have been indication enough that no one, especially a policeman who looked intimidating, should be anywhere near her.

As more tribal and state police arrived on the scene, I snapped back at him, "She can't and she won't."

I stood abruptly without unwrapping Ollie from my body. She held me tightly as I whispered to her, "You want your purple shoes, baby?"

Her answer, a simple "no" cut through the wind, through my soul, and through her innocence.

I squeezed her tight ot my chest, trying to hold in that part of Ollie's personality that made her fearless, that made her a giggling little girl who believed there was no evil in the world.

When the police officer stepped toward me, Jax, who I'd completely forgotten about for one of the first times in my life, moved between us. He turned to a stone wall, impenetrable and solid. Heat and fury swirled in the air from all of us but Jax's was palpable, overpowering, and crushing.

When Jax spoke, every policeman, along with Jerry sitting in the squad car, turned his way. They all strained hard to hear exactly what came from his mouth, quiet and low. "Don't do something you're going to regret, Officer. Another step toward them won't end well for you."

"Are you threatening a man in uniform?"

"I never threaten anyone."

"Then, what would you call that?"

"A complimentary warning that you won't get again."

Most of the time, antics like that against a police officer would have escalated the situation. Jax wasn't in his city, and we probably should have been more careful. But with state police and tribal police there, maybe we had an advantage.

At least, that's what I told myself.

Luckily, the police officer immediately took on a more respectful tone as he tried to disentangle himself from Jax's wrath. I didn't know if Jax had just read the man correctly, and knew what buttons to press, or if his Stonewood name had traveled quickly enough through the town that the officer knew he had to tread lightly.

Either way, I didn't care. Repercussions of breaking the law be damned. I backed away with Ollie still in my arms and started for Jax's car, ready to take her anywhere but here.

The squad car carrying her mother pulled up.

Ollie's mother looked much more sober, like reality had set in. She jumped from the car and ran toward us.

Ollie looked her way and waved to her mother. "Mom! You came. I thought you might be too sick to come."

Her mother's expression fell just a little and her step faltered. She lifted her hand toward Ollie's face where the red mark was but closed it and pulled it away before she made contact. "I'm fine, Ollie. What happened?"

"I'm fine too. But I wasn't good." Ollie looked up to the sky, eyes glassy enough to spill tears at any moment. "Jerry's going to say I didn't listen. I don't want to be in trouble with you and the policeman. I know I should have taken off my shoes. He told me I couldn't wear them where we were going. I didn't really want to go anywhere with him, and so I said no."

"Then, what happened?" her mom asked, so slow I wasn't sure she even wanted the answer.

The look Ollie gave her mom was the exact look I used to give my mother. They both looked at me, ready to lie and keep the secret of abuse in the darkness where no one could document it.

That look, I'd never known exactly how frustrating it was until it had been turned on me. A helplessness rolled through me like it must have rolled through Mrs. Stonewood every time I looked at her when she asked me what was wrong.

I'd been a victim though. I'd been a part of the secret before, and I wasn't going to allow it to consume two others that day. "Ollie, you're safe. You didn't do anything wrong. You keep your shoes on all the time. You know that, right?"

She nodded but her eyes bounced to her mother like she wasn't sure she should answer.

"Jerry was wrong to hit you," I emphasized my statement and let my gaze land on each of them, slowly and solidly.

Her mother started to say something, and I knew it would be defensive. I didn't let her get anything out. "This is your daughter. You are her mother. You are all she has. Don't do what my mom did. Don't lie for him."

She took a step closer like she'd fight me but her daughter chimed in. "Brey, Mom's not sick today." She giggled as she leaned away from me and held her arms out for her mother to take her. "She knows I'm her daughter."

We shared looks as I handed Ollie over. Every muscle in me wanted to retaliate. My mind screamed not to let go. My heart hoped my mind was wrong.

Either way, I couldn't hold on to her. She wasn't mine. I had no claim on her, and I had no control over what her mother did with her.

"That's right, Ollie. You are mine." Her words were just as direct as mine were and held enough meaning that I had to swallow my knee-jerk reaction to yank Ollie back.

Instead, I rolled my lips between my teeth before I said, "She is. But if something had happened today, she'd be a part of the missing bulletin instead."

Her eyes widened. She snapped her mouth shut and kept a steely gaze on me for a few more seconds. "I love her more than anything, okay?"

I nodded because I believed her. Maybe she was like my mom, thinking that giving in to Jerry was best for both of them. "Take care of her."

She dipped her chin so slightly, I almost missed the gesture. She spun on heels then and took her baby with her.

Crumbling in front of them wouldn't have served anyone well. Jax slid up to me and wrapped an arm around my waist like he knew I needed the support. I sagged into him and answered the questions for cops as quickly as I could.

Answers we wanted didn't come as readily. They repeated again and again that the investigation was ongoing, like that cleared up my concerns and fears. We did find that Jerry claimed he wasn't planning on taking her anywhere, that he was just watching her.

His story didn't align with Ollie's or her mother's at all.

And yet, would he be back at their house tomorrow trying the same thing again? The cops assured us that with the evidence of abuse, he wouldn't.

One state policeman mentioned, "Jurisdiction is tricky when it comes to kids on the reservation. The Tribal Police will most likely have to charge him."

A tribal policeman shrugged. "The crime happened outside the reservation. We don't charge anyone off our land."

My brow furrowed. "So, who takes care of it?"

They both waved me off and I fumed on my way back to the car.

Jax took his time following me and shook all their hands. I turned to see him slip an insane amount of money into one officer's hands. My stomach rolled and protested the interaction, but I kept my mouth shut until we were on our way home.

"You paid that officer to do the job he should have been doing anyway."

His eyes stayed on the road. "Every job is a business, Whitfield. I paid him to do his job right."

"This isn't a fucking business, Jax. It's a little girl's life. Jerry should be going to jail for kidnapping, assault, and attempted..." I couldn't finish as I choked and then gasped out a sob.

His eyes darted my way but I turned toward the window, not wanting to share my anger and frustration with anyone.

He cleared his throat before he spoke again. "The laws and jurisdiction are different on and off the reservation, Aubrey. Money isn't. Money talks. I can't know what the hell will happen to Jerry without it. I gave that cop money to get things moving."

I just shook my head because I wanted his answer to be different. I wanted so many things to be different and before I could stop the words from flying out of my mouth, I blurted, "My grandmother vanished into the darkness of the night. My mother used to say a dark cloud rolled through the reservation and swallowed her up. Then, not long after, my mother was raped."

Jax white-knuckled the steering wheel before he swerved to pull over.

We stared out at the open road, me shocked at what I'd just revealed and him trying to digest it. "What do you mean? Your father?"

I shook my head. "No, it isn't important. I just..."

"Start at the beginning, Peaches."

So, I did. I told him what Margie told me and how I'd been questioning everything ever since.

He listened until I finished. "The world is a pitiful fucking place, Peaches. Your mom did her best."

"Was her best just being with another man that abused her so she didn't have to go back to something worse? Did she think she was protecting me?"

Jax didn't answer my questions. He just replied, "We're all doing what we can to make our world a little better. Focus on us doing what we could today and on what we can do tomorrow."

We let silence descend upon us for the rest of the drive, his words echoing in my head.

In that car, after the shock of almost losing Ollie wore off, I changed. I promised myself to do just as Jax said. Focusing on doing what I could to make my life and the world around me better meant facing my demons, stepping out of the shadows and confronting the monsters that had kept me suppressed for so long.

Starting with my father.

CHAPTER
FORTY-THREE

AUBREY

JAX AND I still went back to see the kids that day and tried to make the most of it.

Everything was different though. I was different.

When we got back to my apartment, we tried to unwind by getting lost in each other.

It didn't work.

After showering, I found him on the couch, working on his app. "It's almost been a month since you went to see him. The anniversary of my mother's death is approaching."

Snapping steely blue eyes my way, Jax nodded as he gauged my reaction and tried to process where my head was at before he responded. "Okay."

"So, you're going again soon?"

He shifted on the couch and removed his feet from the ottoman. "Peaches, let's not do this now."

"Do what?"

"Fight about him after the fucking terrible day we've had."

I looked toward the ceiling. "I wish I could stop thinking about it but I can't. You told me to start making days better a little at a time. You know what I thought about? Him. How Ollie had to be a victim to someone even remotely like him."

Jax winced.

"You go visit a man in prison just like Jerry. And you keep going like he means something to you."

He sighed and ran his hands through his hair.

"Are you going to see him again soon?" I asked again.

He stared at me. The cold blue washed over me like a polar vortex blowing through. We were back on the battlefield, measuring one another's army, attempting to figure out who would win and who had the upper hand. "If you're keeping tabs on why and when I go visit him, you can add in that I have the launch of my app coming up this weekend. I go visit him around every big event in my life." Sarcasm and condescension dripped from his voice.

I stood over him, ready to attack, seething at his words. "Great that you've been able to share those big events with someone all these years other than me."

"You wouldn't have wanted me to share anything with you after I left you."

"Really? How would you know when you didn't ask?"

"I know—I called, Whitfield."

"Oh my God!" I threw my hands up. "Are you counting the time you were so wasted you could barely string together a sentence?"

"I was never that drunk…"

My blood boiled from his denial. I stalked over to my laptop on the counter and typed in my password quickly.

"What are you doing?" He asked and I felt his body heat wrap around me as he looked over my shoulder. Even though I wanted to lean into him and forget the whole conversation, I couldn't.

I put the voice mail on loud. His voice cackled through, slurring words of love and then telling me about his record deal. I let him hear the voice mail that haunted my dreams for years.

He tried to grab for me. I pushed him back and held my laptop out. "Keep listening, Jax."

His eyebrows pulled down and his jaw ticked. He turned away from me to run his fingers through his dark hair and pulled at it before he stalked back.

He tried to grab my laptop to stop the message from replaying, but I pulled it out of his reach.

"Why did you save that?" he whispered, pain rasped through his question.

"Does it matter?" I whispered back.

This time, when he stepped up and wrapped his arm around my waist, I let him. I leaned into his chest and let his other hand take the laptop to close it.

"You should have deleted it," he mumbled into my hair.

"Believe me, I wanted to. But somehow, I can't bring myself to delete any part of you from my memory or life."

"Makes two of us, Peaches."

For what seemed like a moment, but could have been minutes or hours, we stood there, arms wrapped around each other. I absorbed him, taking in what I could. His smell. How I fit against his chest like it was the only home I'd ever felt safe in. His arms so secure like they'd protect me from anything and everything.

Except they couldn't protect me from him.

I finally looked up to step back and distance myself.

His hands drifted to my hair. "I can't keep doing this with you. Come with me to visit him tomorrow or wait until it's over. It will be after my launch."

I blinked once. Then I blinked again, trying to see if his face changed, to see if he'd retract the offer.

Like stone, nothing moved though. The frown stayed in place and no smile formed. His blue eyes held fear, and he didn't try to mask it by looking away.

I stared at them like a moth going toward a blinding light in the middle of one of the darkest nights. "Why now?"

"I finally lined up all my ducks. They're in a row and they're ready to end this."

"Why let me go before you end it? After all this time…" I shouldn't have even asked. I should have just taken him up on the invite.

"Because we're here. I'm not going anywhere and neither are you. I saw you today with Ollie, I saw what I couldn't control. This, I can. This thing between you and me is mine to control, and I know for damn sure I'm not letting go of that control because of shit with your father. He's hung over our heads too long."

My world tipped onto a different axis. It not only tipped, it rolled over and snowballed into a freaking new planet.

I stumbled back, trying to get my footing but this planet didn't have solid ground. It was thin ice over freezing cold water. "You can't be serious," I whispered.

He stepped toward me, his footing so sure I wanted to push him, rock him into my unsteadiness, tilt his axis just a little.

"I'm ready to go whenever you are."

It was a challenge just as much as it was him trying to overcome our demons. I saw the cold, calculated determination in his eyes that never wavered when he had set his mind to something.

Most of the time, he was setting his mind to pushing me and this wasn't any different.

Every single time he pushed me though, I rose to the stupid occasion. On our battlefield, no one could back down or show an ounce of hesitation. One misstep out there and life would never be the same.

Could I do it this time? Could I walk into that prison and look straight into those eyes that mirrored mine? After all these years of silence from my father and my silence being reciprocated? Open my mouth to say words I had thought about millions of times but never thought I would get the chance to say?

"Tomorrow I have class."

"Then, Friday."

I sucked oxygen into my lungs. I heard it going in, I couldn't feel it though.

I didn't feel anything when I replied, "I'll be ready."

If someone asked me what I did on the day before I went to visit my father, I wouldn't be able to recall. I assume I ate three meals, went to class, and drank whatever concoction Jax went to buy from Jackie.

I assume I studied or tried to lose track of time with Jax. I wouldn't be able to bet my life on it though.

I didn't remember that day. It paled in comparison to the days surrounding it. I wish I could have told myself that those days, the ones with nothing happening, were the ones to remember.

I should have listened to every whisper of a moment I had with the man I'd fought not to love for so long but who sat with me to stare out a window and appreciate the way the wind danced through the trees. I should have snuggled closer to him on the couch as we sipped the chai tea he'd made us and enjoyed the calm silence of steam off our warm drinks. I should have tried to bottle the feeling of being kissed by his lips, wrapped in his arms, and enveloped in his scent.

Instead, the day came and went like lightning, so fast, I barely saw it.

Like a flash, I was standing in front of my mirror trying to figure out what I would wear to go visit my father in prison.

White.

A color my father insisted upon. White, so clean and pristine.

Like walking into a room with fresh, clean sheets free of any stains. No one would ever guess how quickly you had to wash blood off that white color to make sure it didn't set into the fabric. Or how many times we'd had to clean that fabric to make sure it was white enough for the next event.

White. It was our show color. And there I stood, donning it again just like he would have wanted.

I wondered if my mother would have approved of me bending to his will. Would she have told me to keep the peace one last time, even knowing he couldn't hurt anyone behind bars?

I sighed. She couldn't answer the question and neither could I.

Jax had left my bed early that morning with the excuse of needing to work, but I knew he'd gone to the living room to give me space. Now though, he pushed open the door without a knock as if he owned the place. "Jax, you could knock."

"For what reason?"

"Well, for one it's polite," I sighed.

His smile was slow. "You think I want to be polite with you?" I rolled my eyes. "I could have needed some privacy."

He shook his head. "You don't get privacy with me, Peaches. I've seen every part of you."

I stared at him, wondering if he could see how my insecurity over the day melted away when I looked at him.

When he stood in front of me, all I could see was him. His broad shoulders, how they took up almost the whole width of my doorway, how he dominated every place he was in and didn't have to try. I found myself wanting to swim in oceans of Caribbean blue as I looked into his eyes.

He crossed his arms over his chest.

Without thinking, I blurted, "You're back in a suit."

The small smile that crept over his face held sadness when he replied, "You're back in white."

I didn't know if he was referencing how my mother and I dressed for my father or my lack of colors in general. I didn't ask because I didn't want to know.

Nodding, I tried my best not to stumble when I walked toward the doorway.

I'd go see him to end these years of no contact and to figure out if he'd be sorry or remorseful or anything at all.

I'd do this for me and for my mother.

Jax grabbed my arm as I brushed past him in the hall. He leaned in close. "You don't have to do this, Whitfield."

For years, I hadn't seen any vulnerability like this in Jax, and I didn't know how to take it.

I knew he didn't want me to know what all his visits were about. I assumed he was nervous that I'd figure out something he'd kept a secret all this time. I assumed a lot at the moment and it started to make this trip about finding answers about Jax and my father, not about my mother and me.

The car ride was more of the same. I knew the protocol Jax took. He entered a black SUV, now with me. He took precautions to make sure we weren't seen as I am sure he had in the past and we started the long drive there, both of us in the back with a driver behind a partition.

I paid attention to none of it. I worked on stacking block after block of my defensive wall up in my mind. Each block had some damn memory attached to it, a slap on my mother's face, a bruising of an arm, a locking of a door.

Then, the other blocks came for them both. The calls Jax ignored, the events we'd been at but he'd only politely addressed my presence before leaving, the secrets they kept together. The wall got taller and taller and stronger and stronger.

Jax moved his hand to my thigh but instead of it bringing me any comfort, I jerked from his touch.

His eyes searched mine for a minute but he left his hand there. Maybe he was baiting me to push it away but I saw the look he had and knew I wouldn't win that battle.

I sighed and tried to relax. He sighed too, like the damn visit was causing him anxiety. Like he didn't do this every couple of months.

Maybe it was though. Maybe they had enough secrets to hide from me that he didn't want me there.

Maybe this was a test.

The drive could have taken a year but it felt like no time at all had passed. When we pulled up, the car idled outside the prison's gate.

Like every time before, the paparazzi had found him. Had found us. They were buzzing at the gate like they knew we would be there any minute. They rushed the vehicle as our driver waited to be ushered through.

Flash after flash went off. I heard them yelling questions, trying to provoke an answer out of Jax and me.

Jax's posture didn't change. He kept his eyes forward and didn't address any of them at all. "They can't see us in here. The windows are tinted. Ignore them."

I wanted to growl that ignoring them was impossible.

Who had tipped them off? My paranoia set in and had me thinking that maybe this was all a set up. Maybe my father and Jax worked to set up the paparazzi together. The idea felt ludicrous and completely logical at the same time. My mind was a tornado of emotion, yet I sat there completely still beside the statue of a man next to me.

Maybe we'd both been programmed to deal with trauma and unorthodox situations in this way. Maybe, we were just that screwed up.

As our SUV rolled slowly through the crowd of paparazzi and entered the prison grounds, I realized no panic had overwhelmed me with the cameras flashing. I'd focused on the other problems, and again was able to overcome that illogical fear I used to have.

Now though, my breaths were shorter. My palms started to sweat and my heart beat picked up. As the vehicle pulled to a stop, I looked over at Jax and met his cool gaze. "You haven't said a word to me about what I should and shouldn't say to him."

"He's your father, Whitfield. You can say whatever you want." His tone was soft.

"All these years, and now you're both okay with it?" I accused.

He looked off toward the prison and his hand bunched into a fist before he moved away from me to slide out of the SUV.

Flashes went off from afar as he rounded the vehicle and came to open my door. He ducked his head and watched me.

His stare gave me options. He talked to me through that damn stare, saying I didn't have to do this but he was there for me if I wanted to. Somehow, he let me know he was the fucking rock I had needed all these years and that he would be for a long time after this.

His commitment walloped me like a wrecking ball. I felt how much I wanted him as my rock. I felt my weakness to him, and I felt myself retracting and withdrawing from the whole damn idea of coming here in the first place.

I didn't want to know what they talked about. I just wanted to love him.

I didn't want what we had to be ruined by their relationship. I wanted to ignore it so we could stay this exact way.

I wanted him to stop whatever the hell they were doing. I wanted us to forget it ever happened.

I wanted a damn happily ever after, and I should have known I couldn't run from the biggest problem to get it.

I did just that though.

I shook my head at him as my vision got blurry and rolled my lips between my teeth like I was trying to hold in every emotion I wanted to have burst out of me.

"Peaches, you want to go home?"

I couldn't answer him. I couldn't face my fears out loud. Instead, I just nodded.

He nodded too. But he looked disappointed as he told the driver to take me home and send him another car.

Before I realized what had just happened, the door slammed, and I was on my way back.

Without Jax.

I realized too late that I was a coward and Jax had left me to be on my own as he continued the same damn meetings that slowly bled us dry of faith in each other.

CHAPTER
FORTY-FOUR

JAX

WALKING TO MEET him didn't scare me anymore. Walking away from her that day did.

She retreated. She stepped down and waved a white flag in a way I'd never seen her do before.

The battlefield was where we thrived. We smelled the gunpowder, felt the heat of an explosion on our face, and ran forward toward the enemy.

We fought.

It was our dance.

But she saw something that was too big to lose and backed away from the fight. She didn't charge forward for something she'd wanted for so long. Without her facing this, we wouldn't have anything.

I was a fool to think I could have kept her from him and have our relationship not be tainted. Now, more than anything, I wanted her to come to him with me. For us to face him together. For her to conquer this fear, and for me to conquer him so we could move the fuck on.

His smile was big and so genuine when he saw me alone that I almost turned back around. He didn't deserve any happiness. We both knew that. He'd admitted it to me time and time again. Yet, here he stood, like he'd won the damn lottery.

"Someone tipped me off that I might see my daughter with you today." He tilted his head with that same smile on his face as I sat down opposite him across the metal table.

"She's not here. So, your tip was wrong."

"Was it? Or did I just see you open the door for someone who didn't get out?"

I didn't take the bait. "You want to talk business, Frank? Or you want to talk about your daughter who you have no communication with?"

"Maybe I should be in communication with her."

"Making empty threats about something you don't care about only hurts you, Frank. Not me." His smile dropped off.

"My company's stock is floundering because of that other damn candy company."

I nodded. "The board is doing what it can."

He slammed his hand on the table, eyes wild. "Do something more. You wanted to go fucking public with my company, and I took your advice."

Frank always blamed a bad deal or idea on someone else. Normally, that person was me, and normally, he was right to blame me. He just didn't know it.

"You're a richer man because you went public, Frank." My tone was neutral. This was all something I'd listened to before. It was routine.

"You should be apologizing for your misstep." I stared at him. He knew I wouldn't.

He waved me off. "Fine. What can we do to pull back up? I want to propose the casino idea on the reservation. We could fund most of it. The profits would be huge."

That was the problem with Frank. He always tried to have power over his family. That used to be his wife and now it was his daughter. He'd somehow found out about her trips to the reservation, knew he could taint her love for something and tried to constantly move in on it.

Whether he did it consciously or not, I saw his pattern. He'd used his business to cover up the dirt he threw at his wife first. He'd bought her nice clothes, put her in a nice home, made it look like he gave her everything. His business allowed him to cover up the pain and abuse underneath. He would do the same thing with Aubrey's haven at that reservation. He'd ruin it. I'd been working toward making sure that business was never there to cover up his dirt again.

"I can propose it at the next meeting."

"Don't just propose it. Make it happen. Then, you need to be back here soon. I need an update."

I let a small smile slip as I stood. "Sure, Frank. I'll make sure you get that update by next week."

With that, I walked out. I was ready.

No one else was.

On my way back from visiting Frank, speculation rose in the media about who had been in the SUV with me. Most of them were guessing right. They referred to her as Frank's daughter or the victim of the "Whitfield Downfall." She was moving to the forefront of the media frenzy.

I'd hired a PR team to take Isabel's place, but none of them could stop the snowball from growing. I knew that, and so did they. We'd have to let time pass and wait for another story to catch their eye.

I called Aubrey over and over. I texted her. I even left voice mails which I wasn't inclined to do most of the time.

She didn't answer and didn't return my calls.

I called my brother but couldn't persuade him into getting involved, and then I even called Roman. That man answered his phone enough that I knew he was purposely ignoring me, too.

The idea of him consoling her or even being there when she was upset with me had me fidgeting like a jealous fucking lunatic as my driver sped toward home.

I couldn't shake the itch to see her. I needed this shit ironed out. The infuriating woman wanted me to come there too. She had to. If she didn't, she would have picked up or called me back or even texted me.

So, I rerouted and headed in that direction, knowing the time I spent on her cut into the preparation I had to do for my launch this weekend. My stock had to skyrocket with this launch for everything else to work. Yet, my mind couldn't work through preparing for anything if she kept fucking ignoring me.

When I got to her place, I noticed Roman's truck in the parking lot. I also noticed a couple of media outlets camped out, ready to catch a glimpse of us.

I slammed the door after telling my driver I'd call when I needed him.

As the cameramen swarmed me, I met them all with glowering eyes. "You're on private property. I promise my team will disassemble your career if you don't get the fuck out of here."

Half of them dispersed and the other half I plowed through to get into Aubrey's apartment.

I banged on her door. "It's too late for this shit, Whitfield. Open the damn door."

This felt like déjà vu, and if I met Roman in the hall, I'd probably lose it.

The locks clicked quick enough, and she appeared in her small shorts and tank top.

"That's not an outfit to wear when you answer your door."

"You were screaming through it, genius. I knew it was you. Who's to say your outfit is one to wear when you're banging on someone's door?"

I stepped forward and she opened the door to let me pass. I caught how quickly she sidestepped me though. I saw the distrust and distance that was there again.

I sighed. At least we weren't going to have this conversation in the hallway.

"You're ignoring my calls, Whitfield."

"I figured you didn't want to talk since you sent me on my way this afternoon."

Shaking her wouldn't do me any good but the woman made me want to. "I told him I would be there."

Her green eyes widened. "I don't care what you told him!"

I tried to step toward her again but she retreated around the island and into the kitchen. "We can't keep having this fight."

"And you can't keep visiting him without telling me what the fuck is going on," she practically screamed.

"I tried to start that conversation today!" My mouth snapped shut as I realized I'd raised my voice too.

"I don't want to have that conversation with you. You know who I want it from? I want it from him. I want him to explain everything. Then, I want to tell him his explanation isn't good enough. Then, I'll come home and you can do the same damn thing he did. Try to explain yourself."

I saw hints of red tunneling my vision as I listened to her, I felt the damn hairs on the back of my neck stand up, and my jaw clenched tighter than it ever had as I responded, "We go at this together, you hear me? I don't want you going there alone."

She smoothed back her hair and stood taller like she could take on the world.

"You don't get to go there without me, Whitfield," I repeated.

"Don't I? He's my father, Jax." The fight in her was back. I wondered why I wished for it and how I could want to engage in it.

"He's nothing but a man who gave you life, then took the life that was most important to you."

She stared deep down into the dark depths of me as she said, "Are you talking about my mother or are you talking about you? Because I lost both of you to him."

Her words knocked the wind out of me, and she didn't seem phased at all as I gasped for a breath. When I rushed to her that time and threaded my fingers through her loose hair, she didn't resist. She met me halfway as I crushed my lips to hers.

When I moved to lift her legs, walking us back to her room, I told her the truth, "You never lost me. I've been with you every fucking step of the way."

She didn't respond except to bite my lower lip and wrap her legs more tightly around me.

We got to her bedroom and I fell onto her bed with her. She belonged under me and my body always, always, always longed for that, knew that, and fought for that. I slid my hand down her shorts, and she arched into me as she spread her legs.

Her body always knew where it belonged too.

When she gasped against my lips, I pulled away to bite at her collarbone, and moved her panties out of the way. Then, I was sliding my fingers in her and rolling my thumb over her clit just the way I knew she liked.

She barely moaned before I saw the color in her eyes deepen, her pupils dilate, and her teeth bite her lower lip.

"Don't bother holding back, baby. We both know you want this."

She groaned, "Please just shut up, Jax."

I smiled and whispered in her ear as I started to pump three fingers in her. "Listen to me when I tell you we do things my way, Peaches." My words had double meaning and she knew it as she narrowed her eyes at me. "It's easier my way. Even if it's not, my way is our only way."

She started to respond but I curled my fingers to just the spot I knew she couldn't handle. She writhed under me and screamed my name like I owned her and she knew it.

After that, I milked the aftershocks out of her until she was so damn pliable, she didn't even try to help me move her when I flipped her over and took both her ass cheeks in my hands to massage them. "Glorious, Whitfield, fucking glorious."

She mumbled something but I didn't hear it. My mind was ruled by my dick at that point. I pulled her hips up and entered her from behind. I slid my hand down her back and wrapped it around her neck, feeling her at her most vulnerable spots. I pounded into her, claiming her over and over.

She took it. She wanted it. She loved it. Just like I loved her.

We came down from our high and as we lay in the bed, I whispered, "I don't do music anymore because of this."

She looked at me with question in her eyes. "It's too raw for everyone to hear."

"Music is your gift. People love that you shared it with them."

"I never wanted to share it with anyone. I wanted to share it with you and you weren't there. So, I shared it with the world, hoping you'd hear it."

"Some days I wished you would have just stayed and shared it with only me. It's completely selfish."

I shook my head. "I'm singing for the launch tomorrow and that'll be it."

"Why?"

"I love being in the background of it but nothing else. What I feel for you, I can't share that with anyone else anymore."

She snuggled closer to me and I held her tightly, hoping to hold on to her just that way forever.

CHAPTER
FORTY-FIVE

AUBREY

SOMETHING ABOUT THE night with him was perfect. Every part of it was ours. We'd owned one another. I'd felt his highs and his lows. He'd fucked me and then made love to me. He'd made me feel ravaged and then like a treasure.

I wanted to box the night up, put it in a safe and go back to it every time I missed him.

And I would miss him. Very much.

Because today, I knew we were over.

I slid out from under his arm and made my way quietly to my closet that morning.

I pushed all the clothes aside until I got to the black dress I'd worn for my mother's funeral.

Black bled all the colors together, dark and ominous and full of everything. I applied a heavy eyeliner to match the dress and took in the end result.

I'd barely gotten ready in silence while the man I loved slept in my bed. I'd left my hair mussed from the bed, lips bruised from the night, and cheeks flushed from knowing what we had done.

My dress tightened enough at the waist that my breath felt a little shallow before it flowed out to accentuate that I was in fact a woman, not a girl anymore.

My eyes burned boldly green against the makeup. They were the only color that stood starkly out.

I looked at Jax one last time; took in the way he swallowed up the room even while sleeping. That presence, that infallible magnetism, and that boldness that radiated from him couldn't ever be compared to anyone else. I knew I was walking out on the one man I'd never be able to get over.

Yet, as I took in his sun-kissed skin and his dark hair, his full lips and his sculpted chest, I knew that I'd never, ever find the strength to walk away again and do this on my own.

And I did have to do it on my own.

I'd faced my father for years with my mom as a shield. I had to face him alone now.

Jax would try to shield me. I didn't want that.

I'd done the proper thing, the right thing, things for everyone else for far too long.

I quietly made my way out of my apartment and texted Rome that I needed his truck to see my father. He met me outside with his keys.

No questions. No words.

He handed them over as he stood there in his sweats and then pulled me in for a hug. After kissing the top of my head, he turned back to our building and let me go.

The drive lasted as long as any drive would of that length. This time I didn't dwell on memories or conjure up walls and barriers. I just focused on the road, on me, and on who I'd become without him in my life.

The past few months with Jax had changed me. I'd changed me too.

I had more trust in myself. Confidence. Determination.

As I pulled up to the same building I'd been to the day before, I focused on getting through the gates, not on the cars that had followed me here, on the media I knew had been assigned to my apartment throughout the night to try and get a glimpse of Jax or me or both of us together. Only a few had caught me leaving in Rome's truck and those few got pictures of me now.

Jax would soon know I was here. Soon, so would the world.

I didn't focus on that because I was focused on this being about me. Today, I didn't come here for Jax or to see my father.

I came because I needed it. This was for me.

After being patted down and following the guard, I turned the corner to where he sat, waiting.

Frank. My father. A tormentor and an enforcer throughout my life. Someone I hadn't seen in years, yet remembered vividly in all my worst dreams.

The memories had faded but his face, the one that held so much anger and rage, hadn't.

That face, the one that hardened before he struck my mother, was one I would never forget. I would see it forever. Even if today, his face was relaxed and subdued. He squinted a little as if he was just a little curious, eyes bright and clear from being sober.

He looked older, more worn down, and a little skinnier. His silver hair was still combed to the side nicely, and he didn't look as bad as I had hoped.

When I sat down across from him, neither of us smiled. We took each other in like we were both a species neither one of us had come across.

Maybe I thought he would start the conversation. Maybe I thought it would flow naturally. Maybe I'd been hopeful. Nothing came out of his mouth though. Nothing came out of mine.

I just stared at the eyes that looked so much like mine and wondered how we'd gotten here. How I'd not come sooner. How he'd not contacted me sooner. How Mom would have felt about it all.

Not that it mattered.

She was gone and it was because of him.

I cleared my throat. "I'm here just this once."

My voice felt weak, even to my own ears. I must have appeared small, insignificant, and still so young to him. So many times he had overpowered me and made me feel just that way, I couldn't shake it.

"I'm glad you finally came." His voice chilled me to the bone. Somehow, it had remained starkly precise and cut through all my thoughts. I wondered if that voice and his mannerisms, the way he held himself to this higher standard, had allowed him to build his company, to maintain it even while behind bars.

I wrung my hands together under the metal table and tried to hold his stare. "There hasn't been a reason for me to come visit you in the past."

"And now?"

"Now, I've come to terms with how I want to live and it doesn't include wondering about you or how you feel." I shifted and held that gaze as I said my next words. "It doesn't include wondering what you and Jax talk about."

His eyes narrowed in the slightest, then he broke eye contact to really study me. Study my posture. Study my clothes. Study my hair. I saw him focus on every single detail. I let him.

I didn't squirm or fidget under his analysis. Never had I wanted to move so bad though. He didn't deserve to get to take in his own daughter. It wasn't his right when he'd taken so much from me. Yet, again, I let him.

I wondered if that's what he wanted or if he wanted to make me feel small, wanted me to shift and show him weakness.

"You've grown up, Aubrey," he finally replied when he was done taking stock of me. He frowned, and the wrinkles that weren't so prominent years ago on his forehead stood out. "I'm not sure I'd agree with your choice in showing off how you've grown up. But you have and ... "

I cut him off. "I'm not here for your approval. Quite frankly, I don't care about it."

"Don't talk over me, Aubrey." His jaw ticked. "I'm your father." Those three words. How I hated those three words.

They used to foreshadow so much pain. Today, I'd change the course of what they meant to me.

"You've never been a father to me, Frank."

His eyes widened, but I just shrugged.

"Fathers take care of their children. They love them. They protect them. You didn't do those things for me. I lived in fear of you." My heart pounded as words poured out of me. Words meant to hurt but also meant to release me from years of frustration and resentment. "Mom should have left you. I should have run away. We should have told someone or buried your name in truths with the press."

He slammed his hand down on the table and got a reprimand from the guard before he spit out at me, "You didn't do any of those things. You did as you were told because that's what a daughter and a wife does."

"And does a husband and a father try to light his family on fire?"

His face got so red, I thought he might burst across the table. Instead, he whispered, "It should have been you trying to save me in the fire. Not your mother. Your mother listened. She tried. She kept her wits about her. Unlike you."

I could only imagine that my face got as red as his. That I looked like I wanted to jump across the table at him too. "You think it should have been me but it shouldn't have been *anyone*. We should have let you burn, Frank. We should have let you die there. Now, instead, I'm without the one person who loved me from my very beginning. I have to carry her memory with just the trust fund she left me. Believe me though, I will carry on her memory even if you won't. Even if you try your best to continue to never acknowledge her death, her life, her spirit."

His smile was slow but it crept up as I talked and was a bright, blinding white like I'd made his stupid day by the time I finished what I had to say.

"You want to know why your boy comes here to visit every now and then?"

I didn't answer him but he knew I wanted that. He knew I was basically salivating to know. His smile told me I shouldn't. His smile reinforced what I thought I knew when I'd left Jax this morning. Whatever I found out today would end us for good.

"He comes to help me keep my business afloat."

My stomach churned as bile rose in my throat. I wanted to ask why but knew I didn't have to. Frank looked too excited. He was leaning over the table like he couldn't wait to continue his story.

"He didn't want me to tell you. He started coming here from some guilt. You know, he could have woken me up in that fire, saved us all a lot of trouble. He didn't though, and it scared him as a little boy. He wanted some sort of redemption by coming to visit me. He threw that trust fund in my face and I laughed, Aubrey. I laughed so hard."

I looked at him bewildered, not understanding what he was getting at.

"Neither of you knew—your mother never had access to my money. To any money. That trust fund was set up by the Stonewoods for you. They didn't want you to feel like a charity case. Without me though, and without them, you are. Your mother never could have left you anything because I made her. I owned everything. I still do. Well, except for some of my company now. You know who owns a part of it?"

I shook my head, wanting it all not to be real, wanting this to be a dream, wanting to wake up.

"Jax owns a part of it now. So, I would have kept our little trust fund secret like he's always wanted me to in order for him to come here and keep helping me, but now he's invested enough in my company that he wouldn't dream of screwing me *and* himself over."

"You made this agreement to not share anything with me?" My voice sounded far away. So far down a tunnel that I could barely hear it.

"It was the only way, sweet daughter of mine."

I stood up so fast the chair I sat in tipped back and clattered to the floor.

He chuckled to himself, like I'd made his day.

I knew I told him he was sick, that there was no redemption for a man like him. Something along those lines but I couldn't be sure of anything else except that he yelled to me as I walked away, "My daughter should wear white and dress like a lady. Remember that next time you come to visit me."

There wouldn't be a next time, I told myself as I rushed to get out of there. I couldn't remember how I stumbled to the truck, how I managed to get it started and maneuver my way out of the gates and around the frenzy of paparazzi that must have caught wind of me visiting. I didn't even remember the drive home.

I almost expected Jax to greet me when I got through my apartment door but the place only had a lingering smell of him.

As I shut the door, I gasped for a breath of air. It felt like the first breath I'd taken since I'd run from the truth, from the reality that I wasn't sure I'd ever be able to stomach or get over.

Jax had made a deal or two with the devil. Deals he'd tried to keep from me. Secrets he'd hidden from me for so long. With all this time together, he'd never told me.

I started for my room but before I got further, Katie and Vick barreled in the front door with Rome following behind them, looking somewhat bored and a little irritated.

"You ready for the launch?" Vick belted out like she was yelling across a stadium.

"Launch?" I racked my brain, stumbling through the chaos of emotions to figure out what she was talking about.

Vick looked surprised and then frowned with a little bit of disgust as she replied, "Brey, Jax has been working on this music app forever. Pull it together!"

I probably looked stunned because they all looked at me like I was crazy.

Vick continued as if I was a child that she needed to explain the situation to. "His concert to launch the app is a huge deal. The media has been covering it for weeks. He never, ever performs! They say he won't ever again after this. Do you think that's true?"

I opened my mouth and then snapped it shut. I knew the answer but now I wondered. Did I really know him at all? Was anything he'd said true?

"Girl, you okay?" Katie stepped forward but I stepped back. I needed a minute. Or a freaking lifetime.

Rome stepped in front of Katie and blocked me from their view as he turned to them and said, "I need to talk to her for a minute."

Silence descended over my apartment, and I knew they were all throwing looks at each other. Rome must have won because he spun and grabbed my arm to pull me to my room.

I followed, probably because I couldn't find a thing to say to any of them. I couldn't explain what I was going through. I couldn't explain my feelings. I couldn't do anything because I didn't know anything. My world had crumbled, the floor was gone from beneath my feet, the air had been sucked from my lungs, and my vision was probably playing tricks on me.

"What happened this morning?" he asked as he closed the door.

I sank onto my bed and stared at my knees like they would give me an answer.

"Brey, you have to talk. You have to let it out. Whatever it is."

"I can't," I whispered. "I don't know how."

"Try, baby girl." He sat down next to me.

"Everything I thought, everything I knew, it isn't." I sighed and put my face in my hands. "Nothing is as it seems."

"Life normally isn't. Remember, you've been through the worst, and you still got through it."

"Was it the worst though?"

"Even if it wasn't, you're strong enough to get through it. You're you. You fight, you bleed, you fall, you get back up. You don't give up. You survive."

"What if all I've been doing is surviving?"

"Then you'll start living today, baby girl. Life's not over."

I let his words roll over me and let myself absorb it, know it, and own it. I had to. It was the only way I was going to get through the rest of the day.

As I stood up, I pushed the flurry of emotions down and mentally pulled up my big-girl pants. "You're right."

As I said the words, both of our phones chimed and within a couple seconds both Katie and Vick were bursting into my room.

Katie yelled, "What in the flying fuck, Brey?"

Vick, at the same time, yelled, "You went to visit that monster without telling us?"

Both pummeled at me then hugged me without an answer. I didn't return their embrace. I just said, "I can't talk about it, you guys. I just can't."

Vick started to protest but Katie threw a death stare around the room. "Vick, don't. And, Rome, you fucking knew."

He started to deny it but she cut him off. "Don't try to lie. I'm already thinking of a way to kill you slowly."

His mouth snapped shut.

My phone rang, but Katie moved as fast as a python striking to turn it off.

"Everyone should probably silence their phones," Vick announced. "So, the media got the word out about me going to see him then?"

"It's out there." Katie let out a frustrated sigh.

"Fuck." I let the swear slip. "I forgot about the launch. I forgot about everything when I went this morning, honestly. And after today, it doesn't matter. Jax and I are over, but I didn't want to harm his launch or the app. I just ... I had to go."

They all stared at me like I'd spoken in a different language. Katie was the first to say something. "You and Jax aren't over."

Vick and Rome stayed silent as I tossed my glare around the room. "Of course we are, Katie."

"Whatever you learned today, girl, you are going to talk to him about it." She didn't ask, she commanded.

"What he says won't matter."

"Maybe, but you are not done getting your closure. You say what you need to. You go to that launch today. Let Vick get you ready. Or better yet, let me get you ready if you want to go there and kill him."

I shook my head like I couldn't fathom the idea. "Don't retreat back into this shell." Her determined stare showed so much more than she said. Katie knew me better than all of them, and I knew her. She'd gone through enough to believe she was giving me the right advice. She didn't care if she was pushing, she thought the pushing would save me.

"It's not a shell, it's survival and … " The words died on my lips as Rome cleared his throat.

Start living today.

Closing my eyes and breathing hard before I said my next words wouldn't wake me from this nightmare because it was real. If life blew up in your face, you had two choices: stare down at the explosion, lament what was and what could have been or chose to fight your way out, become someone new, and build something new for yourself. I wanted to be someone better, someone different, someone stronger.

"Fine." One word that would change the course of the rest of my life. I knew it. I knew today would be the turning point.

"Fine?" Katie retorted like she couldn't believe it.

"Yep. Fine." I straightened a little and pushed my wild hair back from my face. "Let's get ready. Katie, you're helping me get ready, not Vick."

Vick grumbled.

"I'll talk to Jax after the launch."

CHAPTER
FORTY-SIX

AUBREY

THE WEATHER COOPERATED as we walked to the launch party. The breeze picked up just enough to cool off the crowd even as the sun shined down through intermittent clouds.

As we made our way to where he leaked the launch location, we saw swarms of people dressed for a concert. I hadn't read much about what exactly the concert would consist of but Katie and Vick must have known what to expect because my outfit, and their own, fit right in with the crowd.

We looked like the epitome of summertime girls. Katie and I had a ruthless twist to our outfits. My tank top was tight but a light green that brought out my eye color. It was cut on the sides to show more skin and pinned together with little sparkly buttons. It drew attention in a subtle, sexy, sort of unforgiving way. My jeans were a boyfriend cut that sat low on my waist and were ripped in

413

so many places they could barely be called jeans. With stilettos and smoky eye shadow, I hoped I looked ready to kill, because I was.

We pushed through the throngs of people. The campus's epically large hill was covered with fans, and the streets that sidelined the stage were filled. From above, I saw drones taking in the sight and it must have been a great one. I'd never seen this many people flood the area.

Jax was notorious for having amazing openers for his concerts, but surprisingly, he took the stage first. He let the crowd roar on and on for a time and looked over the streets and campus. The sight might have humbled him, or maybe it just built his ego. I couldn't be sure what someone with so many fans felt up there.

I'd have felt panic, fear, anxiety, and a need to hyperventilate.

He probably felt all that with a rush of adrenaline and excitement. His smile shined bright and genuine as he raised his hands and motioned for the crowd to quiet down. Then, his voice boomed over the speakers, filled with authority and amusement. "All right, come on guys. You have to be quiet if you want to hear the damn songs."

The crowd just responded with louder cries, and I completely got it. He stood there in a tight black T-shirt and jeans that looked so good on him, I knew they must have cost a fortune. Somehow, they looked faded and worn on their own though. Like he'd just come from a stroll in the park and was somehow still the perfect man you wanted to serenade you.

It was a stark contrast to the suits he wore most of the time and could easily play to the idea of the app. This was their artist, away from the everyday working grind, here to stroll through the park with them and sing the songs they wanted.

He waved for more silence and the crowd finally started to listen. Jax chuckled and thanked them all again. "My family's front and center to see you all fawn over me today. I'm a little embarrassed that you're making it so easy."

He pointed to where the Stonewoods were. They'd been fenced in and security was all around them, typical for the infamous

American family. Jax had asked me to be there with them, and Nancy Stonewood called, along with Jay, to try and persuade me. Now, more than ever, I was so happy I hadn't taken them up on the offer.

Instead, we'd pushed through the crowd to a building where security let us in. They directed us up to a suite where we could watch from above.

I stared down at the family I thought I knew.

Did they all know about my trust fund? I wanted to scream at Jay to tell me what he knew, but sometimes it was better to be kept in the dark. Truths and honesty between best friends hurt sometimes more than the omission. I wanted our friendship untainted for just a bit longer.

As for Mr. and Mrs. Stonewood, even Jett who'd always handled my investments of the fund, I'd have to find a way to forgive them. Their generosity and compassion to try to help me had tainted their rationale.

Jax and forgiving him, that was different.

Maybe he knew that. As he glanced up at our building and straight to the window where I stood, we locked eyes. We were close enough that I could read the strain on his face, I could see it simmering there. I just didn't know if it was the simmer before a concert or if it had started when he'd found out I'd gone to see my father.

His eyes snapped back to the crowd and he mumbled back to his band, "Let's give them what they want."

The first strum of his guitar quieted the crowd so much, I swear I heard the lapping of the lake nearby and the whoosh of the wind. The sun had started to set as Jax and his band mesmerized the crowd with the start of their set. No words flowed through the speakers. They let the instruments have their time for the introduction.

The slow build worked in his favor because when they stopped to let his voice come in completely acapella, I honestly saw some in the crowd start to weep.

The first song was about waking up to your lover and living that small moment to the fullest before you left them for the day. Some had argued it could have been forever. I wasn't sure what he meant by it either. He'd written it after leaving me. So, I imagined it had been about him leaving me for good and my heart broke, shattered, and disintegrated every time I heard it.

Today, for the first time, hearing it live transported me to our mornings together. I wanted to lie in his arms forever. Yet I knew I never would again.

People mingled around me in the suite, talking about how everything was going smoothly. These were his close friends, ones that had seen him in concert before. They maybe weren't as mesmerized, but I couldn't look away.

Song after song stabbed my heart. Some were ones I'd known from the day we started walking down to the lake together. Some were ones I'd heard over the years. Some were completely new to me and everyone in the crowd leaned in close, trying to memorize every word and absorb the enigma that was Jax Stonewood.

His heart was on the line with each song. He loved the music, bled the music, and died for the music. One of his friends leaned in close to me at one point and said, "I can't believe he'll leave the world holding this talent hostage."

"What do you mean?" I asked.

He shook his head. "I don't think he'll perform again. The fame isn't what he wants. He did this for the launch, so he can have a part of it without all of it."

I understood but didn't know how to respond. His friend was a high-profile musician as well. So, there was no denying Jax had the talent and that he may never share it with anyone again. That was his choice.

I shrugged. "Maybe, maybe not. At least we have today…"

Katie, Rome, and Vick came to stand beside him. I knew they'd given me space as I watched him, but they seemed to realize they had a moment as I talked with his friend.

Katie shoulder bumped me as his friend faded back into his own world, "It's going well, but it's almost over. He'll probably be up here after to celebrate."

The warning in her voice was clear. If I wasn't ready and if I didn't want an audience, we needed a better plan than being near his close friends.

She kept going. "I could intercept him for you to talk in private but I vote for you telling his ass off in front of everyone."

Vick was shaking her head no, and Rome oddly kept silent like he couldn't decide which side he was on.

"What I have to say won't take long." I'd hidden from crowds by doing the right thing for so long, I just didn't care who heard or where I said it at that point. I was here, he would be too, and I didn't intend to make a scene. "Let's not complicate it."

They all nodded, but none of them seemed convinced. I turned back toward the window. For once, I wasn't going to worry about how convinced they were or weren't.

We all listened to Jax who announced that a few more surprises were coming but he had to sing just this last song. He smiled to the crowd but when he looked up toward me, his glare was obvious, "It's one all of us know but one I always save to see if I can really perform it the right way for you. Today, cut me some slack. It'll be a little different."

The band quieted and didn't join him like they normally did when he started the introduction to "Sweet Sin." He hummed with his guitar and then a violinist joined him on stage. The high notes from the instrument added an eerie sort of darkness to the melody and when his voice joined it, the effect sent chills down my spine.

Boldly, he changed the words from love to pain. His voice twisted and scraped like gravel grating on my heart as he built to the hook.

Sweet Sin, Sweet Sin,
You pulled me in
Like an apple from the devil

Like a moth to a flame
I'd have followed you to hell
But you couldn't wait,
Sweet Sin, Sweet Sin,
you pulled me in
I was a fool, such a fool
To think this wasn't a game

The words had changed so much. They eviscerated me, cutting deep in my soul. This was why he had looked at me with cold determination. This was why he glanced up again as he sang those words and his eyes got colder and colder.

I stared back just as coldly, I hoped. The battle between us had just begun.

The screaming after his set finished rivaled the Super Bowl, I swear. Jax went down to meet his family. They walked into our building together where the media and crowds tried to swarm them. It took a while for Jax and Jay to enter the room upstairs, but it looked like the rest of his family had taken a private exit.

Jax and his band instantly had the women and men he'd invited crowd him with congratulations.

The place had turned into the equivalent of a backstage party that I didn't want to be in attendance for. With the concert still going on and Taylor Swift now taking the stage to say she was, of course, backing one of the best artists in history with his new app, it was hard to hear or comprehend anything.

Jay pushed through the crowd of people to get to me. He didn't say anything, just moved in to hug me tightly.

I knew he knew. He'd called about a hundred times. I just didn't want to address it with anyone yet. He pulled back and held my face in his hands so I could look up at him. "When you're ready, I'm ready, Brey."

I nodded and held back the tears I could have shed from just those few simple words.

He stepped back like he knew I needed the space or maybe he knew Jax did because all of a sudden, Jax appeared in back of him, moving toward me with purpose.

Without addressing anyone else, he grabbed my arm. The shock from his touch jolted with pain this time. Not lust, not want, not desire.

"We need to talk," he stated.

The magnetism between us had flipped and my body wanted to repel him. I didn't protest though. I walked along beside him without looking back at anyone else.

This moment, this downfall was ours alone. Anger and betrayal pumped through my blood, building my body up to attack him.

I was so coiled, so pushed to the brink, so teetering on the edge that every camera could have been flashing lights on me, and it wouldn't have mattered.

When we rounded a corner to a small seating area somewhat closed off from the room, he spun me so I faced him. "What the fuck happened today?"

I lifted my chin. "A lot. Where would you like me to start?"

His eyes widened like he couldn't believe I snapped back at him. "From the beginning, apparently. Since I was under the impression that after we slept together last night, you weren't going to do anything without me."

"I don't know where you got that impression," I countered.

"Oh, I don't know. When I was buried inside you and there weren't any fucking protests about not going without me."

I stuttered at his callousness. "When you were … I'm sorry … excuse me?" I barely kept my voice from rising. "I don't have to protest or confirm anything with you, Jax."

"No, I guess you don't. I guess that's not the type of relationship we have, is it, Whitfield?"

"The type of relationship we have? You want to talk about relationships? You want to talk about how deceitful you have been this whole time?" I took a step toward him, so sick of the lies hanging over our heads. "You couldn't tell me after all these years that you'd been investing for him. Or that you knew I was investing your parents' money into the reservation?"

A small jerk escaped his body as he blinked with the words I spoke. He hadn't known I knew. That was my first sure sign of that. He recovered quickly though, as if a little jab of a knife could slow him down.

His counterattack was faster and it slashed at my heart. "So what? You went to see him without me and found out things you didn't want to learn. Surprise, surprise." He slowly clapped.

"You are so disrespectful."

"I could have told you that was going to happen, Whitfield."

Maybe it was the callousness or lack of feeling in his voice that got to me. Maybe it was the sheer lack of remorse. I couldn't say for sure. All I knew was the thin thread holding me together didn't just unravel. It snapped.

"You're a real fucking asshole, you know that, Jax?"

"Me? I'm the asshole even though I took you the day before to go see him? I took you, wanted to be there for you, Peaches. I needed this to be something we did together."

"*You* needed? This wasn't about you." I pushed my finger into his chest. "This was about me. Me facing my father."

"I should have been there with you."

"Why? So, you could control what was said? So, I wouldn't find out?"

"You can't be serious with that accusation."

"What if I am? What's the point in investing in his company? You've basically been helping him stay afloat all these years. Helping him! Not hurting. Not leaving him alone. Not considering how that would make anyone feel. How that would make me feel. What's wrong with you?" I emphasized the question, so sick with the idea of them in business together.

"Whitfield, there's a lot you don't know … "

"Because you've never told me!" I screamed as I threw my hands up. "And I can't help but wonder why."

"What's that supposed to mean?"

"Is this all a game to you or are you so selfish that investing in his company actually helped you, made you richer and that's all you care about?"

He stepped toward me like he wanted me to take back what I'd said immediately. "Don't fuck with me, Whitfield. You know better than to say that shit to me."

"I don't though. I don't know anything about you anymore. What I thought I knew isn't real."

"Cut the bullshit. You're fishing for something to be mad at when you know you don't have to. Don't let this ruin us again."

"How can you think there's even an us when you were never once truthful with me?"

"Everything we've had has been the truth, Whitfield."

His voice held a warning but I pushed on. "I can't possibly believe that now. Not after all the lies."

"Peaches, you know what we have is real."

"It can't be." I whispered, letting go of that fragile little thing that was our relationship.

"Yes, it can." He stepped toward me but I stepped back. "I fucking love you, woman."

"No!" I screamed. "Don't say those three words to me like this. You did it just as badly before."

"I meant it then just like I mean it now."

"You don't know how to mean it. You don't know how to love me. I don't believe it."

"You better because I'm not fucking around."

"How can I believe it, Jax? It would make me an idiot. Fool me once, but more? I'm not that naive."

"You're being paranoid just like him."

His last words rang over and over in my head as I stared at him. Those words that so ruthlessly compared me to the man I hated. They were my only excuse, my reason, my only justification for acting how I did after.

I don't remember flying at him. I just know I did. Katie said she was proud and Vick said I looked unhinged. I reached him before anyone could stop me and the slap could have been heard throughout the campus. Jax's head flew to the side with the impact. Then he turned back to face me. His eyes blazed with such emotion I wasn't sure if I would have chosen that or the apathy I saw in them before.

He rubbed his cheek. Then he whispered with a voice that seemed so dead and lifeless after being so full of life during his concert, "Like father, like daughter then, Aubrey Whitfield."

My friends, the people who seemed to show up even when it didn't pay to, took away my opportunity to hit him again.

Rome was there wrapping his arms quickly around me before I could unleash the violence that took over me.

I screamed at Jax, "We're done. This is over. Don't ever talk to me again."

I fought Rome as he carried me away, wanting to inflict physical pain on Jax. Rome kept whispering, "Calm down. Calm down, baby girl. It'll go viral in the media."

Katie said later that instead of settling down, an animal force took over, Vick said she was sure she imagined how hard I fought, my stare locked on Jax.

I suppose I'd been fed up with keeping appearances for so long that lashing out finally felt right, liberating, like I shouldn't have held back even if I wanted to. I know I lunged for his face, ready to claw him, arms and fingers stretched, ready to tear him down and make him feel the pain I felt. It wasn't just what I wanted, it was the only thing I could do. And yet, Rome held me off, pulling me back away from him and the circle of people that had formed.

Through the haze of what I remember, one particular image stood out, clear as blood on white linen. Jax's stone-cold face as he looked on at me fighting to get to him. He didn't look scared or sad or remorseful. He didn't look like any emotion at all.

Then, Jay walked right up to him and punched him in the face so hard, everyone gasped.

I stopped fighting Rome.

Jax's head snapped to his brother, his mouth bloody. He wiped the trickle of blood from the corner and said low, "I'll let you have that one, little brother ... "

Jay cut him off, "I told you not to fuck this up." Jay glanced my way. I saw pain as deep as mine, like he couldn't believe his brother had done this.

I cracked then. My body convulsed and instead of fighting in Rome's arms, I crumpled. The sobs that racked me were ugly and brutal.

I felt the loss of someone I'd loved for so long, it was like death, plain and simple. Our relationship was dead, and the vision of who he painted himself to be was dead too.

I heard him call my name. Maybe I imagined his voice cracking and finally sounding like he gave a damn, but Rome was carrying me away by then.

I wasn't looking back.

Not for anything.

CHAPTER
FORTY-SEVEN

AUBREY

THE NEXT WEEK PASSED. I made it through just fine. Katie saw me rolling with the punches and although she looked a bit worried, she nodded like this was the way to do it.

Vick pleaded with me to let my feelings out. Rome said I needed to heal in my own way, that it would come with time.

I told them all I was fine and that this heartbreak wasn't like last time.

And it wasn't.

The day my class resumed, I got up to get ready and found Jay in my living room.

"Have you packed to get back to LA yet?" I asked as I started getting my coffee ready. It wasn't a chai tea or even a coffee with sugar mixed in. It was black. Bold. And straight to the point.

"I'll pack my bags when I think you're ready for me to leave." I laughed a little. "I'm good, Jay."

"Yeah, so you keep saying. I think you're too good though, which is bullshit."

I nodded at his assessment. To everyone, over these past few days, it must have appeared that way. I hadn't wallowed or cried like I'd done in the moment. I wasn't dwelling on losing Jax like I had the first time.

I wasn't sad, I'd told them over and over. And it wasn't a lie. I was numb. Dead. Empty. Those were better words.

I'd told myself I wouldn't fall for him again and I had. I'd fallen so hard and so deep into that hole of love, I couldn't see a way out.

The heartbreak poured into that hole too, like oil and tar pouring into an ocean. It was inescapable and toxic. I'd tried to claw my way out of the hole but the heartbreak stuck to me, pulled me down even deeper and suffocated me.

Worse, it infected everyone around me. I saw the way my friends looked at me, like I was so fragile and breakable.

I shook my head at Jay. "I'm moving on, Jay."

"No one moves on that fast from what you just went through."

"Do most people go through what I went through?"

He leaned forward on the couch and put his head in his hands before he ran them through his dark hair. When he did that, he reminded me so much of his brother, I almost winced in pain.

When he stood and looked at me though, his blue eyes held compassion and love for me, unlike Jax's last cold stare.

Jay had never been one to hold a grudge or get so mad that he'd freeze someone out with just a look. Jax, on the other hand had perfected that.

"I don't know another damn soul that has fucked with a person the way you two fuck with each other."

I just hummed in agreement as I poured coffee and held up the pot to see if he wanted any.

He nodded. "And I also don't know another damn soul who's gone through surviving the trauma you both have. I know you're strong, but it doesn't mean you can get over all this so fucking quick. I witnessed how hurt you were last time ... "

I cut him off. "Last time, we were young, and I didn't know what I was getting into. This time, I made the decision knowing what could happen. I took that risk willingly."

"It doesn't mean you can't be hurt that it didn't work out the way you wanted it to."

"True." I nodded and handed him a mug of coffee. "But I'll live. I'm just not going to fold under the pain this time."

"You never folded," he balked, like a good friend protecting me against my own criticism.

"I did and I don't feel inclined to again. I learned my lesson, Jay."

He leaned against the counter and took a sip of his coffee as he studied me. "What lesson is that?"

"Love doesn't take sympathy just because you were heart-broken before. I should have known better. Love gives us what we deserve."

"He deserves to have the shit beat out of him," he grumbled into his mug.

"You already punched him."

"And he didn't fight back. You know why? He knew he fucked up."

I smiled. "You should be happy he didn't fight back. You need your pretty face."

He scoffed. "I can handle my own against my brother."

I raised my eyebrows.

He pushed off the counter and moved to pinch my side but I sidestepped him. "Don't be a Sass Pot. I'm a damn good fighter."

I shrugged and took my coffee to the couch. "If you say so."

He followed and sat down so close, I fell into his side. "I know so."

I eyed his large body next to me. "Personal space ever been an issue for you?"

"Not when I'm next to a hot piece of ass like yours."

I rolled my eyes and switched on the TV. Of course, the enter-tainment news blared over the screen because it was Jay's job to know exactly what was going on in the industry. He reached to grab the remote quickly and change the channel but I moved it out of his way.

"It's fine, Jay." I stared at the TV as they showed picture after picture of Jax and my family on the screen. "I know what the news has to say. I've been through it before."

And I had been through it before. He just expected me to react to it the same way I had in the past. I crumbled under the media last time and retreated into a dark lonely shell I'd built for myself.

Now, the host on the TV waved at her face while she gazed at a picture of Jax. "He's the hottest bachelor who apparently is back on the market, and he's worth millions, ladies. Last week, during his launch, sources claim he fought with his brother's ex, Aubrey Whitfield. She's the lucky woman who has been with not one but two Stonewoods, it seems. They say she broke both of their hearts, and I am willing to bet—"

Jay grabbed for the remote and got it this time. He switched the TV off and gawked at me. "I think you're turning into a masochist."

I rolled my lips between my teeth before responding, "If I am turning into one, at least I'll be an informed one when I get swarmed by paps later out there."

Jay tensed a little, which meant there were still paparazzi waiting to get my picture somewhere outside. "It'll all blow over, Brey. Give it a week, and they'll be on to a new story."

"I'm aware." They would be on to a new story, and I would be stuck with this same one, trying to get on with my life.

"If it's any consolation, he hasn't left his penthouse in the city. He asked if you were—"

I held up my hand. "I don't want to know, Jay."

It took every ounce of control I had not to scream for more information. We hadn't spoken to one another. I hadn't called him, and he'd only called once. I ignored it and when the voice mail came through, I deleted it before even listening.

I could want to know everything about him, what he was doing, how he was feeling, but it wouldn't help. I had to move on.

I jumped up. "I have to get to class. Last week before I can officially graduate."

Jay smiled. "I can't believe you aren't walking in the commencement ceremony."

"Yes, you can because you know I hate the attention."

He shook his head as he stood up. "My driver can drop you off on the way back to my place. I need to talk to you about my dad and Jett's proposal anyway."

I agreed to drive with him but didn't agree to Senior Stonewood's proposal.

"What do you mean you can't?" Jay pushed on my way to class.

"I have to find a way to pay back your parents for the trust—the charity they gave me. I can't take a handout of a job from your dad too." Jay breathed deep, pulling in air like he was trying to suppress the anger that wanted to blow out of him instead. "You. Are. Not. Charity. Brey."

"Easy for you to say. They're your parents. That money actually could have potentially been yours." I winced. "Oh, God. I probably ate away at your trust fund, Jay."

He yelled to the driver to keep going around the block when he stopped in front of the building for my class. Then his eyes snapped to me. "Get fucked, Brey. My parents have a shit ton of money. That money would have just gone into the fucking business and made us more money."

"All the more reason I need to pay it back."

He shook his head, frustrated. "Alice, call Dad." My eyes widened. "No, Alice! Don't call him."

"Jay," Alice said through the speakers. "I am calling your dad."

Jay chuckled and patted my thigh. "Alice only listens to who she's programmed for."

When Senior Stonewood's voice boomed out over the speakers, I eyed the door handle. I could have jumped out and made a run for it but Jay locked the doors when he saw me contemplating it.

"Dad, Brey thinks your job offer is charity."

My eyes bugged out at him as I shoved him hard in the shoulder. "She should know I wouldn't risk someone being a part of my business for charity."

He didn't know I was in the car. I mouthed to Jay that I wasn't there. I motioned that I would slit his throat if he mentioned it.

"Brey's here. Can you talk some sense into her?"

"Oh, good," Senior Stonewood said, his tone flat like he didn't care one way or the other. "Brey, you'll take the job. We can have you start in a few weeks. When do you graduate?"

I cleared my throat. "I'm done with class after this week but it doesn't matter, Mr. Stonewood. I owe you and Mrs. Stonewood enough as it is. I appreciate the offer—"

"You owe us for what?" he questioned.

"The funds you said were from my mother and for all Mrs. Stonewood did for me when—"

"You owe me and my wife for taking care of our family?" Mr. Stonewood's voice was frigid. So cold, I shivered back into my seat.

"That's kind of you to refer to me as family," I started, eyeing Jay for help.

He lifted his eyebrows and shrugged like I deserved whatever I had coming to me.

"I don't care about being kind, Brey. I don't waste my time on niceties to make someone feel good. You're family. You think you owe me for giving a person in my family a trust? Fine. I need time off and Jett will need an intern to help. You can pay me back by being that intern for Jett."

"I don't think me working for Stonewood Enterprises is a good idea. Jax works—"

"He works in a different department. And you can work remote when need be."

I shoved Jay again who had started to laugh quietly from his side of the SUV.

"I just don't think … It's probably a better idea … "

"I have to get back to work. Jett can iron out the details with you later, and if my wife calls, don't offend her with the idea of paying us back."

Before I could reply, I found out where Jax got his habit of hanging up on people from. Alice announced that the call had ended. Jay laughed loudly while I sat there with my mouth hanging open.

When he sobered enough, he leaned back in his seat. "Dad doesn't really take no for an answer."

"I know that, Jay!" I moved to shove him again but he held up his hands in surrender. "This is all your fault. I have to do this now."

"Yup." He patted my back as I leaned forward to put my face in my hands. "You'll be fine, Sass Pot. This will all work out. In the meantime, you need to get to class."

I don't remember what was said or done in class that day. I was playing out scenarios of how to get out of the internship.

Every scenario had me cowering under Senior Stonewood's demands though.

It wasn't the path I had conjured up for myself. For so long, I thought I'd invest my own money and help Margie with the kids. I thought I could make a difference that way.

Now, I was indebted to Senior Stonewood, to the whole Stonewood family really. Every way I looked at it, the internship would help me pay them back.

So, I succumbed to the idea.

CHAPTER
FORTY-EIGHT

AUBREY

THE TWO WEEKS before my internship flew by more quickly than I would have liked. I passed my class with an A but couldn't bring myself to call Jax and share the news.

So, I dove into focusing on ironing out my internship schedule, figured out a plan to move to the city by continuing to rent my apartment month-to-month until I found a place, and spent as much time at Margie's as I could.

Each time, she would tell me that we could find a way to tell the kids I wouldn't be around as much. I just told her they were a big part of my life and I would still be there every week. A lot of me had changed, but my love for that place hadn't. My goal was still to learn to invest well enough that I could keep them afloat in the future.

One particular day, the kids were so hyper when I arrived, I asked Margie what had caused it. She sheepishly admitted that

Jax had started to visit. I didn't comment on that news, but I left with my blood boiling.

He knew better than to start coming to visit and then drop it all when he decided they weren't convenient anymore for him. And that would happen.

He'd done it to me, and he'd do it to them.

I tried my best not to seethe about it. I went running that day, I talked it out with my friends, and I even went running again.

That night, I dialed his number. "Peaches, you all right?"

Hearing that voice again laced with sleep had me forgetting the real reason I called and remembering all the reasons I shouldn't be. I wasn't immune to him yet. I still loved that voice, still wanted to wake up right beside him and hear it. My body ached knowing I wouldn't ever be able to again.

I whispered out a lie, "Of course, I'm all right. Why wouldn't I be?"

He cleared the grogginess from his throat. "It's the middle of the night."

I glanced at the time on my phone and winced. "I didn't realize it was two in the morning."

He hummed. "I'm glad you finally called. We should talk—"

"I didn't call to talk about us," I snapped, knowing I didn't have the strength to rehash our issues. "Margie said you went to visit."

He sighed.

"I specifically asked you not to do that! They need stability."

"Who's to say I can't be stable?"

"Are you kidding?" I said.

"Whitfield, don't say some shit you're going to regret," he warned, his voice low.

"Oh, please. You're one to talk about saying shit you'll regret! You couldn't wait to throw my father in my face."

He groaned. "I never should have—"

"It doesn't matter," I said quickly. "God, none of this matters. Except you are not going to see the kids anymore. They've been through enough lately."

"I'm not going to put them through any more. I plan on being around. I won't let them down with that."

"Like you planned on not letting me down?" The question jumped out of my mouth before I could stop it.

"You know damn well you made the decision for both of us to stop what we were doing when you went to see him. I didn't let you down, Peaches. And I've called. You don't answer."

"I can't make the same mistake my mom did."

"What the hell does that mean?"

"She stayed in a toxic relationship—"

"Don't you dare compare what your mom had with him to our relationship."

I laughed but it was hollow. "I can't make a comparison but you can? Like father, like daughter, right?"

"Peaches, baby, I should have never said it. I meant what I said in the voice mail—"

"It's fine. I'm fine. It doesn't matter what you said in the voice mail, I didn't listen to it."

He grumbled.

I didn't wait to hear what he had to say. "It's true, anyway. A part of him is in me. He raised me. So, maybe I'm twisted from that. Maybe seeing them together as the only real relationship I knew for so long, maybe I justified what we had as healthy. But it's not. I have to take what I learned from them and know when something is toxic. We're toxic and unhealthy, Jax. And I have to walk away from something like that even if my mother couldn't."

He stayed silent for so long, I figured he'd come to terms with what I'd said. His fight to keep us together finally died, and something in me that felt a lot like hope and happiness died along with it.

"Can you just stop going to Margie's too? We don't need to be making this any more complicated than it is, and the kids need people who will stick around."

He grunted and then growled, "They need us. So, I don't plan to go anywhere, Whitfield. Mark my words, I'll always be there."

I knew he wasn't talking about the kids anymore. "Jax, please just let us go."

"No," he practically yelled. "If what we have is unhealthy, I don't want to be healthy. I'll take the fucking heart attack." His voice cracked. "Inevitable, Peaches. We're inevitable. Watch the news tomorrow."

Then, he hung up.

That very next day, I stared at the TV in shock. Katie and Rome came over to stare at it in shock with me.

"He did the impossible," I whispered to them.

Neither of them responded. We just listened to the news anchor go over the millions he must have lost in his latest deal to close down Whitfield Candy Company. The numbers were staggering, yet the feeling of my father stripped of all his power was even more overwhelming.

To me, he'd done what I thought no man could do.

The man on the TV said it had obviously taken Jax years to gain the trust of my father and take over the majority of the stock. They were baffled that someone who'd never faltered and had Stonewood as his name, could've made so many mistakes so quickly after taking over that he was forced to close up shop for good.

The hit to his name and bank account would be monumental, they said. Speculation swirled on other channels too. They said he'd slotted everything into place for that app launch, that money was flooding in from it. No one really believed he'd lost his investing touch after all the right moves he'd made with that, and so this was a calculated plan to purposefully take a loss and shut down the company. They speculated he'd done everything for me.

For once, I believed the media.

"I think you should call him," Katie blurted.

I put my head in my hands, "To say what?"

"Everything you ever wanted to say," Rome answered.

"This doesn't erase how crazy we are together, you guys."

"Better to be crazy together, than nothing at all apart," Rome said matter-of-factly as he got up. "Kate-Bait, talk some sense into your friend."

Then he walked out of my apartment.

I blew a raspberry and looked at Katie. "I'm getting through this the best way I know how. Talking to him won't help."

She patted my thigh. "It's not the best way. It's your safe way. Time to buck up, bitch, and fight for that creep of yours."

"Katie, I can't call him."

"Then, he'll find you. He always does."

Her omen echoed through me for the next few days and on the first day of my internship, I told myself over and over that Jax hadn't called. We weren't together. We worked in different departments. He wouldn't seek me out. He wouldn't come looking for me.

I took my first two-hour train ride into the city and walked the rest of the way to the Stonewood Enterprises building. The height of it humbled me as I looked up before walking in.

When I stepped through the doors, there Jax stood, just as tall in my mind as the building. Dressed in a dark navy suit with his hair slicked back, he was just as foreboding and awe-inspiring too.

He stood in the lobby with two coffee cups, looking at me expectantly. Like I should go to him, like we were meeting here. I took him in and saw circles under his eyes. Those blue eyes didn't hold much sparkle and he didn't smile. He just looked me up and down as if he were measuring me up.

I didn't move, my stilettos had frozen to the ground. I congratulated myself on wearing the white dress that fit so well, that he swore he'd destroy. I knew, at the very least, I looked good standing there like an idiot, holding on to my briefcase as if it would save me from having to talk to him.

On the phone, yelling at him, I could do. Seeing him and knowing what he'd done for me, for us, I didn't know if my knees would give out or I would end up crying on the floor on my first day.

He walked to me, and I tried to ready myself for a conversation.

When I opened my mouth, he shook his head and shoved the cup in my hand. "It's a chai latte."

"I don't drink—"

"Humor me, okay?"

My eyes started to water at those words. "Jax."

He shook his head again. "Not today, Whitfield. Enjoy your first day. White looks phenomenal on you."

He walked away, and I whispered that blue looked phenomenal on him too.

My first four days flew by. Every morning, he met me in the lobby, offering a chai latte and a compliment on my attire. My work day then consisted of fretting over our minute-long encounter and trying to absorb every little lesson Jett had to offer. When we dove into different portfolios, I remembered I could do all of it, that I enjoyed doing it.

By the end of the work week, I'd found a rhythm. I got ready by dressing in a simple black pencil skirt and flowy black top. I wondered if Jax would have something to say about it as I entered the lobby and waited for my chai latte.

When I stopped to look around for him, I was surprised to find he wasn't there.

I tried to shake it off, but his absence weighed on me throughout the day. When Jett asked me what to do about a particularly tricky portfolio, Jax's words from so long ago popped into my head. "Let yourself fly a little."

I thought I saw him in the halls and around the corners or smelled him in the conference rooms. He was nowhere to be found. At lunch, I got in the elevator to go find something quick to eat when he appeared.

No one followed him on and when I saw his face, I knew why. He looked ready to cut down anyone who got in his way.

"Whitfield," he nodded as the doors closed.

"Jax," I nodded back and glanced around, wondering if anyone could see us enclosed in the elevator by ourselves.

"You look good," he grunted.

"Thanks," I whispered because it was all I could manage. We were alone, and I smelled the mint I missed, felt the presence I longed for, and saw the man I couldn't quite figure out but knew I loved.

"We need to talk."

I shook my head. "That's not a good idea," I blurted.

He just looked down at me and mouthed inevitable. Then he stepped forward and swiped his key FOB.

"Jax! I have work to do."

"You're on your lunch."

"Well, I'm working during lunch." I crossed my arms. He smiled a little. "Now who works too much?"

I shut my eyes, frustrated as the elevator doors opened to his penthouse. When he waved me in, I went.

Two coffee cups were sitting on his counter and he nodded to them. "I had a meeting this morning that I couldn't miss."

I grabbed one. "Please stop getting me these."

"You know I won't."

"Why, Jax? We aren't together." I motioned between us. "This doesn't work and seeing each other every morning doesn't work either. It's painful."

"It *is* fucking painful, Peaches. I should be waking up to you every morning and making you that chai latte."

"Oh, no." I started to move toward the door but he stepped in front of me. "I am not doing this. We had our end. We can't keep having it over and over."

"You ended it because of your father. He's out of the picture now. He's fucking done."

His words resonated with me. Like a dehydrated animal hearing the first drops of rain, I wanted to weep with relief.

The feeling was wrong. "You shouldn't have done all that, Jax. You shouldn't have spent your time and money to destroy him for me."

"It wasn't just for you. It was for myself. It had to be done. For both of us."

His words nearly broke me. "That doesn't erase everything, Jax."

"I know." He combed his hand through his hair. "It's a start though. It's a fucking base that might be cracked and messed up, but it's something. We build from there. If not for us, then lets at least do it for my brother and family. We work in the same place here. We have to get along."

I shook my head and set down the latte. "No way." I pointed a finger at him. "You used that as a tool before to start this all up again. And look where that got us."

He stalked toward me. "I'll use whatever I have to. This isn't over. It won't ever be."

I stepped around him and he let me pass. "I can't talk about this. There's nothing left to say. I have to get back to work." I walked onto the elevator and he let me go.

His blue eyes held deep determination as the doors closed. I knew our conversation wasn't over.

After work, I was so tired I could barely keep my eyes open on the train. I sat at a window seat and leaned onto it as I closed my eyes.

Just as I was about to drift off to sleep, a familiar mint smell filled the air, and the hairs on my arms stood up.

An intoxicating voice whispered in my ear, "You shouldn't ever sleep on a train, Whitfield."

My eyes snapped open to see Jax sitting next to me. I had to lean back just to make sure I wouldn't lean in instead. He looked so good wearing his suit pants with a button-down shirt that I knew had a suit jacket over it earlier in the day. Now, he sat there with his sleeves rolled up and looked at me with love in his stupid, perfect blue eyes.

"What are you doing here?"

"We need to finish our conversation."

"I already said we have nothing to talk about."

"I figured you said that at work. That you would be able to talk after."

I looked around and knew I couldn't escape for the next hour. My resolve to avoid him was already cracking, and I didn't know how I would withstand him for long. I moved to get up. I needed to put some distance between us.

He grabbed my bicep, the pleading look in his eyes made me stay. "I rewrote "Sweet Sin" for you."

"I heard it at the launch." I glared because the words he'd changed it to had been heartbreaking.

"No." He pulled out his phone and two ear buds. He slid one in my ear and his hand lingered on my cheek. The spark as he touched me had me leaning into him before I could stop myself. "The lyrics that day were out of anger. This version, I wrote for you out of love. I love you, Peaches. I don't ever say it right, but I mean it every time. Shit, woman, I mean it even when I don't say it all."

I rolled my lips between my teeth to hold onto the words I wanted to respond with. I loved him, I couldn't stop loving him even if I wanted to. "I'm not strong enough to keep doing this, Jax."

He took his hand from my face, and I felt the loss of warmth immediately. "Don't be strong anymore, then. I'll be strong for both of us."

He turned on the song from his phone and sat back.

An acoustic guitar played at first, soft and sweet. We both stared ahead as the train rolled on.

When his voice came over the ear bud, it mixed with him there right beside me as he sang along.

> "Sweet Sin, Sweet Sin. You pulled me in.
> You're my beacon in the night,
> won't ever stop being my light.
> I loved you before, ever more, ever more.
> Sweet Sin, Sweet Sin, I love you now.
>
> Stop fighting it. Just fight for this.
> For this. For us.
> Ever more, ever more.
> Sweet Sin."

He harmonized every word and people on the train started to turn and stare. His voice mixed joy and sorrow together and wove them up so beautifully, I didn't know whether to cry or smile.

The guitar took over and he slid his hand to my thigh to rub circles as tears streamed down my face.

He stared at me staring at him. Then, he mouthed at me, "Okay?" I nodded and mouthed back, "I love you."

EPILOGUE

JAX

PEOPLE WHO SAY all is fair in love and war haven't really loved or fought in a war. I like to think the saying should be all is fair in business and money. Even then, when someone says, "Don't take it personally. It's just business," you sure as shit take it personally.

Love and war are different though. There are lines on a battlefield that aren't crossed. Women and children shouldn't be hurt, those unarmed shouldn't be harmed, mustard gas can't be used. Sure, those rules have been broken before but history never shined a positive light on those incidents. Those were the incidents that weren't fair, that had rules broken, and that broke down the saying.

The relationship I had with Whitfield should have followed the saying. I'd figured it would.

All's fair in love. And. War.

And damn, weren't we at war with each other half the time.

But I loved loving her and loved warring with her just as much every day of my life.

I'd come to terms with knowing the moment I met her, I've loved her in some capacity.

I loved her smell, her hair, her sassiness, the way she challenged me, the way she lit up when I challenged her. I fucking loved that girl.

So, my twisted way of showing it was messed up. Selfishly, I had wanted to take down and beat the monster who'd ruined her childhood at his own game. I wanted to own him and know that he could never own or ruin another part of her life again.

I didn't go visit him to give him the satisfaction of telling me off. It was another step taken to crush his spirit and let him know I had ruined everything he'd ever built. Instead, I received a report on how he'd taken the news.

To say I was satisfied with the report was an understatement.

And yet even knowing all this, knowing I'd accomplished what I set out to do, didn't really matter.

Because all wasn't fair in love and war.

There were rules.

There were standards and lines that shouldn't be crossed.

I'd crossed all of them.

I knew the second the words left my mouth in that room, staring down into her green eyes, that I'd stepped over an edge I couldn't climb out of. Her face shuddered with agony I knew I wouldn't be able to take back. And for moments, I didn't want to take it back. She'd made me so damn mad, I wanted her to feel the fucking betrayal I felt after finding out she'd gone without me.

I was supposed to be there for her. I was supposed to protect her from him. From anyone. And she hadn't let me. She hadn't trusted me enough to let me be that person. So, I'd crossed the line. I'd hit below the belt. I'd stabbed her in her back and watched the love she had for me bleed out.

When she hit me, I wanted her pain, I wanted to feel it and absorb it and keep feeling it because the damn woman evoked every emotion in me that I couldn't control. I wanted her to feel the chaos too. When I spewed more bullshit about her being like her dad, I was looking for her—and the room—to erupt.

Maybe I wanted it all along, for us to combust and explode. I had accused her of creating bullshit so we couldn't be together, but I was just as guilty.

Mostly though, I think I couldn't see past the burden of my feelings for her. I loved her so fucking much, I'd barely been able to get on the stage at my launch, I'd barely been able to launch everything my team had worked so hard for because I'd been consumed with where she'd gone.

She controlled my heart in high school, my soul when I left her mother and father to die, my music when I left her, and my career when I wanted to get her back. I was a fucking slave to her, and she hadn't even known it.

So, I tore us apart by crossing the line, by doing the one thing not fair in our dance of love and war. I compared her to the man she hated and made sure she understood that I knew them both well enough to say they were the same.

When Rome carried her away, and she finally broke down to cry, my resolve cracked. Her broken sobs wrenched through me like they were my own. Souls connected somehow had the uncanny ability to make you feel the other's pain. That pain brought me to my knees, literally.

In the middle of my backstage party, to celebrate the biggest success in music history for a man my age, I tried to suck in enough air to breathe through the turmoil of losing her. Of feeling our souls ripped apart. Of something burning my other half away from me.

My brother stood next to me but it wasn't out of concern.

He bent low to face me and I remember his low whisper. "You deserve all this fucking pain, man. All of it. Losing her will be your biggest mistake. So, you better get the fuck up and start working to get her back."

I did exactly as he said.

Now, I'm staring at her in our bed on the anniversary of the fire and her mother's death. Today will be hard for her. She still struggles with trusting anyone after finding out why her mother stayed with her father. She'll think about it today, and I'll try to carry that burden with her. It won't be easy. I know she still has a wall up because I kept the trust fund from her.

It's something we still fight about and probably will for a long time. We aren't perfect together but no one is.

And yet, as I look at her sleeping, I know I'm damn lucky because she's perfect for me. Her dark hair is loose across the pillow, and she doesn't have a piece of clothing on. She's let go of all her insecurities around me and it's a beautiful thing to witness.

She works hard and takes some of the biggest risks while investing for Stonewood Enterprises I've ever seen. She's good at what she does and it helps her to invest for Margie and the kids. Not that she needs to. We'll always take care of them, but she tells me that's not the point.

We bickered for about a day on where she was going to live. I got my way. There was no way my girl was going to continue to come to work on the train every day.

Now, I'm finding I won't get my way with decorating the place though. Her decorating has turned more colorful and vibrant than anyone who's seen her wardrobe could have imagined. The woman loves colors so bright, I'm concerned we'll outshine the rainbow. She claims she's living for her mother, her grandmother, and herself. That all their dreams show through her colors and her long, dark hair.

I would have let her decorate all of Stonewood Enterprises with that answer.

Still, I am proud to say I put my foot down with our bedsheets. A man deserves to have just white sheets if he's going to stare at pink bedroom walls all day. Today, those white sheets look even better with a bright red engagement ring box sitting on top of them.

Today will be hard for her, but I'm hoping this will make it a little bit better.

The End.

Keep reading for an excerpt
of Jett Stonewood's REVERIE

REVERIE

REVERIE is an angsty, enemies-to-lovers standalone romance where opposites definitely attract.

VICK

Rude. Harsh. Severe. Jett Stonewood.

The billionaire businessman refused to even crack a smile while vacationing in paradise. But I broke him down, introduced some fun into his life.

If we had a bit too much by sleeping together, so be it.

The overly practical man revealed that he could also be caring, thoughtful—and before long he was the one wrecking me.

He pulled me into a complex dream I needed to forget when we returned home.

The problem: Jett acquired my company.

He's everywhere now, a constant reminder of the unattainable.

JETT

Bubbly. Airy. Wildly optimistic. Vick Blakely.

She needed a lesson in safety precautions. Not that she would have followed it if our recent tumble in the sheets was any indication.

She was too peppy... so naive it was dangerous. Someone needed to break down her fortress of positivity, teach her that warnings weren't meant to be invitations.

The solution: I took on the job. I infiltrated her life and began disassembling it. The little pixie flutters around in reverie.

Let's see how well she flies when I reduce her fairy-tale bubble to dust.

VICK

"**YOU'RE FIDGETING," THE MAN** with eyes as dead as stone but as piercing as a sharp knife pointed out.

"I am not." I squirmed one last time in the black dress. The tulle hung loosely over my waist and down to my mid-thigh. Unfortunately, the corseted lace across my bodice left little to the imagination.

I should have ordered a size up.

My best friend, Brey, was marrying a musician-turned-music-app-nerd and every person was recognizable past the lush, expansive row of bushes. If I was going to walk down the aisle as a bridesmaid, I needed to look freaking amazing doing it. I just didn't know how if I couldn't take a breath. I pulled at the strapless sweetheart neckline digging into my cleavage one last time.

"Are you about done? You'll look fine if you just stop squirming like a bee flew up your dress."

Jett Stonewood. The groom's brother. And the devil of a man who Brey paired me with for this ceremony. The other bridesmaid had been paired with Jaydon, the younger, fun-loving brother of the groom. Jett, on the other hand, was who you talked with if you wanted humor to die, your smile to disappear, or your belief in all things joyful to disintegrate.

Still, my knees buckled a little when I saw him in his suit.

Stonewoods wore suits better than any other men on the planet. Jett wore his best. His broad shoulders set a perfect line for the jacket to sit on, accentuating his thick neck and strong jaw. Every part of him screamed masculinity and my body responded.

I licked my lips, turned toward the ceremony, and pointedly ignored him as best I could. The music started, a soft instrumental version of one of Jax's songs. His one album had gone triple platinum, an album he admitted he wrote just for Brey. Then he effectively retired, saying he wanted her to hear it and didn't care about the rest of the world.

My eyes watered thinking of their story.

Lush green rolling hills swelled up from the horizon of the private golf course. Clouds as white as cotton fluffs spotted the blue sky. The centerstage's gondola overflowed with stargazer lilies and roses. The backdrop of it all was the sea, lapping at the sand. The sun hit the clear water in such a way that it looked as if diamonds sparkled everywhere.

I peeked around the corner to get a glimpse of everyone before Jett and I had to walk.

Jett growled, "What are you doing?"

"Just trying to see how it all looks," I whispered.

"Probably about the same as it did when we rehearsed."

I wasn't sure if he was trying to be rude. So I shrugged. "The wedding planner said the sun would start to set over the ocean. The shimmer on the lilies with the Swarovski crystals would be out of this world."

He looked toward the sky and took a deep breath, like my presence was an annoyance he could barely handle.

Yup, definitely trying to be rude.

Before I could say anything more, the wedding planner cued us. I gripped Jett like my life and reputation depended on it as my heels sunk into the sand with each wobbly step.

I did not want to fall face first in these heels when my best friend was about to get her happily ever after.

When we passed the wall of lush shrubs, I closed my eyes.

Beep. Beep. Beep.

It was a sound I heard only in my head. The same rhythm every time. The same high note, sounding off that I was still alive.

Barely.

I opened my eyes and drowned out the beeping with what was right in front of me. The sun shined on precious stones that had been positioned in white-and-red bouquets along the aisle. The flower arrangements stood tall in glass vases. They'd decorated pillars with more crystals and draped tresses of flowers around and above us. The sun basked every guest in their best light. With the waves crashing in the background, the music couldn't have sounded better.

"This is stunning," I whispered to Jett, choking back a sob.

"It's ridiculous," he said under his breath.

His words were so final, and filled with such anger, I forgot where I was. I halted to glare at him.

He nudged my arm, widening his eyes. "What are you doing?" he whisper-yelled at me.

"How can you say that?" I said behind a forced smile as I took measured step after measured step. "This is the perfect day with the most amazing couple."

"You're just as delusional as everyone else."

My jaw dropped. "Excuse me?"

"This marriage is bound to be chock-full of problems. Probably won't last. Most of them don't. And we'll have to pick up the pieces when it falls apart."

"Marriages last when they're meant to be together and those two are soulmates."

A chuckle—dark and bleak—rolled out of him.

As we neared the altar, I tried one last time to change his mind. "This is going to be a moment in your life you'll never forget. This is your brother and your future sister's happily ever after."

He made eye contact with me for the first time. I gasped at how strikingly blue his eyes were. The blue was direct, cutting. It sliced away at my happiness, so vivid and so stark that it seemed to mock anyone who dared to dream of anything. "Vick, everyone should know by now, there's no such thing as happily ever afters."

With that, his arm dropped mine like I was a very hot, very diseased potato. He turned to make his way over to the groom's side.

I twirled toward the bride's side and made sure I strutted with extra pep in my step.

I'd get him to change his mind by the end of the night.

I could make anyone believe in happily ever afters.

JETT

EVERYONE CRIED AS Aubrey and Jax said their vows. Everyone except me.

Maybe I wasn't meant to be a groomsman. My eyes were as dry as the Sahara in a drought. Shit, even my father shed a tear.

Senior Stonewood, the man who'd molded me into who I was, stood next to my mom looking prouder than ever before.

It was quite possible that everyone had amnesia. My father leaned down to say something my mom smiled at. People would have said they looked in love. Yet, I remembered the year my mom kicked my dad out. They'd screamed at each other about his long hours, about the business coming first.

My mom broke down, crying so many nights, her depression nearly overtook her. She begged him to let her be his first love. My dad swore she was. Still, he couldn't commit to anything but his enterprise. The investments pulled him away time and time again.

On those nights, I remember soothing her as she cried on my shoulder while shielding my brothers from her pain and despair at the same time.

Then I grew up. My mother had been so determined to keep us away from my dad's business that I gravitated towards it. Wave after wave of arguments ensued over my staying with my father. My mother had overcome the sadness and morphed into a ferocious woman who could match my father's ruthlessness one-for-one when it came to the job of raising her children. She didn't want me to turn out like him but also didn't want to suppress my dreams because she feared history repeating itself.

Today they held hands like they missed one another, like they had forgotten the past.

Love hadn't conquered all with them, and somehow everyone thought it would conquer all for Jax and Aubrey.

The bar presented the only solution to my problem. I needed to catch amnesia with a drink or two. The outdoor hut with long stalks of hay and twigs for a roof held every type of alcohol, and I could smell the fruit mixed with rum as I approached. The bartender welcomed me with a wide smile across his tanned face.

The groom and my baby brother, Jaydon, walked up next to me.

Jaydon questioned Jax as they both leaned onto the bar. "When do you think the reception music will start?"

Jax chuckled and nodded out at the guests mingling on the sandy coast we'd reserved for a happy hour. "Are you planning something?"

"I might have one or two people crash the party." He smiled like we had nothing to worry about, like just anyone could show up.

"You can't have some girl off the street come to the reception, Jaydon. It's asking for trouble. They could be the media or ... " I started in on him.

"Lighten up, man. We're in Kauai. The media's not trying to fly to the island to get a shot." Jaydon waved me off.

"You're the most famous person here," I ground out, trying to keep my frustration at bay. He'd been acting for years now and tabloids loved to put him center stage. "You should understand how detrimental crazy paparazzi can be," I responded.

"Oh, I understand. I'm just not going to let them dictate my fun," Jaydon said.

Jax sighed. "You're not having strange women at the reception, Jaydon. Aubrey will kill you and then me for allowing it."

"I'll ask her." Jaydon scanned the crowd.

"If you do that right now, I promise I'll help her kill you," Jax grumbled.

Jaydon didn't seem to care because he started texting someone. I snatched his phone away.

"What the fuck, Jett?" He made a grab for it, but I held the phone out of his reach.

"You're not bringing a girl that hasn't had a background check into this event. Everyone signed an NDA. No one outside our circle comes in. End of story."

Jaydon stared at me a second longer and then slumped into the bar. "You two are fucking buzzkills. Brey would let me bring someone in."

Jax snorted.

Jaydon continued, "She might have married you, but she's still my best friend. She's nice enough to give me the opportunity to get laid here."

"Yeah, she's too fucking nice to you. And everyone. Which is why we have to speak up for her." Jax tapped the bar and the bartender appeared, aligning three hand-cut crystal lowball glasses on the shined wood. He poured whiskey in each.

"She's not always that nice." I broached the subject everyone had been avoiding.

Jaydon laughed and sat down on one of the barstools. "She can be a sass pot. Girl knows when to lay down the law."

"If you say so. You're already married but it's still something you should consider, Jax," I said and slid Jaydon's phone back to him.

Jax turned to me and handed over the glass of liquor. His blue eyes held a warning when he asked, "Consider what?"

Maybe I should have backed off. "Her dad's in prison. You and I both know the media can twist a story."

Jax turned to set his glass on the bar and faced me again. This time, I saw the anger. His muscles bunched with it, and his jaw ticked. Behind him, Jaydon stood up—his phone forgotten—with the same look in his eyes that Jax had.

They both wanted me to retract what I'd just said. They wanted me to apologize and say I didn't mean to talk badly about Aubrey Whitfield.

Aubrey Whitfield, the love of his life, was intelligent, inspiring, and driven. In fact, I'd offered her a job investing with me at Stonewood Enterprises after she'd graduated. My team consisted of extraordinary people and she'd overcome her father burning down her childhood home. She took risk after risk. The girl was strong. Perfect for him and for our family, considering the media that followed it.

But they were naive to think the media wouldn't have a field day with how quickly they were getting married. And stupid to think it wouldn't take a toll. I needed them to last, not crumble under the pressure.

And most people folded under the institution of marriage because the titles, the expectations, the compromises—they pushed people to the brink. My parents were a perfect example of that.

If I had to be the one to consider every angle, I would. Fact was, her father was in prison for arson and the homicide of her mother. My brother was a Stonewood and a retired musician. With his fame and her father's notoriety, the press loved to watch their every move.

"She has done well with being in the news, Jax. I'll give her that. But what happens when she gets stressed? What then?"

"Then she gets stressed, and we handle it," Jax replied, his tone flat and void of emotion.

"You have to consider that fifty percent of marriages end in divorce—" I started.

He cut me off. "I went to visit her father for years, Jett. I made it my business to be there, bring him to his knees, and make sure he never bothers us again."

Jax had climbed a metaphorical Mount Everest to make sure Aubrey's father never had the money or authority to come in any contact with his daughter again. I didn't agree with the amount of money he'd lost by disassembling her father's company, but I understood that he'd done it for her. "If you say so."

His eyes narrowed, a glare meant to wither me. "I've considered every aspect of this relationship more than you can ever imagine. Repeat what you just said and you'll regret it."

"Someone has to protect the family…"

Jaydon snorted and crossed his arms. "Brey's never tainted our name and she never will. If anything, she's lowering her standards by marrying Jax. He doesn't deserve her."

Jax shoved him. "Fuck you."

"What? You know damn well you don't deserve her."

"Look," I reasoned with them both. "You're married, it's all fine. In the future, if everyone folds under the pressure, the divorce will be—"

"Jesus," Jax sighed as if he was tired. "You deserve to get your ass beat."

"Are you kidding me, Jax? I'm trying to make every angle clear." I rubbed the five-o'clock shadow that had spurted one or two gray hairs over the course of last year.

Jaydon's gaze ping-ponged between us, and then he pointedly placed himself between Jax and me. "Come on, you two. We don't need black eyes tonight."

"You're lucky I love my wife and don't want to cause a scene," Jax said.

"No, you're lucky. You forget who taught you to fight?" I glared at him over Jaydon's black-suited shoulder.

The muscle in Jax's jaw worked as his ice-blue eyes shot anger my way.

I deserved a beatdown. He was right.

Running my family's investment company was taking its toll on me. I was taking my stress out on them, on this wedding. I didn't have time to vacation in Kauai, even for something as important as my brother tying the knot.

I straightened my tie and adjusted my suit jacket. "Look, Dad's not been present at work lately. He's spending more time with Mom. Trying to make things work." I resisted the urge to state another point in the case of why the institution of marriage wasn't a smart move. My parents were a perfect example of consistent compromise, of my father not getting to do what he loved. "He can't work and make Mom happy, which means more work is falling on my team. We have a lot of clients that need my attention."

Jax stopped me. "I don't give a fuck about a job. I work there too, remember?"

Jax worked on algorithms. Not deals, not major companies under our name folding, not managing the work of thousands. The weight of people's families having dinner on their table each night sat on my back. That work didn't stop because of a wedding.

He continued on, "You're a groomsman. Start acting like you care."

I ground my teeth together as I once again held on to the words I wanted to say.

Jaydon tried to play peacemaker again. "This is supposed to be bonding time between brothers."

I sighed and nodded my head. "Jaydon's right." I patted his shoulder as we both stared at Jax. "Sorry for bringing it up. I just want what's best."

Jaydon turned toward me and let my hand slide from his shoulder. "You didn't let me finish, Jett," he growled, his glare even meaner than Jax's. "It's bonding time, so let's not talk about my best friend like she's not worth a damn or I'll help Jax hide your fucking body, you prick."

I rolled my eyes and turned toward the bar. "Guess I'd better drink the whiskey down and shut the fuck up. Seems you two aren't into seeing reason anytime soon."

They turned away from me and the bar to walk off, leaving me with the toothy bartender.

"What can I get you?" he asked.

The bridesmaid I'd walked down the aisle with literally skipped up beside me. "Can you get him a strawberry daiquiri? One for me too, please."

Spunky, full of life, and exasperatingly happy, Vick didn't appeal to me. Nor did her taste in drinks, but the bartender spun around to make them anyway.

I pushed the heel of my hand to my temple to ward off the migraine I knew would come from irritation. "You can take both of them. I don't want strawberry anything today."

"They're great, I promise. It's the best drink to have in hot weather like this. You'll see." Her smile didn't reach her eyes as she tried her best to keep a cheerful face.

The girl was pretty. She had long blonde hair that swung with its own weight when she walked and a tall enough frame that she could pass as a model. The black dress she wore accentuated her curves, small waist and substantial chest. With high cheekbones and full, pink lips, her face had perfect symmetry.

Her personality was the problem. The fucking prancing around needed to end here. "Where's Brey? Shouldn't you be getting her a strawberry drink?"

Her honey-colored eyes widened. "OMG." She actually said the letters. "She's only drinking white wine today. She can't spill on that dress. And these drinks"—she grabbed hers as the bartender set it down and shoved mine over to me—"have way too much alcohol in them. This bartender doubles down on the daiquiris, I swear. Being that impaired on your wedding day never ends well."

I grabbed the drink. "Well if it's got as much alcohol as you say," I shrugged. "Bottom's up."

I clinked my enormous glass to hers and took a big gulp. The rum overpowered the saccharine taste to the point that I coughed and almost spit up on her dress.

She smiled wide this time, like she'd won a private fight between us. "Told you it packs a punch."

She stood tall, chest puffed out and eyes sparkling when she got the best of someone. She clearly relished in getting the best of me. For the first time that day, I was a little less perturbed and a lot more intrigued.

"What did you say you do for a living?"

She waited a second before she answered me. She stared out at the horizon and the ocean below it, then dropped her gaze to where most of our family and friends were dancing and mingling. "Brey didn't tell you?"

I chuckled. "Brey and I discuss business. She doesn't share what's not important. I know we're looking at buying up the company you work for. Your job isn't really a factor in that."

She stiffened at my bluntness. "I would think everyone's job is a factor if you want to keep people happy."

"It's not my job to make everyone happy."

"Right. Well, the owner of the company I work for strives to do that. He won't sell unless he knows his employees are taken care of."

"Everyone sells for the right price, honey."

"You'd be surprised what Steven has turned down. I promise he's not in it for the money."

I leaned back on the bar and studied her. Those eyes turned a molasses color when she got fired up. She stood her ground with me, and I liked it more than I thought I would. "You're sure about that?"

She folded her arms over her chest and glared at me. "I'm sure."

I shrugged and downed the rest of my daiquiri before I turned to place it on the bar. "So, what do you do within the company that makes you so sure?"

"I ... well,"—she cleared her throat—"I'm one of the associate contract lawyers for Samson and Sons."

"Samson and ..." I recall chuckling a bit at the name when I'd first read over it. We would have to drop it if we acquired them. I couldn't help but smirk as I cleared my throat. "Doesn't matter. An associate who knows what the owner wants?"

She flipped her ponytail over her shoulder like she was fluffing her feathers. "Look, Steven and I have known each other a long time. Our families go way back. I interned with the firm, and I'm climbing the ranks fast. He's confided in our team—and in me—time and time again. We trust him to do what's right for the company."

"If you say so." The bartender appeared again. This time, I ordered our drinks. "We'll have two tequilas straight up."

"I don't want—"

I cut her off. "I tried yours. You'll try mine."

"It's disgusting."

"It's much healthier than what you're drinking."

"And you think I'm trying to be healthy tonight?" she snapped.

"I think we're both doomed to feel the effects of our drinks tomorrow. Let's just enjoy what the bartender serves us."

"Fine." She narrowed her eyes. "But, if I finish this drink, you have to dance to one song with me and look like you are having an enjoyable time. It's your brother's and Brey's day. We have to make it the best. For them."

I sighed and shoved her drink toward her when the bartender brought it over. "If we keep getting drinks, I'll be able to look like I'm having a magnificent time."

She rolled her eyes and brought the glass to her lush lips. She tipped it back fast, letting the liquid flow into her mouth.

The sun-kissed skin of her neck bobbed as she swallowed. She'd probably been out prancing along the beach every day before the wedding, singing the praises of the sand and seashells.

She didn't cough at all. I was surprised when she kept gulping and finished the drink right then. She set the glass down without a wince.

Her triumphant smile met her eyes this time. "You ready to dance?"

Before I could answer, she spun around so fast her blonde hair whipped me in the face. Then, she was bobbing up and down as her heels carried her to the open dance area on the beach. Aubrey and Jax swayed near a speaker, along with their friends.

I grunted and downed my drink before I made my way over.

The beat of the music moved the crowd, pulsed through the bodies. I sidled up close to Vick and shrugged when Jaydon raised his eyebrows at me.

Vick lifted her hands above her head and rolled her hips while she smiled at me. "I love this song."

I rocked just enough so I looked like I might be dancing. "Do you love everything?"

She laughed at my question. "What's there not to love?"

She didn't give me time to answer, just spun and dropped down low to the beat. Her friends hooted and egged her on. She bounced a little, watching me. Her antics were immature, but I had to admit she looked hot as hell doing it.

Pole dancers looked good while they worked too. It didn't mean they should do it everywhere.

As if Vick read my mind, she leaned into me and slid her body up mine to bring herself back to her full height.

She was being ridiculous, I thought.

She was fucking hot, my dick thought.

I stepped back from her, but she followed me. "Jett, the song's not over yet and you don't look happy at all. This wasn't part of the deal. Are you a man of your word?"

She moved toward me, like a little fox trying to outwit me, and I pulled my frown into a slight smirk.

I slid my arm around her tiny waist and yanked her into me. I moved against her as I leaned down to whisper in her ear, "Sure am, Pixie."

She narrowed her eyes. Then she twirled around and that damn ponytail flew into my shoulder, sliding off it like golden liquid as she walked a few feet away. When she turned back around, her eyes were back to big, honey-colored saucers filled with joy. "Can you do anything other than step side to side?"

I undid the top button of my white collared shirt and when the next song's beat hit, I stepped up to her challenge. I did the damn dance with everyone else.

After one more song, I nodded to Vick. "Man of my word. Off to get another drink."

The woman cracked another grin, like she had an unlimited supply to give out. "I'll come with you."

I headed toward the bar. "I don't want another daiquiri."

"Suit yourself. I do though."

I ordered her another one while I ordered myself more tequila. When the bartender set the drinks down, her hand shot out to grab mine, and she gulped it like a damn shot. When I protested, she held up a finger. "I just need a second before you get all crabby about it."

"The bar is open, woman. Just order one of your own if that's what you want." I tapped the bar and signaled for another.

She stared out at Brey laughing with Jax as she asked, "You don't want to celebrate them. Why?"

"It's complicated."

"Simplify it for me."

"I don't believe it'll last this way. So, it isn't worth the effort."

"So, you think love isn't worth the hassle?"

"Honestly, it isn't."

"What about life?" She turned to me and waited for the answer. The happiness bled out of her eyes, the warmth of the honey sapped away, leaving a worn, dismal mahogany behind. Her stare was cavernous, holding secrets behind layers I wanted to see, to learn, to experience.

When I didn't reply, she lowered her gaze and grabbed her daiquiri. "See ya on the flip side, Mr. Stonewood."

I didn't respond to her trying to end our encounter. I followed her instead. She wove through the crowd and we passed a few tables and chairs in the reception area.

She jumped when she glanced around and saw me standing behind her. "What are you doing?"

"Following you."

"I'm aware. You held up your end of the bargain. We're done playing now. You can go be all dreary somewhere else."

"Why did you ask me if life is worth the hassle?"

She focused on a table covered in a milk white cloth in front of her. Her bubblegum pink lacquered nails ran over the linen, working out the wrinkles. "Well, there are a lot of obstacles."

I nodded, but she continued watching her own efforts to iron out every flaw in the tablecloth.

"Like love, life has hurdles. Peaks and valleys. It's give-and-take. It's a freaking feat just to live. And to love … that deserves serious recognition. So, I wondered what you thought of it all being as pessimistic as you are."

"I'm not pessimistic. I'm realistic."

She peered at me, through me, into something so much greater than me. "And isn't reality the saddest thing there is?"

She waited for my answer with a different type of smile. It didn't spread across her face, and it didn't light the room. She concealed sadness behind it, and she crossed her arms over her chest like she wanted to keep that sadness locked up and hidden from everyone.

"You've been buzzing around this beach like a little pixie, excited to be a part of reality. Now it's sad?"

"I push the bounds of reality to be happy. You have to fight for joy."

I sneered at the ridiculous answer. "You don't change it, Pixie. Reality is what it is. It's all we're given."

A piece of her hair had fallen loose, and she moved her manicured hand to push it behind her ear without answering me. Her somber movement and the way she heaved a sigh fascinated me. Her plump lips parted, and her tongue wet her lips. She ran her gaze up and down my body and those eyes warmed up again.

Her silence hovered in the air, making me wonder exactly what she was thinking. Something had shaken her enough that we'd moved past her default happy personality. I wanted to unravel her and find out what was behind her facade.

"Reality is reality," I continued. "Get lost in it with me?"

She tilted her head. I didn't wait for an answer from her. I walked toward the hotel rooms.

I heard the clicking of her heels behind me and knew that even with the copious amounts of alcohol I drank that night, I would not forget my time with her.

VICK

ALCOHOL WASN'T TO blame for me following Jett on Brey's wedding night.

He spoke of reality, and it jarred me into wanting to experience something other than happiness.

Jett was the epitome of the reality I didn't focus on. I focused on flowers, sunshine, rainbows, and holidays. He focused on mud, darkness, rain before the rainbow, and probably memorials instead of holidays.

He lived in the dark while I lived in the light.

Opposites attract, though, and I was curious as to how the other side lived.

I was also a little tired. Tired of trying not to be jealous of the love Brey and Jax had, tired of not having a date myself. I was so tired of searching for Mr. Right at a wedding when Mr. Wrong was right in front of me.

Jett could barely smile when he danced with me. Still, he could dance, and he could turn me on just as much or more than any nice guy I was going to run into.

I followed him along a grassy pathway and peeked back at the wedding. No one noticed me leaving. My friends were all lost in their own bliss.

We created that. My friends and I had come together to coordinate this celebration of love and life. We planned the reception, tasted the cakes, ordered the flowers, decorated the space, and sent out the invites.

We made a day so perfect no one should have been negative about it.

Yet, there he was. Jett Stonewood. Mr. Negative.

The man had everything going for him. He practically owned a multibillion dollar company, had a family that loved him, and was in Kauai celebrating his brother's happiness. He looked like a freaking god. He stood half a head taller than me even though I wasn't short and I was in heels. His crystal-blue eyes popped against his obsidian black hair. The way he filled out a collared shirt had just about every woman at the wedding salivating. And his face. His freaking jawline and cheekbones and full lips. The combination, honestly, was unfair to every other man.

So how Mr. Everything could also be Mr. Negative was very confusing to me.

Frustrating.

Exhilarating.

Interesting.

I blamed my lack of foresight on it.

I hurried along behind him. He never slowed down for me or looked back. I wondered if he even knew I was following him. When I stumbled over a rock in the path, though, he spun around and caught me before I fell.

"Careful," he grunted.

I mumbled a thank you as I righted myself and tried to step back from him.

He slid his hand down my arm and threaded his fingers through my hand. He slowed his pace as we walked toward the hotel.

I looked out at the horizon and pointed. "This is the most beautiful sunset I've ever seen."

"It's the same one you see everywhere, Pixie," he replied with a smirk, like he knew I had a point.

I laughed. "You know my name's Vick, right? And, come on, it's setting over the same mountains they used to film *Jurassic Park*. It has every color bleeding out into the ocean. It's not the same everywhere and you know it."

"Real is real, doll. It's the same."

I halted on the path, and he turned to look at me. "Sometimes seeing something in a unique light brings a whole new view. You have to admit that."

He squinted at me. He dropped my hand and stepped back. Then he tilted his head as he dragged his gaze up and down my body. "You're in a different light in this sunset."

I didn't shrink at his assessment. I was confident about how I looked even if I was standing in front of one of the most attractive and powerful men I'd ever met. "And? Am I different?"

I didn't realize I was searching for a compliment until he replied with an insult. "No different, Vick. You are who you are. You look how you look. A sunset isn't going to change that."

I rolled my eyes and shoved past him. When we got to a fork in the path, I stopped and asked, "Which way to your hotel room?"

He halted at the fork too. He put his hand on the small of my back before he asked, "You sure you want to come to my hotel room? Will you remember any of this in the morning?"

He wanted to make sure I hadn't drank too much. Or that I wouldn't regret the decision I was about to make. He was giving me a way out, and for some reason that made the way out much harder to take.

"Which way?"

"We should probably call it a night."

I glared at him. "Which way, Jett?"

He sighed and turned to his right without answering. I followed.

Our hotel rooms sat on the edge of cliffs that overlooked the ocean. They were more like condos or suites, so big and inviting that they each had their own entryway. We walked up to his door, and he swiped the keycard while looking at me. The beep sounded, and he twisted the handle but didn't look away. "We walk in here, we lose the facade, Vick. I'm too on edge to play any games or recite some fairy-tale poetry you might want for your happy ending to your day."

I shrugged and walked right past him into his place. "I intend to make you recite poetry because you want to, Jett. It's never forced. It's—"

I didn't finish my sentence because he grabbed my face and devoured my mouth.

I gasped in surprise, but he didn't let up. He dove in deeper, pressing his body against me. The way his tongue tasted mine, the way he didn't hesitate but gripped my face like it was the only thing he ever wanted made me feel like we had something more than just tonight.

He kissed me like he wanted there to be more.

Maybe I imagined it, because then he pulled back and held my face in his hands. His blue eyes looked almost black, and he stared at me like he wanted me to see into his thoughts. "This is reality, Vick."

I leaned in to kiss him, and I didn't hold back. I wrapped my legs around him and let my dress bunch up. I felt him against me. He was long, hard. Ready.

He slid his hands down to my butt and groaned when he felt just a thong beneath my dress. He lifted me up and carried me to his bed.

I didn't look around or take in how he had set up his suite. I didn't care. When he fell back onto the bed with me on top of him, I lifted myself so he could slide my dress over my head. Then I was back on him, sucking his bottom lip, biting it, and working his belt and zipper underneath me.

His hands slid up my back, and one wrapped around my ponytail. He pulled it hard enough that I leaned back and moved to the side. Then he was on top of me, taking over. He ravaged my neck, biting it roughly and then licking it better. He didn't waste time taking off any more of his clothes. He grabbed protection, slid my panties over to the side and plunged into me.

I was ready for him, so ready that I orgasmed on his first thrust. I pulled him close and screamed into his shoulder as stars brighter than the freaking sunset burst through me.

I rode my high and he let me, watching me the entire time in the darkness of that room.

When I came down from it, legs still wrapped around his waist and him still deep inside me, he said, "You're in the darkness now. You want to know if you look any different than when you were under the light of the sunset?"

I barely comprehended what he was talking about but I nodded. "Sure," I mumbled in a state of shock at how blissful it was to get off by none other than Mr. Negative.

He looked down at where our bodies connected and then back up at me. "Still the same. You look exactly the same. Truth, doll."

I shrugged, not caring that he hadn't given me a poetic line. I'd just had a fairy-tale orgasm.

His next words seared into me though. They left a tattoo on my heart.

"Beautiful as fucking ever. Most beautiful thing I've seen in a long time. Light or dark. Under any light." He waited a beat. "Truth."

Then he rocked back to thrust into me hard, not giving me a moment to respond.

I blame alcohol for the idea of love that swirled in my head. He balanced me and showered me with compliments throughout the night. His whispers of how perfect this was, how good I felt, sparked my own dreams of a wedding day, of a happily ever after. The way his hands smoothed over my skin like it was made of pure gold and the way he ran his nose along my nape.

He wanted me the way I wanted him. I knew it. He wanted the love, the future, and the commitment.

Like stars glittering against the night sky, I felt like I shined damn brighter than ever before with him beside me.

After we made love again, he fell asleep, and I raked my eyes over his entire body. He breathed in air like he dominated it, his muscles rippling with the effort. The frown he normally wore disappeared, as if his dreams freed him from the drain of reality. He looked at peace and he needed that. Worrying about every war the world waged at every moment of the day wasn't healthy.

I could attest to that. Once upon a time, there was no happily ever after for me.

I fell asleep after snuggling into his arms. I was excited for what the morning would bring. We would talk over the future and enjoy the sandy beaches of Kauai.

His arms weren't around me when I woke. I stirred and found not even a sheet covering my body. I woke up cold and sat up to look around.

The sun shined into the bedroom, and I smiled as I breathed in that humid air, listened to the rustle of the trees, and thought about our extraordinary night.

I stretched and winced a little, knowing I would need water and ibuprofen to fend off the headache that was sure to come after the amount of alcohol I'd consumed. Even more so because Jett had ravaged me last night. I was sore in places I wasn't sure I'd ever ached before.

He strolled in from the bathroom, a white towel hanging from his hips and a few stray droplets of water glistening on his chest.

Part of me couldn't believe I'd slept with that amazing specimen all night long. Every muscle cut into the next with precision and they moved in beautiful sync with one another as he entered the room.

He hadn't looked toward me yet as he dried his hair with another towel. I let the sheets hang loosely on me as I tried for a sexy rasp, "You look good this morning."

Jett jumped in surprise and then his whole body went rigid. "You're still here?"

I frowned. "Well, yeah. I just woke up. I figured we could lounge in bed…"

"I don't have time for that." He stepped back as if offended by my suggestion.

I scooted off the bed and found my dress in a ball on the floor. "You're totally right. We should start the day off by getting outside to explore this amazing island. Do you have some sweats I could borrow? My dress…" I held it up and shrugged, knowing that guys loved when a woman wore their clothes. I hoped he'd think I looked cute standing there completely naked.

I was excited to see his face when I slipped on the shirt he would give me, excited to spend the day with him too.

He didn't move to get me a change of clothes though. He stared at me like gum on the bottom of his shoe. My smile dropped a little.

Did I imagine that look of annoyance?

He raked his eyes up and down my body and then rolled them. Dramatically. "You can't just wear that dress for a minute to get back to your place? It can't be far from here…."

"But I thought we—"

"We?" He spit the word out like it was gasoline in his mouth. "There's no we, Pix."

"Last night was…"

He held up a hand to stop me. "Last night was last night. Now last night is over."

"But you said—"

"Nothing to make you think this would last till morning. Honestly, why did you even stay the night?"

Shock ping-ponged through me. And the reality that he'd spoken so damn highly of dropped down on me like a lead weight, crushing all my hopes with that one question.

"I stayed because I thought we were enjoying each other."

"I enjoyed fucking you. I think it's safe to say you enjoyed that part too."

I wanted to throw my dress at him, but I didn't want to retrieve it completely nude. So, I took my time stretching out the wrinkles all while I looked at him.

He didn't shrink away from my glare. He met it head-on by crossing his arms and pointedly looking at my deliberately slow movements. "I don't have all day, Vick."

"Wow, you know my name now. Not your little pixie anymore, huh?" I fumed. "And you had all night. You can spare me a precious few minutes of your day so I can at least look presentable when I do the walk of shame."

"Oh, please,"—he turned toward the living area—"half of the island is probably doing the walk of shame. You could call it a normal stroll at this point."

"Where are you going?" I quit trying to smooth creases from my dress and threw it on as I stomped after him. "You don't get to whisper sweet everythings in my ear all night and then act like a complete jerk the morning after."

His face held a question. "'Sweet everythings'?" He burst out laughing, like the answer he found was the most comical thing ever. He laughed so hard he bent at the waist and held himself up on the island counter near the living area. The towel barely clung to him as his whole body shook.

Maybe he's joking with me. Maybe he's laughing because he's about to tell me he really does see us going somewhere.

"You." He wiped his eyes quickly and then shook his head as he righted himself. "'Sweet everythings.' That's ridiculous. You know what a one-night stand is. I know you do."

My laugh died as my jaw dropped.

"Come on." He rolled a finger in front of him, motioning for me to start moving. "Let's get moving. I need to get dressed."

I snapped my mouth shut. I straightened up. And I stepped up to face the terrible morning this was turning out to be.

"You know what?" I stalked toward him, not waiting for him to respond. "You're exactly what is wrong with this world. Don't tear me down because I had a fucking hope that this was more, you dick."

His eyebrows slammed down. Good, I wanted a reaction.

"I know where I'm not wanted. And I'll walk out of here happy, Jett. You want to know why?"

He lifted one shoulder, but he watched me like I finally wasn't a joke to him or just a one-night stand. All of a sudden, I had his attention. His sapphire eyes held mine, and they didn't look away. It was almost like he wanted my disdain. When most people would have shied away from being reprimanded, he reveled in it.

"I'm thankful I enjoyed a couple orgasms from you and now I get to leave you and all your negativity behind. I thought you might be deeper than it, that you just saw this world differently from me, but you're only searching for grim places, and I've been down that boring road before. I want the light, and I'm good enough at finding it that I can honestly say"—I slipped my shoes on, glancing at him while I did—"this will be one of my better mornings because I got to leave misery—you—in the dust."

With that, I swung open his front door and flipped my hair over my shoulder as I walked out.

Smiling.

JETT

THAT GIRL WAS SOMETHING.
   I smiled as she turned to leave. I waited for her to turn back and catch one last glimpse of me. I wouldn't have minded one last look at her too.

Sleek and well-packaged woman that she was, her body would drive any man insane with her long legs, tiny waist, and curves in all the right places. I wanted her to turn so I could see her face and the smooth, soft skin right where her jaw and neck met, the place I now knew drove her fucking crazy when I bit at it.

I wanted to see those honey-colored eyes burning with resentment and fight in them. She bled confidence when someone cut her. Surprisingly, I found that blood attracted me.

I prided myself on not caring about the women I brushed off. I never gave them a promise, just like I hadn't given Vick one. Yet, she targeted the jugular by calling me on my flaws and leaving me to think about them.

Normally, women knew what a one-night stand looked like.

A shiny outlook on the future blinded her to all we had last night. I wasn't the one at fault, but there I was questioning myself.

She was the best I'd had in a long time. I practically got hard just watching her walk away. My body wanted her in a way I didn't want a lot of other women, but I wasn't stupid. I knew I could find someone to fill her shoes any day of the week. There were billions of women in the world and she was only one of them.

She was only one, and yet, when she didn't look back at me, I almost went after her.

Almost.

She flipped her long blonde hair like it was waving goodbye and good riddance. I had wrapped that hair around my hand and owned her last night. Saying goodbye shouldn't have been that easy for her. To most of the women I slept with, it wasn't.

I shook off our encounter and got to work. Businesses had to grow. Money had to be invested. I had to focus. The world my family built had to run and run well. People depended on that. I wasn't in Kauai to play around.

I took breaks here and there.

Jax and Jaydon would have killed me if I didn't.

But I wanted to take my own life when I found out that day one of our excursions was a paddleboard lesson on a private beach across the island. We sat in a large van, piled on top of one another. And our driver looked completely incompetent.

I surveyed the van. "Put your seatbelt on, Jaydon."

He smirked, "Sure, Dad."

Everyone else complied without me pushing further. If I had to be the one with the stick up my ass so that everyone would live, so be it.

Somehow, Vick ended up next to me. We didn't talk because, thankfully, I'd brought my laptop so I could catch up on emails.

I lost my patience after watching cars take turns to cross a one lane bridge though.

"Who booked this?"

Vick jolted a little at my tone, and Brey answered meekly from behind me, "I did. I didn't know there would be so much traffic or that there was only one lane."

Jax's hand was on her thigh and he smiled like we had all the time in the world. "It's fine, Peaches."

Vick wiggled next to me like excitement was about to burst out of her. "We get to take in so much of the island. Look out that window!" She pointed as she practically shouted, "The fog hugs those mountains like a cocoon around a caterpillar. I love this! I could spend days doing this."

I grunted. "No one has days to spend bouncing around a damn island."

The tension in the van thickened. No one responded to my lashing out at Vick, and the woman just looked down at her phone as if she hadn't heard me.

Suddenly, from her phone, I heard an excited weedy voice, "Vicky! You FaceTimed me finally."

Her face lit up like a firefly in the middle of a warm summer night. "Steven," she breathed and held her phone just far enough away from her face that he got a damn good angle of her neckline. The neckline I had ravaged the night before. "Kauai is gorgeous."

"I told you it would be. How was the wedding? Brey and Jax with you?"

"Everyone's here!" She swung her phone around to showcase all of us. Then she practically dangled her phone out the window. "And we are enjoying the freaking fantastic views. Isn't it absolutely breathtaking?"

His low hum came out as a squeak over the phone's speakers. "Vicky, I really wish I could have come with you. My apologies to you all. I'm sure the wedding was amazing." Then he cleared his throat and said in a voice I am sure he hoped was casual, "And I see even Jett's taking a break from work to sightsee."

She angled the phone so we were both in the frame for Steven to see. "Jett's still working. Laptop came along for the ride."

Steven chuckled, but it was strained. "I see. Well, good to meet you through the phone, Jett." He didn't really think that. Anxiety bled out of his smile. "I know we may do business together soon."

"Right. My lawyers and the financial team are reviewing some details before we reach out. I know you've been working closely with them and my investment reps. I'll be sure to personally take a look before we make our final decision." Because I hadn't looked at all. I didn't scope out every company we absorbed. I trusted my team to do that.

He looked relieved as he sighed into the phone. Then, his eyes shifted over, and I knew from the smile that stretched across his face, he was looking at Vick. "Well, that makes me so happy, Jett. Vicky, you are always influential and indispensable, I swear."

Her friend Katie grumbled behind us about him calling her Vicky, but she ignored it and said, "I'm excited to get back to work. I'll look over the contracts you sent me tomorrow morning."

"Perfect. Call me once you do."

"Sounds good. Talk soon."

He smiled and then the video chat ended.

"Seriously," Katie piped up from behind her. "Can he stop calling you Vicky? You hate that nickname, and I do too. It's fucking gross."

"It is not gross," Vick retorted. "He doesn't mean any harm."

"Harm? Ha! He's practically pissing on you by calling you something no one else does. He wants to bone you."

Vick didn't deny it. She smiled like she hoped that was the consensus. "I hope you're right. We've been friends for a few years, but I think he's starting to really make an effort. Brey was there last time we all went out for drinks and he totally looked like he was into me, right?"

Brey smiled and rested her head on Jax's shoulder. "He seemed thrilled to see you."

"And he sounded sincere when he said he wished he could have made it right?"

Brey nodded.

I went back to typing and cut their conversation short. "Is this ride ever going to end?"

My tone must have come off rude because Jaydon kicked my chair from behind. "Loosen up, you prick. We're not working."

"You're not working," I grumbled.

The conversation in the van went on without me. Rome, another one of the newlywed's friends who'd flown in for the wedding, bothered Katie by continually calling her Kate-Bait. Jaydon complained that he should have been able to invite a few girls. Jax kept telling him to fuck off while Brey kept my two brothers from coming to blows.

I worked.

At one point, Vick leaned right over my lap to take a picture of the view. "You want to trade seats since you're so intent on capturing every damn thing on your phone?" I asked quietly so we were the only ones privy to our conversation.

"We'll never get a better view than this," she whisper-shouted back at me.

"Then put your phone down and look at it."

She glared at me, but clicked off her phone's camera. "Fine. Trade seats with me."

I slid my laptop into the case at my feet and unbuckled my belt. She started to stand but there was enough space for me to just grab her by the hips and lift her. I held her as I slid into her seat and set her in mine. Her eyes widened and stayed on me the whole time.

"What?"

"Don't grab me like that in front of everyone," she whispered so discreetly I could barely hear her.

"Why?"

"Because it looks like you ... we've ... well, you know." I smirked. "Maybe I don't. Care to enlighten me?"

She rolled her eyes and looked out the window. "Don't be a jerk and don't grab me like you know my body intimately."

I looked her up and down. Then I reached past her to pull her seatbelt down across her chest. I took my time, and I felt her chest heave in a breath, hold it. A little bubble, one I didn't want to exist formed around us. I snapped the seatbelt into place and popped our moment. "But I do know your body just that way, Victoria."

She scoffed, "No one knows about our night, and I want it to stay that way."

"Why?"

"Because!" she said loudly and some of her friends looked over. I was finding she had a hard time keeping her voice down.

"Are you ashamed, Pix?"

She smiled at everyone and they lost interest quickly. "I'm not ashamed. I just don't think it was memorable enough to share."

I hummed low. "Okay. I'll let you have that one."

She pursed her lips like she wanted to say more but knew it wasn't in her best interest. Her honey-colored eyes followed my movements as I reached back into my bag to grab my laptop.

"What are you working on that is so much better than all this, anyway?" She leaned in a little as I opened my laptop, and her blonde hair slid from her shoulder onto mine.

She was so damn close I could have turned and bit the bottom lip I'd spent so much time nibbling the other night. It tasted like a sweet strawberry, and I could smell that she was probably wearing that same lip gloss.

My body reacted, and I was surprised to find I could barely focus on the email I pulled up. "Just business as always. I may need to research that little company of Mr. Stevie's too. Huh?"

She recoiled. "His name's Steven. Or Mr. Samson. And I highly doubt Steven will think your company buying out ours is a good idea, not after our conversation about you not giving a damn about employees."

Her defensive tone tempted me to push her more. "Honey, for the right price, every man thinks my ideas are fan-fucking-tastic."

She narrowed her eyes. "Not Steven."

The bus driver announced that we'd arrived and everyone cheered.

I let Vick's comment go. She could live in her bubble forever. She probably would too, because I wouldn't pay an arm and a leg for a company that wasn't willing to bend to my will. If Mr. Stevie wanted to keep Samson and Sons, he could.

We paddle boarded on the private beach for much longer than I would have liked to. Fortunately, Rome was also one of the clients I personally invested for. We discussed how his clubs and bars were doing and where we could put extra money. It was close enough to a business meeting that I didn't feel I'd completely wasted my day.

When Katie, Brey, and Vick approached us, I figured I could succumb to a little play. They all goaded Rome into going out to paddleboard. Katie and Brey didn't bother with me, as if they knew my answer would be a withering look.

They practically dragged Rome out, but Vick lingered behind, eyeing me in my black swim trunks. "You dressed to get into the ocean. Are you planning to?"

I looked at the bikini she filled out. "I don't think you're dressed for paddleboarding at all."

She crossed her arms. "Jett, I'm wearing a swimsuit. Of course, I dressed for it."

"You barely kept it on with that last fall."

"So, your attention wasn't just on your work this whole time," she remarked, hands falling to her hips.

"If you're insinuating that I was paying attention to you, I can admit to that. Every guy is paying attention to you. The paddleboard instructor can't look away. He's too damn nervous he'll miss when the strings you call a bikini top inevitably come loose." I wasn't kidding either. He was still staring at her even while she talked to me.

I understood though. Vick drew eyes wherever she went, I was starting to realize. She dressed for attention and she got it. She had chosen to wear a bubblegum-pink bikini top and thong today and the color popped against her tan. Her blonde hair was down and slicked back by the ocean water. With her long legs and loud personality, she drew every eye on that private beach.

She put her hands on her hips and leaned in closer. "Jett Stonewood, stop trying to insult me and get your workaholic ass into that beautiful water. No one should be sitting here working, not even you."

I stared at her for maybe a moment too long. She surprised me by not fighting back when I insulted her. Most everyone would have been defensive, would have retaliated in some way. She, instead, wanted me to have an enjoyable time.

Before I realized what I was doing, my laptop was back in its case and I was standing up. She backed up a step, and her eyes widened as I loomed up to her. She didn't shrink away. Instead, she blatantly looked when I took my shirt off.

"Careful, Pix, someone might think you had an unmemorable night with me."

VICK

THAT MAN COULD sit on a laptop all day, and somehow, I would still salivate over him. When he took his top off, I wasn't going to look away for anyone. I didn't care if everyone in the world knew I'd slept with him right then.

Kauai somehow made everything more vivid, colors more saturated, life more vibrant. And under that sun, Jett became a man I wanted more and more. His arms looked bigger, his chest wider, his abs more defined. His skin already looked bronze even though I was sure he didn't spend extra time tanning.

I didn't respond to him, knowing that's what he probably wanted. I just met his gaze and held it.

He cocked his head as if assessing me. "Paddleboarding won't make me enjoy this trip."

"Have you ever paddle boarded before?"

He grunted and then walked past me to grab a board. "Of course."

I rolled my eyes. "Not everyone has done it. It isn't just common practice, Jett."

I grabbed mine and followed him out.

"Have you not?" he asked the question like he knew the answer.

"I just learned on this trip."

As he waded into the water, I followed. When he veered around a large rock that blocked the others from view, I did too.

"So, you just suntanned when you went to the beach before?"

I let the cool blue water lap at me while the sun warmed my skin. I breathed in the humid air and felt the breeze in my hair before I answered. "My family only went to the beach when I was young. I haven't been to one since high school. This is my first time."

Before he jumped onto the paddleboard, he asked, "Why?"

I shrugged. "Life sometimes gives you lemons and you make lemonade. Other times, you can't make anything."

It wasn't an answer. We both knew it. I waited to see if he'd pry, but he jumped up on the paddleboard instead.

I got to my feet, the board shaking beneath me, and steadied myself. Jett paddled ahead with confident strokes. When I stuck my paddle in the water, I overbalanced and belly flopped in with a splash.

Jett looked back and laughed. I managed to right myself and paddle a few strokes after him, but it wasn't long before I fell again. Each time I fell, he laughed harder.

Under the sun and in the sparkling water, I could swear Jett was finally enjoying himself.

After about my tenth fall, I stayed in the water and rested my elbows on the board as I stared up at him. "You have to admit this is kind of fun, Jett."

He paddled up so close, looming over me. Droplets of water glistened on his legs and he smiled down at me like Zeus would at an ungodly soul. "I'm getting my exercise in for the day instead of having to work out when I get back to my place, so that's a plus."

"Oh, come on," I whined. "You are the epitome of a bad mood. Nothing will make you enjoy this trip, will it?"

As soon as the words left my mouth, Jett crouched on his paddleboard. His smile disappeared and his brows drew a little closer together. Determination glittered in his eyes.

I took a small step back in the waist-deep water. He jumped off his board, unhooked himself from it, and came toward me. I backed away and tried to put my board between us. "What are you doing, Jett?"

"Showing you exactly what will make me enjoy this trip."

He ducked underwater and suddenly I felt his hands skating around my ankle, removing my board's band. Then, he was back above water, pushing away my board so he could grab me around the waist and bring my body up against his.

I glanced around quickly. "Are you joking? We can't…"

He didn't shift his eyes away from mine for a single second, not even checking his surroundings to see who might be watching us. He just pulled me closer with his hand on the back of my neck and kissed me.

Devoured me.

Branded me with that kiss. He didn't leave room for me to object or resist or even breathe. No part of me wanted to do any of those things anyway.

My stomach flipped, and my heart rate picked up. My mind got lost in the illusion of a world where we were lovers, the only people who existed. The waves lapped at my back, cooling it while Jett heated me everywhere else.

"This bikini top…" he groaned as he kissed down my neck.

"You love it?"

"Me and every fucking man on the island."

He untied the strings around my neck. "Is that a problem?"

"You enjoy men looking at you?"

I smirked and shrugged. "I don't really care whether they do or not. It's all about fun, Jett. Enjoying yourself on a vacation. I enjoy feeling sexy, and if men enjoy looking, I guess everyone wins. They're just looking."

He hummed but didn't say anything else. He let my top slide off of me and drop into the water. The breeze felt liberating against my bare skin. His hands skimmed down my neck to my breasts.

"They don't deserve to see this body, Vick. Not like it's a piece of meat. It should be a crime."

I didn't answer him, didn't tell him that his idea of hiding it all away was silly. Because at one time, I'd thought I would never get to display it again or even have a body to display, for that matter.

I looked down at his hands squeezing me. I rubbed my hands up and down his chest. Then, I did what any woman would with Jett Stonewood in front of them. I hooked my arms behind his neck and jumped up to wrap my legs around his hips. He grabbed my ass with both his hands and hummed low in my ear, "Woman, next time we go to a place you have to wear a swimsuit, wear a damn one piece."

I bit his neck. "No fun."

"And we all know you're all about fucking fun."

He slid my bikini to the side. When his fingers brushed over me, I should have glanced around to make sure my friends weren't looking for me, that people weren't catching me in the act.

I didn't though.

Beep. Beep. Beep.

This was my moment and the little sound in my head reminded me of that. In the middle of Kauai's bluest bay, under the brightest sun, with one astonishingly hot guy who wanted me here, and I wanted him.

I catalogued it, saving it for a future daydream when I'd pull it out of my imaginary Rolodex. I noted the way his blue eyes darkened, the way his jaw tightened when I slid my hand down the front of his swim trunks, how he thrust into me and every one of his muscles rippled under me. I would have taken a freaking picture of his face if I could have, so perfectly symmetrical and angled just right that every woman in the world would probably drop their bikini top for him.

I didn't need to record the way his hand moved in me though. He had learned how to work each inch of my body into a frenzy the first night we were together and there in that crystal-blue water, he used every skill he knew to drive me to the edge.

I writhed against him, wanting to race to my release, but he kept a steady pace. "Jett, stop playing with me."

"I thought you liked to play," he quipped as he walked us into deeper water.

I squeezed him hard and quickened my strokes. "I like to have fun."

His hand moved in me, and I moaned. "This fun enough?"

I didn't answer, just rode his hand and stroked him at the same pace.

He grunted, "Looks like you're having a great time, Vick."

He slid another finger in, and I bucked against him. "Jett, can you please ... "

"Please what?"

I moaned, "Please shut up and fuck me here. Please. Please. Please."

He laughed at my chanting but didn't move to take his shorts off. He curled those two fingers in me and rubbed in just the right place.

He kept strolling deeper into the water. And just as I was about to scream, he submerged us.

We looked at each other as I pumped him faster and faster, and he fingered me at the same speed. The water clouded my senses, disoriented me with lack of oxygen, and shook me to my core. When I orgasmed, I didn't see stars or explosions or lights. I saw his blurry figure under the water like a foggy dream taking over my damn mind.

He owned me, held me where I couldn't breathe, couldn't feel air against my skin, or witness any life other than him.

I felt him spasm right after me, his muscles tightening. I saw his neck go taut and knew he was getting off just as intensely as me.

We were under the water, in an unfamiliar world made for us alone. I told myself to forget about the fairy tale, to stop living in reverie, but I lost myself to it with him under that water.

After Jett got me off, he swam away, then reappeared with my swim top. "Here."

I grabbed it and retied the strings as he front crawled over to where the tide had washed our boards out. When he pushed mine toward me, I said, "Should I go around the rock first or you?"

"Or we could both go at the same time?"

I narrowed my eyes at him.

He laughed. "Vick, no one cares what we're doing."

"Speak for yourself. My friends are nosy."

"Are they? Or are you the nosy one and think they'll ask the questions you normally ask them?"

"Brey knows…"

"She might know something is up, but that girl would never ask."

I huffed and straightened my bikini top before I paddled my board toward the rock. "Whatever. It doesn't matter."

"I know it doesn't. We're adults. We can do whatever we want in the damn water."

I ignored him and swam toward Jaydon and Brey who looked like they had resorted to sitting in shallow water looking at seashells.

"Where did you guys go?" Jaydon asked.

I looked pointedly at Jett behind me. "There's some beautiful coral reef on the other side of that rock."

Jett rolled his eyes and walked past all of us without engaging in the conversation.

"Guess Jett didn't enjoy it?" Jaydon practically yelled after his brother to irritate him.

Jett turned to respond, catching all of us off guard. "Oh, the reef was exceptional. Under the water, in this light—absolutely exceptional."

My face heated, my stomach flipped, and my knees went weak enough that I slid down lower into the water to hide my reaction to his words.

ORDER TODAY OR READ FREE IN KINDLE UNLIMITED:
US: amzn.to/3eoqRjN
Universal: mybook.to/ShainRoseReverie

ABOUT SHAIN ROSE

FACEBOOK PAGE:
facebook.com/author.shainrose/

INSTAGRAM:
instagram.com/author.shainrose/

SHAIN ROSE IS an author of Contemporary Romance and New Adult novels. She fights for love one word a time. Those happily ever afters can sometimes be a bitch to get to.

When she isn't writing, she's spending the days with her husband, daughter, son, and terrible cat. She and her husband drink way too much coffee, eat way too much candy, and laugh way too much. Life is good when the kids are behaving.

On the off chance she's not writing or spending time with family and friends, she's calling them to talk. And if no one answers, then she's reading and watching trashy TV.

LET'S STAY IN TOUCH

RECEIVE UPDATES ON all things Shain Rose and get an email once the pre-order is live! Subscribe to Shain Rose's newsletter here so you can be the first hear about all the news:

shainrose.com/newsletter

JOIN SHAIN ROSE'S Lovers of Love Facebook Group to keep in touch and get sneak peeks into the Stonewood Brothers' lives:

facebook.com/groups/shainroseslovers

AMAZON AUTHOR PAGE:
amzn.to/37Nfejt

BOOKBUB PAGE
bookbub.com/authors/shain-rose

GOODREADS PAGE:
goodreads.com/shainrose

WEBSITE:
shainrose.com

Made in the USA
Las Vegas, NV
20 September 2024

95553831R00272